MW00910964

Lynn Langley Whirled Around and Started Back up the Hill Toward the Gates to the Horrcove Cemetery.

A chill trilled down her spine, and she knew without looking that the dark, shadowy figure was following her.

Then she heard the sounds, low and rasping like the labored breathing of an asthmatic. But the rhythm and volume was all wrong. What she was hearing sounded more like the slow-motion pumping of a blacksmith's bellows, harsh, loud, irregular.

She began to walk faster . . . and faster. Then she broke into a run. She ran blindly past the massive gates and on up the hill toward the single street lamp thirty yards away. She needed the light. Craved it. The light would shine down on what was behind her, give it substance, make it real. Once she knew what it was, she could deal with it.

She reached into her purse and pulled out an old rusty butcher knife with a ten-inch-long serrated blade. Throwing her purse aside, she gripped the knife with both hands, and slowly began to turn to face her assailant. She'd teach him to pull a practical joke.

When she completed her half-turn, she lifted her eyes to look at what was coming into the light. What she saw blew her mind into total oblivion . . .

OUT OF THE NIGHT

PATRICK WHALEN

POCKET BOOKS

New York London Toronto Sydney Tokyo Singapore

An *Original* Publication of POCKET BOOKS

POCKET BOOKS, a division of Simon & Schuster Inc.
1230 Avenue of the Americas, New York, NY 10020

ISBN: 0-671-67994-5

First Pocket Books printing September 1990

10 9 8 7 6 5 4 3 2 1

This book is for my parents, Violet and Bill Whalen

Acknowledgments

My thanks to John Scognamiglio, my editor and Joanna Cole, my agent.

Thanks also to Dr. Bernard Rudis and Debra Bertorelli, the world's best typist.

Finally, my appreciation to Lynn Garner for help with the first one and Kathy Wengerd for the encouragement, suggestions and the energy.

Prologue:
Part One

**Ravina, California
October 1889**

The instant the clouds covered the moon, the mob from Ravina started up the hill. Moving as one, a black mass against a black hill, the crowd swept past the newly built mortuary and continued on up the slope, scrambling around tombstones and grave markers in a frantic, driving effort to get up the slope before the clouds parted.

At the top of the high hill the shadowy figures grouped around the coals of a dying fire sensed the threat, but they were near the end of their ritual and were weak. Helpless, drained of all strength, all they could do was stand there while the humans closed on them from below.

Moments later the mob arrived. They swarmed over the motionless figures, slipped nooses around their necks . . . and hanged them from the branches of a nearby oak tree.

The lynchings had been carried out in silence and near total darkness. It took a moment for the townspeople to realize it was over. When they finally did, a few cheered and others offered up prayers of thanks. But most just sagged in relief. Their nightmare was over, and proof that their lives would return to normal hung now from the tree: six silhouettes. Six human-shaped shadows were swinging slowly back and forth in the black night.

There would be no more terror. The grotesque nightly slaughter of their friends and neighbors would stop. Children would no longer disappear from the locked and shuttered homes of their parents.

They were free of the strangers who had come in the night six days earlier. The newcomers had grouped their sheepherder wagons high on the hill just west of town. By day the wagons appeared to be deserted, their dirty canvases flapping in the wind like shutters on deserted buildings.

But at night the strangers' shadows could be seen lurching about their nightly fire. From the valley below the townspeople had no idea how many were up there or what they were up to. All they knew was that the strangers had camped atop a hill owned by a strange reclusive man named Horrcove. Horrcove was a newcomer. He had come to the valley some months earlier, purchased the town's only cemetery, then overseen the construction of Ravina's first funeral home and mortuary. Since his arrival Horrcove had not seen much business. Ravina was a young town, a healthy town. There was only a limited need for those particular services Horrcove offered.

But all that had changed . . . because after the wagons arrived, people began dying. One every night for the past five nights. The deaths had been horrible and beyond comprehension.

The town's doctor was the first to die. His body, puffed and distorted like a dried-apple doll, was found on the outskirts of town, its teeth and fingernails missing. A young sheriff's deputy was the next to die. A drunk found the deputy's body in an alley just after midnight, and by noon the next day the corpse had dissolved into nothing. The owner of the town's newspaper was killed on the third night, and on the fourth, a prostitute was ripped to shreds.

2

Fear as palpable as fog swept through the town. People locked and barred their doors. A few moved away. The sheriff and his remaining deputy locked up drifters, hobos, and strangers. Still the horror continued and even escalated. On the fifth night, not only did another death take place, but two male children disappeared from the locked homes of their parents. It was then that rumors and stories about gypsies began to circulate through the town: gypsies killed for pleasure, worshipped the devil, and used the bodies of dead male children in their rituals to glorify their deity. And it was the same rumors and stories which unified the town, brought them together and gave them the strength to attack and kill the unseen evil that was killing them.

But now it was over. The gypsies were dead. The townspeople from Ravina had hanged them in the old tree on top of Horrcove Hill.

The town's tanner, a big man named Rawlins, called for silence. When he got it, he spoke. "Light the torches. I want to see 'em. I want to see what they look like."

Agreement rippled through the crowd. More than a dozen torches were lit at the same time, then shoved high into the air, their flames bleaching the darkness and the limbs of the old tree a brilliant white. Amid a growing chorus of victorious cheers, the mob looked up at what they had hanged, and the shouts of victory turned to stunned silence.

For it was then they could see they had not hanged gypsies . . . or humans. In the darkness they had hanged hideous malevolent Beings that even in death had the power to look down on them with eyes that seemed to see, seemed to track each and every one of them, and in those eyes the crowd on the hill saw not death but victory and hideous visions of the future: their futures.

Flinging aside their torches, the townspeople blindly stampeded down the hill, running to homes too fragile to keep out the monstrous horrors the night still held. They hid, cried, prayed, and before the night was over, two had taken their own lives and a third took the lives of his family before taking his own. Those that died that night established a pattern—a legacy—which would continue in Ravina for a generation to come.

Just before dawn a man and two children in a horsedrawn wagon made their way slowly up the hill. A misty gray fog provided the man with the privacy he needed in order to accomplish his task. The scene at the top of the hill caused him no terror, only immense sadness. He guided his wagon under each of the suspended bodies hanging from the tree, and as gently as he could, he cut the ropes and laid each body in the wagon with care and reverence. The heavy mist in the air glistened on his face, and the droplets blended with his tears.

When he finished, he stepped down from the wagon, and with his bare hands he dug a deep hole in the earth near the hanging tree. Then he slowly sifted through the ashes of the cold fire, carefully removing the blackened bones of two male children. He put the bones in the hole, covered them over with dirt, then led the horses and wagon over the spot until all traces of the burial were obliterated.

Still shrouded in fog, he climbed back onto the wagon, and without a word to the twin boys sitting beside him, he urged the horses toward the road. Halfway down the hill he guided the animals onto a rutted seldom-used path which would take him and his cargo back to the town's only mortuary.

ITEM: RAVINA WEEKLY GAZETTE, January 4, 1890 (Excerpt) . . . the body was discovered by his wife Nora Hobbs. Mrs. Hobbs had gone to the family business after Mr. Hobbs failed to arrive home for his evening meal. It was known that Mr. Hobbs suffered from a painful malady which necessitated the continued use of laudanum. It is believed that in his pain he accidentally ingested a lethal quantity of the chemical. Services for Edwin Hobbs will be held on . . .

ITEM: RAVINA WEEKLY GAZETTE, February 12, 1890
(Excerpt) . . . visibly shaken by the grisly discovery at the Bleeker home, Sheriff Teal said, "He must have shot his wife first, then gone from bedroom to bedroom killing the children. When he was done, he shot himself in the head."

Mr. Bleeker's actions left friends and neighbors stunned, for the man was considered to be a loving husband and a devoted father. Services for William and Mary Bleeker and their six children will be held on . . .

ITEM: SAN LUIS OBISPO COUNTY CORONER'S INVESTIGATORY REPORT July 17, 1890
Subject: Carl Rawlins
(Excerpt) . . . in conclusion, I am forced to believe that Mr. Rawlins placed a workbench next to the vat he used in his business to boil animal hides. He then climbed onto the bench and stepped into the boiling vat. That Mr. Rawlins was alone in his business and the doors to his establishment were locked from the inside allows me only one conclusion: the man purposefully, and I should note in a horrible manner, did take his own life on July 7, 1890.

Respectfully submitted to and for the County of San Luis Obispo on this, the 17th day of July 1890.

William H. Waldren, M.D.
San Luis Obispo County Coroner
and Guardian of the Public Health

ITEM: SAN LUIS OBISPO COUNTY CORONER'S INVESTIGATORY REPORT October 18, 1890
Subject: Reverend William Hinkle
(Excerpt) . . . did intentionally take his own life. I am at a loss to explain why a minister in his prime

would end his life in such an excruciatingly painful manner, and it is also impossible for me not to add that this is the fourteenth such occurrence I have investigated in the town of Ravina within the past ten months.

William H. Waldren, M.D.
San Luis Obispo County Coroner
and Guardian of the Public Health

Prologue:
Part Two

On the Plains of Monsul, Kurdistan (Iraq) June 1931

Four men knelt in the hot desert behind the truck, waiting for the fuses to ignite the dynamite. When the explosion finally came, the earth shuddered under the force of the blast and shards of rock rained down on the truck and men for almost a minute.

The expedition's archeologist was the first to get to his feet. Wiping grit from his eyes, he peered around the edge of the truck to survey the site of the explosion. Even through the thick veil of dust which clung to the earth like a shroud, he could make out the stark black shadow of a now open cave in the face of the cliff. "Well, you did it, Mr. Patton," Martin Larchmont said, turning to look at a taller man who was brushing dust off his tailored safari jacket. "You got it open. Nothing to do now but wait twenty-four hours."

Patton gave the young archeologist an indifferent look, then motioned for the two other men to come as he set out for the cave fifty yards away.

Stunned and appalled at what Patton was about to do, Larchmont ran up beside him and grabbed him by the arm. "You're not going in there now, are you? The air in there could be poisonous, contaminated with neuromyces spores and—"

Patton jerked free and continued on.

Larchmont slowed to a stop and watched the men pick their way over the rocks and boulders that had been blown away from the cave's entrance. "You don't understand!" he screamed through cupped hands. "If those rocks formed an airtight seal, then the air in there could be filled with neuromyces spores . . . the spores are deadly . . . you'll breathe them in and there won't be anything anybody can do . . . Jesus Christ, don't you understand? . . . You could all die!!" No one gave him a second look.

After they disappeared into the black opening, Larchmont wandered over to a large boulder and crouched down on his haunches in the scant shadow of the stone, seeking relief from the sun and heat. But there was no relief, not in this desert, where the daytime temperature often exceeded a hundred and thirty degrees. The shadowy opening of the cave looked cool and inviting, but his fear of poisonous air overrode his desire to get out of the sun.

He had lost two colleagues in the Valley of the Kings. They had broken into a sealed chamber in the back of a cave they'd been excavating. In their excitement they'd entered the chamber immediately rather than wait the twenty-four hours it took for the poisonous airborne spores of the neuromyces, a deadly fungoid that grew in warm airtight enclosures, to dissipate. Their excitement cost them their lives. In school his professors had compared neuromyces to mustard gas. Larchmont had thought that was an exaggeration until that day in the Valley of the Kings, when he saw his friends die.

So he waited in a Kurdistani desert under a blast furnace of a sun, waited and sweated and wondered what the others were doing in the cave until a man named Smathers scurried out of the opening. Larchmont stood up and watched Smathers run to the truck, then return to the cave, lugging two large cans of petrol and several torches. "Good God," Larchmont murmured. "They're going to burn what they found. . . ."

He slumped back down beside the stone and continued to wait, passing the time by watching the drops of his own sweat splatter down on the hot sand.

A half hour later he heard the sounds of men laughing and congratulating one another long before he saw them. He rose to his feet at the same instant Patton and the other two burst out into the sunlight. The men were jubilant and clapping one another on the back as if they'd just won a soccer game. Smoke trailed out of the cave behind them, and Larchmont could smell it now; it was the smell of petrol and burning wood and flesh. The odor sickened him.

The archeologist walked back to the truck to avoid the thickening cloud of black smoke billowing out of the cave. He leaned against the truck, folded his arms, and studied Patton as he and the other two approached. A zealot, a dictator, and an asshole, he thought. Once again he cursed the day he'd signed on as the archeologist for the madman's expedition.

Patton stopped directly in front of Larchmont, and for a long moment neither man spoke. Finally Patton broke the silence. "Your caution cost you an interesting slice of history. It was just like the scroll described. They were all in there. Trapped. Dead. Mummified. We must have stepped over the bodies of three hundred men, women, and children to get to the coffins."

Stunned, Larchmont looked up at the taller man, squinting his eyes against the glare of the sun. "Then everything in the scroll was true. There were coffins in the cave?"

"That's what's burning now."

Tired of squinting, Larchmont looked down at the sand. "What were they like . . . the coffins?"

Patton shrugged. "Large, ornate, solidly built, and still on the wagons that brought them here. It was an incredible sight: all those bodies and six wagons holding six coffins. The horses were still attached to the wagons. Some of the horses were still standing. They'd died on their feet, mummified just like the humans.

"You could tell the people in there had died horribly. It must've taken them a long time to suffocate after the cave was sealed off. Not a good ending, but appropriate for those that worship evil, don't you think?"

"Did you open any of the coffins?" Larchmont asked, still staring at the sand.

"Absolutely not," Patton said, almost snarling. "I didn't go into that cave to examine the devil's spawn up close. My duty was to carry out God's good work. The coffins were there, and that was all I needed to know. I sent Smathers out for petrol, and then we set fire to everything in the cave."

Larchmont shook his head. "You should have opened at least one of the coffins. Then you really would've known if *everything* in the scroll was true."

Patton paused to wipe his face and neck with a handkerchief. "I'm tired of you, Dr. Larchmont," he said in a controlled voice. "You've been a cynic and an irritant since the day this expedition began. At this point I don't believe the expedition needs an archeologist anymore, especially one who will not follow me into a dark cave. Naturally, I'll cover any travel expenses you may incur in getting back to the States, and Smathers here will see you get a full month's severance pay to tide you over."

Larchmont didn't have to look over at Patton's executive assistant to know that Smathers was looking smug and writing a note to himself in the spiral notebook he always carried. All Smathers ever did was look smug and write memos to himself . . . even out here in the desert.

Angry at the contemptuous way he'd just been dismissed, Larchmont started to walk away. He'd gone about ten feet when he stopped, turned, and smiled at Patton. "You know the scroll specifically said there were twelve coffins . . . not six. You still have six to find."

"I know what the scroll said!" Patton bellowed, the hysteria and terror in his voice catching Larchmont off guard. "I don't need you to remind me that my search for this evil spawn is only half over. I know what you're trying to do, Dr. Larchmont. You're trying to frighten me, trying to undermine the mission that God has given to me. But it won't work." Patton gestured savagely at the cave. "God led me here so I could destroy the evil that lived in that hole. I have no doubt He'll guide me and protect me while I search for the remaining coffins."

"Whatever you say, Mr. Patton," Larchmont said, turning his back on Patton and walking away.

"Let me remind you," Patton screamed, "that I don't have to give you anything if I fire you! No severance pay, no ticket back to the States, and I will fire you if you try and plant doubts in my mind. Stay away from me, Dr. Larchmont, keep out of my sight. When we get back to the main camp, I want you packed and gone by sunset. Is that clear?"

"Perfectly!" Larchmont shouted back, still stunned by Patton's strange outburst.

A few minutes before sunset Patton used the last of the dynamite to seal up the cave forever. It was too late in the day to return to the main camp. Patton and his two executive assistants set up their camp next to the truck. Larchmont pitched his tent out in the desert, well away from the cave and the other men's camp.

It began a few hours later.

The violent spasms of coughing and cries of terror and pain could be heard for miles. Larchmont did nothing. There was nothing he could do. The men who'd entered the cave were already as good as dead.

Later, when the screaming grew louder and more frenzied, Larchmont left his camp and spent the night hiding deep in the desert. He had to hide. Like rabies, neuromyces induced uncontrolled savage insanity while it killed. For as long as they lived, the three dying men were as dangerous to him as a pack of rabid wolves.

He returned to the men's camp at dawn. What he found in the early morning light was worse than anything he had imagined. All three were dead, and they'd died hideously. Their faces were covered with dried frothy bubbles of blood and bits of lung tissue expelled during their violent fits of coughing. Evidence of insanity was everywhere. Sometime during the night Smathers had mutilated his own body with a hatchet. Patton had blinded himself and peeled the skin off his face with his fingernails. The third man had been murdered; either Patton or Smathers had pounded the man's head to a bloody pulp with a large rock, then thrown the body onto the fire.

As the morning sun began to streak the desert, Larchmont wrapped the bodies in sleeping bags and carried them back to the truck. He worked rapidly, knowing that the desert sun would turn the truck into an oven long before he got back to the main camp. Just before he left, he found a rag and half a can of petrol and put both in the cab. He knew that before the trip was over, he would be forced to dip the rag in the petrol and wear it like a face mask. Three hours from now, only the harsh smell of gasoline fumes would block out the rotting and repugnant odors that would engulf him from the back of the truck.

Chapter
One

"I tried to do what you wanted," Oley Gillespie said, wiping his hands on a grease rag and shaking his head. "I really tried." The best mechanic in the town of Ravina was glaring contemptuously at a brand-new black and white police car. "After I pulled all that catalytic crap off, I pulled the engine, bored and stroked the valves, put on a bigger carburetor, did some other things, dropped the engine back in, and basically that car's still a piece of junk. Sorry, Henry." He looked up at Henry Sutton, the police chief of Ravina. "When you brought her in, you said trying to give this car more guts would be like trying to get blood from a stone." He tossed the grease rag onto a stained workbench and shook his head again. "More like trying to get blood from a dirt clod. This car's a piece of junk. It may be new, American-made, but it's still a piece of junk."

Henry Sutton had no choice but to shrug. "I knew that when the city council ordered twelve of these, but what could I do. They're into fuel efficiency and low costs."

"That's exactly what they got. A cheap piece of junk

13

that doesn't use much gas," Oley Gillespie said. "I just wanted you to know I tried." He shrugged again.

Henry Sutton eyed the new patrol car woefully. "How 'bout the front seat?"

The mechanic smiled. "I had to drill some new holes in the frame and remount the front seat. The car won't catch any bad guys, but at least you can get in and out." The mechanic sized up Henry Sutton. The police chief of Ravina was a large man, probably over six foot five with at least a forty-six-inch chest and a forty-inch waist. The man's wrists were larger than his own biceps, and at times, Sutton reminded Gillespie of the broad-shouldered, barrel-chested wrestlers he saw on TV. Not overweight, just damn big. He handed the police chief the bill.

Sutton glanced at the bill, then began writing out a check for the full amount.

"Aren't you gonna get the city council to pay the bill?"

Sutton handed Oley the check. "Our economically minded city council bought that miserable excuse for a car," he said, gesturing at the small patrol car, "and eleven others just like it. They're still bragging about the money they saved on the deal. You think a group that tight's going to lay out money just because I want mine customized?"

Oley Gillespie grinned. "Well, I know one thing. If you ever want to get rid of that car, just find someone in a wheelchair and drag race 'em for pink slips. Ain't no way you'd win against competition like that." Still grinning, he moved off to wait on another customer.

The police chief of Ravina eased himself into the compact patrol car. As he pulled out onto the town's main boulevard, he floored the gas pedal. The car coughed twice, then slowly began to pick up speed. Sutton moaned and eased off the gas. Oley was right. There wasn't anything anybody could do to give a car like this more guts.

Still, all things considered, he was pleased with the surgery Gillespie had done on the car's interior. The mechanic had pulled the front seat and drilled new bolt holes in the frame so that when the seat was remounted, it sat back away from the steering wheel an additional ten inches. The modification had virtually eliminated legroom in the backseat, but that didn't bother Sutton. What did bother him was that the cost of moving the seat back a few inches had come to more than two hundred dollars. It may have been a small price to pay considering the amount of time it had been taking him to squeeze in and out of the new patrol car, but still, he felt he shouldn't have to foot that part of the bill. He was just improving his job performance. After all, what good was the chief of police if he couldn't get out of his car at the scene of a crime?

Sutton stopped for a red light and began drumming his fingers on the steering wheel while he tried to figure out a way to get the city council to pay for that part of the bill. The council might go for it. The hard part would be getting it past the city auditor. The man was a tightwad, a bureaucrat with political aspirations, and a transvestite. The light turned green and Sutton continued down the boulevard. Every night the auditor went home, locked the door, closed the curtains, and paraded around wearing high heels, fishnet stockings, and a garter belt. Interesting pastime, Sutton thought, wondering if there was a way he could use the man's hobby as a way to get the man to pay the bill, knowing full well he would never be able to bring himself to use anything like that to blackmail the man into cooperating. It just wasn't the way he worked.

In his own way Henry Sutton was a virtuous man. By reason of at least one of those virtues, he could never bring himself to use another man's weakness as a stepping stone for his own gain. Henry Sutton was an anachronism. He was by virtue of his virtues an honest and moral man. It was that simple. In a society that pushed situational ethics and "degrees" of right and wrong, Sutton stood out like a dinosaur in a car lot.

As a police officer, he was much the same. He was an old-fashioned man; an old-fashioned sheriff. He was also fair, hard, rigid, and proud of those qualities. He looked upon criminals as criminals, not as by-products of deprived socioeconomic environments. To Sutton, a man was innocent until proven guilty, and once that happened a man stayed guilty. A society that let criminals go because a typist had omitted a comma on a search warrant was, as far as he was concerned, committing suicide in the abstract.

In spite of his rigid perspectives and old-fashioned philosophies, Sutton had the ability to work hard and intelligently within the confusing guidelines of the law.

The rigid internal qualities that would not allow Henry Sutton to blackmail the auditor were a constant factor in his professional and private life, both in his position as the police chief of Ravina and during fifteen years he'd spent on the Chicago police force. The same internal qualities had also cost him two marriages.

His first marriage, a nine-month hiss-and-scratch catfight, pleasurable to neither, ended when he refused to go on the take for his wife's sake. In those days a Chicago policeman pulled down twelve thousand dollars a year. One on the take stood to make twice that much.

His second marriage ended after he discovered his wife had been having affairs with a number of his friends. He didn't divorce her because she'd made a fool of him. He left her because she had made a fool of herself.

Sutton had spent fifteen years with the Chicago police force before coming to Ravina. When he had first joined the Chicago police, he stood out because of his size. When it was later found out that he was also intelligent, resourceful, and devoted to his profession, his rise through the ranks had been meteoric. The future could not have looked brighter for Henry Sutton. He was well on his way to becoming the youngest precinct captain in the history of the Chicago police force . . . or so it had seemed.

On a snowy night three days before his thirty-seventh birthday, Henry Sutton and his partner, an experienced veteran with eighteen years on the force, had gone to an old warehouse in pursuit of a felon with a gun. Both men were nervous. The man they were after had killed a cop three days earlier. The warehouse was dark and cold, and in the midst of the search for the suspect, Sutton's partner saw movement and fired twice. The first bullet caught Sutton in the left hand, tearing off his thumb. The second shattered his shoulder.

Sutton spent four months in the hospital. After his discharge he was ready to go back to work. A stiff shoulder and no left thumb wouldn't interfere with his duties. A Chicago police force medical review board thought otherwise. The board retired Henry Sutton four and a half months after his thirty-seventh birthday with a commendation for valor and a three-quarters salary pension.

Henry Sutton still loved police work and was not about to retire. He saw an ad in a law-enforcement journal. A small seacoast town in California was looking for an experienced chief of police. He applied. The Ravina City Council took into consideration his experience, administrative talents, commendations; duly noted he had no thumb and a stiff shoulder; and hired him on the spot.

They had never come to regret the decision; neither had Henry Sutton. Sutton loved his job. He liked the power and prestige that came with the position. The salary was good, the working conditions excellent, the men under him top-notch. Best of all, he was his own man. The city council and the mayor left him alone. The united consensus had been for some years now that Henry Sutton was a competent sheriff who performed his tasks in a manner described by most as flawless.

Year after year he had dealt with the seasonal invasion of summer tourists in a tactful and competent manner. It was this particular quality that endeared him to the council, for Ravina was largely dependent upon its summer tourist trade for year-round economic survival. When it did become necessary to arrest a rowdy tourist, Sutton made sure it was done in a tactful and polite manner. The council appreciated Sutton's skills and the way he supervised his men, and they showed their appreciation by giving him all the freedom and latitude he wanted.

Henry Sutton lived alone and didn't like it. More often than not, his house seemed like a strange possessive animal whose only purpose was to cut him off from the warmth of the world. He tried to make himself comfortable at home; he had a den overflowing with books, but when he picked one up, the house seemed to breathe on it, making the print unreadable. Sutton knew it wasn't the house. It was his lifestyle. He didn't like living alone, but at this point he had no choice in the matter. So he lived with it as best he could. Which wasn't very well.

To avoid going home at the end of the day, Sutton often stayed on duty and drove his patrol car through the streets to keep an eye on his town in a possessive, protective sort of way. He especially enjoyed cruising Ravina during the winter months, when the tourist population was gone and the people that he encountered were neighbors and friends. He felt close to them, and that made the job of looking after them all that more important to Henry Sutton.

Two miles from the raging California coastline, Ravina was small, with a summertime population of thirty-five thousand, which dwindled to twenty thousand in the wintertime. An oddly shaped hill rose up between the town and the ocean, and while some groused about the hill because they couldn't see the sun set in the sea, most appreciated it. The hill protected the town from the continual winds and harsh storms that battered the California coast. The hill was nicknamed "Hang Hill." The name came from an event that supposedly had occurred in the late 1880s, when some townspeople had hanged some gypsies at the top of the hill. The chamber of commerce and the Ravina Historical Society had never been able to document the hangings, so the hill's name remained as it always was: Horrcove Hill. The name came from the man who had established the town's first mortuary and cemetery and whose descendants still owned and worked the business.

Ravina draped itself around the bottom of Horrcove Hill like a sprawling crescent-shaped necklace. The older residential neighborhoods were clustered at the base of the hill. From there the old town fanned out in an easterly direction with the architectural styles of its homes and businesses changing over the years like the rings of an aging tree, changing from classic and stately to squat and modern.

Sutton's favorite part of Ravina was the old section of town closest to the hill. Most of the homes there were classic two- and three-story Victorian-style homes built in the early nineteen hundreds as summer homes for the rich. They were ancient and massive structures with gabled roofs, hand-carved shingles, dormers, and porticoes supporting ornate widow walks and thick blankets of green ivy.

The easterly side of Ravina depressed Sutton. Six elevated lanes of U.S. Highway 101 passed through that part of town, and somehow the freeway colors and ugly cement on ramps seemed not to stand out in the mixture of tract houses, metal and glass buildings, cheap motels, fast-food restaurants, and used car lots, all dutifully laid out in monotonous tic-tac-toe patterns.

The town's major industry was its summer tourist trade. During the winter months, Ravina existed almost as an afterthought on dairy farms, milk processing plants, fruit and fish canneries, two lumber mills, and a recently built jeans manufacturing plant.

All in all, Ravina was a town like many others along the desolate California coast with one exception: it was Henry Sutton's town. As he cruised it now, his eyes flicked relentlessly from shadow to shadow in the carnival of lights that lined the boulevard. He was looking for trouble, and if it was there, he'd spot it. Henry Sutton possessed an almost prophetic ability to see trouble where others saw nothing. There was nothing strange to him about his talent. It was genetic. His grandfather had been a policeman, and he had had it. So had his father. Sutton had always had it. In the fifteen years he'd spent on the Chicago police force, he had honed his intuitive ability to a scalpel-like sharpness.

The Ravina police department had become aware of Sutton's ability shortly after he'd come on board. He had been out on a routine patrol with an inexperienced deputy named Colefield. They had just driven by an all-night drive-in restaurant when Sutton ordered Colefield to turn the car around and park in the alley behind the restaurant. As they pulled up behind the restaurant, Sutton jerked the twelve-gauge shotgun from the rack on the car's dash. With Colefield at his heels he'd walked through the shadows to the front of the restaurant where they'd come face to face with two men. One had a paper bag in his hand. The other was carrying a narrow package wrapped in butcher paper. With a move that Colefield later described as "faster than grease on ice," Sutton aimed the shotgun at the nose of the man carrying the tan package. Then, without saying a word, Sutton pumped a round into the shotgun's chamber.

The man Sutton was aiming at didn't say a word either. He just dropped the package on the sidewalk and raised his hands. Colefield searched both men. He found the restaurant's money in the small sack and a "hog leg," a shotgun with no barrel and a stock cut down to a pistol grip, in the butcher paper. Afterward, Colefield asked Sutton how he'd known that something was going down at the restaurant. Sutton tried to explain it was a combination of gut feelings and intuition. When Colefield asked how long it had taken him to develop the talent, Sutton had smiled while answering. "Three generations."

The boulevard took him under the freeway, and he automatically slowed down. This was the rougher part of Ravina. The flashing neon signs of bars, lounges, taverns, strip joints, and massage parlors cast blurred electric images across his rain-streaked windshield. As he neared the end of the boulevard, he glanced at his watch. It was just after seven, and he decided to call it a day. Normally he wouldn't have gone home this early in the evening, but the wet October was beginning to play hell with his bad shoulder.

He wheeled the patrol car into an alley separating the massage parlor from the Hi-Low Bar. It was an ugly alley, narrow, littered with garbage. It was also the source of one of Sutton's most pleasurable memories. This was the place where he'd come face to face with a man called the Door. The Door worked as a crane operator for a nearby logging company. Prior to that he'd been a semipro football player, professional wrestler, and a bouncer in some of the roughest bars in Los Angeles. He was called the Door because of his size. The man stood six foot eight, had shoulders broad as an ax handle, and fists the size of pot roasts. He was called the Door because he was as big as a door. It was said that when he stood in the doorway of the Hi-Low Bar, a playing card couldn't be pushed between his body and the door frame. The Door's real name was Francis Lillian Flowers. To call him by his Christian name was to be saddled with a back brace. For life.

The call had come over Sutton's radio early on a Saturday night. The dispatcher described a disturbance at the Hi-Low Bar, then added, almost as an afterthought, that the Door was involved. Sutton turned his patrol car around and headed for the bar. He had never met the man, but knew his reputation.

Three months before Sutton had been hired, the Door

had permanently retired a Ravina sheriff's deputy in a fight at the Hi-Low Bar. The deputy had used a nightstick. The Door had used his fists. The deputy ended up in intensive care with massive head trauma and extensive skeletal injuries. The Door had a slight bruise over his ear. It had taken four deputies to handcuff the Door and throw him into the backseat of a patrol car, which he trashed with his feet on the way to jail. Like the deputy, the patrol car was also retired as a result of injuries. Because the deputy had used excessive force, the court dropped all charges. The Door walked.

When Sutton pulled up in front of the Hi-Low Bar, it looked as if every deputy on the force was standing out in front, waiting expectantly for him. Sutton knew his career was on the line. If the new police chief couldn't handle what he expected his men to handle, he might as well retire on the spot and go into social work.

Suddenly the door to the Hi-Low Bar exploded open and the Door stepped out onto the rainy sidewalk. Sutton was appalled at the size of the man and mildly surprised to see he was carrying three men. Something about the two older men clamped under the Door's left arm suggested they were gay. Sutton knew the man caught up under the giant's right arm. It was the Hi-Low's bouncer. Sutton asked what was going on.

The Door grumped something about an invasion of faggots and how he was going to teach them a lesson. He added that the bouncer had tried to break up the fun and now he was in for a lesson, too. When Sutton asked what that lesson was, the Door had said he was going bowling. The men were balls. Parking meters were the bowling pins.

By now a large crowd from the bar had flowed out onto the sidewalk and were cheering the Door. His deputies were getting nervous. Some had pulled out their nightsticks. Sutton figured he was thirty seconds away from a riot, so he did the unthinkable. He challenged the Door to a no-holds-barred fight in the alley. Just the two of them. No deputies. None of his friends. Just the two of them: man to man. The Door smiled and dropped the three men on the sidewalk. "You don't have to ask me twice."

Sutton handed his gun belt to a wide-eyed Colefield, then told his men not to come into the alley no matter what. Colefield looked as if he wanted to give Sutton his last rites.

Walking side by side, Henry Sutton and Francis Lillian Flowers entered the alley. As they approached a group of garbage cans, the Door took out his dentures, laid them on top of one of the cans, then flashed Sutton a toothless smile and charged. Sutton brought his fists up and braced himself.

It was then the Door slipped on a piece of wet trash. Both legs flew out from under him, and for one long moment he was suspended in midair, feet pointed at the sky, an expression of dumb surprise on his face. Then he crashed to the pavement, cracking his head against the back wall of the Hi-Low Bar.

Sutton waited for the Door to get up. When he didn't, Sutton moved in, knelt down beside the man and could see why the Door wasn't moving. Frances Lillian Flowers had split the back of his skull wide open when he'd hit the wall. Sutton probed the wound with his fingers. The fissure in Flowers' head was deep, spewing blood, covered with bone chips. The Door was in a bad way.

When Sutton walked out of the alley, even his own deputies seemed surprised. Sutton motioned to Colefield and in a whisper asked the man to call an ambulance. Then Henry Sutton turned to face the crowd from the bar. He had blood on his uniform, blood on his hands, and he knew what the crowd must be thinking. He played it for all it was worth. "Next?"

The crowd instantly melted into the night. Ten days later the Door came out of his coma and couldn't remember a thing. He automatically assumed his head injuries were the result of his fight with Henry Sutton. Sutton let the man think what he wanted. Only a fool would argue with Francis Lillian Flowers.

Smiling at the memory, Sutton checked his watch again. It wasn't that late, but his shoulder was cramping up on him and he didn't have any aspirin in the car. He raised the dispatcher on the radio, told him where he'd be for the rest of the evening, then headed home, hoping there was aspirin in his medicine chest.

Chapter
Two

Cable guided his car off the freeway at the main Ravina exit and turned into the first motel he came to. He shut the car down in front of the motel's office and gestured at the blinking Vacancy sign. "I'm beat. I can't drive anymore, not tonight."

The young woman sitting beside him shrugged and adjusted the car's mirror so she could see her face. Then she set to work on her appearance. She put on eyeliner, darkened her eyebrows, brushed her frosted hair into place, then finished up the intricate ritual with a coating of shiny dark red lipstick.

"You going to be okay?" he asked.

She capped her lipstick and glanced out the rear window at the bars and taverns lining the boulevard behind them. "Yeah. I'll be fine."

He watched her climb out of the car, her movements sleek and fluid. Just before she shut the door, he leaned over in the seat and looked up at her. "You know anybody in this town?"

The makeup and lipstick had aged her a good ten years. She glanced over at the boulevard, then back at him. "No," she said, smiling. "But give me a half hour and I will."

While she headed across the parking lot toward the brightly lit street, Cable went in and registered for a room. The night clerk had watched the woman get out of Cable's car and walk away. "Can I ask you a question?" he asked when he finally handed over the room key. Cable shrugged. "Your friend's got a walk like two cats fighting in a bag. Why'd you let her get away?"

"She's a nun," Cable answered, taking the key.

The clerk made a face. "Sure."

"Asshole," Cable grumbled as he pushed open the glass door and left.

"Prick," the clerk called after the door closed.

Cable went directly to his room, tossed the suitcase on the bed, and flopped down beside it. His eyes hurt, he was tired, his back ached from nine hours' worth of freeway driving, and he was disappointed at the indifferent way he and the girl had gone their separate ways. Hell, she hadn't even bothered to thank him for the ride.

Not that their relationship had been that meaningful. They had met seven hours earlier when he spotted her standing on the freeway trying to thumb a ride. Bored and tired of driving alone, he'd pulled over and for the first time in his life picked up a hitchhiker. His first hitchhiker turned out to be a stunningly beautiful woman, beautiful enough to tongue-tie him. They spent their first half hour together in silence. He couldn't think of anything to say; indifferent and preoccupied with her fingernails, his passenger didn't bother to say anything. Finally, to break the silence, he asked her her name, then asked what she did for a living.

"Street work," she had said. When he looked at her questioningly, she'd added, "You know, world's oldest profession and all that stuff."

"You're a farmer?" he quipped.

When she saw he was smiling, she started laughing herself. Moments later they settled into a comfortable relationship which tensed slightly a half hour later when she got around to offering him "a blow job for twenty-five dollars . . . well, fifteen, seeing as how you're giving me a ride and all that stuff."

He'd turned her down and felt an overwhelming need to explain why, citing the trauma of a recent divorce and pointing to a sheer cliff on one side of the highway. In turn, she had picked her teeth with a fingernail during his explanation and yawned like a cat at the end of it. Well, at least she doesn't feel rejected, he had thought.

Oddly enough, she turned out to be an interesting traveling companion, and Cable had enjoyed her during the drive. When she wasn't talking about her favorite topic, herself, she proved to be amazingly knowledge-able about a wide variety of diverse subjects: men, women, the police, the law, prescription drugs, designer drugs, and of all things, the stock market. She didn't talk much about her work, but from what she did say, Cable picked up that she had worn out her welcome in San Francisco, San Jose, and was on her way to Los Angeles to try her luck there.

Her name was Lynn Langley, and Cable had enjoyed her company. Now that he was alone in his motel room, he found he couldn't stop thinking about her. He rolled over on his back, laced his hands behind his head, and stared up at the ceiling, haunted by floating images of her face and figure, images that sent pleasant electric sensations through his body. Suddenly he grabbed a pillow and threw it violently at the door. Christ, it had been a long time since he'd been with a woman.

He sat up abruptly and began to massage his temples as he mulled over what a mess he'd made of his life.

Four months earlier he'd been an American living in Vancouver, Canada, under a special work visa. Four months earlier he had been a recently tenured professor at the University of British Columbia. His areas of expertise were anthropology and archeology.

Four months earlier he was doing what he wanted to

do, was good at what he did, and was well on his way to carving out a niche for himself in the best of all possible worlds . . . or so he had thought up until the moment his wife left him.

It was still difficult for him to accept the fact that a marriage of ten years was over. Even harder for him to accept was the fact that he alone was responsible for the destruction of the marriage. Since the split he had spent an inordinate amount of time looking at himself and delving through the memories of his marriage, and had come up with one major insight: what his wife had done had been his fault, and now he felt as if she had died and not just walked away. As for him, this trip to California was an effort to come to grips with his mistakes; his loss; his grief.

The nature of his work demanded that he spend four to six months a year digging up and researching remains of ancient Indian tribes along the Canadian coast. He had taken his students on the expeditions, but never once considered taking Karen; she would have gone. He knew that now, but the idea of asking her to come along had never occurred to him. On those other occasions, those months when he was at home and in the same room with her, he had been too interested in books, research, and broken, dusty pottery shards to pay much attention to her. It was a life of teaching, research, and publication deadlines. In the process he had forgotten how to hold hands or sit by a fire and talk to someone he loved.

She had been and still was a beautiful woman. She possessed strengths that she was only now beginning to fathom. She had invested ten years in their marriage and in return had been treated like an expensive coffee-table book. No wonder she'd become involved with another teacher in the anthropology department.

The younger professor had always struck Cable as immature, naive, and pompous. Basically an asshole. However, he did possess one quality that Cable didn't.

He knew how to pay attention to a woman in need of attention.

Cable had been blind to their affair. It had gone on for almost a year without his knowing. The whole thing finally surfaced when she met him for lunch at the university's faculty cafeteria. After they sat down in the noisy, crowded room, she'd announced in a clear low voice that they were no more; she was leaving him. Her lover—his colleague—had sat nervously and protectively by her side during the lunch, looking as if he expected Cable to punch his lights out. Cable hadn't.

A week later the full impact of his loss hit him like an avalanche, but by then it was too late. She was gone and wasn't coming back.

Now, sitting on the edge of a lumpy bed in a seedy motel in California, John Cable wished his wife well. His wishes were sincere. He wanted good things for her, and one of the few things that made his situation tolerable was that her new lover worshipped her and wanted to do everything he could to give her a good life.

Easing himself off the bed, Cable walked into the bathroom and turned on the shower. While he stood there waiting for the water to turn hot, it again occurred to him that he'd acted like a spineless jellyfish that day in the cafeteria. He'd just sat there, calm, controlled, a poised picture of lethargy who had even gone so far as to shake hands with the other man as if the whole scene had been a game governed by gentlemanly rules.

As he moved into the stinging hot spray of the shower, he recalled an old theory he'd heard about the nature of man. It suggested there were only two types of men: men of action and men of theory. One group did. The other group just speculated. Painters painted; art critics theorized. Boxers boxed; sportswriters described and analyzed. In essence, men of action lived life, experienced it. Men of theory philosophized about it. It didn't take much insight to figure out which category he fit into, Cable thought. He was a researcher, a teacher, a man who rarely grappled with life. He was indeed a man of theory, who, while watching his wife leave with another man, did nothing, except maybe think about it. Even now he wished he'd decked his rival and gone on to throw his wife over his shoulder so he could take her home and correct his mistakes. But that was the whole problem. Men of theory wished; thought wistful thoughts about what they should have done. Men of action did. Even now Dr. John Cable was still only wishing.

He finished, stepped out of the shower, and shook off his melancholy train of thought by focusing on the purpose of his trip to California. He had come down to visit a longtime friend and his professional mentor, Dr. Martin Larchmont. Larchmont lived in a small town forty miles north of Los Angeles. Cable planned on knocking on his door sometime tomorrow afternoon. Cable wasn't deceiving himself about his reasons for visiting the man who was almost a father to him. He was having a hard time dealing with the loss of his wife, and he had no one else to turn to. He needed to see his friend again.

Prior to the start of the fall term, Cable had requested and received a three-month leave of absence from the university. He had intended to use the time to get a handle on his life and grief, but had ended up spending the first two months of his leave just sitting in his apartment, contemplating the emptiness of it and his existence. That was when he decided to come to California to see Larchmont.

Martin Larchmont was a retired professor of archeology. Cable had met Larchmont just after he started pursuing his Ph.D. at the University of Washington. Larchmont was a respected professor in the University's graduate program, and he'd been assigned to Cable as his academic professor. Initially their relationship had started out as pupil and professor, but during the years it took Cable to pick up his doctorate, the relationship changed from student and mentor to that of close friends in spite of the forty-year difference in their ages. It never ceased to amaze Cable that they were friends. He had always felt privileged simply to be in the older man's presence. Dr. Larchmont was one of the most brilliant men Cable had ever known.

Larchmont had embarked on his academic career long before Cable was born. The man had started out as a Rhodes scholar and had gone from there to establishing a worldwide reputation for himself in the field of Far and Middle Eastern archeology. He was a gifted teacher, researcher, and the author of some thirty books, many of which were still considered classics in his field.

The interests Larchmont and Cable shared went beyond archeology. Both enjoyed opera, theater, and old movies, and each had an extensive classical record collection. But the essence of their relationship involved something more. Over the years they had evolved into the relationship of a father and a son, and this suited both, for John Cable had never known his father and Martin Larchmont had never had a son.

After obtaining his Ph.D., Cable accepted a teaching position at the University of British Columbia. In the same year he married Karen, and often the two of them would drive down to Seattle to see Larchmont and his wife. Those years, the early ones, were good years for Cable, and he had thought it would go on forever. It didn't. A mandatory retirement policy forced Larchmont out of the university shortly after he turned sixty-seven. He and his wife moved to California, where he continued to pursue his interest in Middle Eastern archeology with a strong emphasis on a little-known Kurdistan religion. In his letters to Cable he wrote of this new project as if he were born again.

Nine months later he lost interest in the project when a doctor discovered a tumor at the base of his wife's skull. It took less than three months for the multitentacled growth to kill her.

After his wife's death the man shut himself off completely for almost six months. Then he stepped out of the shadowy world of grief to accept a part-time faculty position at UCLA in the Westwood area of Los Angeles. The position required him to reenter the classroom, where, as he later said in one of his letters, "the students and the research made me whole again."

It was Cable's hope to draw upon the older man's strength so he, too, could come to grips with his own unresolved grief. He knew his trip to visit Larchmont was a selfish one, but he also knew that selfish or not, Martin Larchmont wouldn't mind.

A headache brought on by hunger put an end to Cable's mental wanderings. He dressed, got the name of a restaurant from the motel clerk, and walked up the boulevard, too tired and hungry to notice the chill or the incoming fog.

Cable kicked himself and the motel clerk as he approached the restaurant. It was one of those prefab franchised outlets cloned by a neurotic computer which had cross-tabulated population densities with established traffic patterns and then spat out a program that said: build here.

Cable entered, expecting the worst, and he got it: chrome tables, vinyl chairs, plastic roof beams, and a rug that hadn't been vacuumed in days. Open twenty-four hours a day, the restaurant was staffed with teenagers whose inability to keep the restrooms clean was surpassed only by their inability to prepare food. Still, he was starving, so he grabbed a tray and went through the serving line.

As he carried his tray into the dining area, he noticed the young hitchhiker he'd brought to town earlier. It was hard not to notice her. Lynn Langley was waving with both arms and motioning for him to join her.

The dinner was bad, but the girl sitting across from him was stunning. It was difficult for him to keep his eyes off her, especially with his mind and body toying with the idea of propositioning her. More than once she caught him staring at her, and Cable was always the one who looked away.

Finally, as Cable suspiciously studied his dessert, trying to decide if it was green Jell-O or old pudding, he heard her say, "Can't make up your mind, can you?

" 'Bout what?" he asked, feigning innocence.

"About whether or not to fuck me after dinner."

She had a way of coming to the point, he thought. "It had crossed my mind."

"From the minute you picked me up until now." She smiled mischievously.

He gave her a sheepish look. "You're pretty good at reading minds."

She traded her empty dessert bowl for his full one. "Yeah," she mused. "I guess I am. You got to be in this line of work. I mean, if I go out and hustle the wrong man, I could end up getting busted or worse. I could get hurt. I guess it's sort of something I developed. You know, like a talent." She smiled at the prospect that she might have a talent.

She spooned up some of Cable's dessert, let it slide down her throat like a raw oyster. "I know you want to; what I don't understand is why you don't. You told me about your marriage and all of that, but one bad scene shouldn't turn you into a monk."

Her observation irritated him, probably because it was accurate. "It's more than my marriage," he said defensively. "There're other things like . . . like feelings and the idea of money—"

"You think I'll ask too much?"

"No. It just seems there should be something more than money involved. Making love requires feelings, emotions. I need an investment to make love, and it shouldn't come from my wallet. Without emotions, it's just an exercise in friction." He shrugged, hoping she understood.

She didn't. She glanced at her watch, then at him. "Friction? You're talking three feet above my brain." She checked her watch a second time.

"You got an appointment?" he asked.

"Yeah . . . but I can break it if you want."

He shook his head. The cold way she had consulted her watch had put a stop to whatever feelings he'd had for her. Instead, he found himself wondering what would happen if he didn't finish within the allotted time. Would he have to pay her overtime? Or just stop when the alarm went off? Her soft voice interrupted his sarcastic train of thought.

"Did you hear me? I said I could break it."

Cable found himself staring down at her empty dessert bowl. "No. Nice offer, but no thanks." He looked up at her curiously. "How'd you meet someone so fast?"

Lynn Langley shrugged. "I found myself a friend five minutes after I left you. My appointment tonight is with a friend of my new friend."

"You work fast," Cable said, trying not to sound sarcastic and failing.

She picked up on his tone and a hardness came into her voice. "Comes from liking your work." She stood up and began to put on a nylon windbreaker. "Anyway, thanks for the ride . . . and hey, thanks for not asking me all the standard questions about what I do."

"Questions?"

"You know . . . like how'd a girl like me get into this business? Do I climax? Do I pay taxes? All the standard shit guys ask when they find out what I do."

Cable smiled. "Do you?"

"Do I what?" She gave him a cold look.

"Pay taxes?"

She faked a laugh. "What do you think?" She zipped up her windbreaker, flipped her frosted hair back over the collar, started to turn away, then stopped. "If you see me tomorrow on the highway, give me a ride. Maybe we can renegotiate and get away from this wallet stuff so it's not just friction to you. Okay?''

Feeling alone again, Cable nodded and watched her walk out of the restaurant and down the foggy boulevard. He lit a cigarette and exhaled the smoke pensively. She was a sensuous woman, and he had wanted her badly. A man of action would have gone with her and enjoyed her. But not him. All he'd done was make excuses and speculate and theorize about money, friction, love, and emotions.

Damn, he thought, isn't there any way to break out of this mold?

Chapter
Three

Lynn Langley was tired and down to her last twenty-seven dollars. The trick set up for her by the man she'd met and fellated in his car in an alley behind a Safeway supermarket was two hours late. Shit, she thought, the asshole's ability to send her extra business was on par with his ability to get off in under five minutes.

She swore to herself, released the pinball lever, and watched disinterestedly as the ball bolted forward, then looped downward into a gaudy maze of lights and bells. She hated playing pinball, but shoving quarters into the machine was the only way the 7-Eleven night clerk would allow her to stay in the store at this hour of the night. She glanced at the clock on the wall. It was almost eleven. Her eyes drifted downward until they connected with the face of the clerk. He was looking at her with disgust. She wasn't used to that. The looks she got from men were usually looks of approval, if not straightforward looks of gut-level desire.

She thought about giving the pimply clerk one of her smoldering sexy looks, but decided against it. The asshole was probably one of those religious types, probably

36

carried a Gideon's Bible in each pocket. She fired off the last pinball, then in an act of disgust aimed more at the clerk than the game, she clubbed the machine with both fists, causing it to tilt. Pleased with herself, she walked slowly past the cash register. Just before she pushed her way out the door, she turned and smiled at the clerk. When he finally smiled back, she gave him the finger.

She walked across the foggy parking lot, heading toward what she thought was the heart of town. She was looking for an all-night restaurant so she could drum up some business. Once inside, she would order a cup of coffee, pull out some stationery, and begin writing a letter. It was a way to look busy while she checked out the men. If she spotted a likely john, she'd eventually approach him, her opening line being: "Got a stamp I could buy?

At twenty-two, Lynn Langley was an experienced hooker. She had lost her virginity some eight years earlier at a drive-in movie. Her reaction to the fumbling three-minute event was one of indifference coupled with some irritation over having missed the previews. In the years to follow, her cold impassionate attitude about sex never changed.

When she was sixteen, she discovered her body was a gold mine. The revelation came to her when her high school biology teacher offered her a passing grade and twenty-five dollars in return for a quickie on a laboratory table. By April of that year she had upped her grades in four out of seven classes, and the school's old janitor had begun following her down the hall. She made the mistake of turning down the janitor, and it was he who brought her extracurricular activities to the attention of the school board. On the same day that three male teachers and one female teacher resigned, Lynn Langley got kicked out of school and then kicked out of her mother's apartment.

She left town and within a month was a full-time

professional. She did oral encounter sessions in Berkeley, outcall nude modeling stints in Stockton, then spent the better part of three years working the massage parlors in San Francisco.

She stopped abruptly on the sidewalk and checked the dark foggy surroundings. This sure as hell wasn't the center of town. What do they do around here, she wondered, turn off the streetlights at sunset? She picked a new direction and headed off. The sounds of her high heels glancing off the sidewalk was hypnotic, conducive to thought. Lynn Langley had no false illusions about herself or her profession. She had no heart of gold, and knew no rich customer would come riding out of the sunset to rescue her from a seedy line of work. She was a seasoned veteran who had seen and done it all. Nothing bothered her; nothing surprised her anymore. During her seven years as a hooker, she'd been sodomized, wrapped in Saran Wrap, dressed up in latex underwear, spent time on the S and M circuit, been involved in some bondage, endured golden showers, and had recently had several encounters with the sixty-year-old owner of a chain of pizza parlors. The man had paid her good money to jerk him off into clear plastic freezer bags. Amused, she'd stood by and watched the king of the San Jose pizza parlor franchises seal the bag with a wire twist and store it in the trunk of his car, where it took its place amid dozens of other identical bags.

Lynn stopped on the sidewalk and looked about once again. It was slowly dawning on her that she was lost and the fog was getting worse. She knew she was in an older section of town. It looked and smelled old. The sidewalk had been fractured and heaved by the massive roots of giant oak trees lining the street. Silhouettes of century-old two- and three-story homes loomed up on both sides of her like a double row of black tombstones.

Irritated, cold and nervous, Lynn Langley trudged on, hissing to herself in a muted whisper. "Where the fuck am I? *Where the fuck am I?*" It was hard going. The sidewalk was leading her up the slope of a steep hill. As she continued to walk, she noticed she was leaving the houses and the street lamps behind.

A quarter of a mile on, a tall fence of cast-iron spears thick with ivy emerged from the fog directly in front of her. She slowed and approached cautiously, hoping the road didn't end at the fence. As she closed on it, she could see the street didn't end; it angled off to the right and followed the fence around the side of the hill.

Briefly, she contemplated her choices. She could try to retrace her steps back down the hill, and with luck she might be able to find the 7-Eleven store. Or she could continue to follow the sidewalk and fence around to the other side of the hill.

At that moment a gust of wind parted the fog, and she caught a glimpse of a greenish light shimmering off in the distance up on the hill. As the fog closed around her like a curtain, she took off again, walking with long strides toward the source of the light.

She felt good again, relieved. The light had to be a neon sign, and a neon sign meant people, a gas station, a bar. Hell, she'd settle for a phone booth. All it would take would be one fucking phone call, a cab would come out, and she'd be out of this desolate neighborhood. She hurried on.

She was almost running now, and suddenly the light became brighter as the ivy on the fence stopped abruptly. She slowed to a stop, turned, and found herself standing before a set of massive gates. As she stepped up to the gates and peered through the bars, she saw the source of the light and burst into tears.

Set some yards back on the other side of the fence was a simple sign mounted on brick pillars. Stark green neon letters said: HORRCOVE CEMETERY. Lynn Langley hit the gate with her fist and sobbed. "Shit . . . all this way for a cemetery, a fucking cemetery!" She hit the gates a second time and wiped the tears from her face.

Lynn Langley turned away and began walking slowly

down the hill, the sharp taps of her heels echoing in the fog. She'd walked only a few yards when she saw a large black shape coming out of the fog in front of her. She stopped instantly. There's nothing out there, she thought. It's just a shadow. She willed her body to step toward the dark mass and her body balked.

She just stood there, rooted in the sidewalk, waiting for the wind to dissolve the phantasm of fog. The wind gusted, leaves skittered along the street, but the dark figure remained in front of her, still and foreboding as a giant black statue.

Lynn Langley whirled around and started back up the hill toward the gates to the Horrcove Cemetery. A chill trilled down her spine, and she knew without looking that the apparition was following her.

Then she heard the sounds, low and rasping like the labored breathing of an asthmatic. But the rhythm and volume was all wrong. What she was hearing sounded more like the slow-motion pumping of a blacksmith's bellows, harsh, loud, irregular.

She began to walk faster . . . and faster. Then she broke into a run. The sounds behind her refused to fade away. Oh, fuck, she thought, it's staying up with me.

She ran blindly past the massive gates and on up the hill toward a single street lamp thirty yards away. She needed the light. Craved it. The light would shine down on what was behind her. Give it substance. Make it real. Once she knew what it was, she could deal with it. She was almost to the light when she skidded on the wet street. Her feet skated out from under her, and she went down hard, rolling hip over shoulder into the circle of light the street lamp splayed out over the dark street.

Unhurt, she scrambled to her hands and knees. The harsh irregular breathing sounds from whatever was out there in the darkness just beyond the reach of the light brought her to her feet. She turned her back to the sounds, reached into her purse and pulled out an old rusty butcher knife with a ten-inch-long serrated blade.

It was her best friend. She'd carried it for years. It had more stopping power than mace, was bigger than a switchblade, and just as sharp as a straight razor. More than once it had saved her life.

Throwing her purse aside, she gripped the knife with both hands, fighting the temptation to look over her shoulder at whatever was coming toward her. "I've got a knife, you asthmatic son of a bitch . . . come and get it, fucker." Slowly she began to turn to face her assailant. As she moved, she noticed her hands were steady. The knife was steady. She could handle the son of a bitch who was out there making those scary sounds. She'd teach him to pull a practical joke. . . .

When she completed her half turn, she lifted her eyes to look at what was coming into the light.

What she saw blew her mind into total oblivion. Her consciousness tripped out like an overloaded computer. Her brain's synapses snapped, the circuitry became inoperable, and Lynn Langley was immersed in a merciful nothing. Her brain's last act was a massive effort in self-defense. It shrouded her completely in a numbing cloak of darkness.

Had she remained alert, and able to see what was now approaching, she would have died from heart failure or terror. But she couldn't see it, and so she just stood there, still holding the knife, her eyes registering nothing, while the beast continued to slouch toward her.

The creature was huge with translucent skin that shimmered in the night with a kind of strange untapped energy. Its shape was human, but that was all.

As it came for her, it studied her with eyes that had no pupils, no corneas, or irises. Instead, there simply existed eye sockets filled with yellowish liquid and covered over with clear nictitating membranes, like the eyes of a crocodile.

It lurched to a stop directly in front of her and studied her with glowing yellow eyes. Then it brought its massive right arm up, and with a slow sweeping motion it brushed its claw along the side of the girl's jaw. Her muted body jerked and vibrated uncontrollably until her features were blurred by rapid trembling motions. Searing white flashes of light encased her body in arc-welding brightness.

Slowly the creature brought its giant paw downward; hideous claws, black as the world's last midnight, gently touched the hands still gripping the knife. The spasmodic explosions of light began again, and the girl's body was enveloped in vivid white flashes brighter than lightning.

A microsecond later it was over. As the creature with the countenance of a demon dropped its paw away, trails of smoke drifted off of the girl's body to blend with the fog, and the knife dissolved into ashes.

The creature stepped back away from its still standing victim and pondered her for a moment with eyes that glowed yellow in the fog. Then, almost as an afterthought, it lashed out with a massive arm and slapped her. The effect was like a dandelion puffball in a windstorm. Lynn Langley literally flew across the street, landing with a sick splat in a thick bed of ivy growing near the base of the fence on the far side of the road.

Slowly, painfully, the creature lurched out of the light and back into the fog.

Moments later a weak gust of wind blew the ashes of Lynn Langley's butcher knife into an infinite nothing.

Chapter Four

Sloams's pickup hit a deep pothole in the road. The sudden jarring intensified his hangover to the point where it felt like shotguns were being fired off in his brain, and he cursed.

His name was Johnny Joe Sloams, and he was a full-time maintenance man for the Horrcove Cemetery. He was also an alcoholic, and like many drunks, he was a wife and child beater; or at least, he had been up until eighteen months ago.

A year and a half earlier his fifteen-year-old son had decided to end Sloams's reign of terror. While Sloams was at work, the boy packed his and his mother's belongings in the trunk of the family car, then waited for Johnny Joe to come home.

As had been his pattern for years, Sloams arrived home at seven, already drunk. By nine he was sound asleep on the living room couch.

The boy put his mother in the family car, then returned to the house, intending to put his plan into effect, a plan that would forever guarantee his father would never hit him or his mother again.

After getting a frying pan and a serrated butcher knife from the kitchen, he walked into the living room, where his father still lay passed out facedown on the couch. The boy stared down at his father for a long moment, remembering all the times this man had hit him and beaten up his mother.

The boy hit Johnny Joe Sloams in the head with the frying pan. He hit him just once, not hard enough to kill him, just hard enough to anesthetize him. Then he sat down on the backs of his father's legs, and without hesitating, he took the knife and hacked through both of Johnny Joe Sloams's Achilles tendons just above the heels. The severed tendons snapped and parted like tightly strung cables.

The boy tossed the pan and the knife in the sink, phoned for an ambulance, and joined his mother in the car. By the time the ambulance arrived, they were ten miles out of Ravina, heading south on the freeway.

The doctors tried, but there wasn't much they could do. After hearing he'd walk on his tiptoes for the rest of his life, Sloams had daily fantasies of how he would kill his son and his wife after he got out of the hospital. When he was discharged, he didn't do anything. It came to Sloams one night that anyone who could do to him what his son had done was just as capable of doing something worse. He figured if he found them, the boy might turn the tables again. This time he might just cut off Johnny Joe's legs.

As he rounded a curve in the older part of Ravina and drove on toward the cemetery, Sloams hoped nobody had croaked recently. He was in a bad mood, his hangover wasn't going away, and he'd hurt one of his heel tendons while trying to dance in the bar last night. He was in no mood to dig a grave today. It was out of the question. Rolling up sod would hurt his tendons, and with the shape his head was in, running a noisy tractor with a backhoe might just kill him.

Suddenly the tall gates to the Horrcove Cemetery loomed up in his windshield. Sloams gasped and stabbed the brakes, bringing the pickup to a noisy rocking stop. "Shit," he whispered, glancing about to see if anyone had witnessed his near collision with the gates. Too close, he thought, remembering the time the Horrcove brothers had come down out of their monastery to chew him out for driving too fast in the cemetery. Their cold malevolent eyes had turned his spine to ice. He'd driven very slowly after that. Very slowly.

The Horrcove brothers terrified him. They lived in the huge stone mansion near the back of the cemetery, and while they rarely emerged from their mortuary, when they did, Sloams's stomach always did a slow lurching roll.

He unsnapped the key ring from his belt, found the key to the gates, then wondered why his employers, two twin brothers who had to be old as the hills, should frighten him. He'd thought about it often, but had never come up with a reason, not one he could put his finger on.

He opened the door, started to climb out, and froze when he noticed a large pile of rags half buried in the ivy over by the fence. Then he noticed something else. A gray leg was sticking out from under the rags. "Another fucking practical joke," Sloams muttered, remembering the time some kids had hung a dressed mannequin from one of the trees inside the cemetery.

He eased himself out of the pickup and began tiptoeing toward the mannequin. He was five feet from the pile of rags when a sharp gust of wind blew away part of a shredded windbreaker, revealing a pale face and frosted hair. God, they make dummies realistic nowadays, he thought, until he noticed the eyes, eyes that were staring straight at him. Then he knew.

Johnny Joe Sloams whirled away from the body and took off running for the pickup on his tiptoes. He clambered into the truck, made a screeching U-turn in front of the gates, and started down the hill toward town.

He needed the police. He needed a drink. He decided to stop at the first bar he came to and call the cops.

Chapter
Five

"Look, Henry," Dr. Mark Childress said loudly, "this town's got an orthopedic surgeon, a psychiatrist, several ENT men . . ." Childress had been looking at the floor, but now he lifted his eyes and stared up at Sutton. ". . . but the one thing we don't have in Ravina is a forensic pathologist. And that's what this situation calls for."

As Dr. Childress's words echoed off the tiled walls of the hospital's doctors' lounge, Sutton shrugged in a gesture of frustration and walked over to the coffeepot. Childress slumped down in a slick vinyl chair. He felt guilty about raising his voice, but the sheriff shouldn't have hounded him for answers he didn't have. He thought about the dead body in the morgue three stories below and shivered. "Look, Henry, I just don't have the answers. I don't know what could have done that to the girl." He turned in his chair in time to see his friend coming toward him, a cup of coffee in each huge hand. He accepted the cup and eased back in the chair.

Mark Childress was a forty-year-old physician specializing in the field of emergency room trauma service. He practiced his specialty almost nightly in the Ravina County Hospital's emergency room.

Before Sutton arrived, it had been a quiet shift that started at ten P.M. and should have ended at eight A.M. He'd almost made it. He had put in his ten hours and was starting to take off his smock when Henry Sutton had walked into the emergency room to ask for a favor. A simple favor. Just come down to the morgue and take a look at the body they'd just brought in.

His examination had been rapid, superficial, and it had left him with a queasy stomach and a bad taste in his mouth. Afterward, they'd gone into the doctors' lounge, where Sutton had begun pumping him for answers he just didn't have.

Now, as he drank his coffee, he looked up at his large friend. "It's got me stumped, Henry. I don't know what could have caused all that. Hell, the girl's teeth and fingernails are missing and her skeletal system has been pulverized. The tissue surrounding her sockets and the tips of her fingers show evidence of granulation—even crystallization—and the only way I know for that to occur is through the application of high heat . . . very high heat."

Childress slumped deeper into the chair and pinched the bridge of his nose. "Couple years back, I saw the body of a mountain climber who'd been hit by a big bolt of lightning. Certain areas of his skin vaguely resembled the dead girl's fingertips and the tissue around her tooth sockets. Other than lightning, maybe a laser beam could have caused burns like that, but I'm not sure."

Deeply puzzled, if not frightened, Childress talked on as if the sound of his own voice would ease his tension. "Then there's the dead girl's skeletal system. Something or someone literally jellied every bone in that body, and it was done without breaking the skin. Going back to my own experiences, I've examined the bodies of people who've jumped off forty story buildings. Their skeletal systems come closest to that of the girl's skeleton, but the similarity ends there because their skin was anything but intact. Hers is." Childress shrugged with his hands. "You know, the only reason that girl looks anywhere near human is because of the tensile strength of human skin. I get the feeling if you poked her with a pin, her body would deflate like a balloon.

"Now do you see why I don't have any answers?"

"Christ," Sutton grumbled, "all I saw was a puffy body with no teeth." He lit a cigarette and inhaled deeply. "You mentioned something about a forensic pathologist. Can you get ahold of one?"

"Yeah," Childress said. "There's one down in Lompoc. He's with the Air Force, stationed out at the Vandenberg Base Hospital. He's good, real good."

"Think you can get him to come up here and take a look at the girl?"

Childress nodded as he put aside his coffee cup and pushed himself out of the chair. "Probably. It's good PR for the Air Force when they can get one of their experts to help out us lowlife civilians. Besides, the guy loves a good mystery and this one's a real beaut."

"Can you get him here this morning?" Sutton asked, pushing his luck. "I'm under the gun to get some answers to this mess fast."

Childress glanced up at the clock on the wall. "I'll give him a call. He's a colonel and shouldn't have any problems clearing it with his commander. Lay you odds he's here by nine-thirty."

Sutton exhaled a cloud of smoke toward the ceiling and willed himself to relax. For the first time in years he felt grateful for having an Air Force base located only twenty-two miles away.

The clock in the doctors' lounge registered nine-forty-two in the morning when Colonel William C. Seafront finished slipping on his surgical smock. Turning toward Childress, Sutton, and a male nurse, he smiled congenially. "Well, gentlemen, let's go see this body you got."

The men rode the elevator to the basement of the hospital and walked rapidly down an empty corridor until they came to the morgue. Childress unlocked the door, and the men entered a green tiled room. All eyes were immediately drawn to a large stainless steel table in the center of the room and the sheet-covered body lying on top of it.

Childress drew back the sheet. Seafront briefly surveyed the body, then reached above his head to a suspended hook which held a small pencil-sized microphone. He unhooked the microphone, clipped it to the front of his smock, and glanced over at Childress. "Voice activated?" Childress nodded.

Seafront strolled across the room and opened the doors to a stainless steel cabinet. He pulled on rubber gloves and then went on to throw some surgical instruments onto a portable steel tray. He pushed the tray back to the autopsy table.

With a keen sense of drama, the forensic pathologist allowed himself a slight smile. "There are no mysteries in this universe, just elusive answers. Now, let's solve this mystery."

Sutton made a face at Seafront's comment, but continued to watch the pathologist intensely, barely noticing the heavy odors of alcohol, formalin, and asafetida.

The pathologist began to dictate in an unemotional mechanical voice: "Date, October twenty-fourth, time" —Seafront glanced at his wristwatch—"Oh-nine-fifty-five. The subject is a relatively young white female whose age is . . ." Seafront glanced at Childress. Childress gestured to Sutton.

Sutton said: "The ID we found in her purse said she was twenty-two. Her name is . . . was Lynn Lee Langley."

Seafront repeated the information into the microphone and continued with his monologue. "I am now proceeding with the external examination. The upper portion of the torso is pale to gray in color. The lower quadrants of the body, especially the areas of the lower thighs and buttocks, are purplish in color, suggesting body fluids have been settling for approximately seven to ten hours.

"The body appears relaxed and supple; there is limited evidence of rigor mortis, possibly related to the massive trauma done to the skeletal system. There is a slight but noticeable cadaveric odor.

"The hair is abundant and multicolored. Coloring appears to be chemically induced. Hair is brown at the roots. Facial features are swollen and not pronounced. This would be consistent with the trauma done to the skull.

"There is a multicolored tattoo of a butterfly on the subject's right breast and a second tattoo, that of a small devil, located approximately two centimeters above the subject's pubic hairline."

Seafront touched the dead girl's face with his fingers. "The eyelids are partially open, pupils are round and fully dilated, irises brown in color, cornea appears to be firm and translucent.

"The upper and lower lips are relatively rigid; closer examination reveals subject's teeth are missing. Extractions have been recent. There is no evidence of clotting, suggesting the removal of the teeth occurred after death. Upper and lower gums are gray to black in color. The tissue in this area is granulated, with the texture of the granulated particles being similar to sand."

With his gloved hand still holding the girl's mouth open, Seafront glanced up at Childress. Sutton caught the brief look of puzzlement on the forensic pathologist's face before he resumed his examination. "The color and texture of the granulation suggests that intense heat was present in the immediate area of the subject's mouth. Source of heat is currently unknown."

Seafront clapped his hand over the microphone and glanced over at Childress. "Jesus Christ, Mark. It looks like someone lasered this girl's teeth out."

"Told you this one was a bitch," Childress said,

pleased that he wasn't the only one who found this case confusing.

The Air Force pathologist continued with the examination. "The subject's hands are small, supple with no rigidity. Like the rest of the skeletal system, the hands and arms show evidence of massive trauma. Based on a visual and digital examination, it would appear there are no bones intact in any part of the body. Oddly, the subject's skin is sound and undamaged. The fingernails on the left hand are missing. There is more evidence of granulation in the cuticle areas of all digits, again suggesting the presence of intense heat similar to that which may have been induced around the area of the mandible and maxillary. End of external examination."

Seafront picked up a scalpel, announcing he was beginning an internal examination. "Scalp opened with an intermastoid incision."

Sutton watched the pathologist jerk at the dead girl's hair. "Am now removing skull flap." An instant later Seafront yanked the girl's entire scalp up and away from the fragmented skull and laid it, hair down, over her face like a wet doormat. Sutton groaned and walked away from the autopsy table. He could still hear the pathologist's droning monologue. "Skull is fragmented and held together only by the exterior membranes. Largest single fragment of the skull measures approximately two centimeters across and is roughly the size of a dime. Sections of the calvarium are embedded in the outer tissues of the brain."

Sutton took several deep breaths. I can handle this, he thought. That's just a piece of meat on the table. In the background Seafront continued. "It is not necessary to saw through the skull cap for this extraction, as the skull is already fragmented. I am now separating the medulla oblongata from the spinal cord."

"Just a piece of meat," Sutton said. "I can handle this."

He turned and started back toward the autopsy table.

At that moment the pathologist scooped up the dead girl's entire brain in both hands and dropped it into a stainless steel pan the nurse was holding.

"Oh, fuck," Sutton mumbled, heading for the door.

Alone in the hallway, the police chief of Ravina lit a cigarette. Four cigarettes later the two doctors and the nurse walked out of the morgue. Sutton studied the men as they walked toward him and knew instinctively they didn't know what was going on. All three looked tired, distraught, frightened. Seafront pulled a cigarette out from under his surgical smock. Sutton lit it for him. The pathologist coughed and blew a cloud of smoke toward the ceiling and followed it with his eyes rather than look at the sheriff.

Finally he coughed again. "I know you want answers, Sheriff, so I'll tell you the five things Childress and I are sure of. One, the girl is dead. Two, her teeth and fingernails are missing. Three, some power turned her skeletal system into dried oatmeal. Four, her skin is intact and it shouldn't be, not with the internal injuries she had."

"And five?" Sutton asked.

"Number five," Seafront said, glancing over at Childress before he looked back at Sutton, "is that this is just one question after another. I don't know why her skin is intact, I don't know why the tissue is granulated. It's a big bunch of *I don't knows* from beginning to end—" The pathologist broke into a rasping cough. When he stopped, he glared at his cigarette, then ground it out in an ashtray. "I'm afraid that's it, at least until we get the test results back."

"Tests?" Sutton asked.

Seafront pulled out another cigarette and looked at it distastefully. "I quit smoking two years ago. On the day I quit, I bought a package of Camels and I've carried that pack with me for the past two years and never touched a one. It was like a symbol of my own will-power. Now look at me. I'm so shook up over a dead girl's body, I'm smoking two-year-old Camels." He accepted a light from Sutton. "What were you saying? Oh, yeah, the tests. We're sending tissue, blood, and body fluid samples to Los Angeles for toxicology, spectral analysis, and radiation tests. The results'll be back in forty-eight to seventy-two hours. Maybe then we'll know what we're dealing with."

"Radiation tests?" Sutton said, raising his eyebrows.

"The tissue in the areas of the tooth sockets and fingernails was strange stuff. I've never seen anything like it. It doesn't resemble anything like human skin, even skin subjected to high heat. Basically, it looks like its structure's been altered. I think the process is called molecular reformation, but I'm not sure. I'm not up on my physics, but I think the only way that can happen is through the inducements of radiation. But then that brings up the problem of where did the radiation come from." Noticing Sutton's expression, Seafront smiled wryly. "I told you this was a mess. One unanswered question after another."

Sutton walked out onto the steps of the hospital and was immediately hit by a cold, hard wind. Before he could turn up his collar, his bad shoulder began to ache and he hunched over in the wind, massaging his shoulder as he made his way to his patrol car out in the parking lot.

He eased himself into the car, started it, put it in reverse, and started to back out until a loud rap on the driver's window made him hit the brake. Whipping around, Sutton rolled down the window and stared up at the windblown figure of Deputy Robert Calms. "You just scared the shit out of me, Calms."

"Sorry." Calms hunkered down beside the car so he could see Sutton. "But you did say you wanted to be notified if something developed." Sutton nodded, turned off the engine, and slumped back in the seat. He considered inviting Calms into the patrol car, but didn't. He didn't like the man.

Robert Calms was an experienced deputy who'd been

on the force some five or six years before Sutton had arrived. Competitive and lacking in insight, Calms pursued professional success in all the wrong ways. Essentially, he was an ostentatious ass-kissing backstabber who didn't seem to realize that Henry Sutton promoted his men on the basis of performance, not on how they wore their uniform or how many times they tried to kiss his boots.

Sutton studied the deputy through the partially open car window. Robert Calms's uniform was super-starched, its creases sharp enough to slice bologna. Sutton couldn't see the man's boots, but he knew they were shining like new patent leather. He'd heard the rumors about Calms spending two hours a night with shoe polish, alcohol, spit and cotton balls to keep up the shine. Sutton believed the rumors. He'd seen the baby diaper Calms carried in his hat for dry shines.

"What is it?" Sutton impatiently asked.

"We ran the ID," Calms said, his words sounding rehearsed, "and you were right about her being a hooker. What else could she have been with all those naked pictures she carried of herself in her purse? What do you think she did with those photos? Sell'em to her customers? Some souvenir."

"What about her rap sheet?" Sutton asked, wanting to get on with it.

Calms pulled out a small leather notebook with a sheriff's badge and his initials embossed on the cover. He opened it and began reading. "During the past five years she was busted nine times for prostitution. The first bust took place in Santa Rosa when she was seventeen. That was followed by busts in San Francisco, Oakland, then Stockton. Her most recent arrest occurred three weeks ago. San Jose Vice picked her up in a raid on a massage parlor—"

"Any known associates?"

"You mean like pimps? Boyfriends?"

"Is there anybody out there who'd want to kill her?"

Calms shook his head. "No, sir."

"Thanks for the update," Sutton mumbled, irritated at the lack of information. He began rolling up his window, not realizing Calms wanted to continue the discussion. An instant later Calms squealed like a hurt puppy, and Sutton realized he'd closed the window on the man's fingers. He cracked the window slightly, allowing Calms to jerk his fingers free. "We do have one solid lead going for us, sir."

For the first time since the conversation began, Robert Calms had Henry Sutton's full attention. "Well, Jesus Christ, why didn't you say so?" He rolled his window all the way down.

"While you were in the hospital, we hit the town with all available units. We had a good description of the girl's clothing and a better description of her face because of the photos in her purse."

Sutton considered shooting Calms on the spot. The Polaroid pictures Langley had of herself showed everything but her face. "So you showed the photos to a lot of people?"

"You bet," Calms proudly boasted.

I'll kill him, Sutton thought.

"And I got lucky. A night clerk just going off duty at the Sunset Motel remembered the girl. She came to town last night with a guy who spent the night at the motel."

"Did they check in together?"

"No. The man checked in and the girl took off walking west on the boulevard."

Sutton gave out with a bitter sigh. They were right back where they started from. "Get the man's name and see what he knows."

"He knows a lot, Sheriff. Seems that later on this guy asks the night clerk for the name of a restaurant. The clerk recommends the Speedy Steak. So on a hunch, I go down there and catch the night manager just before he gets off. I show him the picture, ask him some questions. Sure enough he remembers seein' the dead girl and the guy the clerk described to me eating together. Now, he doesn't remember seeing them leave together, but he thinks they might have.''

Wondering why Calms had saved the best for last, Sutton fished a cigarette out of his pocket. Immediately Calms pulled out a gold-plated Zippo engraved with a police badge and his initials and lit Sutton's cigarette. After Calms pocketed the lighter, Sutton lit his lit cigarette with his own Bic lighter and exhaled ruefully. ''Sounds like we got a possibility. Get the make of his car and his license plate from the motel and put out a wanted for questioning all points.''

''Don't have to.'' Calms grinned broadly. ''The perp's still at the motel, and he's not going anywhere until you clear it. I've got two men watching his car and two men watching his room.''

Well, at least they had someplace to start, someone to question, Sutton thought. ''Pick him up. I'll talk to him downtown.''

''Consider it done,'' Calms promised. He started to salute, saw Sutton start to scowl, and thought better of it. He turned and headed off.

Sutton started his patrol car, then shut it off. ''Calms!'' The deputy stopped in mid-stride and looked at Sutton expectantly. ''Nice job. You did well.''

''Thanks, Henry.'' Calms started off again.

''Calms!''

Calms did a quick about-face. ''Sir?''

''Two things,'' Sutton said. ''First, this guy is not a perp. Perpetrators are people who've done something. We don't know if this guy has. Don't treat him like a perp. Second, doing a good job doesn't give you the right to call me Henry. That's something we'll talk about in twenty years if you keep doing a good job.'' Calms nodded, did another military about-face, and jogged off to his patrol car.

Sutton stubbed out a cigarette and watched Calms pull

out of the hospital parking lot. God, it was hard to be nice to that man, he thought, remembering the three resolutions he'd made on the previous New Year's Eve: I will not work on holidays, I will not show up for work early, and I will be civil to Deputy Robert Calms. On New Year's Day, he'd gone to work a half hour early, and fifteen minutes later he'd reamed out Calms's ass for something or other.

Sutton sighed, rolled up his window, poured himself a cup of coffee from his thermos, and reached for the aspirin in the glove compartment.

Chapter
Six

Cable was not impressed. He was not impressed with the four deputies who had stopped him in the motel parking lot as he was walking to his car, and he was definitely not impressed with the runty deputy in the starched uniform who'd shoved him in the back of a patrol car and then wiped his boots off with a baby diaper.

Ten minutes later the parade of police cars stopped in back of the Ravina City Hall and five silent deputies hustled Cable up a corridor, past a receiving counter, down another long hallway, and up to a closed door. The spick-and-span deputy with the shiny boots knocked on the door. A moment later it was opened by a large uniformed man. Filling up most of the doorway, the officer stared at Cable for what felt like an eternity. "Bring him in, Calms," he said finally.

While other deputies walked away, Calms escorted Cable into the office and pointed to a chair in front of a large desk. The sheriff took a seat on the other side of the desk, pulled a tape recorder out of a drawer, and began fiddling with it. Cable twisted around in his chair and surveyed his surroundings. It was a functional office, nothing ostentatious. Deputy Calms was standing right behind him, leaning against the closed door, one hand on his pistol. He returned his gaze to the sheriff and the tape recorder, which looked about the size of a Q-tip in the man's huge hands.

Tired of the silence and being kept in the dark, Cable coughed, cleared his throat, and opened his mouth to speak, but the sheriff stopped him with a wave of his hand, turning his attention back to the task of setting up the tape recorder's microphone. A slow irritation began to build in Cable as he sat back in his chair and waited.

Finally satisfied with the tape recorder, Sheriff Henry Sutton focused his attention on the man sitting across from him. "I'm required to tell you this conversation is being tape-recorded. Do you understand that?"

Cable nodded.

"You were not read your rights," Sutton said, "because you have not been charged with a crime. Do you understand that?"

Cable nodded again.

A slight smile crossed one side of Sutton's face. "Should you be charged with a crime, your rights will then be read to you, and you'll have a chance to telephone a lawyer. Understand?"

Cable nodded, pleased with himself.

The sheriff's smile broadened as if he were enjoying the game. "Now, I'm going to ask you once again if you understand the situation, and if you nod, you'll sit in that chair until I can get ahold of a videotape machine so we can put those cute little nods on television." He glanced up at the ceiling. "Let's see, the last time I needed a video camera, it took me almost twenty-four hours to dig one up. That's a long time to sit in that chair. Now, do you understand this matter concerning your rights?"

"Yes," Cable said, his "don't fuck with me" expression fading away.

"For the record and your information, my name is Henry Sutton. I'm the police chief of Ravina." He put a large forefinger down on a legal-sized yellow pad. "According to your car and motel registration, your name is John Cable and you're from British Columbia, correct?"

"Correct."

"Mind telling me what you do in Canada and what you're doing in Ravina?"

"I teach archeology and anthropology at the University of British Columbia in Vancouver. I'm in Ravina because I got tired of driving and I needed a place to spend the night."

"Just passing through?"

"Just passing through. Look, can you tell me what's going on? Nobody's told me a thing about why I'm here or what's going on. Unless I'm mistaken, that may be one of my rights even if I haven't been charged with a crime."

Sutton nodded. "Couple more questions, then we'll get down to basics." He picked up a pencil. "Since you're just passing through, I assume you're traveling from Vancouver to . . . ?"

"Point Hueneme, California."

Sutton wrote the name of the town on the pad. "Why? What's there?"

"A friend. An old friend named Martin Larchmont."

Sutton scribbled something on his pad. "He know you were coming?"

"Yes."

The deputy with the starched uniform and shining boots magically materialized at Sutton's side as he tore the page from the pad. He gave the deputy an irritated look and the page. "I'll get right on this, Chief," the deputy said, scurrying out of the room.

Sutton refocused on Cable. "A girl with frosted hair was seen getting out of your car at your motel last night. Want to tell me about her?"

"Not much to tell. Her name's Lynn Langley. She

was hitchhiking. I picked her up north of here, and she rode down to Ravina with me. After I found a motel, she took off. I saw her later at a restaurant, and we ate together. That's it.''

"Where exactly did you pick her up?"

"I'm not sure. It was near a state park, but I don't remember the names of any nearby towns." Cable shrugged. "If I looked at a map and saw the name of the park, I'd remember it."

"Nothing else? That's all you know about her?" Sutton asked, writing something down on the yellow pad.

"That's it," Cable answered, deciding not to tell Sutton that Lynn Langley was a prostitute. She was probably in trouble, and he didn't want to add to her problems.

"Did you know she was a hooker?"

Cable sighed. "Yes."

"Did you buy her wares?"

Cable found the question amusing. "Did I what?"

There was nothing amusing in the sheriff's expression. "Did you fuck her for money?"

"No."

"Did you have an argument about how much she wanted to charge you?"

"No."

"Did you have an argument or fight about anything?" Sutton asked, his voice becoming harder.

Suddenly Cable's voice became as hard as the sheriff's. "No. We got along. And we didn't do anything. Like I said, I gave her a ride, dropped her off here, and later I ran into her at a restaurant. By the way, she paid for her own meal."

"Hard to believe," Sutton said skeptically. "She was a pretty lady. You spent all that time with her and never so much as—"

"Sheriff, I don't give a good goddamn what you find hard to believe . . . and what do you mean *was?*"

"She's dead," Sutton said, his eyes fixed on Cable. "She was killed last night."

Cable felt as if he'd just been kicked hard on his gut. He stared at the sheriff, but didn't see him. Instead, he saw Lynn Langley in the restaurant, flipping her hair over the collar of her windbreaker just before she walked out alone into the fog.

He pulled himself back to the present. Sutton was looking at him like a hawk studying a field mouse. "Is that why I'm here?" he asked. "You think I killed her?"

Sutton shook his head. "I don't think anything yet. I'm just trying to fit the pieces of an ugly jigsaw puzzle together. Right now you're here because you're the only one we know who even talked to the girl. That doesn't make you a murderer, but it sure puts you in the ball game." He gestured at the tape recorder. "It also makes anything you have to say worth recording."

"I didn't kill her. I gave her a ride and watched her walk out of a restaurant. I didn't kill her." His palms were wet. He wiped them on his pants.

Sutton picked up a pencil and glanced at his yellow pad. "What time did she leave the restaurant?"

"Nine-fifteen, nine-thirty. I'm not sure." Cable suddenly sat up. "Wait! I just remembered. She didn't leave because she had finished her meal. She left because she had an appointment with someone. She didn't tell me who. She just said she'd met someone after I'd first dropped her off, and this person had made an appointment for her to meet someone else." He shrugged with his hands as he realized he'd given the sheriff no information whatsoever.

"No names? No idea where she was meeting this friend of a friend?"

Cable slumped back in his chair. "No."

Sutton stared at the yellow pad, then slowly shook his head. "The pieces don't match."

"What do you mean?"

"Remember when I said this was like a puzzle? Well, at this point the pieces don't fit. They don't even come close." He put his pencil down and leaned back in his chair. "Mr. Cable, I'd like you to stay in town for a few days."

Cable shook his head. "I told you I didn't kill her. I told you everything I know. You got it all. Everything. Keeping me around here isn't going to do you or me any good. It sure as hell isn't going to help you put together your jigsaw puzzle."

"Look," Sutton said calmly, "I've got a dead girl on my hands and she was a stranger in town. You knew the dead girl and you're a stranger in town. I don't know why she was killed. I don't even know how she was killed. All I do know is she's dead and you brought her to town, Mr. Cable. So stick around.

"I'm only partway into this investigation. There're other people I want to talk to, and I'm waiting for some special tests to come back from Los Angeles. With luck, I'll have these things checked out in forty-eight hours . . . seventy-two at the most. During that time I'd appreciate your cooperation. All I'm doing is asking you to stay in town at the county's expense."

Cable knew Sutton's request was reasonable, but he didn't want to stay in town, not now, not after what had just happened. "You said there were no formal charges, right?" Sutton nodded. "Then I'm going. I'll leave the name and phone number of where I'm going, but I don't want to stay." He started to get to his feet.

"You'll never make it out of town."

"Meaning?"

"If you try and leave, I'll see you're legitimately busted for at least five different offenses before you hit the city limits."

"How do you figure?"

Henry Sutton smiled. "Studies show that even good drivers break the law at least three times during an average mile of city driving. If he has a cop behind him he gets nervous, and then during that same mile his errors climb to seven. Seven citable traffic offenses. The bottom line is if you try and leave town, I'll follow you and you'll make the mistakes. Then I'll bring you in for those mistakes. It'll all be very legal and above-board.''

Cable numbly shook his head. "Looks like I'll be staying on in your town for a couple of days.''

Sutton continued to smile. "No need to tell you that you'll be watched. If you decide to change motels, give the office a call.

"I'll keep you posted on the results of our investigation. If everything checks out like you said, you'll be on your way in a couple of days. Any questions?''

"How did she die?" Cable asked.

Henry Sutton looked at John Cable. There was pain and sadness in the larger man's eyes. "We don't know . . . horribly, I suspect." For a moment Henry Sutton wasn't a police chief. He was just another human being feeling sadness over the death of another human being, someone he wouldn't have cared about, but a human being nonetheless. Cable noticed this and liked Sutton for it. The police chief of Ravina jabbed a button on the intercom box. "Mr. Cable will need a ride back to his motel, and I want whoever takes him back to tell the manager to send the bill for his lodging to this office.''

Chapter Seven

It was dark when the deputies dropped Cable off at the motel. He entered his room, turned on the lights, and wished he hadn't. The room was more depressing than he'd remembered. The furniture was mismatched, scarred, and stained. Paintings picked up at a Salvation Army store had been nailed to the wall. A black and white television set was padlocked to its stand and the stand chained to a radiator. He tried to move a table lamp closer to the phone, but it was bolted to the nightstand.

He slumped down on the bed and called Martin Larchmont collect. After the operator told him to go ahead, he couldn't think of anything to say except: "Martin, it's me, John."

"John, I've been worried. You were supposed to be here this afternoon. Is something wrong? Of course there's something wrong or you wouldn't be calling me collect."

Cable smiled as he remembered his friend's habit of asking questions, then answering them. "I'm in a town called Ravina."

There was a long silence on the phone. "Ravina . . . what are you doing there?"

66

"It's a long story."

"Why should you worry about that? I'm paying for the call. Tell me about it."

Cable did, omitting nothing. He started with how he had picked up Lynn Langley and ended with the sheriff's way of keeping him in town legally.

"But why Ravina?" Larchmont asked, sounding apprehensive. "Why did you stop in Ravina in the first place?"

Cable didn't understand the tension in Larchmont's voice or the reason for the question. "It was just here," he said. "Just a place to stop and get some sleep. What's the big deal about Ravina? Do you know the place?"

Larchmont was silent for a moment. "Yes, I know that town, quite well, as a matter of fact. It's not my favorite place in the world. Tell me where you're staying."

Cable did and Larchmont shuddered audibly into the phone. "You always did have tacky taste."

Cable smiled, his first of the day. "Tacky but cheap, Martin."

"Does that place have bedbugs?"

"Good God, no," Cable said, still smiling.

"Good, I'll be up in an hour and a half. Go reserve a room for a friend."

"You don't really have to come up," Cable said without much conviction.

"Cut the crap, John. You can't come down here, so I'll come up there. Look, while I'm driving up, why don't you scout out a liquor store and pick us up some wine, preferably a rosé."

"Consider it done. How about some cheese and apples with your wine?"

Larchmont laughed. "You have a good memory. By the way, if you can't get a decent rosé, pick up a bottle of Ripple. Living in California has done strange things to my palate."

"Does Ripple go with apples and cheese?"

"Ripple goes with anything," Larchmont retorted before hanging up.

Two hours later Cable jerked the door open and warmly shook the hand of a little man wearing a huge cardigan sweater.

Like many accomplished men, Larchmont's physical appearance didn't match up to all he was and had done. As Cable continued to pump his friend's hand, he reflected on Martin Larchmont. He was considered to be one of the world's greatest living archeologists. He was a dynamic speaker with a powerful voice and an onstage charisma that both moved and fascinated large audiences of university students all over the free world. Yet in spite of all this, Martin Larchmont was a fragile little bald man, barely five feet tall and weighing less than most racehorse jockeys. Years of research had taken their toll on his eyes, and he desperately needed the thick wire-framed trifocals he wore to keep himself from tripping over small everyday things like davenports and parked cars.

Cable welcomed the man into his bleak room, and they broke out the wine, apples, and cheese. For a while they talked about a variety of boring and mundane things, but then the pressure became too much for Cable. "Martin, this whole mess is incredible," he blurted out. "I just don't know what to do."

"It would seem," Larchmont mused, "that the moves aren't up to you. They're up to the sheriff. He really can't go on holding you like this forever. After all, you do have your rights. If he messes with you for too long, the AF of L or the NAACP can hang the sheriff up by his heels."

Cable smiled. "You mean the ACLU?"

"If they want to help, then that's one more for your side."

Cable shook his head. "I've tried to look at the situation as if I were the sheriff, but I can't. I'm too close to it to be objective."

"From my perspective, the sheriff's actions aren't particularly unreasonable, but then I'm not the one who can't leave town." Larchmont pushed himself out of his chair, walked over to a window and looked out. "I must say you could've picked a better town than Ravina to get stopped in. Do you know anything about this town?"

"No, but I've been meaning to ask why you got so concerned when I mentioned Ravina over the phone."

Larchmont returned to his chair, but continued to stare out the window as if something beyond the glass was fascinating or terrifying. "It's an ugly story and a long one."

"I got time," Cable said. "Boy, have I got time."

"About twenty-five years ago . . . no about twenty-eight years ago, I came down to Ravina on a sabbatical leave from the university at the invitation of Dr. Patrick McKenzie."

Cable looked at Larchmont with interest. "*The* Patrick McKenzie?"

"The very one. As you recall, McKenzie was a renowned psychiatrist in the late forties and fifties. His specialty was suicide, and he wrote several notable books on the subject."

Cable nodded. "His books rivaled the works of Emile Durkheim."

This time Larchmont nodded. "Had McKenzie lived, his theoretical perspectives would have surpassed those of Durkheim's."

"But what was McKenzie doing in Ravina?" Cable asked.

"McKenzie organized a research team to study Ravina in the early fifties. It seems that back in the 1880s, a large number of this town's population took their own lives. It was almost like a plague; numerous residents killing themselves and sometimes their families. These suicides and murders kept occurring sporadically through the 1890s and into the first part of this century. All told, about eighty people took their own lives or were killed by someone who later took his own life.

"McKenzie organized a research team to study the phenomena of Ravina's mass suicides. It was to have been researched in a multidisciplinary fashion: historical, psychosocial, anthropological, and medical. I was to have been the anthropological consultant. I think the study would have eventually set the academic world on its ear, but it never got off the ground."

"Why?"

"McKenzie came to Ravina first to do some groundwork for the study. He came with his wife and daughter. His wife was stunning and his daughter, who was maybe five years old at the time, had the brightest blue eyes I've ever seen. . . ."

Cable sighed. His friend was in a rambling mood, but eventually he'd get back to the topic.

"She still lives here, you know."

"Who? The daughter?"

Larchmont shook his head. "No. McKenzie's wife. She stayed on here after her husband died, which by the way was why the study never got off the ground. He died hideously just after I came down here from the university."

"Hideously?"

"He killed himself," Larchmont said grimly. "Of course it was hard on his family, what with him being Catholic and all. She never forgave the church for not allowing him to be buried in the Catholic cemetery, and she had a lot of doubts about his death being called a suicide. She felt he wasn't the type to take his own life, and she stayed on to investigate his death. Eventually she grew fond of this place and decided to stay on." He slumped back in his chair and loosened his tie. "She and I communicated often after Patrick's death. She was a good friend, both to me and to Mandy, especially during Mandy's last months. She actually moved in with us when Mandy was near the end. She helped us both, and I've always been grateful for all that she did."

Cable nodded, liking the McKenzie woman sight unseen.

Larchmont leaned back in his chair, lacing his hands behind his head. "She's a bright, articulate woman. I think she's pursued some of her husband's original plans to study Ravina's strange history. I don't know if she ever found out much about the suicides, but I've been meaning to get back to her to find out what kind of information she was able to turn up in the years she's lived here. Anyway, when you meet Jen, you'll like her."

"Jen?"

"Short for Jenny."

"Beautiful name. I hope I get to meet her sometime."

"You will," Larchmont chortled. "You'll be spending the night at her house."

"I can't. The sheriff wants me to stay put."

"Nonsense. I called Jenny after we hung up. She was adamant about us staying with her while we're in town." Larchmont glanced around the room, shuddered, then pointed to something. "John, I think somebody's nailed that painting to the wall. Why would somebody do that? Who on earth would steal something like that?"

"I don't think it's a good idea," Cable replied.

"You're too timid, John. All we have to do is call the sheriff's office and give him Jenny's name, address, and phone number. What could be simpler?"

Cable gave in. He was sick of motel rooms, especially this one.

"Besides, there's an added benefit," Larchmont said, smiling slyly. "During our conversation, Jen mentioned her daughter had moved back in with her."

Cable eyed Larchmont warily. "Martin, you're not going to play matchmaker, are you?"

"Just pack and follow me in your car over to her place. I think I can find it in this fog."

Cable began packing. As he closed the suitcase, he glanced at Larchmont curiously. "I got the impression there was more to Patrick McKenzie's death than you mentioned. Suicide isn't all that uncommon."

Larchmont's face paled. "It is if you know the details." He picked up a full glass of wine and downed it in one motion. "Patrick McKenzie left one morning to interview some people. He never returned. Two days later the police found him in an old motel out near the cemetery. He was dead. A coroner's inquest ruled that McKenzie's death was suicide since the doors and windows were locked from the inside."

"Why an inquest if all the facts pointed to a suicide?" Cable asked.

"The police and the coroner were skeptical. They felt that no one could have done what McKenzie had done. They said the pain would have been too great, that he wouldn't have been able to do it, take his life that way."

"How did—"

"Patrick McKenzie bit through the blood vessels in his wrists with his teeth, and then he bled to death."

Cable reached for the wine and filled both their glasses. "Sweet Jesus, no wonder there was an inquest."

"And that's why I don't like this town," Martin Larchmont said, looking out at the blackness beyond the motel window. "There's something strange about it. All those deaths a hundred years ago, and then McKenzie's suicide. It's almost like it has a secret, something hidden it doesn't want unearthed." He finally tore his eyes away from the window. "We'd best be off."

While Larchmont called the police department to tell them of the younger man's new address, Cable checked out of the motel. Then they climbed into their cars, and Cable followed the tail lights of Larchmont's '57 Rambler into the fog.

On the west side of town Larchmont pulled over and stopped in front of a handsome home located on a corner lot in one of Ravina's older neighborhoods. Even in the fog Cable could see that the home was at least seventy years old, and a two-story monument to a time when carpenters and craftsmen took pride in what they built.

Walking up the brick pathway to Jenny McKenzie's home was like stepping into an arboretum. Huge cedar deodars framed the house, and graceful aleppo pines and giant oaks lined the sidewalk on two sides of the yard. The house itself was white with brown trim arching over its gables. Maidenhair and sword ferns, ancient azaleas and camellias surrounded the house in abundance. Thick wisteria vines threaded the trellises nestled on both sides of the covered screened-in porch.

A large oak door swung open as soon as Larchmont and Cable stepped onto the porch, and Jenny McKenzie flew out the door to hug her old friend with unabashed emotion. Turning to Cable, she hugged him tightly as if he were Martin Larchmont's son.

Cable's first impression of Jenny McKenzie was she could have been Larchmont's sister. Like Larchmont, she was small, fragile, and energetic. Then, as she stepped under the glow of the porch light, he revised his impression. Though she was in her seventies, the woman was healthy and wholesome looking. She could have gotten a job as an actress for one of those all-organic and natural food commercials on television, he mused.

Jenny McKenzie escorted them into a large living room furnished with elegant antiques. Cable had to be prodded by his hostess before he could bring himself to walk on the valuable and fading Oriental carpet.

The woman was a charmer. Within a matter of minutes Cable felt as if he'd known her all his life. She was comfortable to be around and had the unique ability to make him feel as if he were the center of her universe and every word he uttered inspired. He didn't allow his impression to go to his head. He suspected she treated everyone with the same focused intensity, from postman to President. Hers was a gift that couldn't be faked. It wasn't an act. Everyone that came into Jenny McKenzie's life was important to her.

Comfortable as he was with Jenny, he was surprised to see Larchmont wasn't. Odd, he thought, here's a man who has calmly guest-lectured at most of the world's great universities, and right now he's sitting on a couch next to a pretty gray-haired woman, and he's stuttering. Dr. Martin Larchmont is stuttering. The man is nervous, Cable realized; he really likes this woman. In his mind Cable began playing Cupid. Both were widowed, bright, witty, and both lived alone. The scene he played out in his mind was pleasing, a matched pair, if ever there was one. It was like looking at a perfectly balanced equation.

Jenny finally broke the spell and ended the conversation by going off to the kitchen. After she left, Cable winked at Larchmont. In turn, Larchmont glared at Cable. Jenny returned with large mugs filled with chamomile tea. Cable accepted his mug and balanced it on his knee. They were starting to pick up the conversation when the front door opened and closed with a bang. Jenny McKenzie's daughter, Charlcie, bounded into the living room with an armful of groceries, hastily purchased at the 7-Eleven store for the two guests.

Cable had been expecting her, had even been looking forward to meeting her, but her beauty caught him off guard and he got to his feet without thinking. Then remembered too late. Some of the tea splattered his crotch as the rest sloshed over the carpet.

Cable looked at his pants, then at the carpet, then at Charlcie McKenzie, and then at Martin Larchmont. Charlcie went out for paper towels. A moment later Martin Larchmont rose to his feet and spilled his tea all over the rug. Cable instantly caught on to what his friend was up to. He was trying to lessen Cable's embarrassment by duplicating the same accident.

Charlcie McKenzie came back into the living room carrying a wad of paper towels. She stopped abruptly, looked at the stain at Cable's feet, then looked at the stain at Larchmont's feet, and went back for more towels. When she returned, she got down on her hands and knees and began mopping up the tea. Cable joined her and at that moment Jenny McKenzie decided to introduce the two to each other. Then she picked up some of the towels, gave some to Larchmont, and they began mopping up his puddle.

"Sorry about this," Cable said, still on his knees and almost nose to nose with Charlcie McKenzie.

"No sweat," she responded. "What's an eight-hundred-year-old Persian rug?"

Cable died. "Eight hundred years old?" he asked aghast. He looked at her, but she wouldn't look back at him.

"Eight-hundred years old?" Jenny McKenzie asked from across the room. Charlcie ignored her mother and continued to dab up the tea. "Don't feel bad. After all, it's just a rug. What should it matter that a dozen women in Persia went blind while they tried to weave the threads into this rug?"

"Who went blind?" Jenny McKenzie asked from across the room. Like Larchmont, Cable, and Charlcie, Jenny was still on her hands and knees mopping up tea.

"The women who made this rug," Charlcie replied, still keeping her eyes and face hidden from Cable.

Eight hundred years old, women going blind, Cable thought, wishing now the sheriff would have executed him. God, this woman was beautiful.

"I don't want you to worry about this," Charlcie McKenzie said as she crawled past Cable on her hands and knees. "Just because the rug cost my mother a hundred and fifty thousand dollars—"

"A hundred and fifty thousand dollars!" Larchmont and Jenny McKenzie said at the same time, both looking at Charlcie as if she'd left her brains out in the fog.

Vigorously scrubbing the tea off the rug, John Cable multiplied his salary times the cost of the rug and figured it would only take four years.

"A hundred and fifty thousand dollars," Jenny and Martin said again in unison.

Charlcie finally lifted her head and looked over at Cable, who was still on his hands and knees, scrubbing away at the tea. "Well," she said, "would you believe five hundred dollars?" Cable looked at her. Then Jenny looked at her. "Well," Charlcie said, starting to smile, "would you believe two hundred and fifty dollars?"

"Would you believe," Jenny said, "one hundred and ninety-five dollars, and would you believe I bought it at Sears two weeks ago and it's guaranteed to be stain-resistant for two years?"

Cable kept his stare fixated on Charlcie McKenzie. "Eight hundred years old? Women going blind? A hundred and fifty thousand dollars?"

"I think I'll go into the kitchen and make some more tea," Charlcie offered, bounding to her feet and starting down the hallway.

Laughing, Cable got to his feet, caught Charlcie by the hand and pulled her back into the living room. They collapsed on the couch while Martin and Jenny went off to the kitchen to make some more tea and talk about "old and boring memories."

Cable turned to study the beautiful woman before him. Then, like her, he began to laugh. It was the kind of laugh that began with an embarrassed chortle and ended up with Cable holding his sides and trying not to fall off the couch. After he got a grip on himself, they settled back and both began working at getting to know each other.

Only Cable kept screwing it up. One moment his mouth was dry as sandpaper, the next he was chattering like a nonstop blatherskite in a voice that was cracking and breaking like a boy at his first sock hop. Least I can't do any worse, Cable thought, trying to console himself. Then Charlcie laughed and Cabled liked her laughter and her dimples. "You have gorgeous nipples," he said.

Her smile broadened, her dimples becoming more pronounced. "You like my nipples?"

Cable died. Again. He shook his head fiercely. "I mean to say nipples . . . I mean dimples."

She touched her cheek with one finger, looked down at her chest for an instant before looking up into Cable's eyes. "Well, either way, I guess I can't lose. A compliment's a compliment, right?"

Suddenly Cable stopped the conversation by holding up both hands and shaking his head. "I'm not sure what's going on with me, but whatever it is, I don't think I like it." Charlcie cocked her head and continued to look at him. "You know what I'm talking about. One minute I'm a chatterbox, talking on at ninety miles an hour and bragging about something I've done in archeology. The next minute my voice is breaking up like a teenager with a hormone problem. Alien things are coming out of my mouth. My mouth is dry, my hands are shaking, and my pants . . ." He looked down at his tea-stained crotch and sighed. "And my pants . . ."

"So, are you sick?" Charlcie asked. "Or should I be flattered?"

"Flattered!" Cable exclaimed. "This business of relating to an attractive woman on a personal level is harder than I remembered. I told you I was going through a divorce. What I didn't say was that my inability to pay attention to my wife cost me my marriage. I'm out of practice with this business of putting myself on the line and relating to another person, and it shows. But I do have a theory. Want to hear it?"

"By all means."

"I wanted to impress you—I still do—but I wanted to so much that I messed it up. You know, the bragging, the dry mouth, the screwed-up compliments. I suggest you take my bumblings as a kind of flattery."

"In other words, your liking my dimples-nipples is a form of flattery?"

"Absolutely."

"Then I'm flattered." She grinned. "By the way, did you notice your voice just dropped a full octave during your confession?"

"Like maybe puberty finally arrived?" They both laughed, and this time Cable felt himself finally feeling comfortable in the presence of this woman.

As they continued to talk, they discovered they shared a lengthy list of likes and dislikes. They liked Chicago jazz, old homes, Italian operas, pizza, *Star Trek* on Saturday mornings, mystery novels, Bogart movies, and disco music. "You realize that dates us, John," Charlcie observed. Their list of dislikes started with brussels sprouts and went on to include salesmen who use the telephone, Lawrence Welk, religious TV, incompetent politicians who got taxpayers' money to fund their election campaigns, the smell of sauerkraut, and people who killed whales.

Eventually they got around to the topic of their broken marriages. Cable told Charlcie about his marriage and its death. He was painfully honest in his chronicle. He wanted this woman to know what had really happened, that it was his fault the marriage had ended, not his wife's. He wasn't trying to hang out his flaws. He just wanted Charlcie to know the truth regardless of the cost.

After he finished, she took his hand. "You seem to have forgiven your wife. Why don't you work on forgiving yourself? You weren't that bad, John. I know. I lived with bad for years, and I've got the scars to prove it."

She had met her husband in college. They'd married after graduation and settled down in San Jose after her husband found a job teaching history at a local high school. Charlcie did nothing during the first two years of their marriage. Then out of boredom she began pursuing a graduate degree, and she finally got it, shortly after their sixth wedding anniversary. Her husband changed immediately. Even now she was not sure if the change was brought on by her accomplishment or the sudden emergence of a long-standing mental illness. Whatever the cause, he began coming home late every night, and it seemed as if he had a seminar or a conference every weekend. At the same time his behavior changed. He became critical and distant and exuded enthusiasm only when he talked about his students. In the seventh year he began battering her. She would leave. He would follow, begging her to come back, promising to get help. She always gave in, hoping he would change; he didn't.

She hung on into the eighth year, waiting for the promised change.

It finally came to a head four months earlier when she came home from an overnight shopping trip one day early. She walked into her living room on a Saturday afternoon and found a naked boy and a naked girl sitting on her living room couch. Neither looked over fourteen. They were drinking Pepsi's, and when she walked in, they looked at her as if she'd just interrupted their break. Later she found out she had.

Stunned, she began searching the house for her husband and found him in their bed. He was as naked as the kids in the living room, and so were the teenage boy and girl lying on either side of him.

Screaming something about his "illness" and need for treatment, he scrambled off the bed, begging for forgiveness. In shock she had simply stood there, looking at him, the naked kids, then back at him, and wondering about the two naked teenagers out in the living room. Finally she walked over to the closet to get her suitcase. That was when he hit her, hard enough to break her jaw.

She spent five days in the hospital, and on the day she was discharged, she filed for a divorce, told the police about what she'd found going on in her home some days earlier, and suggested they talk to her husband's high school principal. She spent that night hiding in a motel in San Jose, left for Ravina the following morning, and arrived on her mother's doorstep, with a wired-shut jaw, some clothes, and a partially completed Ph.D. thesis. Four months had passed since she'd come home, and Charlcie had done little with her time except heal and tinker with her thesis. When Cable asked her what the thesis was about, she shuddered. "It's a dull dissertation on aggressive and passive personality types and public administration systems."

"Sounds impressive."

"Oh, yeah? I just barely started collecting my data, and already it's boring as hell."

Cable chuckled and yawned at the same time. "I'm tireder than I thought. My run-in with the sheriff really took its toll." He yawned again and tried to apologize while he was yawning. "Jesus, what time is it?"

"It's late," she said, glancing at her watch. "Five after eleven. You always stay up this late?"

This time Cable's yawn almost unhinged his jaw. "This is embarrassing. I've been known to stay up till eleven-thirty with no problem. I think that sheriff really did me in." Genuinely embarrassed by the waves of fatigue that were washing over him, he started to reach for her, then stifled another yawn. "That's it. I'm calling it a day." He thought he spotted a brief glimpse of disappointment cross her face at his announcement. The expression delighted him.

The lights in the McKenzie home flicked off one by one as the clock over the fireplace sounded eleven times. The house groaned those settling sounds old homes made in the dark while outside a low fog grew heavier and thicker.

Chapter
Eight

It was just after eleven and technically, Deputy Robert Calms had been off duty for hours. But since he didn't look at his job in terms of eight-hour shifts, Robert Calms was still in uniform, still working, still searching that part of the cemetery where sixteen hours earlier the body of a dead girl had been found.

This was the third time he'd gone over the area with his powerful flashlight. He was looking for something, anything, which might have been missed during the daylight searches, and his failure to turn a single clue had set his stomach ulcers on fire.

A bystander probably would have thought that Calms was a dedicated policeman interested in the pursuit of justice. Nothing could have been further from the truth. Robert Calms was a vain and stunted little man whose perception of himself was directly tied to his work and promotions. Calms had no friends, hobbies, outside interests, or family. He lived for his job, the uniform, the pistol, the power. That was the essence of Deputy Robert Calms.

As he swept his flashlight beam back and forth through

the fog, Calms cursed his luck. He had dreams of finding a clue, a vital piece of evidence that would pin the hooker's death on that Canadian perp. If only he could find something like a credit-card slip, a matchbook, or a rumpled pack of Canadian cigarettes, *he* could wrap up this case. Then Sutton would have to give him his sergeant's stripes. But thus far he'd only found gum wrappers, litter, and pieces of rotting plastic flowers used to decorate the graves.

The dense, thick fog shrouded the deputy in darkness and silence. He couldn't hear the semitrailers rumbling past on the nearby freeway. He couldn't hear the sound of a teenager revving up the high-performance engine of his car eight blocks away.

And he did not hear the cemetery gates swing open behind him. Nor did he hear the sounds of something large padding slowly through the ivy while it stalked him.

And because of the fog, he didn't see a large shape coming for him, its green eyes aglitter, coarse body hair erect like a rabid wolf.

Deaf, blind, and standing just outside a cemetery on one of the foggiest nights he'd ever experienced, Robert Calms gave up his search, turned slightly, pointed his flashlight at the patrol car, and then something with the strength of a bulldozer hit him from behind.

The power behind the blow sent him somersaulting into the air. He landed on his back near the cemetery fence, clutching his stomach with one hand, the flashlight with the other. His guts were on fire and he felt like he'd just been disemboweled by a giant dog. Dog, he thought, as the pain in his guts began to spread through his body. If it's out there, it'll come back, attack again. He aimed the flashlight into the fog. The beam picked up nothing. No dog. Nothing. The pain was becoming worse and spreading. His back felt on fire; the front of his body felt as if it had been splattered with acid. Still worried about the dog, he managed to get to his hands and knees. Waves of agony toppled him over.

He fell forward on his stomach, laid there a moment, then tried to turn his flashlight on his own body. But he was weak, his body felt as if it were melting, and the flashlight rolled out of his hand. He looked at the flashlight lying on the ground in front of him. He wanted to reach for it, but he hurt too much.

He tried to yell out, but his voice didn't work. His throat felt warm and spongy as if his vocal chords were melting. Shit, his whole body felt that way.

With a desperate painful effort, Robert Calms reached out for the flashlight, stretching his hand into the cone of light splaying out across the ground. As he did, he saw his hand.

Only it wasn't his hand. It couldn't be. This hand was old, wrinkled, and growing older by the second, like the hand of a movie vampire who'd just been killed with a stake. Only he wasn't watching a movie. He was looking at his hand. And if his hand was doing this, then so was the rest of his body.

Robert Calms stared at his hand, watching the skin wither and flake and fall away like scraps of dried parchment. He tried to be objective about what he was seeing. It had to be a nightmare. Maybe somebody had put LSD in his thermos. That was it. That had to be it, he thought desperately. This couldn't be happening to him. This couldn't be real!

He lost his objectivity when a small maggot squirmed its way out of a newly opened crack between his thumb and forefinger. It was only then that the withered and decaying old man tried to scream, and the only sound he could make was a textbook-perfect death rattle.

Early the next morning Johnny Joe Sloams pulled up in front of the locked gates to the Horrcove Cemetery. He had a monumental hangover, and it took him a moment to notice a police car parked on the side of the road a few yards away. It took him a few moments longer to notice that the car's headlights were on, its motor was running, one door was open, its radio was crackling, and there wasn't a cop for miles.

He eased himself out of the pickup and tiptoed cautiously toward the vehicle. It was parked close to where he'd found a dead girl's body yesterday. With his luck, he thought, he'd probably find another fucking dead body.

He did.

Chapter
Nine

William Seafront, Mark Childress, Henry Sutton, and a visibly pale male nurse gathered around the autopsy table in the morgue and looked down at the bloated and decaying corpse trapped in a Ravina Police Department uniform, a uniform complete with cloth patches, a badge, and a plastic name tag reading: Robert L. Calms. Seafront had pulled the sheet back several minutes earlier. No one had spoken since.

Finally the forensic pathologist unhooked the dictating microphone. He checked it to make sure it was off. "Personally, I think this is a goddamn practical joke." He raised his eyes from the body and looked accusingly at Henry Sutton. "There's no way this body could have been alive yesterday. If you ask me, some pranksters dug up a corpse that'd been in the ground a couple of months and dressed it in your deputy's uniform." Seafront turned his attention to Childress. "Normally I wouldn't've gotten involved in something like this, but at your request I'll go ahead and do an autopsy." The pathologist motioned for the nurse to turn on the room's exhaust fans.

As the nurse walked over to the switches, Childress came around the side of the table to Sutton. "So what makes you think that body on the table's your deputy? Instinct? Intuition?"

"The name tag," Sutton whispered, "and a baby diaper." Earlier, he'd followed the ambulance down from the cemetery to the hospital and asked Childress to call Seafront again. While all three were walking to the morgue, he'd voiced his opinion about the body's identity. The opinion had irritated the pathologist and embarrassed Childress. Impossible was all either man could say. But impossible or not, Henry Sutton knew.

Exhaust fans whirred on. The air in the room began to move, but the effect was minimal. Even with the fans running full blast, the odor emanating from the corpse made it difficult to breathe.

"Christ, it would take a sick mind to think of something like this," Seafront said, clipping the microphone to his smock. He began to pace around the table, studying the cadaver from different angles. As he moved he talked. "The date is October twenty-fifth. The time is oh-nine-twenty. Upon superficial examination, we have what I believe to be a male cadaver in an eight- to twelve-week state of decay. Age is impossible to determine. Reference to gender is based on the clothing the body is wearing." He clapped his hand over the microphone and glanced at Sutton. "Still think this is your deputy?" Sutton nodded. Seafront smiled. "You're going to feel silly if this turns out to be a female corpse, aren't you?" Sutton forced himself to keep an impassive expression on his face as Seafront went back to work.

The forensic pathologist took a scalpel and began cutting the buttons off the starched shirt encasing the corpse's chest. As the last button was cut away, the shirt flew open and the contents of the body's chest cavity and upper stomach flowed out over the table like cold stew. Nothing was recognizable to Sutton, except the rib cage.

"What we have here," Seafront said into the microphone, "is a body in an advanced state of cariosity. Judging from the stages of maggots and larvae and various cultures of fungus and mold, I stand by my earlier estimate. This body has been decomposing for eight to twelve weeks."

Seafront picked up a surgical probe and used it in combination with the scalpel. "The alar cartilage is rapidly deteriorating. Both arctenoid cartilages have degenerated into barely recognizable states. There's almost no evidence of the cricoid and thyroid cartilages. The skeletal system seems to be deteriorating—rapidly—and the decomposition process appears to be in its final stage."

Seafront straightened up and gave Childress a perplexed look. "Are you seeing what I'm seeing?"

Childress nodded, a strained look on his face.

"Strange," Seafront said, as he went back to work.

Sutton inched over next to Childress. "What's strange?" he asked, his voice barely audible over the exhaust fans.

"When a body deteriorates," Childress said, his eyes locked on the cadaver, "the soft tissues go first. You know, stuff like the skin, eyes, outwardly positioned organs and so forth. Following that, the firmer parts of the body go, cartilages and related bony material. Eventually, all that's left are the bones and teeth."

Childress continued to stare at the body on the table, a confused look on his face. "Now, here we got a body breaking down faster than anything I've ever seen before. The soft tissues and the cartilages seem to be going simultaneously. What's worse, so are the bones. Look at that rib cage. It's already collapsing under its own weight. It's not supposed to be happening like this, at least not at the same time."

Childress tore his eyes away from the body and looked up at Sutton. "Course, having you say that cadaver was a deputy and alive yesterday doesn't do much for Seafront or me. Matter of fact, it makes matters worse. See, if you're right, we got one hell of a medical impossibility on our hands. Someone who died yesterday would be subject to rigor mortis, some bloating, and that would be about it. What we got here is a three-month old body decaying at ninety miles an hour . . . and Henry, that just isn't your deputy."

Sutton refocused his attention on the pathologist and tried to make sense out of what he was hearing.

". . . skeletal muscles are in a highly advanced stage of putrescence; massive profusion has—is occurring throughout the entire body cavity at an almost visible speed. Deltoids, pectoralis majors, and serratus anteriors are liquifying and infested with various stages of verminosis."

Suddenly Seafront angrily threw the scalpel across the room, yet his voice continued to drone on in a calm controlled manner. "Further examination at this point is impossible. With the exception of the skeletal system, what I am looking at basically has the consistency of vegetable soup. Were it not for the presence of larvae and maggots, I would postulate this body had been bathed in a caustic acid or been exposed to a mutant form of bacteria that breaks down human tissue at an accelerated speed. End of external examination."

William Seafront covered the remains of the cadaver with a pale green sheet and turned off his microphone. Turning toward the others, he said, "I don't know what the hell is going on here. And I can't explain the speeded-up mortification, though I suspect it's probably being caused by a chemical with a highly acidic content. Later today I'll run some tissue analysis tests, and I'll also send some cultures to the lab in Los Angeles. If I can't figure out what's going on, the lab in L.A. can."

Seafront's eyes moved to meet Sutton. "One thing I do know, that body on the table is not your deputy." Sutton opened his mouth, but Seafront shook his head. "With the time frame you gave me, that couldn't be your deputy, even if acid is involved. You said your deputy signed out last night at seven. Even if he were killed at seven-fifteen and dumped into a barrel of acid, we would still have more to examine than what's currently on the table. Even acid doesn't work that fast.''

Sutton pulled a manila envelope out from inside his shirt. ''On my way down from the cemetery, I radioed for Calms's dental records. One of my men dropped them off just before you arrived. That cadaver still has teeth. I'd appreciate it if you'd check these records against the teeth.''

Seafront made a face. ''No matter what I say, you won't give it up, will you?''

''If we argue this long enough, there won't be any teeth for you to examine.'' Sutton held out the envelope. ''Humor me.''

''Give me a hand, Mark,'' Seafront said, drawing back the sheet. ''You read off the chart. I'll check the teeth.'' Childress took the envelope, pulled out a yellow card, and walked over to Seafront. Interested, Sutton moved in behind Childress and looked over his shoulder at the dental chart.

There was a series of thirty-two small circles on the chart grouped together in an elongated oval pattern. Each of the circles were numbered consecutively, starting with one and ending with thirty-two. On Calms's chart, some of the circles had been X'd out. Others had been shaded in with a dark pencil. The elongated oval pattern represented the upper and lower jaws, Sutton decided. The numbered circles were teeth. An X meant a tooth had been extracted and the shaded-in areas represented fillings.

Seafront was leaning over the cadaver's head, holding what looked like a stainless steel kitchen spatula in one hand and a dental mirror in the other. ''Let's get this over with, Mark.''

Childress started reading from the chart. ''The wisdom teeth, numbers one, sixteen, seventeen, and thirty-two have been surgically extracted. There are distal amalgams on numbers three and four.'' He glanced over at Seafront, got no response and continued. ''Numbers eight and nine have been capped. It says here the caps are gold with a covering of white baked-on enamel on the facial sides. Nineteen is missing and a gold bridge has been inserted utilizing eighteen and twenty for abutments. Thirty-two has been capped with a gold crown. Unless you want me to go on to the X rays, that's it.''

Except for the exhaust fans, the room was silent. Seafront stretched, working a kink out of his back, then tossed his instruments, gloves, and mask on a nearby tray. After a long moment he turned slowly to face Henry Sutton. "What'd you say the name of your deputy was?"

"Calms . . . Robert L. Calms."

Seafront nodded, then looked away. "The body on the table's your deputy. I can't explain it, I don't know what killed him, and I don't know why his body is decomposing so fast. But I do know that's Robert L. Calms.''

Chapter
Ten

It was just after two when Henry Sutton pulled up in front of Jenny McKenzie's home. He walked up the pathway, stepped up on the front porch, let the brass knocker drop one time, then stood back and waited. He was beat. Two gruesome deaths, the autopsies, and the unanswered questions had taken a toll on Sutton. His neck and back were knotted with tension. There were worry lines around the edges of his eyes. He'd picked up a massive headache during the Calms autopsy, and now it took a conscious effort for him to keep his eyes in focus.

Sutton had come to tell John Cable he was free to leave town; all restrictions were off. The hideous death of his deputy had convinced him that Cable was an innocent bystander caught up in a macabre web of inexplicable deaths. Sweat broke out on Sutton's palms and forehead as he thought about the town's future. He had no idea who would die next, but he was confident someone would, and the next death would be as grotesque as the first two.

He wasn't looking forward to seeing John Cable again,

but he had no choice. His own ethics allowed him no way out. He'd confined Cable to town during a face-to-face conversation. He'd have to clear him in the same fashion.

The massive door opened and Jenny McKenzie stepped out on the porch. "Afternoon, Henry," she said in a voice as cold as the wind. "I assume you're here to see John." Sutton came up with a tired smile and nodded. "Well, you'd better come in. It's cold out here."

Sutton took off his Stetson and followed the small woman through the foyer and into the living room, where she introduced him to Dr. Martin Larchmont. Sutton recalled Larchmont's name from the conversation he'd had the day before with Cable, and it explained why the small man was looking at him as if he'd kicked his best friend. In a way Sutton had.

"Martin Larchmont. I assume you're the man Dr. Cable was planning to visit?"

"Correct."

"I was under the impression you lived near Los Angeles."

"Correct again, Sheriff. However, when John called me about his problem and confinement, I thought I'd come up to see him since you wouldn't let him come down to see me." The sarcasm in the small man's voice was as brittle as late-night frost. "Jenny was gracious enough to offer us accommodations, and as I recall, John did report the change to your department last night before moving out of that motel."

"Which I appreciated," Sutton said. He smiled at both Larchmont and Jenny McKenzie. "Offhand, I'd say you and Dr. Cable made the best of a bad situation."

"No thanks to you," Larchmont countered coldly.

"Dr. Larchmont, I didn't come here to fight with you or Jenny. I came here to see Dr. Cable. Is he in?"

"No, he's not," Jenny McKenzie offered. "My daughter and John left around noon to do some shopping and tour Ravina.''

"That's okay, isn't it, Sheriff?'' Larchmont asked, glaring up at the sheriff. "My friend wasn't supposed to do solitary confinement in his motel room or the McKenzie home, was he?''

Irritating as Larchmont was, the man was growing on Sutton. Larchmont was smaller than most jockeys. Sutton towered over him. One swat from his Stetson would have knocked the man into next week, yet the man was standing up to him and not the least bit intimidated by Sutton's size or uniform. John Cable had a good friend in Martin Larchmont, Sutton thought. "Like I said, I didn't come here to fight, but I did come here to tell Dr. Cable he's off the hook, free to resume whatever plans he had prior to his run-in with me. I'd hoped to do it in person and maybe explain why I had to do what I did, but since he's not here, I can't. Please give him my message.'' He nodded to Jenny, turned, and started toward the door.

"Henry Sutton,'' Jenny called out, stopping Sutton in his tracks. "You just turn right around and come back here.'' Sutton did. "Henry, I think Martin and I owe you an apology. You were just doing your job, and coming here was a nice gesture. Why don't you let me make it up to you with a cup of tea.''

"Jen's right,'' Larchmont agreed. "My manners were atrocious. Maybe a cup of warm tea would make up for a cold reception. I know I'd feel better if you stayed a little longer.''

"It's been years since I've been invited to tea,'' Sutton said, looking down at the small couple standing in front of him. "If you've got any aspirin, I know I'll stay.'' He let Jenny and Martin escort him into the dining room. Jenny started with tea, and later the cold tea was replaced by cups of strong coffee laced with cream and whiskey.

The drinks and company relaxed a mind-weary Henry Sutton. Without thinking about it, he began relating the events that had transpired over the past two days. He talked on at length about the mysteries surrounding Lynn Langley's death and then went on to bring up Robert Calms. For Sutton, the conversation was therapeutic, a cathartic purging.

For Jenny McKenzie and Martin Larchmont, the sheriff's words conjured up images of an ancient and unspeakable horror.

While the elderly couple's world was collapsing, John Cable was deciding his world was a delightful place. The personality and warmth of Charlcie McKenzie had all but eliminated the cloud of depression placed on his shoulders by the giant sheriff of Ravina.

The two had spent most of their time together wandering through a small shopping center in Ravina. The cold winter climate had all but eliminated the tourists, and they had the shopping mall all to themselves. Both had been delighted to find bargains everywhere, and as a result, the backseat of Cable's car was filled with colorful plastic shopping bags containing hand-turned pottery, silkscreen prints, windchimes, and a small oil painting.

Charlcie delighted John Cable. She was bright, witty, blunt, and energetic. The woman didn't just walk through a department store, she zoomed, bouncing from counter to counter like a Ping-Pong ball. Keeping up with her was like working out in a high-impact aerobics class.

They burst out of a Penney's department store and were passing a men's clothing shop when Charlcie stopped abruptly, turned, and looked at Cable critically. After studying him for a moment, she undid one of the top buttons on his shirt.

"What are you doing?" he asked.

She stepped back and gave him another once-over. "Working on your image."

"My image?"

"John," she said, continuing to study him, "you look like a forty-year-old college professor."

"Charlcie, I am a forty-year-old college professor."

She sighed. "Okay, how about a stuffy-looking forty-year-old college professor?"

"Stuffy," he said, examining his reflection in the men's store window. "Dull? Maybe. But stuffy? Never!"

She turned and studied him as he studied himself in the window. "I don't know if I would've used the word *dull*, but *stuffy, stilted,* and *formal* do come to mind." She reached up and unfastened another button, exposing more of his chest.

He rebuttoned the button immediately. "One step at a time. First we get rid of *stuffy*. Then, when I've gotten used to the change, we go on to *stilted* and *formal*." He smiled at her and noticed she was looking at his pants. He knew what was coming next.

"Do you always wear polyester slacks?"

"What's wrong with polyester? They're wash and wear."

"You have a nice ass," she said, looking at him admiringly and smiling. "Ever thought about buying yourself a pair of tight jeans?"

He hadn't worn a pair in years, so at Charlcie's urging he bought a pair.

A few minutes later they picked up a box of chicken, drove up out around Horrcove Hill, and parked near the beach to eat and enjoy the view of the ocean.

After they finished, Charlcie suggested an alternative route back to town, a route she claimed was "worth the effort."

Following her directions, Cable drove away from the ocean and up a narrow winding road that led up the back side of Horrcove Hill. At the top he came to an old iron fence and gate marking the back of the cemetery. The gate was open and Cable pulled off the road just after entering the graveyard. They got out and walked over to the fence.

She had been right. The view was breathtaking. Blurred by a shimmering late afternoon fog, the town of Ravina lay spread out far below them on the easterly side of the hill. To the west was an endless ocean and the rugged California coastline. There was no fog on the westerly side of the hill, and they had a magnificent view of the setting sun casting a red swathe across the gray water, the beaches, and distant cliffs.

A cold wind gusted over the top of the hill. "Seen enough?" Charlcie asked, hugging herself. Cable nodded. "Good," she added. "Let's get back to the car. I'm freezing." They ran back to the car, and Cable started the engine and turned the heater on high.

"We're sitting on top of a very interesting and strange hill, Dr. Cable," Charlcie said, her voice shaking from the cold.

"Interesting?"

She nodded and continued to hug herself. "To begin with, this hill's nickname is Hang Hill."

He looked over at her. God, she was gorgeous.

"Well?" she asked.

"Well, what?"

"Don't you want to know why it's called Hang Hill?"

" 'Cause somebody got hung up here," he suggested.

"How the hell did you know?"

He shrugged. "Just a guess."

"Well, shit," she said, pulling a face. "The least you could do is get enthusiastic over our town's history. Legend has it that some of Ravina's more prominent citizens hanged six . . . *six* mind you, people up here about a hundred years ago in that clump of trees over there on your left." She pointed.

Cable glanced to his left. There was a clump of huge

old weathered oak trees over in the far corner of the cemetery near the top of the hill. He looked back at her. "They do sort of look like hanging trees."

"Damn betcha," she said, her smile beginning to fade. "Ravina's a strange town. I don't think anybody's ever substantiated the hangings. It's more of a word-of-mouth myth, and there's not anything about the hangings in our local history books." She moved her eyes from Cable's face to the distant hanging trees. "I think Mom did some research on it after Dad died, but I don't think she found much. If she did, she never discussed it with me. Anyway, all I've ever heard was that some of the townspeople hanged some gypsies from those trees, and that's the extent of the legend, except that no one seems to know why the hangings took place or why a lot of people went crazy afterward."

"Crazy afterward?"

"Start the car, drive down the road about a hundred yards, and I'll show you."

Curious, Cable did what he was told. He let the car roll down the road a hundred yards and pulled over again.

She took him by the hand and led him to a spot near the hanging trees. It was obvious they were in one of the older parts of the cemetery. The trees were huge and weather-scarred. The grave markers and tombstones showed the effects of a hundred years' worth of harsh coastal winds and rains. Marble cherubs and statues of angels were crumbling. The names on many markers were hard to read. Some of the bigger stones had fallen over. Others had been propped up by old two-by-fours.

Charlcie turned up the collar of her coat against the wind. "I want to show you some tombstones. After you read them, you tell me what you think, okay?"

Without waiting for an answer, she walked over to one of the tombstones overgrown with bracken ferns

97

and morning glory vines. She pushed aside the vegetation, then looked up at him. "Read the inscription, but don't tell me what you think yet."

Cable did. It read:

John Noshcroft. 1844–1891. Beloved Father. Beloved Husband. We rejoice at the pain you no longer feel.

He looked at her and shrugged his shoulders. She shook her head. "There's more," she said, leading him over to another grave marker.

James Martin. You suffered. Now you are free. R.I.P.

Charlcie pointed to another one. The wind had erased the name. Only a date and the inscription remained.

–1891. May the pain and the nightmares end with this thy final night.

She led him to other stones and other inscriptions.

If this be hallowed ground, then surely the sleep that holds thee here will be sweet. Rest now in peace, for you knew none on earth.

The terrors are gone, sleep in peace.

J. J. Sanders. 1856–1891. Life was an unjust reward for just actions in the night.

Carl Rawlins. 1838–1890. The nightmare has ended. Rest now.

Finally Charlcie led Cable to two identical tombstones standing just inches apart. Cable read the one on his left.

William Bleeker. January 10, 1838–February 12, 1890. God understands the terror that drove this man.

The stone on the right said simply:

Cora Bleeker and children: Ned, William Jr., Elizabeth, Selma, Baby Cora. February 12, 1890. A tragedy beyond comprehension. The terror is gone. May all sleep in peace.

Cable took Charlcie by the hand and they slowly began walking back to the car. "Sounds like a lot of people on top of this hill were far better off dead than alive," he commented.

"Exactly. The way they read, their lives were nightmares and death was a release, almost a blessing. Did you notice the dates?"

He gave her a puzzled look. "No, I just read the inscriptions."

"All those people and others died within a one- to two-year span of each other: 1889 to 1891. And the really strange part is," she said, pausing briefly for a deep breath, "is that the lynching that took place on this hill happened in 1889. Mondo bizarro weird, huh?" She smiled, but then the smile faded. "I used to ask mother about these tombstones and the lynching, but all she ever gave me were a bunch of those 'How would I know?' answers. I *know* she knows more than she was telling me, a whole lot more. After Dad died, Mom started studying this town, looking for answers that would explain why Dad did what he did. She's spent years researching this town's history, and every time I asked her about her work, all I ever got were blank stares and illusive answers."

She turned her collar up against the cold wind, turned away and looked out to sea. An incoming fog had turned the setting sun into a muted red ball. "God, it got late fast," she said, sounding very far away. "We should be getting back." Cable looked at the back of her head. He was full of questions—questions about the cemetery, the lynchings, the gravestones, Jenny McKenzie—but he didn't ask them. Instead, he let Charlcie lead him back to the car.

The setting sun had turned the landscape into a mass of tangled dark shadows by the time Cable pulled onto the narrow road leading out of the cemetery. As he drove away, he passed a battered blue pickup truck parked on the grass near a newly covered grave, its square plot of turned earth standing out in marked contrast to the surrounding green grass.

Johnny Joe Sloams had had a rough day. He'd spent the morning talking to the police, his noon hour digging a

grave with a backhoe, and then spent most of the afternoon sitting in his pickup, drinking wine and waiting for
some men from the county to come out and bury an
indigent. When they finally arrived, it was Sloams's job
as the cemetery's caretaker to supervise the proceed-
ings. That meant he continued to sit in his pickup, drinking wine and watching the three men from the county
haul the pine box out of the panel truck, lower it into the
hole, and shovel the dirt back in. After they'd patted
down the grave, and just before they left, one of the
county men had pushed a cement block out of the truck.
Then they drove off, leaving Sloams to position the
cement block and put back the sod. The county did not
believe in tombstones for paupers. It was a waste of the
taxpayers' money. Instead, the county chose to use a
square block of cement measuring twelve inches by twelve
inches. Epoxied to the top of the cement block was a
series of black plastic numbers and letters, having nothing to do with the dead person's name, birthdate, or date
of death.

In the case of Lynn Langley the letters on her cement
block read MMH-4424-5. Not coincidentally, those were
also the same numbers and letters on her death certificate.

After the county men drove off, Sloams took a long
pull from his wine bottle, then climbed out of his
warm pickup truck. The cement block was lying on the
grass, and it took Sloams almost five minutes to push
it into position over the grave. He got to his feet, dusted
off his hands, then moaned. He'd done it wrong.
Dropping down to his knees, he rolled the block over
so the plastic numbers and letters were finally facing
upward.

He was exhausted when he finished and decided he
deserved a drink and a nap. Then he'd resod the grave.
Ten minutes later he was asleep in the cabin of his
truck. He slept away the rest of the afternoon and was
still asleep when Cable drove past.

*   *   *

At the same moment Charlcie and Cable were leaving the cemetery, Henry Sutton was walking out of the home of Jenny McKenzie. If he hadn't been so tired, he might have noticed the efforts Jenny McKenzie and Martin Larchmont were making in order to remain composed in his presence. But he didn't. He was exhausted, and all he really was focusing on was the terror that was steadily overtaking his town.

Alone in the house, Jenny McKenzie and Martin Larchmont sat at the dining room table, holding hands and saying nothing. The impact of all that Sutton had told them weighed down on them like a hideous form of gravity.

Finally, after several long minutes, Jenny McKenzie spoke. "What are we going to do, Martin?"

"Two choices," Larchmont said weakly. "Fight or run."

She squeezed his hand. "You know there's only one choice for us. Fight! We've got to try and stop the Resurrection and stop it now, otherwise . . . Oh, God! This can't be happening."

"But it is," Larchmont said grimly. "What about John and Charlcie?"

"I think we should tell them what's happening here and let them make up their own minds about whether to stay or go."

"You know they'll stay, Jen."

"I know," she said, her voice wavering, "and it could cost them their lives.

"A hundred years ago, They almost destroyed this town. Sixty years later They killed my husband because his research might have revealed Their existence, and now They're killing again. Two deaths in as many nights and you know that someone will die tonight, tomorrow night, and two more nights after that. Then God only knows what kind of evil will be unleashed on the world."

Larchmont put his arm around Jenny and tried to comfort her. "I know, I know, but it'll be okay, you'll see."

"Cut the 'there-there, Jenny' crap and tell me what kind of plan you've got in mind to stop this evil." She pulled away and turned in her chair so she could look at him. But he wouldn't look at her. "You do have a plan, don't you?"

"Yeah," he said softly, still not looking at her. "I have a plan."

"But it's not much of a plan, is it?"

"No."

"Want to tell me about it?"

He shook his head. "I'm still thinking about it. God, I never thought this could happen again, not until the sheriff started talking. So right now all my plan has is a beginning and sort of a middle. But no end."

"Tell me about the beginning then. Maybe I can help."

"You can. We're going to have to get the people who know about the two deaths to meet with us. That means getting ahold of Childress, the sheriff, and the Air Force pathologist who did the autopsies—I think Sutton said his name was Seafront. Since I'm a stranger here and you've got some influence, I think you ought to call Sutton and Childress, and while you're talking to Childress, see if he'll get ahold of the pathologist. I think he may come in real handy."

"Why?"

After a long moment Larchmont finally looked at her. "Because Sutton said Seafront was stationed out at the Air Force base near Lompoc."

"So?"

"I'm still speculating. I haven't worked it out yet, but I think his connections with the air base might be of help.

"But the thing is, we've got to meet with them as soon as humanly possible, like tonight."

It was dark outside and dark in the dining room. A light from another room framed Jenny McKenzie's silhouette as she got up from the table. "I'll go make the calls."

Martin Larchmont stood up in the silent, dark room, his head bowed and his posture slumped as Jenny made the calls.

When he heard her coming back into the room, he straightened up and reached for her in the darkness. She came to him, putting her arms around his waist. Both heard the front door open. A moment later the young couple's laughter filtered up the hallway and into the dining room. "What now?" she whispered.

He pulled her close. "Pray, Jenny. Pray that the people who come to this house tonight will believe what we tell them. Pray that it's not too late to stop the coming holocaust."

A cold wind blowing through the window of the pickup woke Johnny Joe Sloams. He coughed, moaned, opened one eye, and tried to remember where he was. Then it came to him. He'd been drinking, working on a grave—

"Oh, fuck," he groaned. He was still in the cemetery and the sun was down and the Horrcove Brothers would ream his ass if they found him here . . . and Jesus Christ, dead bodies had been found just outside the gates. He knew that, because he'd found the bodies. "Oh, fuck," he groaned again, sitting bolt upright and groping for the door handle. He had to go to the bathroom. Bad!

Johnny Joe Sloams scrambled out of the pickup, tearing at his belt and pants. A split second later he was urinating and sighing at the same time. He realized he was peeing on the newly dug grave he was supposed to have sodded over, but he couldn't stop and didn't care. All he wanted to do was finish up and get out of this cemetery.

He was zipping up when he heard the growling whine of a heavy car in low gear. Turning, he stared into the darkness. Off in the distance, he saw a car with only its parking lights on working its way up the hill, heading in his direction. With a start he realized the truck's door was open. The dome light was on. He shut the door and began backing away from the truck, wondering why he felt the need to hide. Hell, he was the cemetery caretaker. He didn't have to explain why he was out here. In the end he decided to hide, thinking only a pervert would be out in the cemetery at this time of night.

He loped over to a huge old cedar deodar and jostled and fought his way through the lower branches of the old tree. When he was safely hidden inside a thick skirt of foliage and heavy limbs, he crouched down to watch and wait.

With only its yellow parking lights on, the black car approached like an amber-eyed panther moving slowly through the night. As it slowly passed by the pickup, Sloams blessed the tree, the fog, and the night for hiding him. He started to let out a long sigh of relief. Suddenly the black car's brake lights flared on, and Sloams's sigh seized in his throat. A heartbeat later the red lights changed to the brilliant white of backup lights, and the car began backing up the road, moving slowly toward the pickup and him. The car stopped a few yards from his pickup. The backup lights went out and an interior dome light came on as the driver opened the door and got out. Leaving the door open, the driver walked first to the new grave, then over to his pickup.

Holding his breath until he thought his lungs would explode, Sloams watched the shadowy figure walk slowly around his truck, then after what seemed like hours the driver began to retrace his steps toward the idling car. Only then did Johnny Joe begin to breathe again.

As his fear began to subside, Sloams pushed aside some branches and stared at the driver and the car.

There was something vaguely familiar about the car, but Sloams couldn't remember. He began to crawl forward, worming his way through the branches for a better view.

That was when Johnny Joe Sloams noticed a small boy moving frantically around in the car's backseat. The boy was upset, banging on one window with his fists and then another. It was like watching a panicked cat trapped in a glass cage, bouncing first off one window, then the next. Sloams wondered why the boy just didn't jump over the front seat and scramble out the driver's open door.

It was as if the boy read his mind. He backed up into one corner of the seat, then lunged forward in a head-first diving motion that would take him over and into the front seat. Suddenly the boy stopped in midair as if an invisible hand had slapped the kid and knocked him back into the backseat.

"Oh," Sloams said, realizing the boy had dived into one of those glass partitions that fancy cars had to separate the front seat from the back.

Suddenly Johnny Joe Sloams remembered what he'd been trying to remember. He knew that car. It was one of the Cadillacs his employers used to carry relatives to and from graveside services. It was one of the Horrcove brothers' black limousines.

He squinted his eyes, trying to make out who the driver was, but it was too dark, too late. The driver slipped back into the car, closed the door, and the dome light went out. Then slowly, too slowly for Sloams, the car glided away from him like a black mist in a black night.

A half hour later he finally got up the nerve to tiptoe over to his truck. After he got it running, he decided he wouldn't turn the headlights on until he was out of the cemetery.

He stopped just outside the gates to turn on his lights and to wipe the sweat off his face. The abrupt stop of

the truck caused a wine bottle to roll out from under the
seat and bump up against the heel of his shoe. To Johnny
Joe Sloams, it was like the arrival of a close friend. He
picked up the bottle, put it between his legs, and drove
down the road until he came to a stop sign. After stopping, he broke the seal, put the bottle to his lips, and
drank deeply. He went through the same ritual at the
second stop sign, and the third and the fourth.

By the time he lurched his truck into his driveway,
he'd forgotten about the cemetery, the black limousine,
and the boy trapped in the car's backseat.

Chapter
Eleven

When Jenny McKenzie had called Dr. Childress and
Henry Sutton to invite them to her home, her explanation for the meeting had been brief and brutally honest.
She had simply said that she and Martin Larchmont had
important information about the deaths of the prostitute
and deputy, and would they be willing to come over?
Surprised and curious, both men agreed to come. At
Jenny's insistence, Childress extended an invitation to
the Air Force pathologist, William Seafront. The meeting had been scheduled to start at eight.

All three men arrived early.

Jenny escorted the men to the living room and introduced them to Charlcie, John Cable, and Larchmont.
Seafront and Childress were familiar with Martin Larchmont's reputation and standing in the scientific commu-
nity, and they greeted him with enthusiasm that bordered
on awe. Preoccupied with some papers he was reading,
Larchmont almost forgot to shake their hands.

Charlcie and Cable were still in the dark over the
reasons for the meeting. Both Jenny and Martin had
been broodingly quiet during dinner, and their silence

had continued long after the dishes had been put away. It was just prior to the start of the meeting that Larchmont took Cable off to one side to tell him that Sutton had come by earlier with the news that he was no longer a suspect and could leave town if he wished. Cable had stared at his friend for a long moment, wondering why he hadn't been given the news earlier. When he finally asked, Larchmont just shook his head. "I forgot, John. It just slipped my mind."

"Martin, what's going on? Why the silence and the mysterious meeting?"

"You'll see, John," Larchmont had said, absentmindedly chewing on a cuticle.

The seating arrangement fell into a natural pattern with Jenny McKenzie and Martin Larchmont standing beside the small love seat and Charlcie and John Cable sitting down on a larger couch facing the older couple. Sutton and Seafront opted for wing-backed chairs that flanked the fireplace, while Childress hunkered down on the fireplace hearth and leaned back against the bricks.

After everyone had settled in and Jenny had sat down on the love seat, Larchmont turned to face his audience. His face was serious as his eyes moved from person to person. When his gaze finally came to Cable, the older man's expression softened, and he smiled slightly before moving on. Finally he took a deep breath, speaking primarily to Childress and Sutton. "In order to get you here tonight, Jenny told you we had information about the deaths of the prostitute and deputy." Sutton started to stir in his chair as if he thought he was the victim of a practical joke. Larchmont looked at the sheriff and shook his head. "And we do. The trouble is, the information we have is both hard to explain and it will be difficult on your part to accept. For those reasons, Jenny and I have decided to give you a two-part presentation. Jenny will go first, recounting some events which took place in Ravina about a hundred years ago. Then I'll follow with information I've gleaned from my own field of expertise.

"Before we start, there're several things we would like to ask of you. First, save your questions until we're through. What we have to offer is difficult enough to present without having to deal with questions at the same time. Second, listen to us with open minds. To paraphrase Shakespeare, 'There are more things in heaven and earth than are dreamt of in our philosophy.' So push aside your philosophy and listen to us." He looked down at the woman sitting in the love seat beside him. "It's all yours."

Jenny McKenzie got to her feet. She glanced at some three-by-five index cards she was holding, then at her audience. "I'd like to preface what I'm about to present by saying it is not a product of my imagination. I have over the years occupied my time by attempting to carry on a historical study of Ravina, a study originally initiated by my husband some twenty-five years ago. In other words, since his death I have studied this town and its history in depth and in detail. What you are about to hear is factual. I have in my library books, original letters, Xeroxed copies of court reports, old newspaper clippings, and other documents that will document the story I'll be telling you. It's all there, and following our presentations, you may peruse the information at your leisure."

She looked at her notes, then at Martin Larchmont. "Late in October of 1889, a group of what were thought to be gypsies arrived in the night in sheepherder wagons and set up their camp on top of Horrcove Hill.

"They camped on the hill for almost a week, and during that span of time the citizens of this town were terrorized by nightly killings just as grotesque and inexplicable as the ones happening now.

"On the first night the town's doctor was killed, and in his log the marshal described the doctor's body as being soft and spongy, as if the bones were all smashed. More important, the log also noted that the doctor's fingernails and teeth were missing." She paused and looked at the two physicians who'd autopsied the prostitute, trying to gauge their reactions. Seafront stared back at her impassively while Childress chose to look down at the rug and chew on a cuticle.

After a moment she continued. "On the second night a deputy was murdered." Sutton shifted uncomfortably in his chair. Jenny didn't seem to notice. "This time the marshal's log said that after the body was discovered, it was taken over and stored in the dead doctor's office around midnight. By noon the next day there wasn't anything left of the body. To quote the marshal, 'The flesh and even the bones melted like ice until there wasn't anything left.'

"The owner of the newspaper died on the third night, and I came across several eyewitness accounts which suggested that the man looked as if he'd literally been scared to death.

"A prostitute died on the fourth night, ripped to shreds by some unseen force, and a farmer died on the fifth night. Over the span of those nights two male children disappeared from the homes of their parents.

"When the second child disappeared, wildfire rumors began to run rampant through the town about how gypsies sacrificed male children during their rites of worship to the devil. That was when the townspeople began to focus their fear and terror on the wagons camped up on the hill. On the night following the fifth death, a large mob of citizens gathered at the base of the hill, and when the clouds and fog blacked out the moon, they started up the hill."

The flames in the living room fireplace crackled and hissed violently as Jenny picked up the cadence. "Forty-five to fifty people stormed up the hill that night to kill the gypsies. And they did. They hung them all. No one in the mob was injured or killed during the attack, and in a way the people in Ravina won. The deaths stopped and no more children disappeared.

"But in a way the town didn't win. It actually opened

itself up to a far greater horror . . . because each and every individual that went up the hill and participated in the lynchings came down totally and horribly altered.

"Something happened at the time of the hangings. The mob did something . . . saw something so terrifying, so beyond their comprehension, that it destroyed every individual who participated in the hangings."

The faces of the people in Jenny's living room reflected myriad expressions ranging from puzzlement to skepticism. Undaunted, she continued. "I can best illustrate what happened to those people with some statistics. You'll recall that forty-five to fifty people participated in the hangings. Of that number at least twenty-six and as many as thirty-two people took their own lives in a multitude of ghastly ways all within two years of the hangings. Moreover, several killed their own families before they killed themselves.

"Of those who didn't commit suicide, six moved or disappeared from Ravina. Of the six, only two were located. One man, an alcoholic, turned up in a tuberculosis sanitarium in San Francisco, and he died of TB in 1893. The other became a gardener for a Catholic mission outside of San Diego. Incidently, he too hanged himself in 1895.

"Three others went to prison for capital crimes, and in their cases the victims of their crimes were members of their own families. All three pleaded guilty without trial, and the transcripts indicate all three men begged for and received the death penalty.

"Some time back I spent the better part of a year searching through the San Luis Obispo County court records for the years 1890 through 1895 and found that the surviving six members of the mob, who I should note were all normal prior to the hangings, went insane and were committed either to a state hospital for the criminally insane or a state hospital for the feebly minded."

Her strength was waning. It seemed to take a monumental effort for her to finish. "There you have it. A hundred years ago forty-five to fifty men in this town hung what they thought were six gypsies, but something happened up on that hill. They saw something or came face-to-face with something that permanently altered their lives in the most horrible of fashions, and that is the point which I hope you will keep in mind when Martin gives his presentation."

Jenny McKenzie sat down in the love seat next to Larchmont. The small man took Jenny's hand, pulled her close, and said to the others, "Why don't we take a break. There's coffee in the kitchen." He turned his attention back to Jenny.

Charlcie started to get up, intending to go over to her mother. Cable took her by the hand, pulled her back on the couch and pointed out that Martin was doing an excellent job of comforting her. Charlcie nodded and stayed where she was. As Cable continued to hold Charlcie's hand, he looked at the others in the room, trying to guess what was in their minds. Childress and Seafront looked confused and puzzled by what Jenny had said. Sutton, his fingers tented, was staring at nothing, his face deeply creased.

Finally Seafront got up and walked over to the couple. "An interesting story," he commented. "But I don't see the connection between something that happened a hundred years ago and the two bodies I just autopsied."

"You will," Larchmont said, never taking his eyes off Jenny. After a moment the pathologist shrugged and returned to his chair.

Cable and Charlcie went into the deserted kitchen. While Charlcie poured coffee into their cups, Cable propped his elbows down on the counter and looked at her. "Your mother's an amazing woman. That must have been a horrible topic to—" He noticed her eyes were moist and went over to her. "Hey," he said softly. "What's with you and the tears?"

"It's my mother. God, can you imagine what she's

been through, the pressure she's been living with all these years? I've never even noticed. When I think about all the information she's gathered about this . . . this town, Jesus. When I think—" She turned away but continued to talk almost nonstop as if the wall she was facing could hear her. "Shit, all these years and she never once confided in me about what she was doing or going through. That may say a hell of a lot about her, but it doesn't say a whole hell of a lot about me and my ability to perceive pain or anguish in someone close to me. Can you imagine me growing up in this house and never once realizing what kind of burden she was shouldering. What am I? Blind? Deaf? How can anyone be that insensitive to someone else's pain?"

Cable tried gently to interrupt. She wouldn't let him. Finally he put his hand over her mouth, extinguishing her gush of words. "Listen to me. Listen to me hard, all the way through. Okay?" He didn't remove his hand until she nodded.

"Martin told me about your father, about the study he was going to undertake and what happened to him. He also told me that after your dad died, your mother put her whole soul into picking up where your father left off, not just because the work was important to your dad, but because whatever he was doing may have played a part in his death.

"That she concealed her research from you is understandable. Lots of loving parents don't share their personal pain and problems with their children, and because she's intelligent, she did a good job of camouflaging the horrors she encountered in the research. If I'm right, then the only thing you're guilty of is being a poor mind reader, and that's no sin. Over the years your mother put on a good act and put her best face forward for your benefit. That makes her a loving mother and a good actress. It doesn't make you an insensitive daughter."

Cable scrutinized Charlcie closely, trying to gauge the effect his words were having on her. Her eyes were misty and red. Mascara had left a dark trail down one cheek. She sniffed audibly and nodded, still close to tears.

Cable couldn't think of anything else to say, so he pulled her close and put his arms around her. She buried her face in his neck, and he could feel the dampness on her cheek. He felt as if he could hold her like that forever, not moving, barely breathing. Then someone called from the living room. "We're going to start."

Cable reluctantly started to release her. Then, with a start, he realized she was not holding him back. It was like he had his arms around a statue, and suddenly he wanted to be held like he was holding her. "Charlcie," he said hesitantly. "When someone's holding you, it's only fair to hold them back." She didn't move. She just continued to stand close to him, cold and rigid. At that moment Cable felt very silly and his world went out of focus.

Slowly, with stilted movements, she stepped back so she could look at him. "John Cable," she said, "you're an ass."

"Pardon?"

She smiled. "I've got a cup of very hot coffee in each hand. If I hug you, I'll spill the coffee and barbecue the best tush I've seen in years. That's the only reason why I'm not hugging you as hard as I can right now."

Cable's spirits took off like a comet. "Well! Put the coffee down and let's try this again."

"Let go of me and I will."

He did, and she put the mugs on the counter. They were starting toward one another when someone called out from the living room again. "Let's get this going, you two."

"Well, hell," Cable grumbled.

"My sentiments exactly," Charlcie added.

Chapter
Twelve

Cable followed Charlcie back into the living room and
sat down beside her on the davenport. He noticed Jenny
McKenzie was quietly studying him, taking note that he
was holding hands with her daughter. It seemed to him
she gave him a brief look of approval. He wasn't sure if
he was reading her expression correctly, but he hoped
he was.

Martin Larchmont was kneeling beside the love seat,
pawing through the contents of an old battered briefcase. Jenny McKenzie reached out from the love seat
and put her hand on the older man's shoulder. After a
moment he found what he was looking for and stiffly
stood up, a thick manila folder in his hands.

As Larchmont began thumbing through the folder,
Cable suddenly tensed, remembering what Charlcie had
shown him earlier. He leaned close to her and whispered, "You know those gravestones you had me read
this afternoon?" She nodded slowly at first, then more
rapidly. He knew she'd just made the connection between the inscriptions on the stones and her mother's
story.

"I should have thought of that while Mom was talking. Most of those markers verify what she was trying to tell us."

Cable nodded. "Maybe she doesn't know about the stones. Maybe you should tell her when you get the chance."

Charlcie began to nod enthusiastically, as if the idea of adding something to her mother's macabre tale was exciting to her. "She probably knows about the tombstones, but if she doesn't, it would be kind of neat to add something to her research."

Cable started to say something else, but was interrupted by Martin Larchmont's deep strong voice.

"Earlier, you heard Jenny describe what happened to a mob of townspeople after they participated in a mass lynching some hundred years ago. You're probably wondering what they saw or encountered on the hill that changed them so dramatically.

"I intend to tell you what they ran into and exactly why they came down the hill so altered and terrified of life. But first I have a story to tell, only mine takes place in a different part of the world. It begins some forty-two years after the hangings in Ravina.

"In 1931 a man named Patton recruited me to be a consulting archeologist for an expedition he was taking into the desert Plains of Monsul in Kurdistan . . . or Iraq, as it's now called.

"Patton was an incredibly wealthy man who'd made his fortune through the manufacturing and selling of firearms to small countries all over the world. He was also a crazy religious fanatic, although I didn't know that at the time I accepted the position."

Larchmont shook his head as his mind delved through memories almost half a century old. "Patton was a strange man. On one hand he was a maniacal sort of born-again Christian. On the other hand he thought nothing of using his money to fuel a war between two feuding countries so they'd buy arms from his company.

"In any case, he took the expedition into the Plains of Monsul near Upper Mesopotamia to research the ruined remains of a monastery and city that had once been the center for the followers of the Yezidi religion. It's important for you to know that this was a fierce religion that believed the universe was ruled by an ancient evil god called Iblis. The followers of Iblis viewed their god as a malevolent deity—somewhat along the lines of Satan, but also worthy of immense devotion. In essence, they worshipped a terrifying evil god, a god that mirrored the harshness of the land where they lived. The Plains of Monsul was, and still is, one of the cruelest environments in the world.

"To the followers of Iblis, their religion was more than a belief, it was a way of life. Their culture was marked by a caste system with priests at the top, followed by the warriors in Iblis's religious army, the general population, and finally the untouchables, consisting of nonbelievers, slaves, prisoners, and whole tribes the Yezidis had conquered and captured. It was a fierce religion, devoted to fighting and war as a means of survival and a means of spreading their beliefs throughout the land. The warriors were a ferocious lot, completely devoted to Iblis, much like the Vikings were devoted to Odin. Failure to distinguish oneself in battle or failure to fulfill a mission meant an automatic death sentence from the priests, a sentence that the warriors gladly accepted without hesitation.

"Two hundred years ago this religion had sixty thousand followers, and it still exists today, but continual fighting, warring, and an unsympathetic twentieth century have reduced its numbers to four or five thousand . . . mostly hillside people eking out an existence in an inhospitable land.

"As I said, Patton's interest was in the remains of a monastery and the ruins of a city that encircled it. Up until the mid-eighteen hundreds, the monastery had been the hub of this religion. However, beginning in the early

1860s the religion split into two distinct factions which began warring against each other. As a result of this war, the monastery was destroyed, the city leveled, and just about everything ever written about their religion and the reason for the schism obliterated." Larchmont gave Cable a professional look. "That's why we know almost nothing about this religion or its deity today.

"How Patton ever found out about this particular religion, I'll never know. But he was interested in studying the monastery and the remains of the city because he couldn't come to grips with the fact that a barbaric religion with a satanic god could have flourished so close to the geographical roots of Christianity. His own personal theory was that numerous Christians had gone into the Monsul plains to convert the followers of Iblis to Christianity but were slaughtered by the fanatical followers of the demon god. What Patton wanted to do was prove that the area surrounding the monastery was a graveyard containing the martyred bones of hundreds of missionaries. Once he had that evidence, he could claim that the demise of the Yezidi religion was not due to infighting and the twentieth century, but due to the slowly encroaching influences of Christianity.

"Of course it was all crazy. It was an insane theory thought up by a crazy man who had the money to finance an archeological expedition simply so he could prove a point which had no basis in reality or history. By the time I realized what was going on, we were nearly at our destination. I could have walked away from it, but I knew if I did, I would never work in the field of archeology again. Crazy or not, Patton was a powerful and influential man. So I stayed and decided to play any game he wanted, no matter how unscientific or irrational.

"After we arrived at what little was left of the monastery and the city, we began grid-trenching and doing random soil probes. Almost immediately we discovered a mass grave containing the mummified remains of sixty-four men just outside the monastery's south wall. Their rotting leather armor and weapons suggested they'd been warriors in the Yezidi army. It was a strange find, but what made it stranger was that the bodies had been laid out side by side in a uniform pattern like dominoes. Upon examining the bodies, we found that they had been buried while they were still alive.

"I was fascinated by the mystery. Why would sixty-four armed warriors lay down side by side in the pit and willingly allow themselves to be covered over with dirt and buried alive?

"Patton wasn't particularly interested in the find. The bodies were pagan warriors and not Christian missionaries. The mass grave didn't support his theory of Christian martyrs in the region. However, when one of our workers found a scroll wrapped around the chest of one of the dead warriors, he became curious and allowed me to take two days away from my other duties so I could translate it.

"The scroll was made of tin. It had been beaten to a flat, thin texture not much thicker than a sheet of paper. It had been scribed on with a sharp knife or stone. Parts of it were untranslatable. Before his death the warrior had wrapped the scroll around his chest under his outer clothing. When he began to decompose, his acids settled on part of the tin and made it unreadable."

Larchmont opened his manila folder and removed a sheaf of papers, yellow and stiff with age. "This is my original translation of the scroll. It's over fifty years old, and I brought it up with me from my home after my friend, John Cable, told me about a girl's murder in Ravina. Most of you might find it strange that a scroll written well over a century ago in a land four thousand miles from here could have a direct bearing on two recent deaths in Ravina, but as you will soon see, it does.

"Rather than paraphrase it, I would like to read what this warrior wrote just hours before he died. To present

it in any other way would be an injustice to this man and
his purpose.'' Larchmont adjusted his glasses and began
to read the words of a warrior whose body had been
ashes and dust for over a century.

'*My name is Ben-Admid Tomar. I am a warrior
of Paramount-Rank in the Army of Iblis. Tomorrow, before the sun burns the sands on the Plains
of Monsul, I and sixty-three of my fellow warriors
will be put to death by the priests of Iblis in a
manner I know not. We, the warriors of Iblis, fear
not this last sun-coming, for it will bring relief from
and an end to our shame. We have failed our God,
and our failure is as evident to all as are the huge
boulders that now block the cave at the Cliffs of
Charis. Thus, we sit here in the destroyed Temple
of Iblis without guards, without bonds, surrounded
by broken walls and open doors to await the
sun-coming.*

*Our sin was great, and thus we seek our own
ends. The sadness I feel is not for the ending of my
existence; it is for the living, for the lives of my
family, who will continue to live on after I am gone.
I did, at this last sunset, bid my good-byes to my
wife, Bethnay, and my children. They were strong,
as I knew they would be, and I praised them for
their strength. Since their departure, I have three
times evoked the blessings of Iblis upon my loved
ones, asking that they might prosper, and I will do
so three times more before this final sun-coming.
For thus, it is the custom of Iblis, and he will
provide for them in their future hours of need.*

*It was my wife who brought to me these sheets of
tin and the tool with which I write, for it was only
the priests who forbid that this story be told, not
our God, Iblis. In matters of action, I will follow the
dictates of the priests; in matters of conscience, I
will follow the dictates of Iblis. My tale is a matter*

of conscience. It will be told and Iblis will bless my efforts.

Man is composed of two parts, the good and the bad. For me, my good will continue to live on after the sun-coming in the form of my family. The bad I carry with me to my grave in the form of a scroll . . .'

Larchmont glanced up from the papers. "This part of the scroll was unreadable, etched away by the man's body acids. I'll move ahead to where the scroll became legible.

'. . . Somewhere, something must exist to explain the terrors which will live on. My body and I are to be the instruments of this information which may yet serve a purpose long after my death. To deny me this is to deny my life as a follower, a worshipper, a Warrior-Paramount in the service of Iblis. It is also to deny our failures, which did allow His hideous spawn to live on and into the forever.

We, the followers of Iblis, have not the right to question the acts of our God when He chose to fornicate with the She-Beasts below the rocks on the mountain of Herron-Bey. He was our God, and we did not judge His actions when twelve consumers of flesh entered this planet through the birthing labors of those unspeakable creatures.

From the mouths of our priests came the words of Iblis, warning us not to worship that which our God had engendered. But this was not to be. The twelve creature-demons spawned from the seeds of Iblis were great in their power, and greater in their terror. They promised much, a great cleaving did occur among the followers of Iblis. Some chose to remain faithful to Iblis; others chose the forbidden path and knelt at the feet of the twelve flesh-eating sons of Iblis and the She-Beasts of Herron-Bey.

It was then that the great war began, for the

priests spoke to us with the words of Iblis: 'Worship of that which I have fathered is forbidden! Slay my progeny and all those who follow them!'

We, the followers of Iblis, amassed our army and warred heavily upon the son-worshippers. Thousands died on each side in the seven years that followed, but in the end the army of Iblis came to victory. We closed in on them, the twelve creature-demons and their battered followers. It was then that the vanquished chose to place their twelve gods in coffins mounted on wagons and flee from their camp in the blackest part of the night across the Plains of Monsul.

The Iblis priests commanded us to pursue, and to destroy the demon flesh eaters and all those who loved them. We followed them in the heat of the day and in the black of the night. We pursued for eight days. By the light of the sun we followed their tracks in the sand and witnessed the carcasses of their victims lying beside their trail. By night we tracked them by the foul smell they exuded even from their coffins.

On the beginning of the eighth day they trapped themselves by seeking refuge in the great cave in the Cliffs of Charis, and there they prepared for a great siege which was never to come. Our supplies had been depleted during the pursuit, and thus, our priests ordered me and two hundred of my warriors to the top of the cliff high above the cave. For a full day and night we broke away the face of the cliff with steel bars, causing large rocks and boulders to fall forward, sealing the cave that contained the spawn of Iblis. Our efforts were successful. In the end not even a breath of wind could have escaped from the cave.

We departed for home, weary but joyous in the success of our services to our god. We journeyed homeward only in the comfort of the sun, for haste was no longer needed.

One day's ride from the cave we found signs of a trail in the cracked clay of the desert that led away from the cave of Charis. Victory bled from our hearts as blood from a wound as we realized what the signs meant. The creature-demons and their followers had formed themselves into two groups. One group had gone east to meet their deaths in the cave. A second group had gone south toward the ruins of Old Babylon. In our earlier haste to catch the twelve sons of Iblis, we had passed by the signs, which told of the splitting, in the darkest part of the night.

I led two hundred warriors to seek that which was not now entombed in the caves at the Cliffs of Charis. We pursued our prey on foot by day and by night. When the ruts of the wagon wheels disappeared in the hard rock soil of Edir-bin, we spread out like a great angry fan and sought signs of their spoor. Date farmers told of seeing a caravan of weary people and six wagons, each carrying a singular ornate box. We knew now that six creature-demons had been sealed in the cave. Our quarry was the surviving six and the remnants of their following.

We set a fiery pace for ourselves, running south to Karhala, and then on past the ruins of the city of Old Babylon. Near the terraced city of Shatra, we were attacked by the city's frightened citizens. They had thought us to be part of the followers of the demon-creatures and had been sickened and enraged over the flesh-taking rituals that these creatures required for sustenance and rejuvenation. I lost over a hundred warriors at Shatra, one of whom was my brother, but we took no time to bury our dead, for the demons were still ahead of us.

We followed them on, even as they veered west-

ward at Basra and later looped southward near the
Wells of Mir. We ran on, and were close to them as
they entered the seaport town of Ganaveh Bandar
Rig. Finally they were ours. Their backs were to us,
their faces were to the sea. They were trapped.

My two hundred warriors were no more; the heat,
the steady running, the battle of Shatra had reduced us to sixty-four. In spite of this, all of us
were singing victory songs in our hearts as we
marched into the seaport of Ganaveh Bandar Rig.

The citizens of this plague-infested town were
reluctant to point out the route the demons had
taken in their effort to hide from us. We killed
some, and the remainder cooperated with outstretched arms that pointed to the streets our prey
had taken. We tracked the demons down stone streets
and past crowded markets until we arrived at the
rotting docks of this despicable seaport. They would
be ours. There would be no escape. Torches were
prepared. Swords were drawn. Fire would destroy
the sons of Iblis while they slept in their coffins.
Our blades would pierce human flesh. We searched
the wharfs and buildings that lined the harbor. But
found nothing.

Our prey was nowhere to be seen.

Our swords and gold coins secured for us the
final thread of information that would complete this
tapestry of failure. The followers of the six sons of
Iblis had purchased passage for themselves and
their hideous cargo on a ship.

We could not believe it. They had sailed on a ship
only hours before we had arrived on the wharfs.
They had sailed on a ship named for that crafty
rodent which battles the deadly hooded snake. Their
destination was to be that land which grew and sent
out soldiers who wear that strange uniform of red
and black.

Our mission, our purpose, our reason for being

*died there in the slime on the wharves of Ganaveh
Bandar Rig. We returned to the ruins of the Iblis
monastery with our heads hung in shame, for we
had failed our God, our Iblis.*

*Thus, it is now, and I have looked about me in
this prison that has no walls; the night has turned
to the color of turquoise, and the sand quail have
fluttered their wings in homage to a pending dawn.
About me I can see the sixty-three silent shadows
of my men. They, like me, await the priests and the
sun-coming. Like me, they wait and welcome these
things, for it brings a release from the shame we
have brought upon ourselves. I must end my writing now so as to wrap the tin around my body to
conceal it from the eyes of the priests. They will
come soon and they will end our lives. This is not
feared. For it is to us no more than an easing of
tired muscles and heavy eyes, and it will put an end
to my shame, which until now has never been known
by a Warrior-Paramount in the army of Iblis.'*

"That is the complete scroll of Ben-Admid Tomar,"
Larchmont finished, looking at the others in the room.
"This translation has been in my possession for over
fifty years, and I've read it often. I like Ben-Admid
Tomar. I would've liked to have known him."

He slipped the papers into the briefcase, then rose up
slowly. "Patton went wild when I showed him the translation. Within an hour of reading the scroll, he and two
of his aides and I left for the Cliffs of Charis, where we
hoped to find the cave and destroy whatever was in it.

"We drove along the base of the cliffs until we came
upon the signs of what looked like a monumental
rockslide. Two of us climbed up the face, looking for
evidence that might suggest the rock slide had been man-
made. We found it. The top part of the cliff was covered
with grooves and indentations where men had shoved
poles and metal spears into fissures in the rocks so they

could pry boulders loose and topple them over the cliff and down on the cave two hundred feet below.

"When Patton found out the rock slide had been man-made, something happened to him. He'd always been close to the edge, but somehow, that pushed him over. He became obsessed with entering the cave, and it was like working with a madman. For almost a full day we used sticks of dynamite to blast away at the boulders blocking the cave, but it was too slow for Patton and he had us rig up three boxes of dynamite all timed with fuses to go off at the same time. I thought he'd bring the cliff down, but he didn't. The dynamite did its work.

"When it was finally open, he and his two aides immediately went into the cave in spite of my warnings about poison air. They stayed in there about a half hour. When they came out, Patton came over to me and said that the scroll was accurate. They'd found the mummi-fied remains of the worshippers of the sons of Iblis, and they'd also found six ornate coffins in the cave, still on the wagons used to carry them across the desert."

Larchmont massaged his temples, as if the act would make his memories less painful. "I can still remember Patton saying to me that there were still mummified horses chained to the wagons.

"I never did see what Patton saw. While he was in the cave, he set fire to everything that was in there and he later dynamited the entrance closed. That night Patton and his two assistants died from the air they'd breathed while they were in the cave." He motioned to Cable. "Cable's an archeologist. He can tell you about the dangers of neuromyces.

"I probably should have forgotten about everything that happened out there at the Cliffs of Charis, but I couldn't. In the years to follow I researched all I could about the creatures in the cave and the creatures that had escaped, though not a lot was available to me be-cause as I said, the war between the two factions of the Yezidi religion destroyed a lot of what was written about Iblis's spawn, and what did survive was later destroyed by the priests of Iblis.

"Some ten years later, in 1942, I was sent to London by the United States Government. My job was an insignificant research project which left me with a lot of time on my hands. I was still curious about what had happened to the followers and the coffins that had eluded Ben-Admid Tomar and his warriors at the seaport. London was the ideal place to satisfy my curiosity because Tomar had mentioned in his scroll that the creatures had set sail for a land that sent forth soldiers in uniforms of red and black. In the mid 1800s the English were the only people whose army wore a uniform with those colors.

"While Tomar didn't give me the name of the ship the cult and coffins sailed on, he did mention they sailed on a ship named for a rodent that battles the hooded snake. So, while I was there, I set out to find out what I could about a ship called the *Mongoose*.

"My position and title allowed me access to the archives of the National Maritime Museum of England and the Lloyds of London Register of Cargo and Shipping. The museum's archives listed three British-built ships with the name *Mongoose,* but only one fit into the time period I was interested in. That ship had been built for a company called the East Persian Trading Company, Ltd. With that knowledge, I went to Lloyds of London's Register of Cargo and Shipping, where I was able to get ahold of and read the *Mongoose*'s bills of lading and manifests of cargo for the years 1870 through 1885.

"I don't think I actually expected to find anything, but I did. I found written evidence to support the scroll. Detailed on the manifests of cargo for the year 1880 was a lengthy statement about how the *Mongoose* took on six large crates and thirty-one foreign men and two foreign women in the seaport of Ganaveh Bandar Rig. The cost of passage to England was paid by one of the passengers to the captain in gold.

"I had several friends in the British Government, and because of them, I was able to get into the archives of the East Persian Trading Company, where the rest of my story was outlined in the logs of the *Mongoose*. The logs were lengthy, and to save time I'll give you basically an outline of what happened after the followers and their gods escaped Ben-Admid Tomar and his warriors.

"The *Mongoose* left Ganaveh Bandar Rig on June 6, 1880. En route, nine of the foreign passengers died of wounds they had prior to boarding or of exposure to western diseases they had no resistance to. After they docked in England, the leader of the cult met with the board of directors of the trading company and leased the *Mongoose* for an extended journey. Once again he paid in gold, and the price far exceeded the ship's worth and potential earnings for the years to come.

"For three months the ship remained in England, where it was refitted for a lengthy sea voyage, and in May of 1881, it set sail for the United States with twenty-four passengers and six ornate boxes. It took thirteen months to reach Norfolk, Virginia. According to the log, illnesses and storms killed twelve of the passengers and numerous crew members disappeared. After arriving, most of the crew deserted. Repairs to the ship and the hiring of a new crew took nine months. The *Mongoose* finally left Norfolk in February of 1883, and was immediately plagued with more problems, primarily more deaths and desertions. Several crewmen simply disappeared with no trace. And every time the ship put into a port, much of the crew jumped ship. Delays were constant, so much so that it took the *Mongoose* almost three and a half years to sail from Norfolk around the tip of South America, up the westerly coast of Mexico, and into the western coastal waters of the United States.

"In July of 1886 the *Mongoose* put to port in a small California sea town some forty miles south of here, a town called Dove Harbor."

Childress gestured for Larchmont's attention. "I know

this area as well as anyone around here, and there is no Dove Harbor forty miles south of here. Matter of fact, I don't think there's a Dove Harbor anyplace along the California coast."

"Wrong, Doctor." Larchmont retorted. "Check your history books, especially those prior to 1890. The town did exist. It was a pleasant town with a population of about a thousand people. Beginning in mid-1888 it was plagued with a number of mysterious happenings: fires, strange deaths, suicides, and in September of 1889 it was leveled by an earthquake. Actually, the quake did more than level it; it pushed the whole town into the sea.

"A month later, October 1889, to be exact, the strange sequence of events and deaths that Jenny described took place in Ravina.

"I think you will agree with me. It's easy to surmise that the followers of these creatures who were dormant and in their coffins, took advantage of their time in Dove Harbor to explore their new surroundings. For some reason Dove Harbor did not appeal to them and it paid a terrible penalty for this. But there was something about Ravina that was attractive to these followers as a whole. What that was is still a mystery to me, although I suspect that Ravina might have offered them a way to disguise what they really were up to. Bear in mind that there were very few human followers alive at this time, so in order to survive secrecy was an absolute must.

"After they arrived here from Dove Harbor, their followers grouped the wagons on top of Horrcove Hill, and then they initiated a complex six-day ritual that would bring the creatures, their gods, out of their states of dormancy. I should explain that the Eastern concept of dormancy does not mean asleep or helpless. It means resting with only a partial amount of one's complete powers at one's command. In any case, the ritual began, a ritual that over a six-day period would bring all six demons back to life, a ritual that necessitated the taking of a human life by each of the different creatures on each of the six nights and a ritual that also demanded the sacrifices of two male children. The end result of this ritual, if successful, meant that all six creatures would return to life at a full state of incomprehensible powers.

"And then, as Jenny related, the deaths began. A single death on each and every night for five nights in a row.

"Jenny and I believe that on the sixth night, the final night of the renewal ritual, the townspeople came up from the town, and in the darkness they hanged what they thought were gypsies. But in reality the mob hanged six creatures who were caught—suspended midway between a dormant state and a fully active state. For a brief period of time they were helpless and defenseless. When the townspeople finally lit their torches and saw what they had done, what they had actually hanged, the impact of what they saw or the dying creatures' fading powers drove everyone who was up on the hill insane.

"Earlier, you heard Jenny talk about what happened to everyone who participated in the lynchings. Most committed suicide, others killed their families and then took their own lives, while still others asked for death or were committed to institutions.

"Now you know why. Now you know what they came up against and what they saw. Now you know what drove them to do what they later did.

"Some of you may wonder why the worshippers of these demons didn't try and stop the mob. All I can tell you is that there were very few of them, and to be near these creatures during their final moments of resurrection was to be standing inside a circle of death. The human followers were off someplace else in another location, waiting and watching perhaps. Because of this, they escaped the hangings and were able to return to the hill the following morning to carry away their gods and hide them away again. In the years to come, the surviving human followers passed their knowledge and powers on to their sons, who like their fathers, assumed the role of caretakers and guardians of the remains of the creatures.

"I don't believe the lynch mob killed the creatures. I think the hangings or the shock of having their ritual shattered pushed them back into a second state of dormancy. They've been dormant-powerless—waiting the past hundred years for the right time to begin another resurrection ritual.

"God help us," Martin Larchmont whispered. "That is what's going on in Ravina today. Two demons have already attained a partial state of rejuvenation through the taking of two human lives. Four other demons will follow as they did a hundred years ago, using tonight and three other successive nights to bring themselves into a partial state of wakefulness. Then on the sixth night, the final night, they will play out the last aspects of their ritual, and at that point each and every creature will attain its full complement of powers, and a holocaust will begin in Ravina, a holocaust that'll make what happened to Dove Harbor look like child's play."

"I don't believe what I'm hearing," William Seafront said, abruptly cutting Larchmont off. "I'll admit the first part of what you had to say was interesting, as was the scroll, in a fairy tale sort of way. But now you're standing here in front of us, asking us to believe there're six mythical creatures from Iran—"

"Iraq," Larchmont quietly corrected.

"Iran, Iraq, Saudi Arabia, that's hardly the point."

"Agreed," Larchmont said. "But now you tell me. What do you think my point is?"

"Your point?" the pathologist asked. "Er . . . well, you're asking us to believe that some religious cult brought six sons of Satan into Ravina a hundred years ago, and now all of a sudden they're waking up and killing people."

Larchmont smiled. "Very good. That's exactly my point, and your label—sons of Satan—is probably accurate because I've long suspected that if Iblis wasn't the devil, then he was related to him."

Seafront gave Larchmont an angry look. "If you ask me, I think you're asking us to believe in a crock of shit." He glanced at Jenny McKenzie. "Sorry about the language."

"Frankly," Jenny McKenzie replied, "I'm interested in what you're thinking, not in what kind of language you use."

The pathologist sighed, pulled out a wrinkled packet of unfiltered Camel cigarettes, and lit one. He pinched a piece of tobacco from his lip. "In the last two days I've examined two bodies, and to put it bluntly, I haven't the slightest idea how they died. Now, if you can tie in what you've been saying to the two bodies I've just autopsied, I think I might give your story a bit more credence." He coughed, sat back in his chair, smiled slightly, and coughed some more.

When Seafront stopped coughing, Larchmont said, "You have to remember that the information I have about the sons of Iblis is scant. On the other hand, there's far more information about the She-Devils of Herron-Bey and Iblis than their offspring.

"There are stories told in the villages near Herron-Bey of a She-Beast called Garnach. The villagers called her the witch of cutting edges, and her power was sustained through the taking of fingernails and teeth from her victims." Seafront shifted uncomfortably in his chair as Larchmont continued. "There's a high possibility that the creature that killed the girl may have had Garnach as a mother. The parallels between the dead woman you examined and what I found in my research are extremely strong. If you remember earlier, I said that demon-creatures were basically an energy force contained within a restrictive body. In seeking a source of rejuvenation, Garnach's offspring unleashed its energy force when it attacked the girl and took her fingernails and teeth, and that power was responsible for the shattered skeletal system you could not explain." Larchmont's gaze moved from Seafront to Sutton. "You said that

Seafront had speculated on the possibility that perhaps a laser beam type of force had been used on the woman. If that's the case, I would postulate that this creature's power would equal, if not surpass, the power of a laser beam.''

"How would you explain the rotting body of the deputy?" Mark Childress asked. "The body didn't last very long, but as near as we could tell, nothing appeared to be missing. That sort of blows your theory of laser beams and a creature that requires some part of a human being in order to rejuvenate itself."

Larchmont shook his head. "As I understand it, the deputy was brought in in an advanced state of decay. How do you know nothing was missing? From what Sutton said, half the man's internal organs could have been missing and you wouldn't have been able to tell. Still, I think I can account for what happened to the deputy.

"The villagers who live in the area surrounding the Mountain of Herron-Bey are afraid of it. The mountain is taboo; no one goes near it, and one of the reasons is their fear of a She-Beast called Gorthcore. She's the witch of shadows and swamps. No one knows what she requires to sustain her existence, but legend has it that anything she touches rots away instantly.

"Her offspring touched the deputy . . . ." Larchmont gestured with one hand as if there was no need to finish what he was saying.

In the silence that filled the room, Seafront pulled out another cigarette and lit it. "You're saying that the son of the She-Beast of sharp edges killed the girl, and the offspring of the witch of swamps turned the deputy into vegetable soup?"

"Yes. That's exactly what I'm saying."

"Christ," Seafront said, grinding out his cigarette and shaking his head. "I can buy the fact that you found a scroll in Iraq fifty years ago and that some fools died because they entered a cave too soon. And I think I can buy this town going nuts because they hanged some gypsies a hundred years ago. But what I can't buy is your claim that a creature-demon took fingernails from a dead prostitute, and a second demon touched a deputy and turned him into nothing."

Larchmont slumped down on the arm of the love seat, removed his glasses, and massaged the bridge of his nose. "I sympathize with your point of view, Doctor, but you see, I've done the research. I've heard and seen and gathered enough information throughout the course of my career to be genuinely concerned about the plight of this town. The problem is that you have a rational and logical mind—which makes you unwilling to consider the existence of things you can't see, touch, or experience."

Larchmont put his glasses back on, turned slightly, and looked straight at the pathologist. "This evil exists, Dr. Seafront. It's out there hiding in the shadows and hard to document for a number of reasons. The creatures we're dealing with are intelligent, and they don't want us to believe in them until they've obtained their full powers. I think it was Plato who said evil grows openly amid ignorance. By refusing to believe what I am saying, by refusing to even consider that these creatures might exist, you're playing right into their hands. At this point, they only have limited powers and have no wish to do battle with us, so they'll do anything they can to keep their existence a secret. With help from people like you, they will."

Though he was exhausted, his belief in what he was saying seemed to fuse Martin Larchmont to renewed energy. Still staring at Seafront, he got to his feet. "A hundred and fifty years ago your profession didn't believe in germs or bacteria because they could not see them. Fifty years ago you wouldn't have believed in the atom for the same reason. That's what's going on here tonight. This evil is not part of your mind-set. You can't see it, touch it, experience it, so for you it doesn't exist. It's all part of a fairy tale, and your failure to even try to acknowledge this evil is a shame because your particular point of view just might get you killed."

He turned to look at the others in the room. "There is an evil out there hiding in the night. An evil that's growing, becoming, and killing. During the past two nights, this evil has already established its pattern, a pattern identical to what was occurring a hundred years ago in this town. As such, it's my fervent prayer you'll join Jenny and me in an effort to stop what is taking place."

"Pattern?" Seafront shouted. "What pattern? A pattern implies continuity and a certain amount of predictability."

"The pattern is there," Larchmont said. "It's already underway. There have been two deaths in the last two nights"—he turned and looked at Henry Sutton—"and if this goes unchecked, there will be four more deaths over the next four nights. Sheriff, one of those deaths will take place tonight."

He turned and looked back at Seafront. "There's one other element you should add to this pattern. Some time during the next couple of nights, two male children will disappear as if by magic. No one will know what happened to them or how they suddenly disappeared, but the point will be that they are indeed missing. Maybe then you'll begin to believe that this town has a problem."

For the first time since the meeting had begun, Henry Sutton spoke, his voice low and tense. "You keep using the word *creatures* or *demon-creatures*. This is probably a stupid question, but can you tell me what these things look like?"

Larchmont shook his head. "It's not a stupid question, and all I can tell you is I've seen drawings of the She-Beasts done by the villagers who live near the Mountain of Herron-Bey. The drawings were crude and primitive, but what the villagers captured was hideous and malformed. If you ever saw one, you'd know it. Believe me, you would know it."

135

Sutton sat back in his chair and looked at Larchmont intently. "Assuming I believe everything you've said tonight, how would I go about finding these things? More important, how would I kill them?"

Larchmont cleared his throat as if answering the question might be difficult. "As for finding them, I would focus on the area closest to where the bodies were found. As for destroying them, I'm afraid that's a whole different ball game. I have a plan, a couple of ideas, but I'm not sure if my ideas would work."

Henry Sutton continued to look up at Larchmont, his face set in an unreadable expression. Then, when it looked like Sutton was about to ask another question, William Seafront broke out in a fit of coughing. When the coughing subsided, Seafront got up from his chair. "Sorry, Dr. Larchmont, but it's getting late and I've got a busy day tomorrow. I've got to get going. You coming, Mark?"

Childress nodded as he got to his feet. "It's later than I thought. I've got an early shift tomorrow." Avoiding Larchmont's eyes, Childress motioned to Seafront. "I'm ready."

John Cable's stomach did a slow roll as he watched Larchmont's anxious eyes move from the physicians to Henry Sutton. "Are you leaving too, Sheriff?" Cable knew what Henry Sutton's answer would be, but in his mind he begged Henry Sutton to stay and give Martin Larchmont something more than cold indifference.

Sutton was as unreadable as a block of granite. Then slowly he nodded. "Sorry, Doctor, but what you had to say was just too far away from my sense of reality." He got to his feet, picked up his Stetson, and looked down at the small professor with a trace of compassion in his expression. "Personally, I think there's a psychopath loose in Ravina, a psychopath who's responsible for at least one of the deaths and probably both, but whatever the case, I'm sure the killer is human. A demented one, but a human being nevertheless." As Sutton turned away,

Cable wanted to defend Martin Larchmont's beliefs, but he couldn't. He simply didn't have any way to debate Seafront or Sutton. It was then that he realized that like the others, he didn't believe what Jenny McKenzie and Martin Larchmont had said, either.

Martin Larchmont's eyes, hugely magnified by his thick trifocals, sought out Henry Sutton a final time. "Sheriff, I need to remind you of something."

Henry Sutton stopped and glanced back at Larchmont. "The resurrection renewal requires the presence and eventually the bodies of two male children. When the children disappear, and they will, come back and see me. Maybe we can work out some sort of plan, a way to stop these demon-creatures."

Henry Sutton's face darkened into a tight mask of shadows and concerns as he turned away from Larchmont. He put on his Stetson, nodded to Jenny McKenzie, and then followed Seafront and Childress out into the night.

The sound of the front door closing accentuated the tense silence in the McKenzies' living room, and Larchmont slowly turned around in that silence, stopping when his eyes met Cable's. "You didn't believe me either, did you, John?"

Unable to lie to the man who was as close to him as a father, Cable tried to look at Larchmont but couldn't. "I want to . . . I tried."

The older man motioned with his hand. "It's all right. It took me years to learn to believe what I said tonight. I guess I really didn't expect anyone to believe what Jenny and I were trying to get across, but I had hoped—" He shook his head, then walked over to Jenny McKenzie. She was still sitting on the love seat with her daughter hovering close by. Larchmont held out his hand. Jenny took it in both of hers. A moment later, they walked out of the living room together.

"How's your mother?" Cable asked.

"Tired, depressed, frightened . . . not for herself, but for me and you and this town." Then, after a moment,

"Hell, how should I know? After all, I'm only her daughter."

"Charlcie, we covered all that in the kitchen, remember? Talk to her in the morning after you've both had a good night's sleep."

She looked at him. "You always this logical?"

Cable sighed, took her hand, and led her back to the couch. "No, but this particular situation seems to call for something like logic." He sat down beside her and they put their feet up on the coffee table.

She tapped his foot with her foot. "We'll have to do something about your rational responses in the face of emotional situations. That logical mind-set of yours goes along with your old image of a middle-aged professor in polyester pants."

"I don't think I understand," Cable said, staring into a dying fire.

"Don't you ever lose your cool? Get emotional? Rant or rave or scream rather than analyze and assess?"

"You mean am I always this boring?" He yawned, then answered his own question. "Probably. But what you see is what you get."

"You're not boring, damn it. I just want to know if you've ever shouted or lost your cool?"

A hard question, Cable decided, as he tried to remember if he ever had. "I guess I ranted and raved a little after my wife left me. Then there was that time in high school when some seniors pulled off my pants and threw me in the girl's locker room. I screamed a lot until some girls came out of the shower to see what was going on." He shrugged. "It wasn't much of an outburst. When I realized what was on their minds, logic set in and I became very very quiet."

She cuddled up next to him, leaning her head on his shoulder. "If you did what I think you did, you've definitely got potential. How many girls did you say came out of the shower?"

"Twenty-two."

"Huh?" she asked, sounding very sleepy and far away. "Just kidding."

"You definitely aren't boring," she mumbled. "You just have a controlled approach to things."

While Cable wondered if a controlled approach to things meant he didn't have any spontaneity or was a man of theory, Charlcie's breathing deepened and Cable closed his own eyes.

It wasn't that late, and Henry Sutton decided to check in at the station before going home for the night. It was only after he entered the civic center that he found out about Michael Shehane.

Michael Shehane was a four-and-a-half-year-old boy who some three hours earlier had disappeared from his house while his parents were home. When Sutton first heard the news from the dispatcher, he felt as if he were going to throw up. The nausea passed, but Martin Larchmont's prophetic words—"When two male children disappear, and they will . . ."—haunted him for the rest of the night.

Chapter Thirteen

Louellen Mae Harnes liked to think of herself as a devoted and loving mother. Yet she was able to enjoy a black and white rerun of *I Love Lucy* before deciding she was ready to go out and look for her missing daughter.

While she searched her living room for car keys, she heard a television announcer. "Tonight's classic creature feature is definitely not for the squeamish. Tonight we're proud to present *Creature from the Black Lagoon*." Louellen Mae Harnes moaned and turned off the TV. It was bad enough her daughter was a sneak, a liar, missing, and the reason why she was about to go out into the night. But now the little bitch was about to cost her a movie. She swore and tried to remember whether she'd seen the horror flick, but it didn't matter. It just didn't matter. She was pissed.

In the dim light of the dying television Louellen grabbed her sleeping three-year-old son by the wrist and jerked him off the davenport. The boy woke up, but was smart enough not to cry out as he allowed his mother to half-walk, half-drag him to the car and dump him in the backseat like a suitcase. Deaf since birth, he felt his mother climb into the car an instant before slipping back to sleep.

Louellen Mae's mood was black and foul, and it governed the way she drove through the fog. She should've known something was up. Tammy Fae had been too nice; no arguments, no lip, all the chores done right the first time around. Louellen Mae was no dummy. She knew her daughter was up to something and Tammy Fae hadn't disappointed her. She'd made her move just after dinner the previous night.

"Cynthia Wyckoff's having a slumber party at her house tomorrow," Tammy had said while clearing the table. "I'd like to go. I really would."

Even now, Louellen couldn't believe she'd said yes. She could've said no. She'd never met the Wyckoff kid. All she knew about the girl was that her parents were rich and lived in a fancy house with an indoor swimming pool. But no, she'd been stupid, given in, and Tammy had gone over to the Wyckoffs' right after school . . . or at least, that's what Tammy had wanted her to think.

Tammy often reminded Louellen of herself. It was this which prompted Louellen to call Mrs. Wyckoff "just to make sure my daughter had gotten over there okay."

Now, three hours later, Louellen Mae could still hear the preening delight in Mrs. Wyckoff's voice. "Cynthia's here, but I haven't seen Tammy . . . no, Cynthia is not having a slumber party tonight . . . well, I certainly hope you find your daughter, Mrs. Harnes." It wasn't what Mrs. Wyckoff had said that irked Louellen Mae, but the way she said it. The woman had talked to her as if she were white trash.

The memory of the conversation only fueled Louellen Mae's foul mood. She drove harder and faster through the fog, guiding the car toward a small copse of woods near Livermore Creek. When she'd gone to school, the woods had been called Makeout Park. Recently she'd heard it was now called Condom Corners, and that's where she would find her daughter, busily making out with that greasy taco, Joe Santos. They'd be easy to find out there, even in the night and fog. Santos drove a shiny red car with a rear end so low to the ground it scraped its bumper every time it pulled into the driveway.

She'd get 'em. She'd get 'em both. She'd hit Santos with a statutory rape charge and ground her daughter for a fucking year. Then Tammy Fae would have time to do her work. Louellen Mae smiled. The house would just shine.

She spotted the turnoff, slowed, and eased the car off the highway and onto a rutted dirt road flanked by high trees. Contrary to custom, Louellen kept her headlights on high beam, causing shapes to sit up in their cars and give her the finger. Laughing, she continued to keep her headlights on high.

The road she was on was a simple mile-long loop that led back to the main highway. As she continued on, the road became congested with parked cars. Driving slowly, Louellen Mae checked out the cars she passed, looking for a red one with a lowered rear end. It wasn't there.

She pulled the car back up on the main highway and drove away, heading now for the second best parking spot in Ravina, the west side of Horrcove Hill.

The eastern side of the hill was the cemetery, but on the westerly side, where there was a winding gravel road and trees, there were lots of places to pull over and park. In the daytime lovers could sit in their car and gaze out at the ocean. At night the view was the last thing they had in mind.

Preoccupied with anger and revenge, she almost missed the turnoff to the hill. Braking hard, she cramped the wheel to the right, and the car fishtailed off the highway and onto the winding gravel road that led to the top of the hill.

Her earlier trek to Condom Corners had triggered old memories for Louellen Mae Harnes. As she drove, she thought back on her life. Fifteen years ago life had looked good. Fifteen years ago she'd looked good, and she'd had more boyfriends than she could handle. But now, fifteen years later and thirty-one pounds heavier, the choices were few and far between. That scared her because her third and present marriage was on the rocks. Her current husband worked nights at a dairy farm, and he was seeing other women, she was sure of it. No one spends twelve hours with a herd of cows and then comes home smelling like wine and White Shoulders perfume. She would have given him the heave-ho, but the prospect of a divorce frightened her. Louellen Mae Harnes hated being alone, and she wasn't sure she had the ability or the physical assets to catch a fourth husband.

She sighed bitterly as she recalled her first marriage. Tammy Fae had been the motivating force behind the ceremony. That marriage had lasted ten months.

She'd been twenty-six years old when she met and married a truck driver named Anthony Fiori. Now, there was a good man, she thought as she drove slowly past two parked cars on her left. Anthony had cared about her and his stepdaughter. The marriage had worked and worked well for five years, and the boy in the backseat, Anthony Junior, was the only living memory she had of her dead husband. Nine months earlier Anthony Senior had fallen asleep behind the wheel of his huge eighteen-wheeler. The truck and Anthony Fiori and twenty-seven thousand pounds of frozen turkey legs had gone off the road seventeen miles from Ravina.

Not wanting to spend another ten years alone, she'd married the first man who'd looked at her. That man was Eric Harnes, and they'd gotten married just ten weeks after Anthony had been laid to rest. From day one Louellen Mae had cursed herself for being so blind. The whirlwind courtship had been fun, the sex great, but she hadn't bothered to look too closely at Eric Harnes. Now she was stuck with a budding alcoholic and a womanizer who seemed to be able to get it up with everybody in the county except her. They'd been married for seven months, and she wondered if they would last a year.

She crested the top of the hill and cruised slowly along the knoll, passing maybe fifteen cars. None had shiny red paint or a lowered rear end.

She turned off the gravel road and onto a narrow cement road which would take her to the cemetery and back home. She didn't like driving into the cemetery after dark, but this route was a shortcut, and she was anxious to catch the last half of *Creature from the Black Lagoon*.

Driving down through the Horrcove Cemetery brought a whole new set of memories to Louellen Mae Harnes. Both her father and Anthony Fiori were buried up here, their graves less than thirty feet apart. She liked their graves being so close together. They'd gotten to be good friends after the marriage, and Anthony had been just as broken up as she had when her father had died twelve months ago. Then three months later Anthony was gone.

The fog was thicker in the cemetery than on the top of the hill. She gripped the wheel with both hands, slowed the car to a crawl, and stared hard through the windshield. Remorse welled up inside her as she remembered she hadn't visited Anthony's grave in months. After the funeral, she had vowed to visit his grave every day for the rest of her life. For almost two weeks she had. But then she'd met Eric and hadn't been back to the grave since the weekend Eric had taken her up the coast to the Madonna Inn.

A sudden gust of wind swept the fog away from the road, and Louellen gunned the car, taking advantage of the brief visibility. As she came to a curve near Anthony's and her father's graves, the fog reemerged like a gray wall. Before she could slow down, she was into the fog and driving blind. She hit the brakes, felt the tires lock, and skidded on the wet cement. An instant later the front end of the car seemed to collapse, dropping forward as if the road had been jerked out from under it.

Then the interior was filled with shrieking groaning sounds as the frame and front axle slammed down onto something hard.

Louellen Mae didn't have to get out of the car to figure out what had just happened. The car had skidded off the edge of the road, and the entire front end had gone into a deep ditch. Judging from the forward slanting angle of the car, the rear tires weren't even touching the road. Trying to back up the car was probably a waste of time, she thought, but she tried and it was a waste of time. "Fuck," she hissed, hitting the steering wheel and turning to look at the boy sleeping in the backseat. She thanked the stars he wasn't awake. The last thing she needed right now was a bawling, squalling kid on her hands.

Louellen Mae considered leaving her son and going for help, but it was cold, wet, and foggy out, and she suspected she'd get lost before she got out of the cemetery. Inside the car was warm. It was freezing outside. The decision was easy. She'd stay where she was.

She settled back in the seat and turned up the heater. The car's motor was running and its lights were still on. She liked the way the high beams bounced back from the fog and illuminated the interior of the car. The light made her feel safe and comfortable. Just before she fell asleep, she remembered the graves of her father and husband were less than thirty yards away. They were close, and would look after her, she thought. She liked that thought and held on to it while she fell asleep.

A low moaning sound woke her. She stirred, trying to remember where she was. Then she remembered and sat up with a start, looking around. The car's motor was still running; its lights still on, but the fog seemed thinner now, almost translucent. Shaking her head in an effort to clear her mind, she tried to remember the sound that had woken her. She wasn't too sure, but it seemed to her someone had called out her name. But that was impossible. She was stuck in the middle of a cemetery in the middle of the night, and there wasn't anybody around, let alone anybody who knew her name. There was a bad taste in her mouth, and the heater seemed to be pulling putrid smelling cold air into the car.

She turned and looked out the windows. The fog had really thinned out. Earlier she'd been able to see nothing. Now she was able to make out the shapes and outlines of tombstones, grave markers, and pine trees on both sides of the car.

Settling down into the seat, she closed her eyes, praying for sleep and the bright morning that would follow.

Moments later the sound of her name being spoken again rolled out of the darkness and fog. She sat up like a frightened cat, the fine hairs on the back of her neck standing erect. What was going on? A practical joke? Had Santos and Tammy Fae followed her into the cemetery? Were they playing games with her? She'd kill 'em if they were. This wasn't funny.

Then she heard it again. Someone was saying her name, but the way they were saying it was distorted and low, like the sound of a forty-five record being played on thirty-three speed.

Again she heard her name, clearer, closer, only this time there was a hideous familiarity to the sound she heard. Then she gasped. There was only one person in her life who had said her name that way, with those familiar rolling tones. Her father.

Again from the darkness. "Louellen Mae . . ."

"Oh, Christ," she murmured. It really did sound like her father.

The sound had come from behind the car. She whirled around in the seat and peered into the darkness.

"Louellen Mae . . ."

Horrified, she bit her lip, and under her breath she began numbly chanting, "It's not possible . . . Daddy's dead . . . Daddy's dead . . ." She kept turning in her seat, trying to locate the source of the sound. But it was too dark.

Suddenly she reached out, grabbed the shift lever, and shoved the transmission into R. The car's white backup lights instantly flared on. Her fingernails dug into the back of the seat as she looked out the rear window at the tombstones behind the car. Nothing. There was still nothing out there . . . no, wait. There was something, something standing just outside of range of the lights.

Her thoughts began to run together in irrational confusion. It's just a tree, just a tombstone, a shadow. No. It's a tree. But trees don't move and that's moving . . . toward me!!

Crouching down behind the front seat, staring out the back window in wide-eyed horror, Louellen Mae watched the shadow lurch slowly and haltingly toward the passenger side of her car. It walked funny on weak disjointed legs, like a puppet with broken strings, but still it inched its way ever closer toward her and her car.

Spittle dripped from the corner of her mouth as she cowered down in the driver's seat, her eyes locked on the specter lumbering toward the car until its blackness filled the passenger window.

Numbly she tried to comprehend what was standing beside her car. It looked like a scarecrow dressed in the tattered remnants of a black suit. The roof of her car blocked her view of its face. It said her name again, and the spit on her lips turned to bubbly froth as the impact of her father's voice assaulted her senses.

It's not true, she thought, wanting to scream her thoughts at the figure outside her car. But then she saw the fraternal pins on the lapel of the black suit. . . . There was an Elks pin; next to it a thirty-second degree Mason pin. Her daddy had belonged to the Elks club . . . to the Masons. Suddenly she froze as the thing standing beside her car began to lean over, bringing its face closer to the window as if it wanted to look at her.

Mouth open, eyes fixed in a wide unblinking stare,

Louellen Mae Harnes watched as a broken-toothed grinning skull appeared in the window. For one brief second she grabbed at the idea that the fleshless ghoul outside the car was a Halloween mask. The hope died when she saw the grinning apparition's teeth; four teeth were missing . . . the same four her father had lost years before in a barroom fight. The realization of what she was seeing rammed through her mind and Louellen Mae Harnes began to scream at the grinning death-head that was her father.

She shrieked until her voice broke, her throat seized, and in the silence that followed she heard the thing that was her father speak to her. ". . . Louellen Mae, I've brought someone with me." She looked up at the macabre visage just in time to see it point a bony finger at her. The gesture riveted her against the driver's door. She couldn't take her eyes off the skeleton's finger.

"Go away. Get the fuck away from this car!" she rasped.

"I've brought someone with me," her father said. The finger of bone and dried tendons continued to point at her through the car's window.

It was only then she realized the thing was not pointing at *her* but at *something* behind her. Mesmerized by the apparition, her mind and senses nearly gone, she began to turn slowly in the seat to see what it was pointing at. Her movements were slow and jerky, but she continued to turn in the seat until she came face to face with her dead husband. His lipless face, a collage of bones and rotting flesh, was less than six inches from hers. He was staring at her through the driver's window with shrunken wrinkled eyes that did not blink. She saw it all in the reflected glow of the car's headlights. She saw the broken body, the misshapen skull, and all the trauma of a car wreck that a closed casket had kept her from seeing.

"You're not my Tony," she said very softly, her mind

nearly gone and her mouth hanging agape. "My Tony's sleeping in heaven. Go away. Please, just go away."

Her pleas turned to screams and she lost control of her bowels as the visage of her husband attempted to speak through mangled teeth loosely set in a jaw broken and unhinged on one side. It coughed, seeming to almost throttle itself on the decaying remnants of its own throat. But then the sounds, low, rasping, and guttural, came. ". . . Lou . . . Louellen . . ."

It was then Louellen Mae Harnes began to scream. She slapped her hands over her ears, closed her eyes, and continued to scream.

She did not see the bodies of her husband and father topple over and crash to the ground. Nor did she see the massive black shape come out of the fog. She was still screaming when a powerful arm crashed down through the roof, door post, and into the back of her head. She died instantly and never felt the set of razor-sharp fangs pierce the back of her skull and neck.

The deaf child in the back seat stirred slightly when an alien arm gently lifted him out of the car. He opened his eyes and looked up into the eyes of what was carrying him away from the car and into the night. As he did, a strange kind of calmness came over him, and he returned to sleep without struggle or thought.

The beams from the headlights continued to bounce back off the wall of fog, throwing a misty light over the corpses lying beside the car and the dead body within. The power behind the demon-creature's blow had pushed Louellen Mae Harnes's head into the steering wheel, and the weight of her chin on the horn had set off a continuous, almost mournful sound, somehow appropriate for the strange display of death and destruction in the Horrcove Cemetery.

Chapter Fourteen

Henry Sutton broke free of the nightmare and forced himself to wake up. His mouth was dry, and he could taste the salt of his own sweat. As he sat up, he tried to recall the dream. Most of it was blackness now, but blurred visions of mutilated bodies, a missing boy, anguished parents, and Martin Larchmont's creature-demons floated around him in the dark room.

He sat on the edge of the bed and watched the digital alarm clock crank out green numbers. 4:34 . . . 4:35. The numbers irritated him, and by the time the clock registered 4:36, he was in the bathroom, splashing cold water on his face, trying not to think about the missing boy and Larchmont's prophecy.

He spent a long time shaving, a longer time in the shower, and finished off the ritual by turning the hot water to cold and standing in the frigid spray for almost a minute. When he emerged, he was feeling almost human again.

He returned to the bedroom, opened the closet door, and swore to himself. He was out of clean uniforms. Six were downtown at a dry cleaners. The other six were in a hamper in the bathroom. He'd meant to pick up the clean ones yesterday but had gotten sidetracked. He padded back to the bathroom, picked up the shirt and slacks that had the fewest wrinkles, hung them on a hanger in the steamy bathroom, then went off to rummage through the refrigerator for something to eat. It was almost as bare as his closet. He finally settled for carrot sticks, a can of peaches, the last of the bacon, and four cups of instant coffee made with lukewarm water from the kitchen faucet. Still in his undershorts, he pressed his uniform with a travel iron and dressed.

It was still dark out when Sutton climbed into his patrol car and drove through the empty streets of Ravina. He parked his car in the employees' parking lot and took the elevator from the basement to the sheriff's department on the first floor. The instant the elevator doors opened, he knew something was wrong. The hallway was full of uniformed men milling around the briefing room. As he stepped out into the hall, he could hear the strident voice of the night watch commander, Andrew Slatkin, barking out orders to the deputies. Sutton couldn't make out what Slatkin was saying, but the watch commander sounded upset. Now what, Sutton wondered, as he walked up the hallway and stopped behind the men standing in the doorway to the briefing room.

Glancing around, Sutton was puzzled by the number of uniformed men present. He took a quick head count and realized his night shift and morning shift were jammed into the small room. That never happened; his men were dedicated, but when their shift was over, they were gone.

Still trying to figure out what was going on, Sutton stayed in the shadows and studied his watch commander.

Andrew Slatkin was standing behind a lectern at the far end of the briefing room. A cop for nearly thirty years, Slatkin was an easygoing man with a good sense of humor. But not tonight.

"Reber!" Slatkin shouted.

A thin blond-haired deputy sitting near the podium got to his feet. Slatkin pointed at Reber. "I want you and Grayson to get over to the hospital and follow the ambulance out to the scene. Help the attendants any way you can, and when they're done, I want you to escort them back to the hospital." Reber and Grayson started to leave, but Slatkin wasn't finished. "Whatever you do while you're up there, don't let those medics out of your sight. I want one-on-one coverage for both those guys while they're out there." Reber and Grayson turned and worked their way out of the crowded room. As Reber passed by, he noticed Sutton and started to slow up as if he had a concern. Sutton shook his head. Andrew Slatkin was still in charge, and he was not about to intrude on the other man's authority. Grayson and Reber had their orders, and with a motion of his hand he sent them on their way.

"Caruthers," Slatkin snapped. A man leaning against the doorway in front of Sutton stepped into the room and raised his hand so Slatkin could see him. "I want you to go over to the Harnes home and bring in the husband and daughter." Caruthers nodded and started to turn away. The watch commander's voice stopped him cold. "And Caruthers, don't ask 'em questions and don't volunteer any information. Leave that to me or Sutton. Think you can handle that?"

Caruthers nodded and left, an irritated look on his face.

Sutton shook his head at the watch commander's performance. Caruthers was a good cop who didn't deserve sarcastic comments from Slatkin about his ability to handle an assignment.

Henry Sutton had known Andrew Slatkin for years and had never known him to ridicule one of his men. This was out of character for Slatkin, and again Sutton wondered what the hell was going on.

After a moment's indecision Sutton finally decided to make his presence known. He stepped into the doorway. Because he was bigger than everyone else in the room, Slatkin noticed him instantly, and the watch commander's reaction caught Sutton totally off guard. "Well, how about this," Slatkin commented dryly. "The sheriff's decided to come to work. Glad to see you've finally decided to earn your salary."

As he crossed the room and headed toward Slatkin, Sutton kept his expression impassive and his shoulders back. The other deputies scrambled to get out of his way like leaves in a storm.

"Just where have you been?" Slatkin asked, his voice booming over the mike. "I had men pounding on your door all night long and the radio dispatcher tried to raise you by phone. The telephone operator said maybe you'd turned it off. Dammit, Henry, you're supposed to be contactable."

Blanching under the watch commander's tirade, Sutton tried to recall if he'd pulled the jack on his phone. He couldn't remember. As for deputies pounding on his door, all he could remember was his nightmare; he hadn't heard anything, no pounding, no doorbell, and the nightmare may well have been the cause, but this was not the time or the place to debate it, not in front of the entire Ravina police force.

Sutton mounted the podium, walked over to Slatkin, and before the man could say anything more, Sutton wrapped his hands around the lectern's microphone, silencing it. "I don't know what the fuck is going on around here, Andy, but whatever it is, let's not play it out in front of the men."

Slatkin stared up at Sutton and suddenly all the angry emotion in his face seemed to drain away. "It's been one hell of a night. One hell of a night."

"I gathered that," Sutton said. "Let's go to my office. You can tell me about this hell of a night." He removed his hand from the microphone and spoke to the others. "I don't know what happened tonight, but for the time being I want the day shift on the streets and the night crew to pack it in."

Sutton jerked the door to his office open. Slatkin entered and slumped down in the chair in front of Sutton's desk. Sutton kicked the door shut and walked over to his desk, pulling a bottle of Irish whiskey and two Styrofoam cups out of the bottom drawer. He filled both cups and passed one to Slatkin. "Drink up, then talk."

Slatkin downed the whiskey in one motion and held out his cup for a refill. Sutton obliged, thinking the man must have gone through a lot.

"Not that I'm complaining," Slatkin said, "but there's old coffee grounds in this cup."

"I didn't check the cups." Sutton shrugged. "There's no telling what's in mine."

"Screw the grounds. I'll take another shot."

"No."

Slatkin slumped back in the chair. Suddenly he seemed to be at a loss for words. Sutton didn't push it. Slatkin would talk when he was ready.

"Henry, I've never seen anything like what I saw tonight. It was like . . . like something out of the fucking Twilight Zone."

"It all started when we got a call from someone who was complaining about a car horn up near the cemetery. The dispatcher sent a car up to check the disturbance, and they got up there around two-thirty." Slatkin looked down into his cup and shook his head. "They found the car making the noise, only it wasn't near the cemetery, it was *in* the cemetery. I was in the radio room when they called in. Henry, I've never heard cops sound like that. They were scared shitless. They kept babbling about a dead woman with a hole in the back of her head and skeletons and ripped-open graves."

Sutton's guts did a slow roll, but he continued to stare at Slatkin as the watch commander continued. "It sounded bad, real bad out there, so I rolled on the call myself. It took me almost forty-five minutes to get out there because of the fog, and Lord, I wish I hadn't made the trip cause I saw her face. I saw that dead woman's face, and I'm gonna remember it the rest of my life.'' Still staring at his cup, Slatkin's voice dropped to a whisper. ''She was dead, you could tell that right off, but that's not what bothered me. It was her face. Her eyes were bulging out and her lips were pulled back from her teeth. She'd bitten through her tongue, and fuck, she looked like she'd died of fright, but she hadn't. There was dried blood all over her lips. You know what that means?''

Sutton nodded, and his stomach continued to churn. ''It means she was alive when she bit her tongue.''

Slatkin didn't seem to hear Sutton. ''It means she was alive when she bit down on her tongue. Jesus! What would cause someone to do that to themselves? Henry, the woman looked scared to death. I've never seen a face like that. She looked like she'd been dropped into hell and kicked back out again. She died scared, Henry, scared out of her mind.''

Slatkin was starting to ramble. Sutton could appreciate the man's fear and the need to talk out what he'd seen, but he needed information, and needed it now. ''Who was she, Andy?'' Sutton asked, trying to keep Slatkin on track.

''The woman's name was Louellen Mae Harnes. . . , Henry, I've seen bodies, but like I said—''

''What killed her?'' Sutton asked, disliking the cold professional tone he heard in his own voice.

''We don't know. None of us could figure out what could have done that to her.''

''Done what?''

''Something bit the back of her head off. Henry, there was a hole in the back of that woman's head you wouldn't believe. One of the other men said her head looked like an apple somebody'd taken a bite out of. You know what? He was right.''

The watch commander's hand went to the back of his own head. ''You know those two bumps you got at the

back of your head, right above your neck?'' Sutton
nodded. "That woman's bumps were gone, her hair was
gone, the bone was gone and maybe her brains were
gone too. You know what else? We couldn't find the
missing flesh. It was just gone . . . like somebody ate
it.''

"Dear God," Sutton whispered, pouring more whiskey into Slatkin's Styrofoam cup.

"You think this part is bad?" Slatkin asked. He downed
the whiskey in a single gulp. "Well, hang in there,
'cause it gets worse.'' Sutton shook his head and wondered how much worse it could get.

"The doors to the woman's car were all locked. All
four doors. Whatever got to her, got to her by ripping
away part of the roof and tearing out the door post. The
metal was just ripped away. I know it sounds impossible, but when you see the car, you'll know what I'm
talking about. You will see the car, won't you, Henry?
And maybe the body?''

"Yeah, I'll check out both, Andy," Sutton said. "Just
as soon as we're done here.''

That seemed to reassure Andrew Slatkin, and he looked
up at Sutton. "You ready for the rest?''

Sutton nodded, wishing there was a way he could say
no.

"There were two more bodies by the car. I know it
sounds impossible, but one of the bodies was nothing
but bones, dressed in an old rotten suit. The other one
was newer, hadn't been in the ground all that long. It
still had flesh on its face, and when I looked at it with
my flashlight, I recognized it. It . . . he used to be in my
bowling league up until when he was killed in a truck
crash nine months ago. I knew the man. His name was
Anthony Fiori, and he was the dead woman's husband.''
Slatkin gestured with his hands. He was her husband up
until when he got killed. Then she married some shit a
few weeks later.''

"What about the other body beside the car?''

Slatkin held up his cup and Sutton obliged. "The other body, the skeleton in the black suit, had no identification. One of our men checked the back of a Mason pin on the suit lapel. It was engraved with the name Delbert Reasoner."

Sutton shrugged.

"Didn't mean anything to me, either, until I got back to the station and started checking." Sutton took a deep breath. "Delbert Reasoner was Louellen Mae Harnes's father. He died about thirteen months ago."

Henry Sutton's mouth dropped open as the horror of Andrew Slatkin's story rolled over him. A dead woman with the back of her head gone, a car ripped open from the outside, the decaying bodies of her dead husband and dead father lying beside the car. God, how much worse can this get? Sutton wondered.

Andrew Slatkin provided the answer.

"We checked the area around the graves as best we could with flashlights, but the fog made it pretty difficult. Maybe you'll find something in the morning different from what we found. You probably won't, but God, I hope you do."

"What do you mean different from what you found?"

"We found two freshly opened graves. Not freshly dug graves, just freshly opened."

"I don't follow."

"Neither do I," Slatkin said, "but maybe I can explain. There're freshly dug graves, which people dig for dead people. Then there are freshly opened graves, which weren't dug open by anybody, at least anybody living. They were just sort of opened up."

"Andrew . . ." Sutton impatiently prodded.

Slatkin shook his head. "What I'm saying is that there wasn't any sign of cut sod. No shovel marks or signs of anything that would've suggested the graves were broken into. It was more like they were broken open from the inside.

"And then there were the coffins. Henry, you may

not believe this, but I actually got into those graves, and I looked for pry marks, hatchet marks, something . . . anything that would've proved those coffins were opened from the outside. I didn't find anything. The way the wood was fractured and splintered, it looked like something kicked its way out from inside."

Close to tears and probably drunk, Slatkin looked away from Henry Sutton. "Either I'm a drunk old man or those bodies kicked their way out of their own graves and walked down to that woman's car." Slatkin finally turned on Sutton. "What the fuck is going on with our town, Henry? We've got a dead hooker with no teeth, a deputy with a body you could pour through a screen, and now we've got a dead woman with the back of her head missing, and it looks like two of her relatives got out of their graves to see what the fuck was going on. Am I crazy?" Slatkin asked, finally turning toward Sutton, "or can you explain some of this to me?"

It was hard to look at Andrew Slatkin, but Sutton did. "I can't explain any of this, but one thing I do know, you're not crazy."

"There's just one more thing," Slatkin said, staring at the cup in his hand.

There couldn't be, Sutton thought. Too much has already happened, too much has already gone down. There couldn't be anything more. But somehow, he knew he was wrong.

"We got ahold of Harnes's husband at work," Slatkin said, gazing at his cup. "He went home, then called us a few minutes later saying his stepkid wasn't there. He said that Louellen Mae might have taken the boy with her when she left home. Problem is, we didn't find any signs of the boy anywhere. He wasn't in the car. We couldn't find him in the graveyard. We don't know where he is. He just sort of vanished."

Stunned, bewildered, and frightened, all Henry Sutton could do was stare at Andrew Slatkin as he slowly pushed himself out of his chair. "I think that's about it.

Maybe when you go out to the scene later, you'll find something that'll explain what's going on. If you do, call me right then and there. I guarantee I won't be asleep. I might be sick, but I won't be asleep, so call."

Slatkin headed out for the door. "Andy," Sutton called out. Slatkin stopped, but he wouldn't turn around and look at Henry Sutton. "Is there any way the husband, this Harnes fellow, could have figured into this?"

Slatkin shook his head. "The man works the night shift at a dairy, and at least seven of the guys he works with are willing to swear he was with them the whole night, and that includes breaks and midnight meal break."

"You want somebody to drive you home?"

With his back to Sutton, Slatkin shook his head. "No. Getting home isn't the problem. You want to know what my problem is?" he asked, turning slightly so Sutton could see part of his face. "My problem isn't getting home. It's coming back to work tonight. I'm not sure if I can do it. I'm just not sure if I can come in." He turned and walked away, closing the door behind him.

For one brief moment Sutton felt the urge to walk away with Slatkin; quit his job, leave the town, maybe go fishing with Andy, and leave this goddamn mess for someone else, but he knew it was an impotent fantasy. He knew himself too well. He would fight this thing, whatever it was. He would treat whatever was going on like any unsolved crime. He would break it down into its components, rework the pieces like a ghastly jigsaw puzzle, get a handle on it, and then he would wrap it up. Without much conviction, he knew that's what he would do . . . or try to do.

Sutton opened the curtains to his office. Fog and low clouds still blanketed Ravina, turning the sun's rays into a weak peach-colored glow. As he turned back to his desk, Sutton noticed the whiskey bottle and his own untouched Styrofoam cup of whiskey. He poured the whiskey back into the bottle, threw the cup away, capped the bottle, and dropped it into the drawer. Then he sat down at his desk, pulled out a yellow legal-sized tablet, and began to write out a morning agenda.

He wrote out *Louellen Mae Harnes* at the top of the paper and wrote the word *autopsy* beside it, followed by the names *Childress-Seafront.* Directly beneath the woman's name he put *died of . . . fright???* Below that he listed the names of the two missing boys and printed the letters *FBI* and followed that up with the notations: *T.V., Newspaper, reward??*

Near the bottom of the page, almost absentmindedly, he wrote the work *Ceremony* followed by the words *Renewal—Resurrection,* and then he block-printed *Dr. Martin Larchmont.*

At that moment Sutton realized he was beginning to believe in Larchmont's theory. The man's prophecy, his speculations, were too much on target, too close to what was going on in his town. His inclination to believe in Larchmont surprised Henry Sutton. He didn't believe in ghosts, demonic possession, or creature-demons. Evil to him had always been a Saturday night special in the hands of a punk. Car keys in the hands of a drunk. Evil was a lenient judge or a bleeding-heart parole board that let the guilty go and walk among the innocent again so they could hurt the innocent again. His was a pessimistic philosophy where the criminal—whether he be insane or greedy—was the primary moving force. There had been no room in his philosophy for unseen powers that lurked in the night, performing acts of cruelty beyond the realm of human senses. But now the breech was there. A breech put there by Martin Larchmont and a series of events too bizarre and macabre to explain away in any other fashion. He underlined Larchmont's name twice and beside it wrote *See A.S.A.P.*

Finished, he sat back in his chair and found it odd he didn't feel ridiculous about seeing a man about some demons; Henry Sutton had been pushed to the point where he wouldn've walked into hell and consulted with the devil if it would've done his town any good.

Still leaning back in his chair, Sutton pushed a button on his intercom and waited for the door to his office to open. A moment later it opened, and an attractive woman in a crisp tailored uniform strolled into his office. As she approached his desk, Sutton found himself admiring her classic beauty. She had a flawless complexion, wide-set amber-colored eyes, and an aquiline nose. When she was on duty, she kept her dark brown hair swept back in a bun—which she euphemistically referred to as a French roll. But when she was off duty, she allowed her hair to hang down in loose curls which outlined her face like an elegant picture frame. She was, Henry Sutton thought, the only woman he'd ever known who actually looked good in a police uniform.

Jackie Fairmont had been with the Ravina police department for five years. Sutton had first met her at a law-enforcement convention in San Francisco. She had been one of the speakers, and he'd been impressed with her ideas about police administration and communication. So impressed that he'd followed her back to San Jose and offered her a position in his department. Weary of teaching police procedures at the San Jose Police Academy, she'd accepted his offer immediately, then moved to Ravina with her seven-year-old twin daughters, Courtney and Brooke. They were twelve now, and Sutton still couldn't tell them apart.

Sutton's intuitive hunch about the woman's abilities had been on the mark. She was an excellent administrator, with a voracious appetite for assuming responsibilities and streamlining procedures. Occasionally she worked street patrols, but for the most part Jackie Fairmont spent her days behind a desk. She had proven herself more than capable on the streets, but Sutton hadn't hired her to roust drunks; he'd hired her for her administrative talents, and she had never let him down.

That they had been lovers for the past three years had never once interfered in their professional relationship.

"You rang, sir?" she asked.

Sutton was in no mood for an opening like that. "Cut it out," he snapped. "We've got work to do." An instant later he caught the expression on her face and regretted his words. "Sorry, Jackie. It's been a rough morning."

"I know. I heard. Anything I can do?"

Sutton looked down at his yellow pad. "We need to get to the newspaper and TV station and ask for a media blitz on those two missing boys. We'll need photographs of the boys, and somebody'll have to see their families about that." He paused and seemed to mull something over in his mind. "The Shehane boy's family has money, so see if you can get them to offer a reward. Sometimes that helps. Everybody gets real observant if there's money involved."

Jackie shrugged and smiled. "It's done. The Shehane family is offering ten thousand dollars for the return of their son. Channel twenty-six showed the boy's picture on their morning news not more than twenty minutes ago, and they said they'll show it and the Harnes boy's photo on the noon news, again at six, and keep it up until something turns. The *Gazette* promised to run photos of both boys this evening, front page no less." She smiled and shrugged again.

"Damn, Ms. Fairmont," Sutton said, leaning back in his chair and smiling. "What time did you come to work today?"

"Early," she said, still smiling. "But I can't take the credit. Slatkin started the ball rolling long before I got here."

Sutton nodded. In spite of everything he'd been through, Slatkin had done his job and done it well. He went back to his yellow pad. "We're gonna have to assume these two boys were kidnapped and that means—"

"Already done. While you were talking to Slatkin, I called the FBI office in San Luis Obispo. They're sending some lab men and a team of agents down as soon as this fog clears."

"Jesus, Jackie, you're on a roll." He went back to his pad, and his smile faded as he pictured himself telling Jackie Fairmont or some FBI agents about Martin Larchmont's theories about creature-demons. Christ, he'd never live it down.

"How do you want me to handle the media on the three murders?" Fairmont asked, the question bringing Sutton back to the present. "We've been able to keep a lot of the facts away from the reporters, but it's getting harder each day, especially now that we've got three strange deaths on our hands."

"Keep a lid on it. All we need is for this to leak out, and we'll have every newspaper reporter and ghoul in California following us around."

He went back to his legal pad. "See if you can't get ahold of Mark Childress and that pathologist from the Vandenberg Air Force Base. Tell 'em we've got another dead body and need another autopsy."

"It's been done."

"You got Childress and Seafront already?"

She nodded. "Childress was still at the hospital this morning. I don't think he's seen the body yet, but I know he's planning to do an autopsy as soon as possible."

"Damn, you're efficient. If you keep this up, the city council may decide to eliminate my position." He smiled at her. She didn't smile back. "What is it?"

"Probably not much of anything, but we got a couple of phone calls about the missing Shehane boy because of the morning news."

"Any merit to any of 'em?"

Fairmont shrugged and made a face. "Johnny Joe Sloams called in."

"Christ," Sutton grumbled. "I'm surprised he could dial the phone, let alone talk at this time of the morning." He'd booked Sloams for drunk and disorderly more times than he could count. "What did our town drunk say?"

"He said he was working late last night at the cemetery and someone drove by in a black Cadillac. He said he saw the boy in the backseat trying to get out.''

"He thinks this kid was the Shehane boy?" Sutton asked.

"According to him, the boy he saw in the car was the same boy he saw on TV this morning. He also thought the Cadillac belonged to his employers, the Horrcove brothers, but he asked us not to tell them about his phone call.''

Sutton sat back in his chair. If anyone but Johnny Joe Sloams had phoned in this information, he would have hit the Horrcove Funeral Home with every deputy he had, but Johnny Joe Sloams? He was tempted to dismiss the drunk's report, but couldn't. It wasn't that Sloams claimed he saw the boy; it was where: the cemetery. The Horrcove Cemetery. He had three deaths on his hands. Two had occurred just outside the cemetery, and the third had taken place in it. Now a missing boy was seen in a car as it drove through the same graveyard. Coincidental or not, there was too much at stake for Sutton to dismiss Sloams's report.

"What do you think?" Jackie asked.

Sutton sat up and put his palms on the desk. "What do you think of the Horrcove brothers?" As he asked the question, images of the two ancient brothers flashed through his mind. He shuddered.

"I don't think of them at all, if I can help it," she said, shrugging with her hands. "They bury bodies, run a funeral home, own a cemetery, and sit in their mansion all day long. Nobody knows them. God, how long have they lived in that funeral parlor?"

"Forever, I guess."

Fairmont pantomimed a shudder. "I've only seen them a couple of times. They gave me the creeps. You gonna check them out?"

"I've got no choice. Considering what's at stake here, I can't afford to overlook a single lead . . . regardless of the source."

"If you're going out there, you'll need a backup."

"I suppose so," Sutton said. "I'll get Johnson or Lewis to go out with me."

"Hell you will," she snapped. "I'm more familiar with the facts than those two and just as good a cop."

"Okay, you can be my backup."

"It really pisses me off when you get overprotective like this. I like to get away from my desk now and then, and I hate it—"

Sutton looked up at the woman he loved. "Jackie, I said you could back me up."

"Yeah," she said sheepishly, "I guess you did."

At the same moment Jackie Fairmont and Henry Sutton were walking out of the Civic Center toward their patrol car, William Seafront, Mark Childress and a male nurse were walking down the hospital's basement corridor heading for the morgue.

Seafront and Childress had both spent the night at the Ravina Hospital. Unable to get home because of the fog, Seafront had catnapped on a vacant hospital bed. The same fog that had grounded Seafront had also immobilized Ravina. For the first time in his career Childress had put in a full shift in the emergency room without treating a single patient. Like Seafront, he'd slept restlessly on a couch in the doctors' lounge.

Childress had not been surprised when he'd gotten the phone call from Jackie Fairmont. Strange deaths and early morning autopsies were getting to be a routine for him and Seafront. Following the call, he'd woken Seafront, had the nurse paged, and then all three had drunk coffee in silence while they waited for the bodies from the cemetery to arrive.

Now the bodies were in the morgue. It was time to do an autopsy on Louellen Mae Harnes and take a look at her husband, Anthony Fiori, and father, Delbert Reasoner.

Sutton's deputies had filled the doctors in on the scene

out at the cemetery. The brief description didn't do justice to what they found in the morgue.

Louellen Mae Harnes had been placed face up on the autopsy table. She was still dressed in a soiled terrycloth bathrobe laced with blood. No sheet covered the woman, and the stark terror on her face twisted the guts of all three men.

There were two portable gurneys standing off to the left of the autopsy table. The body on the first gurney was dressed in a mildewed flannel shirt and faded denim jeans. Most of the body was covered with tufts of white and green mold, and the cadaver's face was turned away from the physicians as if the body were looking at something on the back wall. The body on the other gurney was dressed in the remnants of a black suit. Childress gestured to the nurse. "Get something and cover those bodies up." While the nurse crossed the room to get some sheets, Childress glanced over at Seafront.

The pathologist was finishing up a yawn. "If you count these three," he said, gesturing at Harnes and the two cadavers on the gurneys, "we'll have done five autopsies in three days. That's almost two autopsies a day."

"So?"

"At this rate we'll be out of jobs in fifteen years."

"How do you figure?"

"If this keeps up for fifteen years, everybody in Ravina will be dead." Seafront grinned at Childress. "There won't be anybody left for you to treat and nobody around for me to autopsy. We'll be out of jobs."

Childress groaned. "That's sick," he said, shaking his head and smiling. On the far side of the morgue the nurse finished draping the two corpses, then returned to a glass cabinet and began to take out the large tray of surgical instruments Seafront would be needing for the autopsies.

"I've heard," Mark Childress said, his back to the nurse, "that after a while pathologists develop a black sense of humor. Was that an example?"

Seafront had moved over beside the body of Louellen Mae Harnes and was getting ready to clip on the dictating microphone. "Probably," he said, still grinning. "It's an occupational hazard. But hell, no field of medicine is safe. I know at least three gynecologists who've gone cross-eyed because of their specialty." He laughed. Childress joined him. Both men knew their laughter was a defense against the grotesque horrors spread out before them in the morgue.

Their laughter was interrupted by a loud crash. Both doctors glanced over at the nurse who'd just dropped the tray of surgical instruments. Childress started to say something but stopped when he noticed the horrified look on the nurse's face. The man was trying to speak, but no words were coming out. All he could do was stare and point. Childress casually turned around to see what the nurse was pointing at.

A heartbeat later Childress, too, was staring at Louellen Mae Harnes in shocked disbelief. The dead woman's eyes had come open, and it looked as if she were trying to sit up. Dear God, he thought as he started to back away, this isn't possible. "William—"

"Relax," Seafront said. "Her muscles are contracting, that's all."

In spite of the explanation Childress continued to back away from the dead woman. She was no longer trying to sit up. She *was* sitting up, her eyes wide open and staring straight ahead. "Muscle contractions?" he asked, embarrassed at the fear he heard in his own voice.

"Absolutely. Happens all the time. During my first autopsy in med school, a body of a grandmother sat up and snapped her fingers. Scared the hell out of me, but like I said, it happens all the time . . . though I'll admit I've never seen a body move this slowly. Usually it's a rapid spasticlike move and not this controlled."

There was a strained note in the pathologist's voice as if he didn't quite believe what he was saying.

Childress forced himself to stop backing up and forced

himself to look at the dead woman, her distorted face now in full view. He could see her eyes now, hideous dry eyes that seemed to be looking at him. "Sweet mother of Jesus," he murmured. "Bill, she's looking right at me!"

"I've heard of bodies doing this before, but I'd always thought they were ghost stories made up by bored morticians." Seafront tried to laugh, but couldn't.

"Fuck your morticians," Childress snarled. "This woman's coming alive."

Seafront was still standing beside the autopsy table. He looked at the back of the dead woman's head and shook his head. "Impossible. Not with a head wound like that."

Louellen Mae Harnes was now sitting straight up on the autopsy table, glaring at Mark Childress. He knew that at the moment of death her eyes had begun to dry out, resulting in a hardening and a flattening of the tissues. But the knowledge didn't diminish the hideousness of her stare. He found himself mesmerized by the lifeless sandpapery eyes of the woman. They almost seemed to be moving in their dry gritty sockets as they continued to track him, focusing on him. "She's looking at me!"

"Impossible!" Seafront yelled. "The back of her head is missing. I can see her brains."

Stunned by the sight, Childress saw something else, new movement. The dead woman's mouth was opening. "My God! She's gonna talk!"

"Impossible!!" Seafront screamed.

Then the mouth formed a word, and Louellen Mae Harnes said, "LEAVE . . . US . . . ALONE." Her dry lifeless eyes continued to stare at Childress.

"This can't be happening!" Seafront bellowed, backing away from the autopsy table and bumping into the gurney holding the dead woman's dead husband. The green sheet covering the body slipped away, dropped to the floor, and at that moment, Mark Childress saw the dead husband's clawlike hand begin to move.

"THIS . . . IS . . . TO . . . STOP," She-It growled, the voice low and ungodly.

Childress barely heard her. He was mesmerized, hypnotized by the sight of a nine-month-old corpse lifting its arm, opening its hand and reaching out for the back of William Seafront's surgical smock. Shocked to numbness, Childress started to scream a warning, but it was too late. The hand grabbed on to the back of the smock. Seafront jerked partway around to see what was holding him. When he saw the hand, bleating animal sounds came out of his mouth. He flailed frantically at the alien hand with his fist, but couldn't break its grip. In desperation he lurched across the room, half walking, half staggering toward Childress.

For an instant Childress thought Seafront had escaped, but then he saw the cadaver's arm still clinging to the back of Seafront's gown. The pathologist was pulling the corpse and the gurney across the room with him.

Childress glanced down at the surgical instruments on the floor. He saw a scalpel, scooped it up, then dashed for Seafront. He grabbed the front of Seafront's smock with one hand and cut a gaping slashing hole down the front of it with the scalpel. Seafront slipped out of the gown and the two of them followed the nurse out of the morgue door.

Just before he closed the door, Childress took one last look at the scene. He saw the woman still sitting up on the autopsy table, saw her eyes were still focused on him, and heard her low grating voice.

". . . LEAVE ALL ALONE . . ."

He slammed the door and heard Seafront scream.

"Lock it! Lock the fucking door!"

Childress did, wasting no time. Only when the bolt slid into the lock did he slump to his knees and begin to cry.

169

Chapter
Fifteen

While Jackie Fairmont guided the patrol car through the early morning fog and traffic, Sutton eased himself back against the passenger door and looked at the woman he loved. Studying her was a pleasant distraction from the pressures of the investigation, and he found himself wondering—not for the first time—what life would be like if he married this woman. The images that came to mind were warm and rich, though the prospect of becoming a stepfather to two energetic twin girls seemed a little overwhelming. But hell, he thought, with the beginnings of a smile on his face, he could handle that. He'd always wanted a family, and he did love Jackie's children, Courtney and Brooke.

But then the smile faded as he remembered why a formal and lifelong commitment between him and this woman would probably never happen.

Jackie Fairmont had been married twice; her first husband, a premed student, had walked out on his family one month to the day after his daughters were born.

She met her second husband, Donald Fairmont, at the San Jose police academy. The six-year marriage had been a good one, and during the course of the marriage, he'd adopted both girls.

Donald Fairmont had been a gentle and caring husband, father, and a good policeman. But it had all come to a bloody halt one night when he and his partner arrested a fifteen-year-old burglary suspect. After searching the boy for weapons, Fairmont had put the boy in the backseat of the patrol car. On the way to the station the teenager removed the sharp fourteen-inch long knitting needle he'd earlier taped to his shin. With no emotion and no warning, the boy then rammed it through the back of the driver's seat. The needle had gone through the seat's padding, grazed Fairmont's spine and gone on to pierce his heart like a heated ice pick through butter. Donald Fairmont coughed, put his foot on the brake and died. His enraged partner and best friend shot the giggling kid three times through the Plexiglas shield separating the front seat from the back.

Jackie Fairmont took a leave of absence from the San Jose police force to be with her children. A year and a half later the police academy offered her a position as a teacher and administrator. She accepted the position, vowing at the same time never to become intimately involved with anyone who had anything to do with law enforcement. She had been through too much pain. Her children had been through too much pain. She was not about to marry another policeman and run the risk of reexperiencing the grief she and her children had gone through when Donald Fairmont had died.

Henry Sutton shook his head as he continued to study Jackie while she threaded the patrol car through the traffic. At work their relationship was professional, cool, and distant, and with few exceptions no one in the department knew Henry Sutton was involved romantically with Jackie Fairmont. The relationship had started five years earlier in a quiet, shy fashion based on respect and genuine friendship. At first both fought the relationship. But in time it grew to love and love-making.

Henry Sutton was confident he'd moved past his fears of mingling a commitment with his profession. But Jackie Fairmont had not. He could not count the number of times she had rebuffed the idea of a commitment, not because she didn't love him, but because he was a cop.

Still, there was some consolation for Sutton in the knowledge that what they did share together was satisfying to both. Over the years they'd fallen into a genuinely pleasant comfortable routine. Usually he would go over to her house two, maybe three times a week for dinner. Afterward, he'd help the twins, Courtney and Brooke, clean up the kitchen, and later he and Jackie would talk or watch TV while the girls did their homework. At nine the girls would go up to bed. An hour later he and Jackie would slip off to her bedroom.

The ritual they shared was almost always the same but, oddly, never tiring or predictable. They would undress each other and then they would lie on the bed, stroking and touching, licking and tasting until he, to keep from bursting, would grasp her by her shoulders and pull her away from him.

This was his time now, and she loved it. With his tongue, he would begin tracing small moist circles on her temples and around the cups of her ears. Still using the tip of his tongue, he would work his way downward, continuing to trace damp patterns first on one breast, then on the other. A patient man, he would stay in this position using his tongue and teeth until she, with a growing sense of urgency, would grab his head and push him down into her warmness. Once there, he would tease and tantalize with his tongue and fingers, listening and marveling as her quickened breathing gave forth cues to a pending climax. Henry Sutton had never regarded himself as a particularly agile multitalented lover, yet with Jacqueline Fairmont he was good. He could bring her to multiple climaxes almost on command. Because he cared for her deeply, this secretly pleased him much more than it pleased her.

After her climax had subsided, he would enter her and they would begin coming together slowly and easily in a rhythm familiar to both. In time he would slow his movements, altering his thrustings in an effort to postpone his pending climax. But she would always speed up, urging him on to his ending. And then he would end, climaxing hard in a never-ending flow of emotions and liquid that left him not sad or empty, but warm and contented. Afterward, they would lie close to each other and caress and touch, and just before falling asleep in each other's arms, he would set the alarm for four in the morning. The twins had never seen Henry Sutton in their mother's bed or in their house in the early sunrise hours. As far as he was concerned, they wouldn't unless Jackie Fairmont changed her mind and a formal commitment were to take place between them.

There had to be a way to get her to change her mind, Sutton thought as he considered the feelings he had for this woman and her children.

The thoughts then faded as Jackie slowed the car and drove through the main gates of the Horrcove Cemetery.

The place where Louellen Mae Harnes had died wasn't hard to find. The road on that part of the hill was crowded with police cars, their red lights flashing in the drifting fog like laser beams.

Jackie edged the car through the maze of patrol cars and around an idling tow truck, then murmured, "My God, look at that," as the Harnes car came into view.

Sutton did, and his stomach did a slow roll.

The metal roof of the car had been shredded and torn apart like a tin can hacked open with a knife. The roof post separating the car's front and rear doors had been torn in two, and the windows on the driver's side had been shattered.

Jackie pulled the cruiser to a stop and Sutton shook his head. Something had attacked that car and shredded the steel as if it were nothing more than tinfoil. Whatever had done that had power beyond anything he could imagine.

Two of his deputies were going over the Harnes car. One noticed Sutton and motioned to him. "I'll be back," he said as he eased his large frame out of the car and started toward deputies Gaylord Bender and Larry Griffith.

Both deputies had been on the force several years, and Sutton liked and respected them. Griffith and Bender had been friends since childhood. They'd grown up together in Ravina, gone to medical school together, dropped out together, returned to their hometown, and then applied for two vacant positions with his department. Smart but immature, Sutton had figured both of them wouldn't last six months on the force, but they'd proved him wrong. They liked police work, especially the investigative duties, and at the end of their first year he decided to take advantage of their interest and background in science. He started by shipping them off to Quantico, Virginia where they took a twenty-four-week FBI course in evidence gathering and analysis. After their return he sent them to Houston for another six-month course in forensic evidence analysis in the laboratory. The end result was that he now had two full-time deputies and two full-time forensic lab technicians.

Physically, the two were a complete mismatch. Larry Griffith was a tall gangly man with an angular face and a crop of wiry hair that looked like a toupee woven from Brillo pads. He was highly intelligent, but that often went unnoticed because of his awkward physical appearance and a slow and easy speech pattern.

On the other hand Gaylord Bender was short, long-armed, and chubby. He had a markedly simian face which he and women adored. Bender was one of the few bachelors on the force and a constant source of amazement to Sutton and the other men in the department. Gaylord Bender attracted women like blossoms attracted bees. Every weekend there was a new woman waiting for him in the parking lot. And not just any woman. Somehow, the runty little apelike man had the ability to attract tall, statuesque, stunningly beautiful women who looked like they just stepped out of the pages of *Vogue* or *Playboy*. No one could ever figure out how he did it.

As Sutton headed toward the Harnes car, he studied the scene around him. It looked like a small war had been fought in the cemetery. The two open graves up on the hill looked like bomb craters. The Harnes car added to the carnage, and a pervasive fog drifted over the landscape like smoke. He glanced up, wondering if the sun would ever come out. It was up there, but little more than a cold gray dime hanging high and distant in a dark gray sky.

The deputies had been busy. They'd filled three cardboard boxes to overflowing with clear plastic bags containing fragments of glass, metal, plastic, strands of hair, and pieces of fiber from the car's seat. It looked like half the crime scene had been bagged, tagged, and tossed in the boxes.

"You guys turn anything yet?" Sutton asked, stopping in front of both men.

Griffith, the shyer of the two, made a waffling motion with his hand and pointed at the cardboard boxes. "We've bagged a lot of stuff, and maybe we'll turn something when we get the stuff back to the lab, but I kind of doubt it." He avoided the sheriff's face and looked over at his partner. Bender nodded in agreement, then looked away.

They're holding back, Sutton thought. Or they know something and they're afraid to tell me about it. "What's going on, you two?"

After an uneasy span of time, Bender sighed and finally looked at Sutton. "Before we started working down here on the car, we were up at the graves, trying to gather evidence up there. We didn't find much, but what we did put together bothered us."

Griffith coughed. "Scared the shit out of us."

What else is new? Sutton wondered. "What'd you find?"

"Come on," Bender said. "We'll show you."

The two deputies led Sutton thirty yards up a hill to the first of two open graves. The jagged hole was littered on all sides with a mixture of dirt, grass, splintered fragments of wood, and chunks of cement.

Bender put his hands on his hips and looked down at the debris surrounding the open grave. "We got up here at sunrise, spent the better part of two hours going over these graves, and couldn't find anything to suggest these graves were broken into."

Sutton gave Bender a strange look. "But the graves are open."

"We know," Griffith said. "But Gaylord said broken *into,* not broken *out of.*"

"Let me explain," Bender said, picking up a hunk of grass with dirt still clinging to its roots. "This is some of the sod that covered the grave. We gathered it up and checked it out. We couldn't find any sign that a tool was used to cut through the grass. If somebody had dug up the grass with a shovel or spade, the sod would have been scored, and some of the pieces would have fit together like a jigsaw puzzle. That wasn't the case here. Nothing fit together; nothing was scored. All the grass has been shredded like this hunk." He threw the grass away. "No marks, no straight edges. You follow me?"

Sutton could remember what Slatkin had said about the graves, how it looked like they'd been opened from the inside. He nodded grimly.

"The second problem," Griffith drawled, "is the layering of debris surrounding the graves. When someone digs a hole, they dig up the grass first and set it a-side. Then they dig up the dirt and pile it on top of the grass. Then when they finally get to the cement sarcoph-agus that holds the coffin, they'll break the top off it, scoop up the chunks, and toss the chunks on top of the dirt. Finally comes the coffin lid. They'll break it up and throw the wood on top of the cement rubble.

"Everything here is mixed together, dirt on top of the cement and so on. You get the kind of mix we got here when there's an underground explosion like when a gas main goes off and blows the dirt and grass and cement into the air and comes down all mixed together. Like this."

"Was there an explosion?" Sutton asked, hoping against hope there might be a logical explanation for all this.

Both deputies shook their head. "No gas mains in this area," Griffith said. "And no signs that this was caused by an explosion of any kind."

Sutton swore and Bender unsnapped a flashlight from his belt, turning it on and focusing the beam on the earthen wall inside the grave. "See how roughly tex-tured the wall is?" Sutton nodded. "You can't get a pattern like that if you use a shovel. If you did, you'd leave lots of smoothed-out indentations on the wall, and there's nothing like that in this grave or the other one."

"So what are you saying?"

Bender looked at Griffith, then back at Sutton. "We're telling you the grave wasn't opened from the outside. It was opened from the inside, forced open like in an explosion."

Sutton sighed, "But you said—"

"I know," Griffith said. "We said there were no explosions."

"What are you telling me?" Sutton asked. "Are you saying two bodies kicked their way out of these graves and walked down the hill to the car?"

Griffith looked at Bender. Bender looked at Griffith, and Sutton looked at both men. "Answer the question," he finally demanded.

Griffith nodded. "How 'bout we just show you what we found? Then you draw your own conclusions. Okay?" Sutton nodded.

"Brace yourself for some really strange shit," Bender warned.

Deputy Larry Griffith pointed to a wide mound of soft dirt on one side of the grave. "We found some hand and palm prints over there. Judging from the pattern, it looks like someone reached up and used the top of the grave to pull themselves out. There are a lot of footprints leading to and from the grave. We can account for most of them, including the ones made by Gaylord, myself, Slatkin, and the other deputies.

"What we can't account for is a single set of footprints leading from the edge of the grave across the dirt and then down the hill."

"What's to explain?" Sutton asked. "Maybe a curious citizen got through the barricades, walked up here, and then walked away."

Griffith shook his head. "There's only one set of tracks leading away from the grave. Whoever made those tracks didn't have any shoes on."

"Why barefoot?" Sutton asked, talking more to himself than the deputies.

"I can answer that," Bender volunteered.

"Be my guest," Sutton said.

"I used to work for a funeral home while I was going to medical school. Everything they do is sort of phony, an illusion. To get that serene look on a dead body's face, they sometimes suture the eyes shut and staple the lips to the teeth. More to the point, when they dress a corpse, they take all sorts of shortcuts. If you think about it, all you ever see is a body in a coffin from the waist up. Those funeral people know that and when they get a body ready, half the time they don't bother to put pants on it. Or shoes."

Sutton looked away for a long moment, then turned back to face his deputies. "You're saying a corpse kicked its way out of this grave, climbed out, then walked down the hill, barefoot."

"No . . . well . . . er . . . sort of," Bender muttered.

"What we're doing," Griffith said, "is telling you what we found and what the evidence suggests. Hell, what do you want us to do, ignore this stuff or not come to you just because it sounds impossible?"

"No. That's the last thing I want you to do. I need to know about everything you come across . . . no matter how far-out. Some very strange stuff's been going on in this town, and it's going to get stranger."

"Shit," Griffith muttered, drawing out the words. "What could get stranger than a corpse walking down a hill?"

"I don't know, but I have a hunch things will. If you find yourself getting spooked or you want to lay a crazy theory on someone, I'm your man. Come to me. I don't know what I'll do with whatever you tell me, but I will listen and stand behind you. I may be the one person in this town that'll believe you. Understand?" Both deputies nodded.

Sutton continued to look hard at his two men. "I want a lid on this. You don't talk to press, friends, or anyone else on the force about what you found up here or anything else that may develop. You report only to me. By the way, did you make plaster casts of those footprints you found?"

The deputies exchanged hurt looks. " 'Course we made casts," Bender said. "After we finish up here, we'll take them down to the morgue and compare them to the feet of the woman's husband and father. God, I hope they don't match, don't you?"

Sutton didn't say anything. He was looking down the

hill at the idling patrol car that held the one important person in his life. It's getting too big, too scary, he thought, almost talking to Jackie Fairmont. Let's chuck it, pull out. We'll swing by your house, get the girls, and leave all this behind. I know this town, north of Sacramento. It sits like a green jewel on the Russian River. I only went through it once, but I liked it. It's an old town, lots of bricks, gray boards with some cobblestones in the street. I could get a job there and we'd be safe. No murderers, no autopsies, no kidnapped children, no ripped-open graves with footprints that don't make sense. Dammit, this thing is too big . . . too unexplainable.

A view of the future suddenly welled up in Sutton's mind. The feeling—the premonition—was as physical as it was mental. His chest pounded and his bones grew cold. And he saw the future. It was a gray nothingness with a black horizon. Then the vision changed, and he saw a black hill and a black horse sitting on top of it. As the horse started to run down the hill, the image faded and Sutton was back in the cemetery, alone and afraid with the sound of a low mournful keen in his ears. Then the sad sound turned into the concerned voice of Deputy Gaylord Bender. "You all right?"

"Yeah," he said, stunned by what he'd just experienced. He shook his head. "Yeah, I'm fine."

"No, you're not." Griffith pointed to Sutton's hand. "You're bleeding."

Sutton looked down at his hands and saw blood dripping from his fingers. "What the—?" he hissed, realizing he'd somehow driven his own thumbnail deep into his forefinger a moment earlier. He pulled out a handkerchief and used it to stem the flow of blood. Then he gave Bender and Griffith a sheepish look. "Cut it on a tin can this morning. Should've put a Band-Aid on it."

The men walked down the hill toward the patrol cars. A wrecker had backed up against the rear end of the

Harnes car, and the driver was wrapping a hook around the car's bumper. Suddenly Bender sprinted across the grass to the car, reached inside, and pulled out several plastic baggies. As he walked back to Sutton and Griffith, he reached into one of the bags, pulled out what looked like a thin, clear poker chip, and tossed it to Sutton. Sutton turned the wafer-thin disk over in his hand. It gathered and held the sun's weak rays like a prism. He flipped it back to Bender. "What is it?"

Bender shook his head. "I was about to ask you the same thing. We found a few of these disks inside the car and some more on the ground by the driver's door. I don't know what they are."

"They're fish scales," Griffith said. Both Sutton and Bender gave Griffith a strange look. "Well . . . that's what they are. Earlier when we found them, they were softer and had an odor. A fish odor . . . like carp. When we get back to the lab, we'll check them under the microscope, then we'll know for sure."

Bender rolled his eyes. "And after we do that, we'll go to the library and do research on what kind of a fish has a scale the size of a silver dollar, won't we, Grif?"

Griffith started to respond, but the grinding noise from the tow truck's winch motor drowned him out. Sutton watched the truck violently jerk the back end of the Harnes car up into the air. The noisy din made further conversation between the men impossible, and they went their separate ways.

Sutton climbed into the patrol car, relieved to be out of the cold and fog and away from the open graves.

"It's about time," Jackie scolded. Surprised at the tone in her voice, Sutton turned toward the woman. "I have a wide variety of skills and talents, all of which go unutilized when my only assignment is to sit in an empty patrol car waiting for radio messages for our great commander-in-chief."

He searched for a comeback and came up with a weak one. "Well, somebody had to handle the radio."

"Next time around you sit in the car and I'll walk around and look important." She was right, but he still had to turn away so she couldn't see him smile. "What was the big deal back there with Bender and Griffith?" She reached for the key and started the patrol car.

It was time for her to hear it all. Leaning his head back against the head rest, he turned and looked at her. "Shut off the car, Jackie. I've got a hell of a story to tell you."

She already knew about the bizarre findings and questions the autopsies on Lynn Langley and Robert Calms had raised, so he started by filling her in on the meeting at Jenny McKenzie's home and ended with Larchmont's prophecy that two children would disappear. Her face impassive, she stared at him while he went on to cover the horrors Slatkin had described and Bender and Griffith had just confirmed.

When he finished, he looked at her, expecting to see signs of skepticism and disbelief. Instead he saw a pale intense woman staring back at him. "You believe it, don't you, Henry? You believe everything Larchmont said about those . . . demons?"

"I didn't last night. But I think I do now."

"Thank you."

"For what?"

"For believing I had the strength to deal with what you just told me and for telling me about what Larchmont said. I don't know if this helps, but I don't think his theory is crazy, either. Matter of fact, the more I think about it, the more it makes sense . . . and it's all we have to go on."

Sutton felt an immense sense of relief as he realized he wasn't alone in his support for what Larchmont and Jenny McKenzie had said. He wasn't too sure what he'd do next, but it was nice to know that whatever he did, he wouldn't have to do it alone.

"Now what?" Jackie asked.

Sutton stared out the windshield, looking up the hill in

an effort to make out the stark lines of the Horrcove brothers' mortuary. The fog rolling over the hillside blurred his view. "I think we ought to start by meeting the Horrcove brothers. At this point I wouldn't be the least bit surprised if Johnny Joe Sloams really did see one of their limousines driving through the cemetery with one of the missing boys in the backseat."

Jackie started up the patrol car and pulled the car back onto the narrow road.

Chapter
Sixteen

Jackie guided the car between two huge stone lions standing sentry on either side of the private road. Thirty yards on she parked the patrol car in a large circular driveway at the base of the Horrcove mansion. While she radioed in their location, Sutton stepped out into a cold fitful wind, craned his head back, and studied the massive building that was both home and business for its two owners.

The Horrcove mansion and mortuary was a massive two-story structure constructed from darkly weathered granite blocks. Large gabled dormers jutting out from the slate roof added to the building's mass and made it seem even larger than it was.

The mansion looming up in front of him was austere, foreboding, and moody. Its arched narrow windows were heavily curtained and framed by large shutters. The only marked departure from the mortuary's severe Gothic exterior was its massive colonnaded front entrance designed somewhat along the lines of an antebellum mansion. Dull gray marble steps fanned out and upward to an elevated veranda almost twenty feet above the foundation. At the top of the steps a series of dark Doric columns soared upward to support a widow's walk type of balcony that was as large as the massive porch it covered.

The Horrcove mansion sat directly at the base of a high hill, and from where Sutton stood, it looked as if the back of the mortuary disappeared into the slope of the hill.

As he and Jackie began to climb the steps leading up to the veranda, Sutton was struck with the strange feeling that the mansion was alive and looking down on them like a dark and evil animal. He didn't like it. The house radiated an intangible brooding quality and it smelled of evil and terror and death.

His mind flashed back to his first year on the Chicago police force. He'd been assigned a foot patrol beat that took him past the stockyard slaughterhouses. Sometimes at night and on weekends, when the plants were closed and cold, he'd heard what sounded like the cries of dying animals. The sounds had unnerved him, and when he'd mentioned them to some of his fellow officers, they'd laughed at him. But the winos who lived in the area hadn't laughed; they knew. They, too, had experienced the unexplained sounds. What he had felt back then was what he was feeling now. This mansion was a place of death, a place of blood, terror, and . . . slaughter.

Jackie's voice pulled him out of his nightmarish speculation. "God, this place is creepy. It's like walking up to that house in *Psycho*." There was no humor in her voice, and Sutton grunted in agreement. They were almost at the top of the steps when Jackie slowed, wrapping a damp hand around his wrist and stopping him. "Henry, look at that." She let go of him and pointed down at the side of the mortuary. "Look at those bushes against the house. They're all fake."

He looked down at what she was pointing at. She was right. Every bush along the front of the mansion was a rubber and plastic imitation of the real thing. The trees and bushes planted out in the yard and in the cemetery which surrounded the house on three sides just beyond were real, but every plant that was close to or touching the mansion was a lush green, artificial, man-made imitation.

"Either they got a strange gardener, or anything that touches this house dies," she observed.

Sutton nodded in uneasy agreement. They moved on, crossing the wide veranda and stopping in front of two heavy ornately carved doors. "You gonna knock?" she asked.

Sutton grabbed the heavy bronzed door handle and glanced at the woman standing beside him. "It may be their home, but it's also a business." He pulled one of the great doors open, surprised at the strength it required. For a moment they stood side by side looking into the dark entrance. Henry then entered with Jackie right behind him.

It was like stepping back into time. An ancient Persian rug muffled their entrance into the foyer. Fourteen-foot-high walls on either side of them had been wainscotted with dark oak paneling, and the ancient wallpaper was cracked with age. Sprites and nymphs had been gracefully carved into the ornate plaster ceiling high above them.

Out of place were the aluminum sprinkler heads of the home's automatic sprinkler system protruding down from the ceiling, as out of place as the plastic foliage out in front of the mansion. Sutton continued to walk slowly down the corridor toward a dimly lit room. He tried to lead the way, but Jackie wouldn't allow it. With quick confident steps, she started out ahead of him and began examining the antiques and tapestries cluttering the hallway they were moving down. Sutton passed a walnut fern stand that had to be a hundred and fifty years old, then stopped. On top of the stand was a Waterford crystal vase just as old. The arrangement of Boston ferns sprouting up from the vase, plastic ferns that could have been purchased at a Woolworth's store, was odd. Equally odd was the large fire extinguisher mounted on the wall next to the arrangement. It bothered him. The fern stand and vase were worth several thousand dollars. The plastic fern arrangement was worth two bucks at the most. What was going on here? Was Jackie right? Was it that nothing living could come into this house or touch it and survive? He shook his head. And why the fire extinguishers? There were two in the foyer and he could see several others in the room they were approaching.

They entered what Sutton guessed to be some sort of gathering room for grieving families. The room carried the same antique theme as the foyer. It was wainscotted, had high ceilings, and was furnished with old musty sofas and davenports. Once again there was an automatic sprinkler system and multiple fire extinguishers every place he looked.

Jackie loved antiques, and while she went off to look at some of the more exotic ones, Sutton took a moment to examine several tapestries hanging from the walls. The central theme in every case seemed to be a gruesomely depicted hunting scene. In one tapestry he was surprised to see the hunters were not hunting boar or stags but other men and boys. In the second tapestry, the hunters were stalking a priest. The fine needlework detailed the priest's collar and crucifix. It also captured the fear in the dying priest's eyes.

Jackie came over and tugged at his shirt. "I think I've died and gone to heaven." Sutton smiled at her enthusiasm. "Do you have any idea how much that Parson's table is worth?" Sutton shook his head. "How about the wall tapestries?" Again Sutton shook his head. "Well, I'll tell you. At least, and I do mean at-the-very-least, fifty thousand dollars. That's just for *one* tapestry, and there are eight of 'em in this room!"

Sutton glanced back at the grotesque tapestries. He was sure Jackie was right. She was an expert in antiques, but who would pay fifty thousand dollars for a scene depicting the hunting and killing of a priest or children? The Horrcove brothers, he thought with a shudder. That's who.

"How may we help you?" a high-pitched feminine voiced asked from directly behind them.

Caught off guard, Sutton whirled around, the back of his neck etched in hoar frost at the ungodly tone of the intruding voice. In the heavily curtained room he could barely discern two shadowy figures standing some ways away from him. They had come in from another part of the house, entering the room through an unnoticed door. Their presence irritated Henry Sutton. He hated to be caught off guard.

Leaving Jackie behind, he began walking toward the two shadows. As the distance narrowed he realized he was approaching two small elderly gentlemen. He was more surprised to see they were mirror images of one another. Twins. Two very old and very tiny twin brothers.

Sutton stopped in front of them, and as he looked down on them, he was surprised by their ages. They were ancient. Both had hollow cheeks and beaklike noses. Their sallow skin had the texture of dried parchment. They reminded Sutton of a grisly exhibit he'd seen in a carnival sideshow years earlier. Displayed in one of the tents was the mummified remains of a gold prospector who'd died a hundred and fifty years earlier in the Arizona desert. The heat and sun had dehydrated the corpse, turning its skin into leather and its face into a grotesque wizened mask, just like the faces in front of him now.

One of the brothers placed his hand on his hip. "My brother asked you a question, Officer. In the face of your uninvited intrusion, surely a response is not asking too much . . . you can speak, can't you?"

Surprised and irritated by the taunting hostility from the little man, Sutton set his face so his growing anger wouldn't show. "I can speak, and you can help me in a number of ways."

The brother who had asked Sutton if he could speak

turned to his twin. "Ah . . . the behemoth possesses a voice, Bartholomew. He may yet answer your question."

Bartholomew Horrcove reached out and stroked his brother's arm in a gesture of affection. "Be gentle, Alexander," he said in a soft feminine voice. "Remember, confrontation begats confrontation." He turned and leveled his eyes at Sutton. "Now, as I said earlier, how can we help you?"

Sutton took in a deep breath, pushing aside the sudden loathing he felt for these two. "I assume you know that three people have died in the last three nights in the vicinity of the cemetery?"

"Yes," Bartholomew Horrcove confirmed. "We heard about the most recent death this morning on the radio. Sounded ghastly."

"Indeed," echoed the other brother, "Though it does seem odd that not a lot of that business has been coming our way."

Sutton's lip curled up in disdain. He was growing tired of this game and tired of suppressing his anger. "Since you've been listening to the radio, then you must know that two children are also missing."

"Two *boys,* I believe," Alexander Horrcove said, overaccentuating the reference to gender while passing a knowing look to his brother.

"Do you know anything about these two missing children?" Sutton asked. His anger was escalating. What the fuck were these two up to?

"Absolutely not," Alexander said.

"What could we possibly know about the two missing boys?" Bartholomew asked. "All we know is what we heard on the radio."

Sutton's eyes moved from one brother's face to the other brother's face, then back again. "This morning we received a call from someone who said that they saw one of the missing boys in this vicinity last night."

"So?" the brothers asked in unison.

"So the caller also said the boy was in the backseat of

189

one of your limousines." Sutton gestured toward Jackie Fairmont. "We've come out to see if there's any substance to the caller's claim."

The Horrcove brothers looked at each other for a long moment. Finally Alexander Horrcove broke the silence. "Are you suggesting that one or both of us might be involved in the kidnapping of a small child?"

"No," Sutton said. "But two boys are missing, and I have no choice but to check out every lead I come across."

"You wouldn't care to tell us who the caller was, would you?" Alexander Horrcove asked, his voice cold as ice. Sutton shook his head.

"I thought as much," hissed the other. "Obviously someone is pursuing a sizable reward without caring who he injures in the process. In any case, I assure you that none of our vehicles were in use last night."

"I still need to check it out," Sutton insisted.

Alexander Horrcove folded his arms. "Then consider it 'checked out,' as you so colloquially phrased it. We've answered your questions, assured you that none of our vehicles left the garage last night, and now since both my brother and I are busy, we would like . . . no, we *demand* to be removed from your list of suspects."

Henry Sutton couldn't believe it. These two men barely came up to his waist. They were as old as sin and they were giving him demands. He glanced back at Jackie. Her wide brown eyes had narrowed into slits of disbelief at the brothers' coldly insolent attitude. He directed his attention back to the two tiny men. "If that's the case, then you'll have no objections if my partner and I look around? Maybe check out the garage and your limousines?"

"But we do object," Alexander Horrcove said.

"We object very much," echoed the other.

Sutton glared at both men in disgust. Suddenly Jackie Fairmont was standing beside him. "You won't allow us to look around?" she asked.

"Absolutely not," Alexander Horrcove answered. "This is our place of business. It is also our home. It is not now, nor has it ever been, open to the eyes of the curious . . . be they tourists, members of the Historical Society, or visitors from the local police department. Do we make ourselves clear?"

"Perfectly," Henry Sutton growled. "But you know I'll be back and I'll have a search warrant. Then, whether you object or not, I'll take this place apart and be legal every step of the way."

Bartholomew Horrcove smiled. "Then by all means, Sheriff, do come back."

"If you can," added the other, smiling like his brother.

Sutton glared at Alexander Horrcove. "What do you mean by that?"

"Nothing," the man said, shaking his head and still smiling slightly. "Just a parting observation."

At that moment Sutton noticed that both brothers' eyes began to glimmer in the dim room like cat's eyes. The strange effect startled him and he took a step back. Breathing deeply, wanting to reach out and crush their heads like grapes, Sutton gritted his teeth, whirling around and grabbing Jackie by the elbow. He half pushed, half dragged her out of the room, down the hallway, and out through one of the massive doors. He slammed the door behind him as if it were made of balsa wood, crossed the veranda, and started down the steps.

"Henry, you're breaking my arm," Jackie protested.

When he realized how tightly he was holding her, he released his grip, apologizing. "Jesus H. Christ! Did they get to me or what?"

"Yeah, they got to you and to me. Those guys have got to be the creepiest . . . the weirdest . . . Jesus, there aren't words to describe 'em." She made a face. "Now what? Go for a warrant?"

"You betcha. Judge Bradstreet's office is the next stop, and I don't want just one, I want three."

"Three?"

"One to get us back into that place and two to stick up their sanctimonious asses."

"Careful, Henry," she said, giggling. "You do that and they'll love you forever."

For the first time in days Henry Sutton found himself laughing. He put his arm around Jackie's small waist and pulled her close to him, his waist-line revolver rubbing gently against her ribs as they walked to the patrol car.

With his hand on the door handle he turned and looked back at the Horrcove mansion looming up behind him. The dark shape framed by a dark gray sky still resembled an animal, an evil predatory beast. Sutton shuddered, turning his collar up against the wind. He climbed into the patrol car and buckled on the seat belt.

While Jackie drove down to the cemetery, Sutton reflected back on his encounter with the Horrcove brothers. He had long considered himself to be an expert—professional in the art of confrontation, verbal and otherwise. But his run-in with those two tiny men had left him numb and angry. He felt like he'd been eviscerated by two ancient alley cats. They had played with him as if he were a mouse, and when they'd finally grown bored with their game, they'd gutted him with the claws of the law and their personal rights, both of which he was sworn to uphold.

But one good thing had come out of the encounter. Their refusal to let him look around and their unreasonable demand for privacy had turned them into tangible palpable suspects on which he could target his energies. The brothers were hiding something . . . perhaps the missing boys . . . perhaps something more. Whatever the case, Henry Sutton now had something to move on, something to go for. He smiled slightly as he began to map out the details of his counterattack.

"Those two guys are guilty as sin," Jackie commented as she pulled onto the main road leading to town.

"Guilty of what?" Sutton asked, only half listening.

"Guilty of something. Why else would they act like that? Don't forget, they threatened you." He glanced over at her. "Well, they did," she insisted. "When you said you'd be back with a search warrant, one of them said something like do come back if you can. The bastard may have called it an observation, but it sounded like a threat to me."

Sutton shrugged absentmindedly while he continued to plot out his moves against the Horrcove brothers. He had already decided to take Embom and Griffith with him when he went back with the search warrant. While he and Jackie searched the mansion, they could go over the vehicles. If the brothers had used one of their cars to transport a screaming kicking boy up to their home, there would be something inside the car to prove it: hair, clothing fibers, scuffmarks, hand prints, something, anything. If there was something there, Griffith and Embom would find it.

"How 'bout I try and raise Bradstreet on the radio?" Jackie asked. "Could we get the warrant faster?"

Sutton nodded and looked around for his clipboard. He needed to write some things out, get himself organized before he went in to see Judge Bradstreet. He reached under the seat and found the clipboard.

"Do you want me to raise Bradstreet on the radio?" Jackie repeated.

"We'd better do this in person," Sutton said, fishing through his shirt pocket for a pencil. "Bradstreet's a stickler—ouch! God dammit!"

"What is it?"

Shocked by a sudden stab of pain, Sutton jerked a bloody finger out of his shirt pocket. "Shit, I've cut myself again."

"Jesus, you sure have." Jackie glanced over at his bloody hand and stained uniform.

Surprised by the amount of blood more than the pain, Sutton held his hand out over the floor of the car and continued to swear. Somehow, he'd reopened the cut he'd inflicted on himself at the cemetery. The cut wasn't particularly deep, but it was dripping blood on the floor mat like a water spigot.

"Henry, you're bleeding all over the car and look at your uniform. There's blood all over it. How'd you cut yourself?" Sutton shrugged and tried to close off the cut with his hand. Jackie sighed, and with one hand on the wheel, reached over and began fumbling through his shirt pocket. "That's what got you." She pulled out a packet of salt encased in a stiff aluminum foil wrapper.

The patrol car started to veer across the yellow line, and instinctively Sutton reached for the wheel. Jackie pushed the salt back in his shirt pocket and turned her attention back to the road. "No problem," she said. "I'm in control. Jesus, I don't believe it. Lacerated by a packet of salt. That's what you get for being a bachelor." She threw him a quick smile.

Sutton made a face, lifted the flap of his shirt pocket, and peered down at the sharp-edged packet of salt. As an absentminded bachelor, he had long ago developed a habit of pocketing all the packaged extras that came with the restaurant meals he ate while on duty. As such, the glove compartment of his car often overflowed with packets of taco sauce, powdered coffee cream, sugar, pepper, and salt. Once every couple of months, he would clean out the glove compartment and drop his collection into his drawer, a drawer he euphemistically called his spice cabinet. He'd noticed the logo of the restaurant where the salt packet had come from, but he hadn't eaten there in over a week. What was the salt doing in his pocket today? Then he remembered. He'd been out of clean uniforms this morning and he'd dug this one out of the hamper.

Jackie glanced over at Henry, uttering her last words to him ever. "Henry, you're a mess. Bradstreet's an important man, and I don't think the love of my life should go into his office looking like—"

Suddenly her body went rigid. Her head was slammed

back against the seat rest, her foot rammed down on the gas pedal, and the patrol car bolted down the residential street like a frightened animal.

The same invisible force hit Sutton. It hit him like a vast unseen wave from hell, a wave that pinned his body back against the passenger seat. He couldn't move and was totally paralyzed. As he struggled against the unseen pressure that was crushing his body, his brain screamed the words: *heart attack*. But there was no pain. Instead he could feel his lips and cheeks being pulled toward the back of his skull as an unseen power tightened its grip around his body. He could feel the car's speed increasing, and with a horrendous effort that threatened to snap the tendons on his neck, he turned his head against the force to see what was happening to Jackie. In spite of what was going on, his mind continued to function. If he was having a heart attack, then what was happening to Jackie? What was wrong with her? Why was blood spurting from her nose, why was the car racing out of control? Why was her face contorted out of shape by what was happening to him?

He tried to speak to her, tried to move toward her, but couldn't. His body felt as if it had been buried in tons of sand. Frozen in position, he had no choice but to sit there and watch Jackie's hands seemingly fly away from the steering wheel and suddenly become pinned against her own chest. With more horror than he had ever known, he watched a bright waterfall of blood begin spurting from her right ear. It gushed out in heavy jerking spurts and sprayed out over her shoulder and the car seat. Henry Sutton had never known such feelings of terror and helplessness.

Then suddenly the hideous gravity force disappeared and Sutton was free of its weight. He leaned forward, his movements hampered by the seat belt. With his left hand, he tried to correct the course of the car. With his right, he reached for the ignition key.

Henry Sutton had one hand on the wheel and one

hand on the key when the patrol car slammed into and ricocheted off a parked car. The impact threw Sutton forward and his head was slammed against the shotgun mount and the car's dash. His mind went dark and his body relaxed and slumped forward against the seat belt.

After ricocheting off the car, the patrol car continued its wild run down the quiet residential street, its speed increasing because the driver's foot was still on the gas. Engine screaming, hurtling along at close to fifty miles an hour, the car careened toward a row of houses and trees set away from the street. The car leaped a high curb, plowed through a thick hedge, then slammed into an old oak tree at better than sixty miles an hour.

Sutton's seatbelt saved him, but Jackie Fairmont's body was thrown through the steering wheel, out the windshield, and into the tree's sharp stubby lower branches.

Sutton, still unconscious, still held in place by his seatbelt, was spared this final horror.

Chapter
Seventeen

Charlcie McKenzie pointed to the cattleya orchid's purple-tinged blossoms. "Beautiful, aren't they?"

Seeing only the girl standing there, framed by a lavender profusion of blooming orchids, Cable agreed. "Yes," he stated simply. "You really are."

Charlcie rolled her eyes, then looked down at the floor. "Gosh, Professor, you Canadian educators are so bold and forthright."

He laughed at her mock modesty and began to walk toward her, a wanting look in his eyes. Charlcie saw the desire on his face. "John Cable," she said, "I know what you're thinking and let me tell you right here and now that my mother's green house is not the place for lustful thoughts or carnal actions."

"Carnal actions?" he asked softly, wrapping his arms around her waist and kissing her full on the lips. She responded, wrapping her arms around his neck and teasing his tongue with hers. He felt himself starting to grow hard. A moment later she separated from him and pulled away.

Cable looked at her questioningly and smiled. "So what's a carnal action?"

Charlcie returned his smile. "A carnal action is what's growing in your pocket right now."

His smile broadened and he looked hard at Charlcie McKenzie. She was a stunning woman and he knew he was on his way to falling in love with her.

They had spent the morning together, talking and joking and enjoying each other's company in a conscious effort to throw off the cloak of depression brought on by the previous evening's meeting. At times they'd attempted to include Jenny McKenzie and Martin Larchmont in their harmless banter, but their strained efforts hadn't succeeded.

Martin Larchmont and Jenny McKenzie were as remote and distant as the house was silent. Jenny had secluded herself in the den with a stack of old books and newspaper clippings, seemingly more interested in reading old newspaper clippings than talking to her daughter or Cable.

Martin Larchmont had spent most of the day in his room. He'd only come out once, and by accident Cable had run into him in the kitchen. During their brief encounter, Cable had asked Larchmont why he had never been told of his friend's interest in the Yezidi religion or the demonic offspring of Iblis.

Larchmont's explanation had been simple and to the point. "You don't share knowledge with someone if that knowledge might get them killed. Some twenty-five years ago Jenny and Patrick McKenzie came to Ravina to find out why all those people committed suicide back in the late 1880s and '90s. I came for the same reason. I also came because I knew this was the final destination of the followers of Iblis.

"Somehow, while pursuing his own investigation, Patrick McKenzie learned something, maybe learned too much, and that knowledge resulted in his death. As I told you earlier, the police called it a suicide, but Jenny

and I believe his death was made to look like a suicide
or he was forced to kill himself by a malevolent powerful force.

"John, the forces that killed Patrick McKenzie are
still out there, and I want you and Charlcie to pack up
and leave before something happens to you . . ."
Larchmont didn't finish because Charlcie McKenzie came
into the kitchen. She realized she'd interrupted something between the two friends and started to back out
when Larchmont stopped her. "Charlcie, I was just
suggesting to John that you and he leave town for a few
days."

She gave Larchmont a quizzical look. "Oddly enough,
my mother just suggested the same thing, and while I
appreciate the concern, I have no intention of leaving."
She swung her gaze from Larchmont to Cable. "Where
would I go? San Jose? The last time I was there, my
soon-to-be-ex husband broke my jaw."

Larchmont turned to Cable. Cable shook his head. "I
know you're concerned, but I don't want to leave, either."

"Fools!" Larchmont flared angrily. "Bloody nonbe-
lieving fools! Don't you realize you could die? Damn,
what does it take to make you two believe?"

"Martin," Cable soothed, "there's no reason to get
angry."

"I know," Larchmont agreed. "I know. It's just that
I like you both very much, and I'm genuinely concerned
for your well-being. You're putting yourself in harm's
way by staying in Ravina." He looked at Charlcie apolo-
getically and shrugged. "I won't bring it up again." He
walked out of the room heading toward the den where
Jenny was.

After Larchmont left, Charlcie and Cable wandered
out of the kitchen into the greenhouse, both feeling the
need to escape the oppressive atmosphere in the house.
The greenhouse was actually an enclosed portion of the
home's back patio. It was a well-designed professionally

constructed greenhouse made from redwood and white-washed glass.

"A fernery," Cable said as he entered and noticed the solid mass of green plants and orchids.

"Oh, no," Charlcie mournfully wailed. "Not another soul lost to the world of potted plants and orchids."

He smiled. "I have a greenhouse myself. I like ferns."

A cloud cover and an incoming bank of fog blotted out the afternoon sun. It was dark and shadowy in the greenhouse. Charlcie hit a light switch, and two overhead neon lights blinked on, revealing green cascades of weeping ferns of all types and varieties. Some hung from the ceiling in moss baskets, their fronds sprouting up from brown and white rhizomes that vaguely resembled squirrels or rabbits feet. Others jutted out from moss-covered boards like giant moose or deer horns. Cable paused before a large fern in a hanging basket. "Lord," he murmured in awe. "Look at the size of this polypodium aureum mandaianum." It sounded like he was showing off, and he was.

Charlcie looked as if she'd just lost John Cable to a big-breasted topless dancer. "Big deal," she snorted.

"But look at the size of it. It's huge. You know what polypodium means?" he asked, still showing off. He couldn't see her face through the foliage. *"Poly* means 'many' and *podium* means 'feet.' Many feet."

"Thank you, Doctor," came her response from a darker part of the greenhouse.

Cable pushed the basket out of his way and gave her a sheepish look. "Sorry if I sounded stuffy."

"You weren't stuffy. Just wrong."

"Wrong? Wrong about what?"

"Wrong about the fern. Actually, it's a polypodium aureum taffelata."

Cable examined the tips of the fronds, noticing the way they separated themselves off into dainty tassel-like formations. "Good God, you're right." He gave a frown, then a smile. "Are you a fern freak, too?"

"Not to the degree my mother is, but I've managed to store away a tolerable amount of information in my seedy little brain over the years."

Coming out from behind the giant fern, Cable watched Charlcie walk over to him. Reaching out, Cable pulled her to him. He tipped his head to one side, leaned close anticipating another kiss, and suddenly found himself with a mouthful of hair. Puzzled, he drew away.

Before he could say anything, she pressed her fingertips against his lips. "I like you, John Cable. I like you very much, but I'm having a hard time handling the messages I get from my mind and body when you kiss me. I want to go with the flow, but then all of a sudden, my mind conjures up all the bad things that went on in my marriage, especially the violence. Then all the horror and violence that's going on around us right here and now comes in and I freeze up." Cable continued to hold her and listen to her talk. "It would be bad enough if all I had to handle were the memories and the pain from my marriage, but that's not all there is. Right now my mother's sitting in the den like a zombie and Martin's walking around the house asking us to leave town and calling us fools for not. I know two doctors and a sheriff who probably have serious reservations about the sanities of the two people we hold most dear in the world. I keep remembering Martin's prophecy that two children would disappear, and if that isn't enough, every time I close my eyes to kiss you, I keep seeing the newspaper headlines."

She was close to tears, and Cable cupped her chin in his hands. "Hey, it's okay. There's no rush. We've got all the time in the world to work through your past marriage and my marriage and . . . what newspaper headlines?"

"The headlines about the two missing boys. Didn't you see the newspaper?"

Cable closed his eyes and shook his head. "No. I didn't see the paper."

"You okay?" she asked softly.

"Yeah," he said, opening his eyes but not looking at her. "I just don't like what I'm thinking right now."

"Which is?"

"That Martin and your mother are right. That everything they said last night might really be coming true. That there really are creature-demons someplace in Ravina." He stared at her hard. "All of a sudden I'm starting to feel uptight about being in this town. Maybe it would be a good idea if you did what Martin suggested and left Ravina for a few days."

"Would you leave with me?"

"I can't. Martin's my best friend. Last night I doubted him. Now, with those newspaper headlines, I'm starting to believe what he said. If he is right, he's going to need all the help he can get."

She nodded. "I think that sums up my feelings, too. My mother's involved in this up to her ears, and not too long ago she became my best friend. I'm staying, too."

She took his hand and they walked out of the greenhouse and into the empty kitchen. She turned to him and started to say something, but Cable cut her off by pressing his lips to hers. They clung to one another fiercely and intense emotions welled up in Cable. He felt a strong desire for this woman. His feelings were half love, half need, and all caring.

When they finally separated, she looked up at him, her eyes wide with focused intensity. "You do know that women sometimes change their minds?" He nodded.

"Good," she said. "Your room or mine?"

"Mine."

Holding hands and trying not to tiptoe, they walked down the hall, heading for the stairway. At the other end of the long hallway, Martin Larchmont was talking to someone on the phone.

They were tiptoeing up the stairs, were almost to the second floor, when Larchmont called out to them. "We've got to get to the hospital as soon as possible."

Charlcie hit the banister with a clenched fist. Cable moaned and shouted back. "What's going on at the hospital?"

"The sheriff's been hurt. He's in the hospital and one of his deputies is dead. That was Childress on the phone. I don't know what happened to him or Seafront, but all of a sudden those two doctors seem to be taking Jenny and me seriously. Hurry! I want to get to the hospital and back here before it gets dark."

Charlcie and Cable stood on the stairway for a moment, looking at each other, then clumped down the stairs to the hallway. At the bottom she hooked her arm through his elbow. "Seems like no matter how hard I try, my virtue's going to remain intact."

"Speak for yourself," Cable grumbled. "I'm beginning to feel like a professional virgin."

"Do you really have a greenhouse in Vancouver?"

"Yeah, but it's not as big as your mother's and—"

"Who gives a damn about how big it is? I just want to know if I can come up and see it when all this is over with."

He pulled her close in the dark hallway. "Look, there's some things you should know about me. I've got some faults. After all, my wife did leave me and—"

"Hey, what do you think I am? Perfect? If we get that chance to go to Vancouver, we can work on your faults, and while we're at it, we can work on mine, too. But that's not what it would be about. Going to Vancouver would be a time for us to get to know each other and maybe see if we've got a workable situation. But my God, don't start gnashing your breasts and beating your teeth before we even get started. Turning searchlights on your faults doesn't become you."

He smiled. "I think it gnashing your teeth and beating your breasts."

"John, are we rushing this? Doesn't this seem premature to you?"

"What?" he asked. "Starting a serious relationship

with you?" He stroked her cheek, then ran his fingers through her hair. "You bet. And I wouldn't have it any other way."

She started to say something more, but her words were drowned out by Martin Larchmont's voice booming out of the living room. "Come on, you two. We have to leave, and leave now!"

Chapter
Eighteen

The four people in Jenny McKenzie's old Mercedes-Benz rode to the hospital in silence. The sun was hanging low in the sky, and like the night before a thick bank of fog was beginning to roll over the town.

The hospital parking lot was filled with black and white patrol cars, but the lobby was empty. They took an elevator to the second floor, where Martin had agreed to meet with Childress, Seafront, and Henry Sutton. Unlike the lobby, the second floor was crowded with people, most of them wearing police uniforms.

Their arrival had been expected. When the elevator doors opened, two deputies stepped forward. One was tall and had curly hair that looked as if it had been crisped by a lightning bolt. The other was a short man with long arms and a face only a mother chimpanzee could have loved. Deputies Griffith and Bender introduced themselves, then directed the four to follow them down the crowded hallway.

The mass of uniforms parted as the six moved down the corridor. The faces of the nameless men they passed were creased with lines of tension, fear, and sadness.

All of them stared at Larchmont intently as he walked past.

The shorter deputy pulled open the door to the doctors' lounge, and Larchmont, Jenny and Charlcie Mc-Kenzie, and Cable entered. Bender and Griffith followed them into the room and pulled the door closed.

William Seafront was sitting in an overstuffed chair, and Cable was startled by the change he saw in the forensic pathologist. The doctor looked as if he'd aged ten years in the past twenty hours. There were new lines in his face, shadows under his eyes, and even from across the room Cable could see a small muscle just below the man's right eye twitch and spasm uncontrollably.

Henry Sutton was sitting on top of a table with his head bowed and his eyes on the floor. Mark Childress was standing beside the chief of police, taking the man's blood pressure. Childress glanced over at Larchmont and the others, then returned his attention to Sutton and began squeezing the rubber bulb on the indicator while listening to Sutton's pulse with his stethoscope. A moment later he began to unfasten the blood pressure cuff from Sutton's giant arm. "Glad you could get here so quickly, Dr. Larchmont," Childress said, not looking at Larchmont.

"You said it was important," Larchmont replied.

"That's gotta be the understatement of the year," Seafront said, slowly getting to his feet. "It's been one hell of a day."

"That's what Mark said on the phone," Larchmont pointed out. "But he didn't go into much detail."

Cable looked over at Sutton and Childress. Sutton was easing himself off the table. The act seemed to require a great deal of concentration and strength, and as the man came to a full standing position, Cable noticed Henry Sutton's eyes. "Hell-eyes," he thought, remembering back to when he'd served as a medic on the front lines in Vietnam, remembering back to the only other time when he'd seen eyes like Henry Sutton's.

"Hell-eyes." Eyes belonging to shocked and dazed men who'd spent too long fighting in the jungle, seen and lived through indescribable horrors not meant for human comprehension. He wondered what could have brought such pain and grief to the eyes of Henry Sutton.

"Bill's right," Childress said. "It's been one hell of a day, as you'll soon find out." He glanced over at Jenny and Charlcie McKenzie, then back at Larchmont. "Can I ask why you brought Mrs. McKenzie and her daughter with you?"

"Because they're safer here with me than they would be alone at home."

Larchmont's reply brought an uncomfortable silence to the room. Finally Seafront broke the silence. "I owe you an apology, Dr. Larchmont." He began walking toward the smaller man. "Last night I thought you were some sort of crackpot and I said some pretty ugly things. But I was wrong. God, was I wrong. I want to apologize." He offered out his hand to Larchmont.

Larchmont shook the pathologist's hand. "No need to apologize. If you'd said to me what I said to you, I probably would've thought the same thing."

Larchmont glanced at his watch, then walked over to one of the windows in the doctors' lounge. Cracking open the venetian blinds, he peered out into the twilight, then turned back to face the group. "We have to get on with this meeting. The sun's setting and we need to take certain precautions before it gets dark. Mark, I think you ought to fill me in on what's been going on."

Childress nodded. "Everything you said last night is starting to come true. Two children are missing. There was another death last night, and a lot of other strange things going on." Childress glanced over at Sutton. "You up to telling Martin about last night and maybe part of what happened today?"

Sutton nodded grimly and filled Larchmont in on what his watch commander, Andrew Slatkin, had found out at the cemetery. Sutton described in detail Louellen Mae

Harnes's injuries and the expression on her face, detailing how the car had literally been ripped apart. He also added a brief description of how the corpses of the dead woman's husband and father were found lying beside the car. When he finished, Bender and Griffith took over. They filled Larchmont in on the open graves and added their own theory on how the graves seemed to have been ripped open from the inside. For the most part Larchmont's expression revealed nothing about what he was thinking. He listened impassively, his face fixed as Bender and Griffith talked about the footprints they found leading away from each grave.

But when Bender mentioned the flat round disks he'd found inside the Harnes car and on the ground beside it, Larchmont stirred uncomfortably and the blood seemed to drain away from his face.

As Bender and Griffith continued to talk, the sun slowly set behind Horrcove Hill.

Three stories below in the hospital's morgue, the body that had once belonged to Louellen Mae Harnes began to move again.

The deputies finished with an apology. They had spent most of the afternoon examining and running tests on the stuff they'd brought back from the crime scene and had come up with nothing. Even a microscopic examination of the clear wafers found in and beside the Harnes car proved to be inconclusive.

"Because of the cellular structure, we think those disks came from something alive," Griffith explained. "But we can't tell you what kind of thing it was. All we know is it was big."

At that point Seafront joined Mark Childress, and together the two physicians tried to explain what had happened to them in the morgue just before they started to do the autopsy on Louellen Mae Harnes. Seafront shuddered as he tried to describe how the dead woman had moved and talked and how a groping hand belonging to a body that had been dead for nine months had grabbed his smock. "What happened down there was impossible," he said, looking at Larchmont. The pathologist sounded as if he didn't believe his own story, but everyone in the room knew he did, and so did they.

Finally Childress turned to Henry Sutton. He had been friends with Sutton for several years, and was one of the few people in Ravina who knew about Sutton's relationship with Jackie Fairmont. "Henry, you sure you want to talk about this? I can tell 'em what you told me, and maybe you could come back later and answer some questions."

Sutton shook his head, pushing himself away from the table and standing tall and massive in the room like a sad and bewildered colossus. Talking softly, Sutton briefly described Jackie Fairmont. In doing so, he used such terms as colleague and second-in-command. Almost instantly everyone in the room knew he had been in love with the woman.

There was a terrible irony to Sutton's location in the lounge. On the wall behind him someone had taped a huge multicolored Charles Schulz poster. A widely grinning Snoopy was leaping upward into a panorama of psychedelic colored flowers. The caption read: *Feeling Groovy!!* It was a terrible contrast to Sutton as he stood there—his eyes haunted, his uniform speckled with his and Jackie Fairmont's blood.

Sutton started with a telephone call his office had received earlier that day from Johnny Joe Sloams. His eyes lost some of their deadness and began to glint with anger as he described the exchange he'd had with the Horrcove brothers and the plan he'd made with Jackie Fairmont to return to their home with a search warrant.

Larchmont interrupted. "Did you discuss your plan to get a warrant in front of the Horrcove Brothers?"

"Yes," Sutton answered dully. Larchmont nodded and let the sheriff continue.

*   *   *

In the morgue Louellen Mae Harnes slowly brought herself into a sitting position. Tentatively, awkwardly, she slid one leg off the examining table. When it touched the floor, she moved the other leg off the table. The dead woman's movements were hesitant and spastic. Her dry and gritty eyes were open, staring straight ahead, seeing nothing . . .

Three stories above, Henry Sutton was trying to describe what had happened in the patrol car a few minutes after leaving the Horrcove mansion. With effort, he was able to keep his voice controlled, but when he reached that point where he had to describe the blood spurting out of Jackie Fairmont's ear, the words seized up in his throat and he had to stop twice before he could go on.

He tried as best he could to describe the powerful and invisible force that had pinned him and Jackie back against the seat just prior to his being knocked unconscious. He did a more than adequate job, but continued to grope for words as if his description was not doing justice to the terrible power that had engulfed the patrol cruiser.

He was ashen-faced and shaking when he finished the story. Unable to handle the expressions of sympathy he could see in the faces of the others in the room, he turned his back to the group and came face to face with the *Feeling Groovy* poster. His eyes grew wide at what he saw. He whirled back around, facing the people once again, his face a mask of fury and anguish— pain and grief. Everyone in the lounge looked away.

"There's no reason for you to be here while I talk to Larchmont about Jackie," Childress said, hoping to spare Sutton further pain.

Sutton shook his head. "Get on with it."

Childress sighed. "I went with the ambulance out to the scene of the wreck. Henry was unconscious when we arrived. The driver thrown from the vehicle was pronounced dead at the scene. I rode with Henry back to the emergency room and treated him for a possible concussion, minor subdural hematomas, and bruises. But for all intents and purposes, he's fine.

"I didn't get a chance to examine Jackie Fairmont's body until later this afternoon. . . . God dammit, Henry, are you sure you want to stay? It's extremely difficult for me to be factual with you here."

"You're doing fine," Sutton said, his eyes focused on a blank wall on the other side of the room. "Finish what you have to say."

Childress persisted. "Henry, this gets down to things you don't need to know . . . things you don't want to know. God dammit, I'm not going to be talking about a piece of meat, Henry. I'm going to be talking about Jackie . . . your Jackie."

Wearily Sutton turned to face Childress. "Okay, let me make it easier for you." His voice was taut and hard like the expression on his face. "I know Jackie was dead before the car hit the oak tree. I also know what the tree limbs did to her body."

"You couldn't have known about the tree limbs. You were dead to the world when we got to you."

Sutton made a sad gesture. "It took a while for the ambulance to get to us. I came to a couple of times. I saw Jackie. I saw what the tree limbs did to her."

"But . . . you couldn't of known she was dead before the car hit the tree," Childress insisted.

"I'm the one who saw blood spurting from her ear before I bounced off the shotgun. Even before I was knocked out, I think I knew. Now get on with it."

Childress turned to the others, his expression reflecting his discomfort at having to talk about Jackie Fairmont with Sutton in the room. He gestured at Seafront. "Our examination of Jackie Fairmont was superficial for several reasons. For one thing, there wasn't much time. For another, the morgue is locked up. We were forced to use a screened-off portion of the emergency room.

"Initially, Bill and I thought Jackie'd died because she'd been thrown through the car's windshield and impaled upon several jagged tree limbs. We were wrong. What we found was that some power or force destroyed Jackie's brain and ruptured her heart, literally ripping it in two before the car ever left the road. Neither Bill nor myself can tell you how this happened, but we both agree that the car wreck had nothing to do with the brain or heart trauma.

Both feet on the floor, buttocks against the autopsy table, Louellen Mae Harnes was trying to stand unassisted. Her movements were uncoordinated, erratic, and fitful like a robot with malfunctioning circuitry . . .

Childress glanced at Seafront. "Quite frankly, the results of this autopsy didn't surprise us, given the number of medical impossibilities we've witnessed over the past few days. But like I said, it was a superficial examination. There's no way either one of us are going back into the morgue with those bodies still there—"

"You mean the bodies from the cemetery are still there? In the morgue?" Larchmont asked, almost screaming.

Childress shrugged. "Where else would they be?"

Larchmont bolted over to the window, split the blinds, and looked out into the night. "Oh, dear God, the sun is down. They'll be stronger now."

"Who?" Seafront asked.

The small archeologist whirled away from the window, releasing the blinds with a clatter. "The evil. It's stronger when the sun sets. We have to leave now. This is not a safe place to be."

"Why?" Childress asked. "This is a hospital, for God's sake."

"There are three dead bodies in this hospital that are somehow related to the evil that's out there. Unless I miss my guess, that evil can command those bodies and send them after us.''

"Us?" Seafront asked. "You sure?"

Larchmont turned on the pathologist. "If a dead body can sit up in the morgue and tell you to leave it alone, then it just as easily can hunt you down and kill you with its own dead hands.''

"Leaving sounds good to me," Seafront said.

"If we're leaving," Henry Sutton questioned, "where are we going?"

"The McKenzie house," Larchmont said. "We'll be safer there. I'll explain why later.''

"What about my deputies out in the hall?"

"They're safe as long as they don't know what's happening. Remember last night when I told you that this evil feared being discovered more than anything else?" Sutton nodded. "Well, I think you were very close to discovering too much about them—it—and that's why they killed Officer Fairmont and tried to kill you. The same thing applies to everyone in this room. We know what's going on and that makes us dangerous to whatever is out there and, therefore, worth killing. The deputies in the hallway are ignorant and as such fairly safe. By the way, your deputies—Griffith and Bender— aren't. They know too much. They'll have to come with us.''

Sutton turned to Bender and Griffith. "You heard the man." Both deputies nodded grimly.

Earlier, when Larchmont had left the McKenzie house, he'd carried a brown paper bag with him and he had held on to it all through the meeting. Now he opened the bag. "There's one other thing I have to do before we leave.''

Louellen Mae Harnes began walking across the morgue's floor. Her body was stiff with rigor mortis, and her movements were restricted and spasmodic, like those of a tightly wound doll. She moved with her arms stretched out in front of her and her eyes were still open. Her face was a death mask of grimacing lips and teeth and her face was flushed with postmortem lividity. She'd died with her head slumped down against the steering wheel. At the moment her blood had stopped flowing, it had settled into the lower portion of her body and face like rocks in a stream. After the hemoglobin broke down, it had stained the blood vessel walls and surrounding tissue. Because her head had been bowed over, some of her blood had pooled and then stained distinct areas of her face: the center of her forehead, her cheeks, the tip of her nose and chin. Those areas were now a blotchy purple color. She looked like a painted Kewpie doll from hell.

Larchmont reached into the paper bag and pulled out several crude necklaces made from string. There was a cloth pouch attached to each string, and he held one of his necklaces up for everyone to see. "All this is is a piece of string, and attached to each is a small cloth folded into a pouch. Inside each pouch is a small quantity of salt. I made up a dozen or so of these this afternoon, and I want each of you to put one on and wear it from now on." Seafront stood up and took one of the necklaces.

"Certain natural elements possess the capacity to repel spells or curses," Larchmont explained. "Salt was readily available, so I made the charms from it." He turned and looked up at Sutton. "I'm still not sure how you survived the spell or force that was put on you this afternoon. Maybe you have some internal power I don't know about. Sometime soon I'd like to talk to you about your background or your family. Maybe we can figure out what saved you, what kept the force that was put on you from tearing your heart in two like your partner's."

Henry Sutton closed his eyes and sighed. After a moment he opened his eyes, reached into his shirt pocket, and pulled out the torn package of salt that had come from the restaurant.

He looked at the tiny packet of salt in his huge hand. So did the others as they got to their feet and shuffled past Larchmont and accepted without jokes or skepticism their crude amulets. Then only Sutton was left. He stared for a moment longer at the packet of salt, wishing the salt had been in Jackie Fairmont's pocket instead of his. Then he tossed the salt into a garbage can and accepted the talisman Martin Larchmont was holding out to him.

The nursing supervisor of the hospital's evening shift locked her car and started to cross the parking lot, heading toward the back of the hospital and a seldom-used door that opened onto a basement corridor. It was after seven. She was two hours late for work, but not worried. As head supervisor of nursing, she practically owned the hospital after the sun went down. She liked her power and being accountable to no one; that was what power was all about.

The director of nursing was good at her job and she ran the hospital like a tightly disciplined ship. Popular with the administration and directors, she was just as unpopular with the people under her. She was aware of the feelings her staff had for her, but didn't care. That also was what power was all about.

One of her favorite sayings was "Do as I say, not as I do," and she lived by it. Coming in late was a luxury she'd earned. She deserved it. Had her staff people tried it, they would have been fired on the spot. Had they protested or tried to point out that she came in late now and then, they would have been reminded of her favorite saying and still been fired.

Rather ordinary in spite of the power she wielded, Elizabeth Bates was a squat, busty, forty-six-year-old woman with a hairstyle that looked like a cross between an old-fashioned bun and a beehive. The hairstyle was the reason why she was late—the hairstyle and the plumber currently resting up on the hospital's third floor.

She had spent the past two hours sitting in a beauty salon over at the mall getting her hair teased, sprayed, tinted, and fluffed. Now she was ready to take the plumber's vital signs. Like many career nurses, Elizabeth Bates possessed a strong desire to care for birds with broken wings, but in her case, she carried it to excess. During the twenty years she'd been a nurse, she had met, nursed, married, and then been divorced from three of her patients. Their ailments had been different, but the reason for the divorce had always been the same. The men had recovered to the point where they no longer needed, wanted, or could tolerate the smothering kind of care she needed to give.

Elizabeth Bates refused to learn from her failures. Her second favorite saying was, "Introspection is like nitroglycerine. A little bit is good, too much will blow your head off." Thus, she was presently stalking a fifty-year-old patient on the third floor. The man was a plumber with gray hair and alarmingly blue eyes. He also had an inguinal hernia, strangulated hemorrhoids, and a prostate problem. The prospect of fluffing the plumber's pillow or checking his IV put Elizabeth Bates in a good mood. She had never been interested in a man with a prostate problem before, and she found the prospect to be an intriguing challenge. The amount of care this man would need after his discharge was positively overwhelming.

She unlocked the heavy metal door at the back of the hospital, entered a dimly lit basement hallway, and started down the corridor. As she passed the door to the morgue, soft scraping sounds caught her attention. She stopped abruptly, whirling around to put her ear against the door. It didn't take much of an imagination to figure out what she was listening to. Two of her staff were hanky-pankying in the morgue. The thought of two people rolling around all naked and sweaty on top of the morgue's dissecting table made her palms wet. The prospect of firing two naked people on the spot set her heart to pounding.

She tested the door. It was locked. As quietly as possible, she pulled out her master key. With slow patient movements she inserted the key, turned it, and stepped back, jerking the door open. "Gottcha!"

The dead body of Louellen Mae Harnes was standing in the doorway less than eighteen inches from Elizabeth Bates. Before Bates could come to grips with what she was looking at, the cadaver reached for her with stiff clawlike hands. Cold hands clamped down on the woman's skull, and the once pretty features of Elizabeth Bates crumpled and then collapsed like a plastic Halloween mask.

The corpse released its grip, and the dead body of Elizabeth Bates continued to remain standing in mute frozen testimony to the terrible power of her killer. The dead nurse's eyes were still open, and they reflected the shock and disbelief of what she'd seen when she had opened the door. No blood had been shed, but the woman's face gave quiet testimony to the massive injuries she had suffered. Her features were bent and distorted like a car that had collided with a cement wall.

Without a backward glance, the thing that had once been Louellen Mae Harnes moved past the still warm, still standing corpse of Elizabeth Bates and slowly lurched down the basement corridor to the door that opened out onto the parking lot.

Moving as one, nine individuals from the doctors' lounge walked swiftly across the brightly lit lobby and out onto the foggy parking lot. They walked close to one another for protection, with the men in uniform automatically taking up protective positions around the group. Sutton took point. Bender and Griffith covered the flanks. Still moving as one, they stopped first at Jenny McKenzie's old Mercedes Benz. While Jenny and Martin got into the front seat and Cable and Charlcie climbed into the back, the two physicians and three policemen headed off for a patrol car Sutton had requisitioned from a deputy still back in the hospital.

Jenny McKenzie was sitting behind the wheel, fishing through her purse trying to find her keys. Just to her right, Larchmont was nervously fingering the pouch of salt looped around his neck. Charlcie was chewing on a cuticle, and John Cable had just noticed an approaching shape, a shadow closing on his side of the car, when all hell broke loose.

Suddenly the body of Louellen Mae Harnes was standing beside the McKenzie car. Before Cable could shout, the car was filled with shattered glass and shrieks as the dead woman pushed her hands through the window and reached for Martin Larchmont. Frozen by the horror of it, Cable saw the hands grab Larchmont by his jacket. Then the apparition began to back away from the car in an effort to drag Larchmont out of the shattered window.

Without thinking, Cable threw himself over the front seat. He landed on top of the two arms trying to pull Martin out of the car. His legs dangled in the backseat and his upper body was the only thing that was keeping the creature from pulling the professor out of the window. Cable reached out and put his hands on the dash. He felt his neck get pressed against the side of the windshield as he felt his ribs begin to cave in as Larchmont's body was pulled tightly against his.

Pinned against the broken window, unable to breathe, Cable managed to reach out with one hand. He grabbed at the finger of one of the hands clutching Larchmont's jacket, bending it back until the stiff finger cracked. Yet the creature outside of the car still held on.

Then, over the screams of the women, Cable heard the scream of spinning tires. An instant later he felt a gust of wind whip around his back as another car passed by them at high speed. Suddenly the hands gripping Larchmont were gone and Cable was falling down between the seat and the door. His shoulder hit the door handle and the door swung open. He crashed down on the pavement. He rolled, came up on his hands and knees, and then looked around.

The lights from the McKenzie car brought the scene into sharp focus. Sutton must have seen the woman attack the Mercedes Benz. He had accelerated his own patrol car and driven it close enough to Jenny's car to hit the attacking apparition. The collision had knocked the woman a good fifty feet away. Now she lay in a crumpled heap, her body dramatically highlighted by the headlights from Jenny McKenzie's car and the one remaining headlight from Sutton's patrol car. As Cable slowly got to his feet, he heard car doors being opened and felt relief when the doctors and deputies converged on him and the others.

He was fine, Martin Larchmont was fine, and everyone started to split up and return to their vehicles. Then Jenny McKenzie screamed. Cable looked into the car. Jenny was still behind the wheel, her eyes fixed straight ahead. He glanced out at the scene captured by the Mercedes' headlights and came close to screaming himself.

The broken and battered body of Louellen Mae Harnes was beginning to move again. It had flopped over on its stomach and was getting up on its hands and knees. It attained a crouching position when Sutton's patrol car bolted into action. Cable knew what was coming next, and he watched intently, almost in awe, as the patrol car hurtled across the parking lot toward the nearly standing cadaver.

The car bore down on the wavering body like a giant locomotive. It appalled Sutton that the expression on the dead woman's face never changed. She glared and hissed at the oncoming car as if it were nothing more than an insect.

The patrol car hit the body at better than fifty miles an hour. The impact flipped the body high into the air and then it crashed down onto the pavement, rolling over several times like a rag doll in a windstorm. Sutton whirled his car around in a slow turn and stopped when the light from his car's one headlight came to rest on the battered woman's body.

For a long moment neither the body nor the patrol car moved. But then one of Louellen Mae Harnes's fingers twitched. A leg jerked spasmodically, and then the woman began to rise again.

Henry Sutton dropped the transmission into drive, shaking his head as he took his foot off the brake. "Die, god dammit!" He stepped down on the gas again.

Cable and the others watched as the patrol car shot forward and the tires rolled over the moving corpse with audible thumps. An instant later everyone grimaced when they heard the sounds of the patrol car being slammed into reverse. Again came the sick thumping sounds as the cruiser backed over the body. Still not finished, Sutton dropped the transmission into drive and started forward once again for another run over the dead woman.

Cable spun away from the McKenzie car and began throwing up. He was not alone. Moments later the tall deputy with wiry hair and an emergency room trauma specialist joined him.

Chapter
Ninteen

After everyone had arrived at the McKenzie home, Cable and Charlcie were given a strange assignment by Martin Larchmont. They were now in the process of following his instructions to the letter. Cable had a large bottle of distilled water in one hand and a paper sack filled with onions in the other. Charlcie was carrying a sack of salt and some empty drinking glasses.

Their task was to place a glass filled with distilled water and salt in front of each outside exit door in the home. Each glass was then sealed on top with a large white onion. When they finished with the doors, they set out to do the windows in the home, both on the top and bottom floors. The windows looked a little strange with water glasses sitting in the middle of the sills topped with onions, but after all that had happened, they were not about to question Larchmont's instructions.

They went from window to window in silence. Earlier that day they had kissed in the greenhouse, talking about the possibility of a future together. Now all that seemed as if it had happened a thousand years ago. Though their feelings for each other were still the same, it was night

Patrick Whalen

out. The house was surrounded by blackness and because of what had happened in the parking lot, the
horrors the night held had suddenly become very real.

When they finished, they returned to the quiet crowded
living room. Most of the people there acknowledged
their return with a look or a nod.

Only Henry Sutton didn't seem to see them. Sutton was
sitting off by himself in a large wing-backed chair, speaking to no one, his eyes fixed on the fire in the fireplace.
He had finally seen the almost incomprehensible horror he
was up against, and it had come in the form of a walking
cadaver that had attacked the McKenzie car. When he
killed it, then killed it again, he'd felt some relief, but it
wasn't enough. Crushing the corpse had not diminished
his desire for total vengeance. Jackie Fairmont was dead,
and there would be hell to pay. Killing the cadaver had felt
good, but the cadaver was only a symbol. He wanted the
energy force, the power that had brought that corpse to
life and made it walk into the parking lot. Only when that
power was destroyed would he be satisfied. Henry Sutton
was a man possessed. Someone—something—had killed
the woman he loved. They—it—would pay. They would
die as painfully as Jackie had died. It was no idle threat,
no vacant promise. Whatever was behind this madness
and horror would perish, even if it cost him his own life.

At that moment Martin Larchmont stood up to address the group, and with considerable effort Henry
Sutton set aside his anger and hate and grief so he could
focus on what Larchmont had to say.

Cold and uncomfortable, Johnny Joe Sloams sat in his
pickup parked in a grove of trees deep inside the Horrcove
Cemetery, trying to shove the remnants of a broken
cork into the open neck of a wine bottle. The wine was
nearly gone and his task was requiring monumental concentration. Finally, after dropping the cork twice and
the bottle once, Sloams ended his problem by finishing
off the wine and throwing the bottle out the window.

222

Johnny Joe Sloams was drunk and in a foul mood. The day had gone badly for him. It had probably been the worst day of his life. After calling the police department to report what he had seen in the cemetery, he had perched on the phone from eight until noon, waiting for the call that would confirm his reward. No call had come. At twelve-thirty Sloams began calling the police department. At first he placed his calls every hour on the hour, but later on, after he'd drank some wine, he was calling the police department every fifteen minutes. He finally stopped calling at six o'clock in the evening when an angry desk sergeant threatened to send out some deputies to remove Sloams's phone and tongue.

Seething with anger, worried about his reward, Sloams went to work on another bottle of wine. By mid-evening he'd finally made up his mind to go back out to the cemetery to look for the boy himself. Sloams's motivation was pure greed. He didn't give a damn about the missing kid. What he cared about was the reward. That was more money than he'd ever seen in his entire life. The thought of how many hookers and wine bottles he could buy with that amount of money fueled his courage more than the wine.

The Horrcove mortuary was less than a quarter of a mile from Sloams's pickup. The lights were off in the old mansion, but the green neon sign on the front of the building glowed dimly in the fog. The sign gave Sloams something to aim for as he began walking unsteadily toward the funeral home with the precise, yet exaggerated, movements of a drunk. His progress was slow, the grave markers irksome, and he took to talking to himself as he maneuvered his way around the tombstones in a giddy stumbling shuffle.

"That's it, J. J., just shuffle to your left, now to the right. Good for you, J. J., missed that nasty old tombstone.

"Easy does it. Just take it slow and easy. We'll just move on up to that old house, have a lookee-see, maybe spot the kid, then roll on down to the sheriff and get us our money. Then it's party city.

"Fuckin' sheriff. Too fuckin' good to return old J. J.'s phone call. Now J. J.'ll show his ass. J. J.'ll find the kid. Won't rescue him, but J. J.'ll find him, then the sheriff'll have to believe old J. J. and cough up the reward and do all those other fuckin' things that sheriffs do—"

When Sloams first heard the sounds, he thought it odd that someone would be beating a rug in the middle of the night in the middle of the cemetery. The noises came to his ears in a deep pattern that grew closer and louder, with each double beat. Whup-whup . . . whup-whup . . . Whup-Whup . . . WHUP-WHUP.

The sounds suddenly grew loud and close. They seemed to be coming out of the air just above his head. He threw himself onto the thick wet grass, landing hard on his stomach, and wrapped his arms over his head for protection as the heavy winds beat down on him in the ever consistent double beating pattern of giant wings. It—something—seemed to hover over him forever.

Then, with agonizing slowness, the winds churning up the grass all around him died away, and as the storm passed, so did the terrible whuping sounds.

Cautiously Sloams got to his hands and knees and looked around, trying to see what could have caused the noise and wind. His eyes instantly locked onto a huge flapping-flying shadow nightmarishly outlined by the green neon mortuary sign. His fantasies about wine, hookers, and women died as his brain registered what his eyes had just seen. Instantly he was up and running toward the pickup as fast as his tiptoed gait would allow, running as if he were being pursued by a winged gargoyle from hell. Which, in fact, he was.

A welcomed silence surrounded him by the time he arrived back at his pickup. It was only after he started the engine that he again heard the double whuping sounds. Then something big flew over the roof of his truck. Horrified and suddenly sober, Sloams literally bent the gear shift lever out of shape in his effort to get the truck into gear. He popped the clutch, pushing the gas pedal to the floor. Divots of grass spurted out from behind spinning tires as the truck shot out of the grove of trees and onto the narrow asphalt road. He hit the light switch, and bright arcs of light flared out in front of the truck. The high beams illuminated the road ahead of him and also illuminated an oncoming winged creature.

Staring out the windshield, Sloams gasped at the sight of a huge man-shaped apparition flying straight at him, propelled onward by its enormous batlike wings. Then it was on him, filling his windshield. The last thing his eyes saw before he threw himself down on the seat was the sight of giant bony talons tearing into his truck's roof.

Sprawled down in the cab, Sloams gripped the seat of his out-of-control pickup while some monstrous shape ripped the entire roof off his truck and carried it away into the night. The truck lurched off the road and nosed down a small incline. Halfway down the hill the pickup shuddered. Then, with agonizing slowness, it began to tip over.

Rolling over one complete time, the truck came to rest on its wheels. Still in the cab, Sloams was unhurt. He'd ridden out the slow rollover in a completely relaxed fashion as only babies and drunks can do in an accident. Silence and fog settled over the pickup. The engine had shut itself off, and only the metallic pings from the overheated engine pockmarked the stillness.

Sloams popped up into a sitting position like a jack-in-the-box clown. Oddly, he wasn't worried about the flying creature. He had already decided the winged apparition was a portent of an oncoming case of delirium tremens. He did a quick check of his pickup, noticed it was now a convertible, and decided that had happened during the rollover.

He tried to start the motor. Nothing. He pulled on the door handle. Nothing. He threw his body hard against the door. It swung open easily and Sloams just kept on going. He did an awkward loose-limbed pratfall out of

the pickup, hit the ground, and found himself lying on
his back in the wet grass looking up at a black sky.

As he lay there, arms outstretched, Sloams began
giggling over his fall from the truck. A heartbeat later
the laughter froze in his throat when he heard a growing
crescendo of beating wings, wings so large they sounded
like huge flags flapping in the wind.

Whup-Whup. Whup-Whup.

Oh, God, he thought, this is going to be bad. That
thing had talons longer than yardsticks.

Whup-Whup. Whup-Whup.

Oh, God, he thought, this is going to hurt. Then he
cursed himself for ducking down when the winged beast
attacked the truck. If only he'd . . . Whup-Whup . . .
just kept sitting up . . . Whup-Whup . . . the thing
would've taken his head along with the roof . . . Whup-
Whup . . . that would've been so much simpler . . .
Whup-Whup . . . so much faster . . . WHUP-WHUP
. . . WHUP-WHUP.

He could see it now as it hovered over him, its undu-
lating wings beating the air, causing the grass to ripple
and churn as if there were a giant helicopter overhead.
The creature began to descend, and as it did, it focused
its yellow serpentlike eyes on him as if he were a hunk
of raw meat. In a moment of terrifying insight Sloams
knew that was exactly what he was.

Martin Larchmont was sitting on the arm of the love
seat next to Jenny McKenzie trying to answer the questions the others in the McKenzie living room had for
him.

"Then who or what killed the woman in the cemetery?" William Seafront asked.

Larchmont angled his head, "Which one? The prostitute or the woman who sat up in the morgue and later
attacked me?"

"The one who sat up and walked across the parking
lot."

Larchmont gestured at Bender and Griffith. "Earlier, one of you mentioned finding some white disks near the dead woman's car. Those disks in combination with the expression on her face and her injuries lead me to believe she was killed by a demon we have no name for. It was the spawn of another demon named Garmath, which frightened its victims to death before taking their blood. Legend has it that Garmath was part woman, part eel, with dragonlike scales." At the mention of scales, Griffith and Bender exchanged glances, both remembering the poker-chip-shaped objects they had found. "I think one of you thought those disks might have been fish scales. Right?" Griffith nodded sheepishly. "I suggest," Larchmont continued, "that they might have been dragon scales if the Kurdistan legend has any substance."

"Why did you have Charlcie and me put the water, salt, and onions throughout the house?" John Cable asked.

"I didn't hear the question?" one of the deputies asked.

"I wanted to know why Martin had Charlcie and me put water and onions and salt in front of all the doors and windows." Cable turned toward Larchmont for the answer.

"In my studies I've come across references to substances that when properly utilized would repel or keep at bay demon-creatures. In China, for example, black sand and rice kernels are used as a barrier to keep evil from entering one's home. In the Philippines hemp rope dipped in the blood of a freshly killed lamb is sometimes strung across doors and windows to keep the unspeakable ones out. Many nomadic tribes in Iran and Kurdistan used well water, salt, and onions for the same purpose. This particular combination made an impression on me because I'd studied some Etruscan tablets in Italy some years back that prescribed the exact same formula used in Kurdistan, though the Etruscans beefed up the water, onions, and salt barrier with the leaves and vines from poisonous plants such as oleanders, wysteria vines, hemlock leaves, and the like.''

Cable nodded to himself. Earlier in the day he had seen several bundles of branches sitting out on the front porch. "I saw some branches out on the front porch earlier today. Your handiwork?''

Larchmont nodded. "Wysteria vines. I believe in covering all the bases.''

"And pray tell, where did you get your wysteria vines?'' Jenny McKenzie asked coldly.

Larchmont continued to look at Cable. "As I was saying, the Etruscans believed—''

"Did you cut up my prizewinning thirty-one-year-old espaliered wysteria?'' Jenny asked as if she were talking to Jack the Ripper.

Larchmont gave Cable a "what have you done" look. "The branches will grow back.''

"In another thirty years,'' Jenny groused.

The couple's bantering over the vines lessened the terrible tension in the room. In spite of his grief even Henry Sutton smiled at the exchange.

"Really, Martin, any poisonous plant would have done. The park is full of oleanders. Why didn't you go and cut them down?''

"I didn't think of it,'' Larchmont said. He was about to say something else when Mark Childress interrupted by walking up to the couple.

"I think it's time I checked your pulse again.''

Larchmont shook his head. "I'm tired of having my pulse taken. I'm tired of having my blood pressure checked. I'm also tired of saying I'm fine. I've got a sore neck and some scratches on my chest, but that's it. There're no pains in my chest, my arm's not numb, my breathing's regular, and I'm okay.'' Larchmont smiled at the young doctor. "But if I do feel a heart attack coming on, you'll be the first to know. Thanks for your concern.'' Childress nodded and started toward his seat.

Larchmont glanced over at Cable. "Speaking of *thank-*

yous, I think it's time I thanked you for the way you helped me in the car tonight. If you hadn't been there, that creature would have pulled me out the window, and Lord knows what would have happened then."

Cable felt himself redden. Charlcie squeezed his hand tightly. He squirmed uncomfortably on the davenport and wished Larchmont would change the subject.

Henry Sutton did. "These repelling agents . . . the salt, the water, the vines . . . can they be used to harm these creatures?"

Larchmont shook his head. "No more than shark repellents would hurt sharks."

Sutton's eyes glittered with hate. "What would?"

"I don't know," Larchmont admitted, looking down at the rug.

William Seafront sat up in his chair. "Dear Christ, if you don't know, who does?"

"No one," Martin Larchmont said.

"What about a priest?" Seafront asked. "What if we got a priest to do an exorcism?" The doctor's eyes darted to the others in the room, seeking support. "Maybe crucifixes or holy water? Maybe we could throw holy water on them, that would work, wouldn't it?"

Larchmont sighed. "We're not up against vampires, Doctor. The creatures we're dealing with are evil in and of themselves. They're not part of the Good God Evil Satan dual system as we know it in western culture. If they were, perhaps exorcism would be effective, but they're not. These creatures we're faced with would laugh at the rites of exorcism and use crucifixes to pick their teeth."

"If that's the case, then what can we do?" Henry Sutton asked.

Larchmont shrugged with his hands. It was a gesture no one in the room liked. "Fire would work. So would water, but both elements pose a delivery problem since we're not sure where the creatures are at this moment."

"What do you mean?" Sutton snarled. "At the hospital I told you about the brothers who run that mortuary; there's no way those bastards on the hill couldn't be involved in this. Those creatures are with them, up on that hill someplace in their mansion."

"I agree with you, Henry," Larchmont said. "I think the creatures have been kept all these years in the Horrcove brothers' mortuary. However, if we attack the mortuary with torches, gasoline, water, or what-have-you, it would be an open act of suicide on our part. The creatures are probably interred in an underground vault below the mortuary. If we went up there—like you would like to do—it would take time to find them, and while we were looking, we would be right in the center of the Horrcove brothers' powers. You see, physical distance from these creatures and the brothers gives us some protection. Not much, but some, and what you're proposing is to walk right into their den, where their powers are the strongest. If we did, we wouldn't stand a chance."

Sutton gave Larchmont a skeptical look as the older man continued. "Sorry to bring this up, Henry, but what you encountered this afternoon just before the car wreck happened several miles from the cemetery, and that would be nothing compared to what would happen to us if we were up on the hill and actually in the mortuary. With the power of their minds and a snap of their fingers, the Horrcove brothers could vaporize us if we were close to them."

Larchmont looked at the others in the room. "I know the answers I'm giving you aren't satisfying, but at least they're honest responses. You have to remember that no one has really gone into combat before with these creatures and the brothers and lived to tell about it."

"Some people in Ravina did a hundred years ago," Henry Sutton said, "and they came out on top."

Larchmont shook his head. "They lucked out. Like I said last night, the mob launched their attack during the creatures' final renewal ritual. The evil was distracted, physically weak. Had the townspeople come up the hill a few minutes earlier or later, they never would have made it to the hill. But in any case they certainly didn't come out on top. If you remember from last night, most of them were dead within two years of the attack. Still, you got to give 'em credit. Their timing was computer perfect." Larchmont paused and smiled slightly. "The comment about computer-perfect timing is as good a way as any to introduce what I think may be our one hope—"

Suddenly the entire house was enveloped in bellowing and crashing sounds as if giant trees were falling against the roof. At the same instant the entire living room floor canted sideways. Trays, coffee cups, and vases skittered off the coffee tables and end tables. Pictures on one wall fell away, hit the floor, then slid across the rug and crashed into another wall. The whole house began rocking back and forth on its foundations. Lamps fell from tables. A chair bounced into one wall.

Mark Childress jumped to his feet. "Earthquake!" he screamed, a fraction of a second before a new tremor hurled him onto his hands and knees.

Charlcie sucked in her breath and grabbed Cable as the roar continued, this time echoing up from below them. The entire house seemed to sway in a violent rolling motion. Porcelain plates flew off the fireplace mantel, adding to the calamity of sounds. A giant brass lamp fell on the floor, an étagère filled with Waterford crystal pitched over in the dining room. Electrical outlets along one wall exploded in showers of sparks, then a giant crack as wide as a man's fist shot up one wall, while plaster rained down from the ceiling like snow. The lights throughout the house flickered, then went dark.

Cable pulled Charlcie's head to his chest and held her tightly, expecting at any moment to feel the floor give way beneath them.

The fire in the fireplace cast dancing shadows around the room, illuminating the destruction, and the terror.

Suddenly the violent tremors and shaking stopped. Everything fell silent. No one said a word. No one breathed.

Then, as though coming from very far away, a new sound could be heard, a whistling sound. Faint yet distinct, it continued to grow, to intensify, from a whistle to a rush, from a rush to a scream, from a scream to a roar, and then a giant tumultuous wind slammed into the house like a hurricane from hell. Without warning, the fire in the fireplace disappeared. The heat, energy, and flames were sucked up the chimney and a curtain of blackness pounded down on the people in the living room.

All was quiet, cold, and dark as a new silence hit the house with the same intensity as the earlier storms. Then, as if by magic, the fire relit itself with a loud whoosh. A heartbeat later the house lights flickered back on.

Cable could see both the sheriff and his deputies were on their feet with their weapons drawn. In that moment Cable noticed Sutton's weapon matched its owner: it was huge with a ribbed barrel at least eight inches long.

The short deputy named Bender called out, "You want me to go outside and look around?"

"You'll be dead before you get off the front porch," Larchmont said. The deputy gave Larchmont a skeptical look and glanced at Sutton. Larchmont shook his head. "Don't let him go, Henry. Those weren't earthquakes. The brothers and the creature-demons were trying to get to us. I'm telling you, if you let your man walk out the door, you'll never see him again . . . at least not alive."

Sutton shook his head and then he and his deputies holstered their pistols. Larchmont turned toward Cable. "Looks like the salt and water worked. But I think we should probably take the same precaution at the fireplace."

Cable didn't have to be asked twice. He released Charlcie's hand and went into the kitchen where he loaded himself down with a gallon jug of water, a bag of salt, and a sack of onions. Juggling his load with both hands, he reentered the hallway and started down the passageway. He was nearly to the living room when the phone in the hallway began ringing. He stopped and looked at the phone sitting on the hallway desk. There was something odd about the ringing sounds. The tones were different, lower than they should have been, and the interlude between the rings was too short. He dismissed his perception as a by-product of tension and began shifting his bundles so he could answer the phone. The deputy who had volunteered to go outside materialized in front of him. Deputy Bender's tone was brisk and pleasant. "I'll get it. It's probably for the sheriff anyway."

He smiled at Cable and reached for the phone. The smile was still on his face as he picked up the receiver and lifted it up.

Just as the receiver touched the deputy's left ear, Martin Larchmont screamed out from the living room. "Nooo! Don't touch the phone!"

"Hello," the deputy said.

Cable was standing less than three feet from the deputy and saw it all. He saw every excruciating detail as if it had been splayed out on a movie screen in slow motion.

The deputy never had a chance to react to Larchmont's order. The instant he said hello, his eyes began to bulge out as if compressed air were being pumped into his brain. A microsecond later twin fountains of frothy blood burst out of the man's nostrils, and a third torrent of blood spurted out of his right ear with so much force that the stream arched across the hallway and splattered onto the wallpaper.

Cable dropped everything and threw himself at the bloody sagging deputy. With one hand he tried to support Bender. With the other he tried to knock the telephone receiver from the man's frozen grip. The weight of the deputy surprised him, catching him off guard. They crashed into one wall and back against the desk.

Cable had only one thing in mind: to break the man's grip on the phone. The deputy was still holding it tightly against his ear. Without thinking, Cable grabbed the phone. When he did, he screamed. It was like grabbing burning steel. It was so hot it had burned itself into the deputy's hand, and now it was searing itself into his hand. Screaming, Cable gripped the receiver, tearing it free of the deputy's grip along with charred hunks of flesh from the palm of the comatose man.

He alone now held the phone, and Cable never wanted to drop anything more in his life. But he couldn't. A terrible laserlike energy was radiating out from the receiver into his hand and body. It was melded to his hand and burning deeper into his flesh.

Put the receiver back in the cradle, he thought dimly. That was the only way to shut off the energy—the hideous power coming out of the phone. He dropped the deputy and staggered toward the desk, his body rigid with charges of electricity and pain. Enduring more agony than he'd ever known in his life, Cable crashed down on his knees in front of the desk, then with sickening slowness he reached out and put the phone onto its cradle. Immediately the pain started to diminish and the lightning bolts ripping through his body stopped. He knelt there for a moment, watching as the receiver began to sink into the soft melting plastic of the cradle. Gritting his teeth, he finally tore his hand free from the receiver. In shock, almost oblivious to the pain, he continued to watch the phone distort and change shape while it melted into a pool of black shapeless plastic.

A heartbeat later John Cable collapsed to the floor beside the deputy. He was tired, in pain, and the blackness rapidly enveloping him was welcomed.

Chapter
Twenty

Cable surfaced from his drug-induced sleep, and without moving or opening his eyes tried to figure out where he was. He knew he was in a bed, naked, his body wrapped in crisp starched sheets. He also knew he wasn't in his room. His seldom-used room smelled of dust and mothballs. This room held multiple scents: flowers, soap, perfume; all pleasant, all female, all belonging to Charlcie McKenzie.

He sensed she was close, then his hearing confirmed it as she began humming "Greensleeves" so low, so faintly, that the ancient folk melody came to him as something less than a whisper. Her voice was soft and melodic and it seemed out of place in the surrealistic nightmare that had been his life over the past days. God, how many days had it been since he'd come into this town, said good-bye to a pretty prostitute in a restaurant, and placed a desperate phone call to Martin Larchmont?

The thought of a phone call kicked off other memories: a memory of a telephone in the McKenzie hallway; a memory of a bloody deputy collapsing to the floor. He stirred and opened his eyes, trying to lift his injured hand up into the shaft of light that broke in from the hallway through a partially opened door. Her hands, Charlcie's hands, pushed his arm back to his side. Her palms were damp. She broke the silence. "The doctors said you weren't supposed to move that hand around."

He heard himself speak, his voice sounding as if his throat were full of gravel. "Why do I feel like I'm dead?"

"Childress gave you a shot, said it would help you sleep and ease the pain."

"It worked. My hand feels fine."

"You may not believe this, but when Childress and Seafront first looked at you, your hand had been burned down to the bone. Then Martin put some salt and water on it. Childress freaked out, screamed that was the worst thing he could've done for you, but it was like a miracle. Your hand started healing. I couldn't see what was going on because everybody else was crowded around you, but the doctors were shocked. They said the charred flesh in your hand just sort of changed, healed in a matter of seconds. You should've seen their faces. Childress wrapped it anyway. He felt there was no reason to take chances with infection."

More of the horror that had happened earlier was coming back to Cable. "How's the deputy?" Charlcie didn't speak. Her silence confirmed what Cable suspected just before he passed out in the hallway. He tried to sit up.

Her voice was firm. "No, you don't." She held him in bed by laying her head and shoulders on his chest. Her gentle insistence took away his desire to move. "You're not supposed to move until morning and that's the way it's going to be. Doctors' orders."

He began stroking her hair with his good hand. "Look, I'm okay and I've got to get back to the meeting. I need to hear what Martin has to say."

She lifted her head off his chest and looked at him. "What for? Everyone's in bed."

"Bed?"

"John, it's three o'clock in the morning. You've been asleep for over five and a half hours."

He moaned. "I couldn't have been out that long."

"But you were, and now everyone's asleep. I doubt if you'll get a rerun from anybody but me, so you best stay in bed."

There was a hint of a challenge in her words. He let it pass. "What happened after I passed out?"

"Lots." Charlcie shook her head in disbelief. "The house was attacked two more times. We never saw anything, but the dishes were shattered, the TV sets, and the radios exploded, and at one point something tried to kick in the front door. It cracked the door, but didn't get all the way in. God, you could hear things clumping around out on the porch and in the yard, but all we could see were shadows with horrible grotesque shapes through the curtains. Then after that, there were explosions that sounded like they came from the center of town. We couldn't tell what was going on, but later we could hear fire engines heading toward the downtown area. Martin seemed to think that when whatever was out there couldn't get to us, it attacked other people or maybe some churches. Ever since the explosions, we haven't heard the bell from the Presbyterian church.

"This is all so crazy and terrifying. It's like the world outside this house doesn't exist anymore. We're trapped here. We can't get out. Childress can't get to his family. Seafront can't get to his, and nobody can use the phone to check on their families—though Martin said he thought they'd be all right since the creatures only attack those who have knowledge about them."

Recounting the night's horrors was beginning to take a toll on Charlcie. Her voice had grown dusky and Cable could feel her tension. He laced his fingers through her hair and pulled her head down to his chest. When she finally composed herself and began to speak again, he could feel her mouth moving against his chest, her breath on his skin. The sensation was arousing. "I'm sort of rambling. Maybe I'd better back up and start with what happened after you collapsed. Childress and Seafront examined the deputy. They said he was dead before he hit the floor. Most of us thought you were dead, too." She tapped gently on his chest with her forefinger. "Don't you ever do that to me again, John Cable. I just found you. I almost died when I thought I'd lost you." She stopped tapping and wrapped her arms around him. Cable's ribs were bruised from the fall in the hallway, and he winced under the pressure of her embrace. "Am I hurting you?"

"No," Cable said, stifling a gasp.

"You wouldn't know this, but while Childress was examining you, you groaned, and we knew you were alive. Martin and I started cheering and crying at the same time. There we were, hopping around, holding each other, and they hadn't even moved the body of the poor deputy yet. After you started coming around, Martin told the doctors to back away and that's when he put the salt and water in your hand. Like I said, your flesh grew back right in front of everyone. Those doctors were speechless.

"After that, Sutton picked you up all by himself, carried you upstairs, and put you here in my room. Childress gave you a shot for the pain and to make you sleep, which was a little odd since you were already asleep. I tried to stay with you, but the doctors said it wasn't necessary. Mother and Martin talked me into going back into the living room so I could hear what was going on and fill you in later, like I am now. Fire away. Any questions?"

An endless series of questions flashed through Cable's mind. Finally he settled for the one most obvious. "What did Martin say about the Horrcove brothers' role in all of this?"

"Martin thinks that the Horrcove Brothers are the

sons of one of the followers who helped bring the demons over from Kurdistan and now they're all that's left of that cult. He thinks their mother and father were part of that group that attempted to take over Dove Harbor where they first landed. They probably met with unexpected resistance and in the end destroyed the town to cover up whatever they'd done to the townspeople. Then they moved on and sent out followers to check out other suitable locations. Those followers eventually found Ravina. They purchased the cemetery and the funeral parlor, knowing it would provide not only a good hiding place for their gods, but it would also provide an ongoing source of revenue. After that they brought the creature-demons to Ravina in sheepherder wagons. After arriving, the followers tried to resurrect their gods and that was aborted when the townspeople attacked and lynched what they thought were gypsies."

Cable stroked Charlcie's hair. "And the brothers?"

"Martin suspects they were born right around the time the cult arrived in Ravina."

Cable gasped. Charlcie kept her head on his chest and continued. "I know—I know. That would make them over a hundred years old. But that didn't seem strange to Martin. He said men from some of those old Kurdistani tribes sometimes lived until they were a hundred and thirty. Martin believes the brothers were raised by the followers to one day assume the role of keepers or caretakers for their demon gods. He believes the Horrcove brothers' legacy is composed of three parts: they protect and safeguard the dormant demons, decide when the time is right for the creatures to return to life, and assist with the Resurrection rituals. They're the ones who kidnapped the two boys, and when Sutton said he'd come back with a search warrant, they tried to kill Sutton so he couldn't search their mortuary and maybe find the dormant creatures."

Cable sighed. "What did Martin say about their powers? They killed Jackie Fairmont when they were miles away from her . . . and tonight all that deputy did was answer the phone. How could they do that?''

''Martin said many of the followers of the Yezidi religion had telekinetic powers. You know, the ability to move objects with mental energy. He believes the Horrcove brothers have taken this ability and developed it to the point where they can not only move objects but can channel their mental energy through the air or through a phone wire like a high-powered bullet. Martin thinks that because the brothers are twins, they can meld their minds and the power they can produce between the two of them is beyond our comprehension. Only a few things can deflect this power . . . salt, water, onions.''

She paused, took a deep breath, and let it out slowly. ''They can even use this power on the dead. That's what made the dead woman sit up and walk and attack the car tonight. He said the dead they command might as well be alive because they'll serve whatever purposes the brothers see as necessary.'' She shuddered, and the shudder turned into quiet sobs.

Cable held her tightly with both arms, and he could feel her tears as they settled between her cheek and his chest. Minutes passed, and when he thought she was able, he spoke. ''Charlcie, just before the first attack, Martin mentioned something about a computer.'' Even as he talked, he could feel her head nodding again on his chest.

''It all sounded very strange to me,'' she said quietly, ''probably because I don't know anything about computers. Martin said he'd been collecting information on these creatures and their religion ever since Dad was killed, and that was over twenty-five years ago. He described it as a stockpile of ''speculative disjointed data'' and added that a lot of the information was basically hearsay, consisting of myths and stories he'd collected from various villages in Kurdistan. I guess it's all historic in nature, badly fragmented, and taken from numerous sources, some of which are unreliable. Some of the data came from the observations made by other archeologists, other information came from the missionaries who worked with the Yezidi followers during that century. I guess even Mother contributed some of the things he has on file because of her involvement and study of Ravina. Anyway, he said he had a vast storeroom—quite literally—a vault of information—that he didn't know what to do with.''

Cable was thunderstruck by the vast amount of undetected energy his friend had invested in the subject matter, much of it done under his nose and without his knowledge. ''God, the man never ceases to amaze me.''

''I agree. But there's more. Did you know that this storehouse of information was one of the reasons why he came out of retirement and started teaching part-time at UCLA? One of the fringe benefits the regents offered when they recruited him was the ongoing access to one of the world's most sophisticated computers, which they have on campus. For the past seven or so years he's been feeding the data he's accumulated into that computer. Seems this computer is quite a machine. It has all sorts of safeguards that allow his particular program to have maximum privacy from other people who use the machine, and its capable of speculative programming. In other words, he can feed it data, then ask it questions, and it will go so far as to surmise an answer. Ever heard of such a machine?''

Cable had. ''Has to be a Telephase Mark IV.''

''That's the name he called it.''

''It's quite a machine, Charlcie. We have one at UBC. I used to feed it random bits of information about some of the Indian digs I'd been working on—you know, like the location of the dig, the manner in which the culture had buried bodies, the chemical composition of pottery shards, how close they were to the seacoast. In return the computer kicked back a kind of reflective analysis as to what kind of culture we were dealing with and even went on to describe the size of the tribe we were studying. Along with their diet, where they hunted, what they hunted, whether or not they were migratory, who they fought with, how they felt about nature, what kind of gods they worshipped. To top it all off, if you don't want an answer printed out for you, it will give you a verbal analysis."

It was a relief not to be talking about the demons and the Horrcove brothers, and Charlcie was intrigued. "You mean it talks?"

Cable felt himself smile. "It has a dual response capability. It can print out answers or it can give you verbal responses. It's not that unusual in today's computers."

"Maybe that's what he meant when he said he'd let the computer deal with the demons," she mused.

"You lost me."

"Martin said his programming had two aspects. One involved the entrance of facts and information into the computer about the Yezidi culture and the Iblis religion. The other part of his programming was how to go about destroying the demon-gods he'd described to the computer. It's all down there in Los Angeles, John: the information on their religion and their creature-gods and the information on how to destroy them."

"Which doesn't do us a bit of good up here."

A spark of excitement came into Charlcie's voice. "Martin's leaving tomorrow for Los Angeles. The sheriff's driving him down after the sun comes up. They hope to get back before the sun sets."

"With what?" Cable asked bitterly. "All they'll have is a computer program. What are they going to do? Throw the tapes at the mortuary?"

"No. It was sort of confusing to me, but apparently there's a compatible computer at the hospital where Colonel Seafront works."

A surge of excitement welled up in Cable as he began to see what Martin Larchmont was up to. "That's right. Seafront's stationed out at Vandenberg Air Force Base. They have some of the most sophisticated computers in the world out there."

Growing weary of rehashing the details of the earlier meeting, Charlcie cut Cable off. "That's what Martin and the colonel said. The plan is for Martin to get his program from the computer at UCLA. Then the sheriff will drive Martin from Los Angeles up to the hospital on the air force base. While the colonel is feeding Martin's program into his computer, Martin and the sheriff'll drive up to the cemetery. At a designated time Seafront will activate his computer and—"

"Wait," Cable said. "I don't understand. The hospital must be a good twenty-five miles from here. What kind of effect would a computer have that far from the cemetery?"

"It's kind of complicated, but while he's at the college, Martin's going to pick up some sort of portable minicomputer with a power pack and a speaker system and a . . . a receiver. The way I think it works is that the air force computer will broadcast the program Martin has put together. The broadcast will be caught by the briefcase computer receiver system he'll have with him at the cemetery."

Cable cut in. He was exhausted and as anxious as Charlcie to end the discussion. "And then this minireceiver will broadcast the spells or chants that Martin's program thinks will destroy the creatures."

Charlcie lifted her head from Cable's chest and moved so she could look at him. In the room's dim light the muted illumination highlighted the classic terrain of her face. She was smiling and Cable didn't like what he was going to say next. "It won't work, Charlcie. It's got too many weak links. Christ, look what those brothers did to the deputy over a phone." He pulled her head back to his chest. "Doesn't he see the flaws in his plan?"

"He knows," Charlcie said softly. "He said it might not work. He just hopes the strength of the computer outlasts the strength of the demons and the brothers."

"What do the others think of his plan?"

"They're like you and me. They're going along with it because it's all we have. Childress is using tomorrow to get his wife and kids out of town; same with Seafront."

"Do you think the doctors'll come back tomorrow night?" Cable asked.

"I don't know. I wouldn't blame them if they skipped town." She shrugged. "I just don't know."

"What about Sutton?"

Charlcie shrugged again. "I don't know. He didn't say much. I'm not even sure if he heard what Martin was saying. He seemed sort of lost, off in his own world. From what I heard, the woman deputy who died this afternoon was somebody special to him. Childress seemed to think they were in love. To me, he just seemed not to be with the group. It was like he was thinking about something else.

"I do know that Martin's glad he's going down to L.A. with Sutton. If Sutton uses his siren and lights, the trip'll go faster. Martin said it was important to make the round trip during daylight hours. If they were on the road after dark, they wouldn't make it back at all."

"I'm going to Los Angeles with Martin," Cable said.

"I knew you would . . . just come back safe, okay?"

Cable nodded as Charlcie pushed herself up and away from him. She closed the door to her bedroom, but a horizontal shaft of light from under the doorway highlighted her standing figure. It didn't surprise him when she began to unbutton her blouse. The shadowy movements that followed were graceful, free of modesty, pretense, and self-consciousness. Cable found the sight of her disrobing to be one of the most erotic experiences he had ever experienced. Transfixed and entranced, he watched Charlcie McKenzie undress, wanting to fix the scene in his memory forever. Part of him said there was no need. The woman would be with him forever. But another part, a darker voice, reminded him that there would be death coming with tomorrow. This would be their first and last night together.

When she was finally naked, she came to him, drawing back the covers and staring as hard at him as he had at her.

He was already erect and nobody was more surprised than he was. After all, he had been attacked by a walking dead woman, then almost killed by a telephone. He grinned at her.

She smiled back. "It looks like you've recovered."

"It's the water and onions," he said, still grinning and reaching up for her, wanting her beside him.

She shook her head, touching his lips with her fingers. "Now," she said softly, urgently. "I want you now." She straddled him, gripping him and guiding him into her. Then she put her hands on his chest, and with infinite slowness she began to move her hips in a slow rolling motion. Cable started to respond, starting to thrust upward with his own hips. She motioned for him to be still. "The doctors said you were to take it easy. Lie still." She leaned close to him, kissing his chin and lips. "My treat," she whispered as she straightened back up and began a rocking gyrating motion with her hips again.

And it was her treat. Moments—maybe minutes—later Cable exploded inside her. When he was spent, she collapsed into his arms, laying beside him with her head nestled in the crook of his arm.

"Nice," was all he could think of to say, knowing it was the understatement of a lifetime.

She cuddled closer to him. "We're going to have to do that with great regularity," she said, her voice dusty with sleep. "I never got off so hard in my life."

Cable turned slightly so he could see her profile. "I didn't do anything. You wouldn't let me."

"You could have fooled me."

Cable kissed her temple and the side of her neck. "Sleepy?"

"Exhausted," she murmured.

Oddly, he felt the stirring of a new erection as he kissed her throat. Then with his tongue he traced small damp circles around her nipples, moving on to lap at the underside of her breasts. "Any chance you might get unsleepy?" he asked, suspecting she was already asleep.

"I am now wide awake, John Cable."

Still surprised by the unexpected return of a second erection, Cable straddled Charlcie's body with his knees and hands. "My treat," he said.

They held one another, touching, tasting, exploring, appreciating and loving all that was the other. This time their movements were slow and drawn out as if they wanted to capture time, stop it, and use their togetherness as a buffer against an ever encroaching dawn.

Chapter
Twenty-one

Sutton sat alone in the living room. Everyone else had left earlier, some heading off to the bedrooms while others, the physicians and the deputy, had slipped away to the den or library after sensing Sutton's fierce need for privacy and solitude.

Henry Sutton sat in the quiet living room in the same wing-backed chair he had occupied all along. He sat in the chair like a dead king on a throne. His posture was rigid, his head high, his unmoving arms resting on the chair's armrests. Everything was still and unmoving. Even his breathing was shallow.

Only the man's eyes suggested he was alive. Glowing red like the coals in the fireplace, Henry Sutton's eyes stared unblinkingly into the darkness.

Anger oozed from Henry Sutton like black sweat. It was a strange kind of anger, the kind of anger that can lower a man's blood pressure, reducing the beats of his heart to a subnormal pattern. The fury that raged within Henry Sutton left him not hot with hellish thoughts of vengeance, but cold. It was an icy calculated coldness, the kind that clears the mind and freezes the soul.

Henry Sutton was wide awake, his mind almost hyperalert, and it was a cruel state of being for a man who'd just had most of his emotional and professional buttresses kicked out from under him. For the past hour his mind had followed a mournful convoluted pattern as it traced over the facets of his life. His train of thought had dwelled upon the mistakes and pain of two failed marriages, the children he'd wanted but never fathered, and led him on into his own aloneness. Briefly it had soared upward to feel the pride he felt in himself over the good years he'd given to Ravina as the chief of police. He had been a good cop in Chicago; done a good job in Ravina.

But then like a crippled bird, the mood, his thoughts, plunged earthward and he began to remember the names.

Lynn Langley . . . dead.

Robert Calms . . . dead.

Louellen Mae Harnes . . . dead.

Gaylord Bender . . . dead.

Knowing the name that would come next, Sutton commanded his thoughts to stop . . . and failed.

Jaqueline Fairmont . . . DEAD.

With her name came the feelings that had been and the words never spoken. He had loved her, needed her, wanted her for life, but had never told her. Now she was dead and he would never speak the words. She would never hear the words, never know the feelings he felt. The words he *could* have said, *should* have said, traveled with him on the painful journey his mind chose to take. The agony and grief that came with his mind's excursion was beyond anything that he'd ever experienced. It was like his soul was committing itself to some sort of painful rite of absolution for the mistakes of his life and the loss of Jackie. His Jackie. In the end, when his mind had run its course, he found himself alone and exhausted and sweating in the cold room.

He found himself no longer trapped in the past, but

focusing instead on that which had brought this all about: the Horrcove brothers and the creatures.

With a new effort he closed his eyes and forced himself to remember everything Martin Larchmont had said about the creature-demons. He ran and reran scene after scene of Larchmont's talks through his mind like a motion picture projector until he could recall every descriptive phrase and every subtle nuance the elderly professor had used in his descriptions of the creatures and their guardian-keepers.

His fingernails bit deeply into the arms of the chair as he rehashed the events that had taken place at the mortuary and home of the Horrcove brothers. It hurt. It hurt because Jackie Fairmont was with him in these memories, but he would not stop.

His memory took him through the massive doors of the mortuary, down the foyer, and on to the harsh encounter with the two strange men. Nothing. No hints or clues, nothing that would aid him in destroying the evil that lived on that hill.

He replayed the scene again in his mind.

It came to him slowly, emerging from the recesses of his memory of two ancient men standing in a room with wainscotted walls and carved ceilings . . . and suddenly it was there. The key. He saw their fear.

In that moment Henry Sutton knew he could destroy the creatures and their guardian-keepers.

Exhausted, soaked in sweat, Sutton slumped back in his chair. He was overwhelmed with relief, tired, but still he pushed his mind on to the process of devising a killing plan which would use the weakness he now knew existed. He sat in the darkness and let his emotions and hate develop a plan.

A plan slowly emerged.

He would go after them with a double-edged sword. One edge would be the plan devised by Larchmont. Sutton knew he would support the elderly man's scheme in every possible way. The other edge of the sword would be his own private plan. In the event Larchmont's plan failed, he would put his own into effect.

Sutton glanced down at his watch. The sun would be up in an hour, and there was still much to do. He got to his feet, making his way across the dark living room. By touch he found one of the few remaining lamps that hadn't been shattered in the earlier attacks. He turned it on, finding a pad of yellow legal-sized paper in Larchmont's open briefcase, and returned to his chair. He paused to organize his thoughts, then he began to write. The pace he set for himself was furious. He didn't bother to punctuate or reread what he'd written. He just wrote, wrote for an hour straight without stopping. When he finally did stop, the sun was coming up in the east. With a cramped hand, he pushed six yellow pages with writing on both sides into a business-sized envelope he'd also found in Larchmont's briefcase. Then he addressed it, folding the bulky packet in half and shoving it into a rear pocket.

With infinite slowness, the rising sun filled the living room with a peach-colored haze. Henry Sutton stood, stretched in the warm glow, then walked over to the badly splintered door. He picked up the glass of water and salt sitting in front of the door and examined it. Last night the water had been clear and the onion placed on top of the glass large and white. But now the water was dark and foul and the onion had withered into a tiny black cinder that floated in the water like a charred fish head.

Sutton pulled the broken door open, started outside, then involuntarily stepped back away from the grisly sight sprawled out in front of him. The body of Louellen Mae Harnes lay twisted and broken on the front porch. "Sweet Jesus," Sutton murmured, realizing the dead woman must have been the destructive force that had hurled itself time and time again against the massive oak door during the assault on the house. Though the body was a twisted mass of protruding bones and crushed flesh totally alien to anything human, Sutton had instantly recognized the woman. Twelve hours earlier he'd repeatedly driven his patrol car over her ever-rising corpse. What he had seen then, outlined in his car's headlight, would stay with him forever.

Shaking his head, he stepped over the cadaver as if it were a garden slug and walked down the walkway to his patrol car. He opened the trunk, pulled out two black plastic body bags and started back to the house, stopping briefly to survey what had once been the well-kept yard of Jenny McKenzie. It looked like a war had been fought in front of the house. Broken branches and scorched foliage littered the lawn. The lush border of ferns and camellias bordering the house now resembled clumps of desert tumbleweeds. The lower branches of the cedar deodars and aleppo pines in the front looked as if they'd been torched by a flame thrower. Wisps of smoke still exuded from many of the blackened branches.

Sutton returned to the house and mounted the steps. Martin Larchmont was waiting for him on the front porch. The small man was dressed, shaved, and was looking down at the corpse of Louellen Mae Harnes, his expression impassive. Neither man spoke.

Sutton knelt down on the porch and began to unroll one of the body bags. Larchmont broke the silence. "I can save you the trouble."

Still kneeling, Sutton glanced up at the fragile older man. Larchmont was holding the glass of muddy water that earlier guarded the front door.

"Move back a bit," he said.

Sutton got to his feet and stepped back. A moment later Larchmont tossed the contents of the glass toward the corpse. The muddy water splashed down on Louellen Mae Harnes, and the reaction was instantaneous. The body began to sizzle like water in a frying pan, and the skin began to shrivel and dry up like an overheated pot roast. The corpse began to twist and writhe on the porch in a kind of slow-motion dance of obscenity. Without thinking, Sutton reached for his pistol. The man at his side placed a hand on his elbow. "There's no need."

Henry Sutton continued to stare at the cadaver's spasmodic jerking movements. It rolled over on its side, then flopped back on its back. Then it made a hissing sound as it drew its knees up to its chest and brought its fists together in a grotesque parody of someone praying. At first Sutton was repelled by the position, but then he remembered this was the posture a body naturally assumed when the manner of death was fire and the resulting heat caused the tendons and muscles to contract. "Sweet Jesus," he whispered again.

The grotesque praying position was visible for only a moment. Suddenly the charred flesh began to break apart like crusts of bread. The body caved in on itself, and then the flesh and bones began to disintegrate until all that remained was a pile of something that looked like it belonged in the bottom of a barbecue. A slight breeze swept across the porch, swirling away some of the azalea leaves and the dust of Louellen Mae Harnes. A moment after that all that remained of the woman were the remnants of a bathrobe and a cheap wedding ring.

Larchmont followed Henry Sutton into the pantry, where Deputy Gaylord Bender had been laid out. Sutton bit his lip as he knelt down beside the deputy and struggled to get the body of the man into the blackness of a body bag. He was about to close the bag when Larchmont stopped him. With a kind of reverence, Martin Larchmont knelt down beside Sutton and poured a clear stream of distilled water over the deputy's uniform. Then he tossed several handfuls of salt over the body and nodded at Sutton.

Gaylord Bender had been Henry Sutton's deputy and more. The man had been Sutton's friend. He turned his face away so he couldn't see his friend's face and then zipped up the heavy bag. The zipper sounded like a shroud being ripped in half.

Larchmont closed the pantry door, blocking it with a new glass of water and salt. He turned to Sutton. "I didn't want to do that to your deputy, but I had to. Forty-eight hours ago that woman on the porch was probably a very nice person who never harmed anyone. What happened to her could happen to your friend."

"You don't have to explain," Sutton said, fishing a cigarette out of his pocket and glancing at his watch. It was later than he thought. He was beginning to feel the pressure Larchmont's trip to Los Angeles was placing on his own plan. He lit the cigarette and exhaled. "I've got to do some things before we leave for L.A." He noticed concern in Larchmont's face. "We need another car. The one I have is a wreck and I should change my uniform. If we're stopped on the way down, I'd be hard pressed to explain why I look like I do now. I won't be long. An hour at the most."

"You know we've got to be back before the sun sets."

Sutton nodded. "How long to get your program out of the computer?"

Larchmont shrugged. "Ten, maybe fifteen minutes to tell the computer what I want. After that it'll take the computer maybe thirty seconds to respond with the program."

Strange, Sutton thought. Thirty seconds to think up a way to destroy creatures that had maybe existed hundreds of years. He hoped the program would work. But if it didn't, there was always his plan as a backup. "Relax. With lights and siren we should be able to make the round trip in six hours, maybe less."

Filtering down from the ceiling above him, Sutton could hear the sounds of footsteps and water running. Somebody flushed a toilet. The world was waking up. Some world, he thought, as he walked out on the porch and surveyed the devastated front yard and his own patrol car. The grille was missing. Both fenders and the bumper were crumpled. Only one headlight was intact, and a piece of Louellen Mae Harnes's bathrobe was hanging from the hood. Sutton jerked it free and let the wind take it away.

He stopped first at his home, showered, shaved, and changed into a cleaner uniform. Before leaving, he went to his desk and took out a huge key ring that held upward of thirty carefully labeled keys. Then he rummaged through another drawer, pulling out his savings account passbook and some other documents. He put the passbook and documents into an envelope, wrote the name of his watch commander, Andrew Slatkin, on the outside of the envelope, and left it on the desk. Then, leaving the front door ajar and unlocked, he returned to his patrol car without ever looking back at his home.

Ten minutes later Sutton pulled up in front of the fence that enclosed the town's motor pool. He used one of the keys on the key ring he'd picked up at home to unlock the gates. It was still early. None of the maintenance employees would be reporting to work for another hour. Sutton appreciated the solitude.

He returned to his car, drove it through the gates, and parked it by a large service garage. He used another key to enter the building.

It was parked in the back of the garage under a heavy canvas tarp. He walked up to it, pulled the tarp off, and stood back in mute appreciation.

Henry Sutton was admiring an old black and white police car, the last of its kind in Ravina. The city had stopped purchasing these heavy gas guzzling beasts years earlier because of a fuel crisis. A year later Detroit stopped turning out cars like this altogether.

Sutton well remembered the day this car, along with others of its breed, had been tagged for public auction to make way for an incoming fleet of toy automobiles made of plastic and tin. He'd purchased it himself before the mechanics had had a chance to strip it of its decals, lights, and siren. It was only afterward that he realized he didn't have a place to keep the machine. He'd called in a few favors and debts owed him by some city people and was able to store the car in the city's garage. The price he had paid for the machine had been small, and since buying it he hadn't paid a great deal of attention to it. But he knew that it had been well looked after because he'd left it in the care of a talented hunchback mechanic cruelly nicknamed Gorgeous George. George's appreciation of the car's all steel construction and powerful engine rivaled his own. His confidence in the mechanic was such that it came as no surprise when the engine started at the first flick of the key.

Instantly the garage was filled with the roar of thunder as the four-hundred-and-forty-horsepower engine exploded to life. Sutton sat back in his seat, allowing himself a fleeting moment of pleasure while he listened to the throbbing rumble of the perfectly tuned machine. Even now he wasn't sure why he had purchased this car. Maybe it was because it reminded him of a time when laws stood for something and the courts labored to protect the common man, not the criminal. There had once been a time in his life when a police uniform meant something and children tugged on it when they were lost. But not now, now it was different. Now everyone, except the innocent, had rights, and there were no such things as criminals, just misguided products of untrained parents or society. Someday, he thought, the pendulum would swing back to the older perspective, but he wouldn't see it; not in his time.

Sitting in the vibrating car, waiting for the engine to warm up, a sad smile played across his face as he recalled Jackie Fairmont's assessment of his impulsive purchase. "Henry," she had said, laughingly, "that car is just a typical macho search for ten-pound balls . . . and if you ever buy a pistol with a twelve-inch barrel, we're through."

The smile slid from his face, and he dropped the heavy transmission into reverse, backing the cruiser out of the garage. He had one more stop before picking up Larchmont.

On the way to the old armory, which his department shared with the National Guard, the car seemed to come alive, and Sutton had to struggle with the machine to keep it from racing the wind.

When he finally pulled up in front of the McKenzie home to pick up Larchmont, he was only remotely surprised to see John Cable clamber into the patrol car on the heels of the professor. It also didn't surprise him when Larchmont gave him another one of his home-made string necklaces with a fresh bag of salt attached. He pulled off the old talisman given him the previous night, and examined it. It didn't surprise him that the white cloth bag and the salt had turned brown sometime in the night. As he drove off toward the On ramp which would put them southbound on Highway 101, he wondered speculatively if there was anything left in the world that could surprise him.

Chapter
Twenty-two

It was starting to get dark. The sun hung low over the Pacific Ocean like a bright red marble on a dull gray carpet. The view from the northbound lanes of Highway 101 was spectacular, and Cable almost missed a sign whizzing by, a sign that said: Ravina 10 miles. Cable was surprised he could read the sign, but then, since he was trapped in a patrol car hurtling northward at speeds up to a hundred and thirty-five miles an hour, he was surprised he could even look at the sunset. That he had noticed the sign and could enjoy the sunset served as silent testimony to his confidence in the skills of the driver.

Cable glanced over at Henry Sutton. The red glow from the setting sun had turned the driver's window into a smear of red, highlighting Sutton's profile, turning the man into a silent brooding silhouette. The sheriff had said little on the way to Los Angeles, and probably less during the trip back up the coast. All he had done was to drive, and drive he had. John Cable shook his head as he recalled the way Sutton would roll up the tailpipes of slower moving cars, his own car's overhead lights blinking out a silent message for them to get out of the way. On those few occasions when the lights hadn't worked, Sutton would swear, hit the siren, allow it to emit a stomach-grinding growl, and then watch as the slower car scampered out of their way.

Cable shook his head again in a kind of silent awe. Sutton had to have set some all-time speed records for the trip to Los Angeles. On three different occasions highway patrolmen had pulled up behind them and radioed for them to pull over, all of them wondering what a ten-year-old police car was doing hurtling down their part of the freeway at speeds up to a hundred and twenty miles an hour. In turn Sutton would radio back, explaining who he was and adding that he was transporting a donor heart to a hospital in Los Angeles. Without fail, the CHP officers bought Sutton's story, and one had even offered to run interference for him.

"Escort welcome," Sutton had said into the microphone. "Hope you can keep up."

The highway patrol officer who was driving a new black and white Camaro laughed as he pulled out around them to take up a point position, but ten miles later, when blue smoke began pouring out from beneath the Camaro, all the officer could manage was: "Mechanical problem. You'll have to go it alone."

Cable thought the small-town sheriff might have finally found himself out of his league when they first started into the massive freeway congestion that was so much a part of Los Angeles. He'd been wrong. Slowing to eighty, Sutton had guided the patrol car through the city's crowded highways and freeways so easily that they'd arrived at UCLA just before noon. Following Larchmont's directions, Sutton drove the patrol car into the heart of the campus and parked in the faculty parking lot outside of the university's science and computer building.

Sutton stayed with the patrol car while he and Larchmont

went in to get the program from a huge space-age marvel called the Telephase Mark IV.

Once in the building, Larchmont's name and reputation got them immediate access to the computer. Later, in another part of the building, all Larchmont had to do was flash his faculty card, and he'd been handed an aluminum box that resembled a tin briefcase. Cable knew the box contained an advanced miniaturized and transistorized computer, complete with a receiver system and speaker system, but he'd been caught off guard when the man handing over the equipment suggested that Larchmont treat the system with TLC since it was worth a hundred and twenty-five thousand dollars.

With Cable carrying the program the Telephase Mark IV computer had devised to destroy the creatures and Larchmont carrying the expensive tin briefcase, they'd returned to the faculty parking lot just in time to see Sutton dropping a thick envelope into a nearby mailbox. Ten minutes later they were back on the freeway, roaring north, heading for home.

The trip to Los Angeles had taken four hours. The trip back should have taken the same. It didn't. Near Camarillo a northbound Shell gasoline truck loaded with fuel jackknifed, and the ensuing carnage, which involved a dozen other cars and two trucks, blocked the north- and southbound lanes of 101. The wreck had happened right in front of them, and before any of them knew what happened, they'd screeched to a stop and suddenly found themselves surrounded on all sides by a frozen river of unmoving cars. Realizing the hopelessness of the mess, Sutton folded his arms across his chest like a great massive Buddha and went to sleep while Larchmont sat in the backseat, looking at his watch, then the afternoon sun, then back at his watch. Cable tried to sleep, but couldn't. He was still caught up in the tender moving memories and feelings from the night before. When he closed his eyes, images of Charlcie floated into his mind. She had slept close to him, giving him warmth and comfort and a serenity he hadn't known for years. And now, hours later, he could still smell her scents, and the scents acted as a catalyst, pushing him deeper into a blurred kaleidoscope of memories, memories of the days and the night he'd spent with Charlcie McKenzie.

Almost three hours later the police and the Cal-Trans workers finally managed to open up a single northbound lane, and as the cars in front of them began to move forward, Larchmont had grimly announced to Sutton they were three hours behind schedule. Without looking back, Sutton had simply nodded. Then the sheriff had showed his two passengers just exactly what he and his patrol car were capable of.

It was like being in a rocket sled and a roller coaster all at the same time. At first Cable tried not to look at the speedometer, but later he'd found himself fascinated by the needle. At one point he shouted, "We're doing a hundred and thirty miles an hour!"

"I think the speedometer's off about ten miles an hour," Sutton said, his eyes locked on the freeway.

"That's good," Cable said. "I feel better knowing we're only going a hundred and twenty."

Taking his eyes off the road, Sutton gave Cable a quizzical glance, then turned his attention back to the road. At that moment Cable realized they weren't doing a hundred and twenty miles an hour. They were doing a hundred and forty miles an hour!

Cable checked his seat belt, turned and checked Larchmont's seat belt, then sat back and stared tensely out the windshield. But as the miles flashed by, he began to relax. There was no doubt about it, Henry Sutton could drive.

An hour after they left the crash site, Sutton pulled off the freeway and onto the narrow winding road leading to Vandenberg Air Force Base. A sign claimed it was twenty-two miles from the freeway to the Base. Sutton covered the distance in eleven minutes.

A worried Colonel William Seafront was waiting for

them out in front of the gates to the Air Force base. As
Sutton pulled to a stop, Seafront ran up to the car and
excitedly explained that he'd gotten ahold of one of the
base's computer experts to help tie the hospital computer into the Telephase Mark IV computer which was
housed in a fortified underground computer laboratory.
He said the expert thought the two computers were
compatible, but wouldn't know until Larchmont's own
portable computer receiver system went on line. Seafront's computer specialist had told him it would take
two, maybe two and a half hours to link the two Air
Force computers together, and it was agreed that the
hospital's computer—with help from the Telephase Mark
IV computer—would begin spitting out Larchmont's program at precisely seven-thirty that evening. After Larchmont had handed over the program, everyone had syn-
chronized their watches like actors in a war movie, then
separated. Ten minutes later Sutton had them back on
Highway 101.

As they roared north, Cable asked Larchmont about
what he thought would happen when seven-thirty came
later that evening. Sitting in the backseat, gripping the
metal briefcase, the older man shook his head and gave
Cable vague meandering responses. The stilted answers
didn't bother Cable. What bothered him was that Martin
Larchmont wouldn't look at him when he did talk.

Cable resumed looking out the windshield. A few moments later Larchmont stuck his chin over the front
seat. "John, I have no way of knowing what'll happen
tonight. I have hopes, but basically that's all I have. If we
win, we win big, and the world will never hear about it.

"If we lose, we'll probably die and so will a part of
the world."

Larchmont continued to sit with his chin resting on
the front seat between Sutton and Cable. No one said
anything for several miles, but Larchmont finally spoke.
"I don't want you to go with me tonight. I want you to
stay with Jenny and Charlcie."

Cable shook his head and continued to stare out the windshield. Larchmont sighed and looked over at Sutton. "Same goes for you. I can handle this myself. It's all sort of automated, you might say." Like Cable, Sutton shook his head.

A mile or so later Larchmont again broke the silence. "I don't believe this. Three men going on a fool's errand where only one is actually required." He shook his head and gestured to himself. "One goes out of pride to test the powers of his accumulated wisdom and to wistfully rid the world of an evil." Larchmont motioned at Cable. "Another goes partly out of ignorance and mostly out of friendship." Finally Larchmont looked at Sutton. "And the last goes because . . . Henry, why the hell are you going?"

Sutton kept his eyes on the freeway. "Because I get paid to go. It's my job."

The sun was almost down, the ten miles to Ravina sign several miles behind them. Ravina was visible up ahead in the dimming light, its lights and buildings obscured by thunderheads and a bank of fog which hovered over the town like an evil winged beast. Suddenly Henry Sutton began swearing and tapping a gauge on the dash.

"What is it?" Larchmont asked from the backseat.

"We need gas," Sutton said.

The car began to slow.

Larchmont moaned in protest. "The sun's almost down."

"If we don't get gas, we'll end up walking to the cemetery."

Sutton took the first off ramp he came to and pulled into a large Arco gas station; it was a huge sprawling place, very modern, very sterile, consisting of a clean white tin building and upward of thirty gas pumps, all sitting in the middle of several acres of black asphalt. During the tourist season, there would have been long lines of cars waiting to gas up. But now it was deserted. There were no other cars in sight.

Two middle-aged attendants came out of the white building. One walked over to the pumps behind the patrol car. The other eased up to Sutton's window, took the sheriff's order, then barked it over the roof at the man by the pumps. "Fill it, Joe. Super, and make sure it's leaded."

"Leaded?" the other asked.

"That's what I said," the attendant said as he began to scrub the bug-splattered windshield.

Inside the car Sutton, Cable, and Larchmont sat in stony silence, waiting for the pumper to finish his task. Sutton had his eyes closed; he looked like he was trying to take a catnap. Larchmont was staring out a side window, watching the upper rim of the sun sink into the ocean. Cable was watching the window washer's progress when he saw a strange look come into the man's face. The washer was staring toward the back of the patrol car and the shock and concern in the man's expression caused Cable to turn in his seat to see what was going on. Looking through the back window, he could partially make out the standing uniformed figure of the gas pumper. Nothing seemed to be wrong. He was starting to turn away when he heard the window washer scream, "Joe, what are you doing?"

Cable scooted down in the seat for a better view of the pumper. What he saw froze his blood. Face stricken, eyes bulging outward, the gas pumper was standing stock still in a rigid contorted position. He was holding the gas nozzle in his right hand, holding it high in the air directly over the trunk of the car. A fountain of pink gas frothed out of the nozzle and washed freely over the back of the patrol car.

For one brief instant Cable thought the man was having a heart attack, but then he saw the pumper's left hand drift up from his pants pocket, the hand clutching a brightly colored butane lighter. Again the windshield washer screamed, "Joe, what the hell are you doing?"

Cable couldn't believe it. The pumper was holding the lighter in the waterfall of gasoline spilling out of the nozzle he was holding, and was trying to light it with his thumb. The Horrcove brothers, Cable realized.

Henry Sutton's eyes were open, and he was sitting up, searching for the source of the window washer's terror.

Cable grabbed Sutton by the elbow. "Get us out of here," he said, in a voice so calm it surprised even him. "Move it now."

The message was clear, articulate, and it elicited a series of smooth coordinated movements from the sheriff. Without hesitation, Sutton hit the key, the gas, and slammed the transmission into drive.

Tires screaming, the car bolted away from the pumps like a frightened gazelle. The sudden movement of the car caught the windshield washer by surprise, and he was swept along with the car, his body straddled across the fender and the hood. The man grabbed onto a windshield wiper and clung to it as the car continued to pick up speed.

Cable whirled around in his seat, and looked out the back window at the insane scene. The other man was still standing like a statue by the pumps, still holding the gas nozzle high above his head, pointing it skyward. Gasoline was spewing out of the nozzle, cascading down over the man and forming a widening pool of liquid dynamite at his feet. The pumper still had his lighter in his left hand. He was holding it under the waterfall of gasoline, and they were still close enough for Cable to see the man's thumb working the lighter, turning the wheel, trying to light the flame.

Nothing happened and for a fraction of a second Cable thought the lighter was too wet to work. But suddenly a ball of flames engulfed the man and the pumps next to him. A microsecond later the pumps exploded, throwing out a ten-foot high tidal wave of liquid fire that went billowing out across the parking lot. To Cable, it looked like the patrol car was being chased by the sun.

A solid wall of hot moving air slammed into the patrol car. At the same time the earth shuddered under the power of the explosion, causing the car to pitch and yaw. The man on the hood screamed as the windshield wiper he was holding onto snapped in half and he flew off the hood of the speeding car.

The man bounced and rolled like a tennis ball over the asphalt. Seemed as if he would never stop tumbling. Cable felt the patrol car slow, and looked at Sutton. The sheriff had been watching the carnage in his rearview mirror. Still braking hard, he yelled at Cable over the screech of tires. "We've got to go back and get him before the underground storage tanks blow—" Then behind them came the sounds of two more heavy explosions, and more waves of hot air slammed into the car. Cable turned in time to see flames spurting up like geysers from huge pits in the asphalt where the long lines of pumps had stood. One of the remaining pumps exploded and shot off into the air like a rocket.

Sutton threw the cruiser into a vicious U-turn and came out of it with the car's nose pointing at the helpless man. He was accelerating when suddenly, directly in front of them, a huge section of flat asphalt began to bulge upward as if a giant creature was trying to escape from beneath the earth. Cable braced himself. From where he sat, it looked like they were about to plow into an ever growing black mountain. He heard someone scream, "The storage tanks are going!!" and realized the words were his.

Sutton spun the wheel, jerking violently on the emergency brake and hitting the gas pedal at the same time. Cable and Larchmont were slammed around in their seats as the car's rear end broke free in a violently controlled skid which whipped the rear end around in a screaming hundred and eighty-degree turn. An instant later they were leaving the window washer and the growing black mountain behind as the powerful engine of the patrol car raced away from the gas station. Everyone knew there was nothing they could do for the man behind them. If the fall hadn't killed him, the pending explosions from the underground storage tanks would.

They were a hundred yards from the gas station when an explosion of volcanic intensity erupted. Hot wind buffeted the car, and a hailstorm of shredded metal and asphalt pelted the machine, turning the rear window into a web of spun glass. Staring through the shattered rear window, Cable watched a huge fireball engulf everything in sight—gas station, pumps, window washer—and rolling steadily onward toward them. Faster than the patrol car, the ball of flames rolled up and over the trunk of the car, blistering paint, turning the interior into a red hot oven of airless pain. Then, as quickly as it had come, the avalanche of flames receded and the patrol car broke free.

They were a quarter of a mile from the flaming gas station and Sutton was still driving the car like a madman. He glanced at Cable. "We're still not out of it. That station had at least thirty pumps. That means there's eight or nine more underground tanks waiting to go up."

He was right. The explosion that followed gave off more light than the sun. The road pitched and heaved like a rope bridge in a high wind. But finally the violence passed. The tremors ceased, the darkness returned, and Sutton turned the car onto the road that would take them to the Horrcove Cemetery.

Chapter
Twenty-three

It was after seven when the patrol car's headlights came to rest on the iron spears that made up the Horrcove Cemetery's heavy gates. Sutton turned off the lights, shutting down the cruiser and turning in his seat to look back at Larchmont. "It's ten after seven. Seafront won't fire up the hospital computer for another twenty minutes. You want to sit here or go on up?"

Larchmont had opened the aluminum briefcase and was running his fingers over the delicate components and buttons in the case. "I think we'd better stay here," he said without looking up. "We don't have much protection as it is, and if we get up there early, the brothers could use those extra minutes to grind us down."

He closed the lid of the briefcase and finally looked up, looking first at Sutton, then at Cable. "I know I brought this up earlier, but I've got to say it again. It's only going to take one person to carry this computer up to the mortuary. I can drive the car and I can carry the computer. What I'm suggesting is that you two leave, make your way back to Jenny's house and set up the same defenses—the water and the salt—that we used last night.''

Both men in the front seat shook their heads, and Larchmont sighed. "Look, you two, what I'm trying to say is I don't have a lot of faith in the program I've developed and I don't have much faith in this electronic marvel." He put his hands on the top of the briefcase. "Will you please reconsider?" The men in the front seat again shook their heads. Larchmont mumbled something they couldn't hear, reopened the briefcase, and went back to examining its dials and gauges.

Cable slumped down in the front seat and stared at the massive gates. His lips felt crusty, his mouth was dry, and he searched his pockets for a stick of gum. Finally he looked over at Sutton's large silhouette. "You got any gum?"

"Check the glove compartment."

Cable did, finding nothing, but didn't want the conversation to end. "You as scared as I am?" He couldn't see Sutton's face, but he sensed the man was smiling ironically in the darkness."

"You'd better believe it."

"When did you first get scared?" Cable asked. It seemed like a dumb question, but he was curious and he didn't want to sit in silence while they waited for seven-thirty to roll around.

Henry Sutton seemed to collect his thoughts. "I don't know. Maybe it was back when they did an autopsy on that girl, Lynn Langley, or maybe it was when they did the autopsy on one of my deputies. I don't know.

"Later, after Jackie was killed, the fear went away. Even when I saw that dead woman walking across the parking lot, I didn't feel fear, just hate. But tonight, when that gas station blew up, the fear came back. The hate's still there and I still want revenge, but yeah, I'm just as scared as you are."

Sutton hooked an elbow over the seat, turned, and looked at Larchmont. "How do you want to do this?"

Larchmont glanced up from his computer and scratched an eyebrow. "Right up the middle, as they say in football . . . or soccer."

"Just drive right up to the mortuary?"

Larchmont nodded. "They already know we're coming. What happened back at the gas station proved that. The sun has set. The powers they have are the strongest now. My guess is they're up there, waiting for us, maybe even looking forward to the sport. I don't think they see us as any real threat, but more as a hindrance that might interfere with the final aspects of the resurrection rites they have to perform tonight and tomorrow night in order to bring all their gods back to life."

"What exactly are the Horrcove brothers?" Sutton asked.

"They're the guardians, the keepers, the familiars of six demon-creatures. Its an inherited legacy handed down from father to son."

"Are the brothers human?" Cable asked.

"I think so. Certainly more so than the creatures they care for. But human or not, they have certain abilities . . . skills developed and refined by their ancestors and passed on to successive generations. Yes, they're human, but they're special human beings with incredible powers."

"Like the telekinetic abilities?" Cable asked.

"Yes. They possess telekinetic powers, mind-control powers, second-sight powers, and the ability to command the dead. In all these cases their powers are truly horrendous because they're twins; thus, their powers are magnified at least twofold."

Sutton shook his head. "I don't follow you. What's second sight?"

"Second sight is the ability to see into the future. I don't believe the Horrcove brothers can do this. I do believe they have the ability to know what's going on around them in the present. In other words they knew where you and Jackie Fairmont were when they set out to destroy you with their minds. The same thing happened last night at the hospital. Somehow they knew we'd be leaving the hospital, going into the parking lot. With that sort of second sight ability of theirs, they were able to send the Harnes woman out to get us. Then there was that . . . that incident at the gas station tonight. Somehow with their minds, they saw us, knew we'd be stopping for gas, knew where, and then they made that poor gas station attendant do what he did.''

"What happens if the Resurrection Ritual gets completed and the creatures come back to life?" Cable asked.

"I'm not sure, but I do know you wouldn't want to live in this world if the brothers are successful.''

Sutton looked at Cable then at Larchmont. "Can the brothers be killed?"

"I think so. In spite of their powers, they're still human.''

"If we kill them," Sutton asked, "will the creatures die with them?"

"No. The Resurrection Ritual is already underway. Children are missing; people are dead. They're almost all the way through the rite. At least four of the creatures have tasted life and are returning to life. With or without the Horrcove brothers, it's just a matter of time.''

Larchmont took in a deep breath. "Everything up in that mortuary has to be destroyed. The brothers. The creatures. Everything. We don't have a choice.''

"What about the two missing boys?" Sutton asked.

Martin Larchmont looked down at the computer housed within the open metal case. "The children are dead. Each died the night they were taken from their parents. The Yezidi religion is a harsh one. Iblis and whatever he spawned are bloodthirsty gods. There was never anything we could've done for those children. I'm sorry.''

Sutton flicked on the dome light, checked his watch, then turned the light off. "It's seven twenty-two. I figure two minutes to get through the gates and three minutes to drive up to the mansion.''

Larchmont nodded. ''I'd like to be in the mortuary's parking lot when Seafront's computer kicks in. Maybe the power surge will blow those bastards and their pets right off this hill. Let's wait three minutes, then go.''

Cable wasn't sure whether the passing three minutes were the longest in his life or the shortest. He felt the patrol car rumble to life when his watch registered 7:25.

Sutton inched the patrol car forward until the front bumper touched the massive locked gates. Then he tapped the accelerator. The car lurched forward, the gates bent inward, but held. He dropped the car into ''D-1'' and accelerated a second time. The engine growled. The rear tires made whirring sounds as they spun against the wet pavement. For a long moment the gates held, but then the weight and the power of the car began to win out, and slowly, like falling trees, the huge gates and their supporting brick pillars toppled away from the patrol car and crashed down on the road in an explosion of dust, rubble, and twisted metal.

Sutton drove the patrol car over the ruined gates. ''Jesus,'' he muttered, shaking his head. ''If they didn't know we were coming, they do now.''

The sheriff nosed the car up the winding hill at a slow, steady pace. Above them they could see their destination, a huge stone building dark and cold as the world's last midnight, its Gothic lines obscured by mist and fog.

Cable felt a rush of cold chills as though a corpse had just scraped its fingernails across a blackboard. The air was dank and seemed to smell of musty things—dead things. Movement off to the right of the car caught his eye, and he peered out into the gray blackness, seeing nothing.

Still staring into the cemetery, he saw movement again. There were flickering fragments of shadows that seemed to be there, but weren't if he looked hard. Whatever he seemed to be seeing reminded him of what he saw when he pressed his knuckles too hard against his eyeballs: specks of light, pieces of shadow, and brilliance that formed no pattern, made no sense.

He glanced over at Sutton. "You get the impression there's . . . things out there in the dark?"

Sutton nodded. "I keep seeing moving shadows out of the corner of my eye, but when I look, there's nothing there."

Ahead of him Cable could see the two huge stone lions that guarded the entrance to the mansion's circular driveway and parking lot. The moving headlights briefly glanced off a drifting taper of fog. No, Cable thought, too thick for fog. It had shape. "Did you see that?"

"What?" Sutton asked.

Cable started to point, then sat back in his seat. "It's gone now. I don't know what it was, but it looked like—like a woman with a dress made of fog." He shook his head. "Never mind. Overactive imagination. Sorry."

"Don't apologize," Sutton said tensely, guiding the car between the two massive stone lions. "You got every right to have an overactive imagination in a place like this. God, this is a creepy night." He started to say something else but was cut short by the hard glare of headlights coming up from behind them. The highbeams reflected off the rearview mirror forcing Sutton to squint. "What the hell—?" he hissed, slapping the car's mirror out of position so the glare wouldn't blind him. "Can you see who's behind us?"

Cable whirled around in his seat. "No. Too far away, lights too bright. But whoever it is, they're coming up fast."

"What kind of car?" Sutton asked.

"Can't tell."

Sutton brought the patrol car to a stop in front of the vast marble steps that led up to the elevated porch of the Horrcove mortuary high above them. The car behind them continued to approach until its bumper nearly touched the patrol car's bumper. As the car stopped,

Cable and Sutton climbed out of their car, their movements illuminated by the other car's headlights. Cable shielded his eyes against the bright lights, trying to see who was in the car. Then the driver in the other car killed the motor and the headlights. In that instant Cable recognized the boxy lines of Jenny McKenzie's ancient Mercedes-Benz. He ran to the car and jerked open the passenger door. His worst fears were confirmed. Charlcie McKenzie was sitting in the passenger seat. He glanced over at the driver, Jenny McKenzie, then back at Charlcie. "Christ, what are you doing here?"

"We couldn't just stand around and wait. We had to come."

Cable's voice was brittle with anger. "God dammit, this is the worst place in the world for you to be! Get out of here!"

Jenny McKenzie got out of the Mercedes and looked sternly at Cable over the roof of the car. "What makes you think we were all that safe back in Ravina?" she asked, her tone as cutting as his. She softened her voice. "We just might be safer up here than back in town."

Cable looked at the other passengers. The lanky deputy named Griffith sat in the cramped backseat, his knees hunched up against his chin. He glanced at Jenny McKenzie, then looked at Cable and silently mouthed the words: "No choice."

With a palms-up gesture of supplication, Dr. Mark Childress nodded in quiet agreement with the deputy.

"We had to come, John," Charlcie said. "We were all at the hospital together when Seafront called in from Vandenberg. He told us what time the computer would be turned on, so we decided to meet you here. Like Mom said, we weren't safe in town. Look what happened to us in the hospital parking lot last night."

Cable nodded. He took her hand and helped her out of the car, putting his arms around her. At the same time Martin Larchmont was putting his arms around Jenny McKenzie. Their coming together was less energetic than the younger couple, but the intensity and the feelings were the same.

Deputy Larry Griffith bumped and bruised his way out of the backseat and found himself face to face with an angry colossus named Henry Sutton. "Griff," he snarled, "I'm gonna have your ass for this. I left you in charge of these people. How the hell could you've let them come up here of all places?"

Rolling his eyes toward heaven, Griffith groped for words. "I didn't have any choice. They just decided to go. I tried to stop them, even tried to stand in front of them." Suddenly Griffith pointed a finger at Jenny McKenzie. "You know what she said to me when I did?"

Sutton continued to stare at his deputy. "No. But you're going to tell me, aren't you?"

"She said if I didn't get out of their way, she'd handcuff my nose to my—" Suddenly he leaned close and whispered the rest of Jenny McKenzie's words to Henry Sutton.

When Griffith finished, Sutton glanced at Jenny McKenzie. "You said that to my deputy!?" The elderly woman put her hands on her hips and nodded. Sutton turned to Larchmont. "If your computer breaks down, we can always replace it with Mrs. McKenzie's tongue." In spite of the terrible tension and the situation, they managed to laugh.

But the laughter stopped as a series of floodlights mounted on top of the Horrcove mortuary flared on, drenching everyone at the base of the steps with a blinding spray of white light. A heartbeat later the mansion's huge front doors opened and the tiny twin figures of Bartholomew and Alexander Horrcove emerged from the dimly lit interior. They strolled across the elevated porch, stopping finally at the top of the steps to gaze down on the humans below.

For a long tense moment neither the Horrcove brothers nor the people standing below them said anything.

Then Alexander Horrcove broke the silence. "How kind of you to visit us, Dr. Larchmont."

Larchmont had placed the briefcase on the lowest step of the staircase. At the mention of his name, he glanced up at the brothers absentmindedly, then returned his attention to the minicomputer.

Alexander Horrcove gestured at the other people standing behind Larchmont. "It was also kind of you to bring the knowledgeable ones to us. It's all quite timesaving, don't you agree, Bartholomew?"

The other brother nodded in the bright glare of the floodlights. "Absolutely. Save for the military pathologist who will shortly die in his hospital, it appears that all who know about us now stand before us. Very convenient, Dr. Larchmont. Please accept our heartfelt thanks."

"Tell us, Dr. Larchmont," Alexander said, "did you bring your electric toy with you?" Both brothers laughed, and Cable felt his spine tingle as if he were chewing on aluminum foil. The Horrcove brothers weren't afraid of Martin Larchmont or his computer or the computers at the Air Force base.

Martin Larchmont seemed to know it. Still fiddling with the knobs, Larchmont looked confused and bewildered. His face was wet with sweat as he picked up the briefcase and got to his feet.

"It's after seven-thirty," Sutton announced, standing off to one side. "Turn it on."

Larchmont did, and the machine in his hands began to hum and vibrate. Holding the case out from his body as if it were a water-witching wand, Larchmont pointed the speakers up at the twin creatures at the top of the steps.

At that moment both brothers moved together until their shoulders touched. They closed their eyes, allowing their heads to loll forward until their chins touched their chests.

For a span of time everything was quiet. Then an unseen force catapulted Larchmont off the steps and high into the air. He crashed down on the driveway ten feet from the stairway. He hit hard, and the still-whirring briefcase went skittering across the gravel, bumping into the tire of the patrol car.

Sutton, his eyes locked on the twin brothers standing high above them, unsnapped his holster strap while Cable ran to help Larchmont. His friend was shaken and stunned, but unhurt. He helped Larchmont to his feet and was surprised when Larchmont pushed him back. "Stay away. If you come near me, you'll get hurt by their power."

Cable watched helplessly as Larchmont limped toward the computer. He put his hand on the patrol car for support and started to pick up the metal box.

Henry Sutton was the only one who saw the Horrcove brothers begin to summon up their powers again by bowing their heads for a second time.

An invisible force suddenly kicked Martin Larchmont in the back, and he was tossed into the air like a rag doll. When he landed, he came down on his face and chest, his arms and legs splayed apart. Jenny McKenzie moaned and cried out in anguish. Cable sprinted for his friend. From high above he heard the almost feminine voice of one of the brothers. "Really, Dr. Larchmont, don't you think this is all quite futile?"

Larchmont was up on his hands and knees by the time Cable got to him. Cable gripped the man by the shoulders, helped him to his feet. "Help me to the computer," Larchmont gasped. Half holding him, half carrying him, Cable and Larchmont stumbled toward the machine under the piercing eyes of the Horrcove brothers. The computer continued to whir and whine as it lay in the gravel by the car. Cable picked up the case and put it into Larchmont's bloody hands. Larchmont was staring up at the brothers, meeting their fierce gaze with one of his own. "Turn up the volume," he said quietly to Cable, continuing to hold the briefcase in both hands. "It's the large knob on the end."

Cable found the knob and was able to turn it all the way to the right just an instant before a powerful wind picked him up and flung him over Martin's shoulder and the patrol car. He was clear-headed as he floated through the air, so alert he could head Charlcie scream his name. Her scream lasted the duration of his flight. He landed fifteen feet on the far side of the car. It was a grinding, bone-jarring landing that shredded his kneecaps and bloodied his elbows. He rolled over on his hands and knees and got up as rapidly as he could. For strength he used his images of Martin Larchmont pushing himself off the ground like a broken mannequin. If that seventy-year-old man could do it, he could do it. He was up now, standing, and starting to walk toward the patrol car. One leg gave out and he fell on his hands. He lifted his head and looked up at the damnable twins.

His view of the brothers was then blocked out by the bulk of Henry Sutton. A massive hand gripped him by the arm and jerked him to his feet. He looked into Sutton's face. "Kill 'em, Henry," he shouted. "Kill 'em now before they kill us."

Sutton released his grip on Cable and stepped away from the man. He needed no urging. He had already decided to kill them before Cable had been thrown over the patrol car. He took a two-handed grip on his .357 magnum Colt Python pistol and brought the weapon up slowly. The green neon glow of the Horrcove mortuary sign reflected brightly off the blue-black barrel. He centered the sight on the end of the barrel on the petite head of Alexander Horrcove in time to see both brothers bow their heads again. Oh, fuck, he thought. Here it comes.

Instantly a thousand rocks were sucked loose from the driveway and hurled at Sutton. He dropped the pistol and covered his face with his arms to keep from being blinded by the onslaught of sharp stones. The pain was scathing. He felt as if he'd walked into a withering storm of bullets and darts.

It stopped as quickly as it had started. Dazed, Sutton

shook his head, trying to get his eyes to focus. One eye was heavy with blood oozing out from a cut over his eyebrow.

His eyes swam back into focus in time to see Deputy Griffith pull out his own pistol. Sutton spun around and looked up at the Horrcove brothers. They were standing shoulder to shoulder, heads high and smiling down at the gangly deputy. Then they closed their eyes and bowed their heads once again.

Sutton whirled back, saw his deputy aiming his pistol up at the two small figures on the porch. He started to scream a warning, but the words seized in his throat when the deputy's pistol exploded in a blinding yellow flash. Sutton shielded his eyes. When he looked again, it was all he could do to keep from vomiting. Griffith was still standing in a classic two-handed shooter stance of legs apart, knees bent, and elbows locked. Trouble was, Griffith didn't have a pistol. But then, Deputy Griffith didn't have hands either. Stunned by shock, Griffith calmly examined the nothingness which had once been his hands. Then the realization set in, the screaming began, and with the screaming came hysteria. Suddenly Deputy Griffith was running away from the group, down the driveway, and toward the two stone lions.

The deputy's panic was blinding; his run from the horror meaningless. He never heard the deceptively mild voice of Alexander Horrcove filter down on the battered individuals in the parking lot.

"Behold, Dr. Larchmont. Behold and bear witness to the full extent of our powers." This time the Horrcove brothers grasped each other's hands like children.

Again they bowed their heads. And again.

The hysterical deputy was running along the left edge of the driveway, running blindly and mindlessly, toward the two stone lions guarding the entrance to the mortuary.

The lion the deputy would come closest to suddenly began glowing with a flickering aura as if blue neon lights were being turned on inside it. At the same moment the giant statue began to hum and crackle like a broken power line. The blue aura grew more intense, more brilliant. Electricity and the smell of ozone filled the air.

Blind with terror, the deputy didn't see it, but Cable did. Sutton did. All of them did.

The deputy was thirty feet from the base of the lion's pedestal when the lion's huge granite head began to turn with crushing slowness to look down at the running figure.

Still bathed in a shimmering blue light, the lion continued to move amid the sounds of granite being crushed against granite. Slowly, yet with purpose, the lion lifted a giant stone paw up from its pedestal. As the deputy ran past, it slashed out at it like a cat slashing out at a mouse. Granite claws sharp as steel cut through the air at the deputy's head and removed it. Like a mindless beheaded chicken, the deputy's headless torso kept on running out into the darkness of the cemetery.

The horrible claws receded into the huge stone paw, and a moment later the limb returned to its original position on the pedestal. Then the lion's head gratingly turned until it was looking at its mate. It was now an identical match to its counterpart which stood on the other side of the driveway. A heartbeat later the intense blue light went dark, and a heartbeat after that the massive stone lion was still. A scream broke from Charlcie McKenzie's lips. Jenny McKenzie vomited and an equally sick Henry Sutton tried to avoid looking at the severed head of his deputy and friend as it lay in the gravel. Cable and Childress started to run toward the scene, then both realized the futility of it all and turned away.

During the nightmarish commotion, Martin Larchmont had managed to pick up the computer. He was holding it in one hand, moving its dials with the other. Almost instantly the computer began to hum louder than before, spitting out unrecognizable sounds devoid of pattern and meaning. Then a servo mechanism activated itself. The machine seemed to pick up speed; the tonal quality increased rapidly until the guttural sounds attained a degree of normalcy and became almost human.

Then the sounds emanating from the computer's speakers did become human. But the language it was speaking was unrecognizable. It was an ancient language, guttural and repetitive like a chant. It was also a dead language. No living person in the world would have been capable of understanding it. But Alexander and Bartholomew Horrcove seemed to understand it.

Cable looked up at the twin brothers and was surprised to see they were finally reacting to the computer. There were expressions of pain on their faces and both had clapped their hands over their ears. One was starting to falter. The other was swaying from side to side. "Dear God," Cable murmured. "It's working."

But his excitement was brief. Almost immediately the brothers regained their strength. The shock and pain they'd displayed earlier over the voice coming from the computer was gone now. Worse, both were standing now, reaching out for each other's hands. Once again, the Horrcove brothers bowed their heads in a grotesque parody of reverence and prayer. It was the same identical posture they'd assumed before inflicting each horrible act on the people in the parking lot. But one thing was different this time. There was a greenish aura of light floating around the clasped hands of the brothers. Cable knew that whatever was coming next would be more horrible than what the lion had done to the deputy. He sucked in his breath, expecting the worst.

It didn't come . . . at least not then.

Soft scraping noises coming from the vast cemetery behind them caused Cable and Sutton to turn away from the twins. Both scanned the darkness. The noises they could hear were strange and unrecognizable, muted and distant; an endless series of odd scraping noises and soft thumps as if earth were being moved about. The sounds were coming from all parts of the surrounding cemetery.

New sounds could now be heard. It was the sound of things shuffling in the darkness like pages of a newspaper being pushed up an alley by a wind. Cable and Sutton exchanged worried glances as if they knew what was about to come lurching out of the darkness.

Sutton picked up his revolver and checked the rounds, slapping the cylinder closed. It was fully loaded, but the weapon gave him no comfort. He lifted his eyes from the pistol to the darkness beyond in time to see the first corpse come slouching into the outer edges of brightness. It was a woman, pale, bloated, and naked. A huge vertical scar starting at her sternum and ending in her pubic region was all too visible as were the black sutures which held the unhealed flaps of flesh together. As Sutton stared disbelievingly at the walking corpse, he heard Cable gasp. "It's . . . Langley. Lynn Langley!"

Sutton continued to stare at the apparition. Cable was right. It was the prostitute he'd seen on the table in the morgue. Behind her, other figures were now emerging from the darkness; they were all around the small group of humans. An army of newly dead and long-dead corpses was coming for them.

They came forward slowly, haltingly, barely able to walk; an oncoming cadaverous horde of corpses, many still wearing tattered rags that had once been expensive suits and dresses worthy of being buried in. Some of the Horrcove brothers' army were incapable of walking. Dried muscles, ligaments, and tendons fell away, and when they did, the skeletons collapsed helpless in the grass. Not even the powers of the Horrcove brothers could create something from dust. Yet the brothers' powers were tremendous. He saw one skeleton collapse into a pile of gray sticks. As he looked on, a single hand bonded together by scraps of flesh emerged from the pile. With a hideous sense of purpose, it stretched out its fingers to grip the earth, then it closed its fingers, pulling itself along, clawing its way ever closer to the humans standing beside their cars.

With sickening disgust, Sutton brought the barrel of his Colt Python up until the sight rested squarely on the oncoming lurching body of the prostitute. He fired one time and the woman's left eye, cheek, and ear exploded. The impact of the bullet spun her around on one leg like a bad belly dancer. She pirouetted away from the sheriff, whirling around one and a half times before coming to rest in a still standing position with her back to him. Sutton watched with sheer awe etched across his face as the naked shadowy cadaver slowly turned around to face him once again. She stopped momentarily to glare at him fiercely with one dry open eye, then slowly, haltingly, she started toward him again.

"Christ," Sutton said, returning the dead woman's one-eyed stare. He considered shooting her again, but knew it was a waste of time. If one bullet in the head didn't work, nothing would work. Even if it had, even if she'd gone down and stayed down, there were just too many corpses coming now and he didn't have that many bullets left. He scanned the encroaching army of cadavers. They were coming, but coming slowly. They wouldn't overrun their position for another four or five minutes, he guessed. There was still time. Time for his plan.

He sprinted over to Cable. "I'm going to try something else. If it doesn't work, get everybody into the Mercedes. You'll be safe there for a while."

"What are you going to do?" Cable asked.

Sutton nodded toward Larchmont, who was sprawled on the lower steps of the mortuary. The strange voice was still emanating from the computer but the voice was fading with each passing second, and Larchmont seemed too injured or exhausted to do anything about it. "That computer's not going to work," he said, glancing up at the Horrcove brothers, noticing they were swaying slightly from side to side as if they were wearing down, exhausting themselves. "Now we use *my* plan. It might work, it might not, but I've got to do it while they're occupied."

He looked up at the Horrcove brothers a final time.

Their eyes were squinted shut in concentration, and they were still holding hands and swaying tiredly on the high portico. Time to go, Sutton thought. He whirled away from Cable and started for the patrol car. He barely heard Cable scream at him in a voice that sounded distant and far away. "Henry, wait! Don't leave. We can still beat them. The computer's still working. Henry!—"

The voice stopped abruptly when Sutton pulled the car door shut. He turned the ignition key and the growling roar from the engine seemed like a fine sound to him. He dropped the car into gear and rammed the gas pedal to the floor. The patrol car responded violently, fishtailing away from the mortuary in an avalanche of gravel and smoke. Sliding sideways at times in its effort to gain momentum, the car veered sharply to the right, then almost on its own it headed toward the steep hill that rose up on the right side of the funeral home. The car careened off the driveway, landing hard in the wet sod, its high speed allowing it to skim over the grass like a pebble skimming across a creek. It hit lurching corpses and plowed through them as if they were dried weeds. Throughout it all, Sutton kept the gas pedal on the floor. The car bucked and lurched and skidded sideways at times as it began its high speed charge up the hill. Several times the steering wheel was jerked out of Sutton's hand. At one point the wheel whipped back and broke his thumb. He never felt the pain. He just drove, slamming the car's transmission into "D-2" and guiding the machine as it continued its violent onslaught up the steep slope, missing some tombstones, crushing others to dust.

In a massive dinosaurlike effort the heavy machine finally crested the hill, and Sutton brought the car to a lurching stop, slamming the transmission into Park. He waited in the car for a moment to see if there was any danger of the car sliding down the hill. The car held its position. He shut the engine down and climbed out. He was right where he wanted to be. The huge machine was precariously balanced on the top of the hill, its rear bumper pointing down the slope, almost aimed at the side of the huge Horrcove mortuary a quarter of a mile below.

"You did good," Sutton said softly, as if the old patrol car could hear him. "Real good."

He looked down the slope at the great foreboding home crouched below him, and his thoughts went back to when he and Jackie Fairmont had visited the Horrcove brothers in that home. "You bastards," he said without emotion. "Without saying a word, you told me what your worst fear was: a fire extinguisher on every wall, sprinkler system in every room, a building made of stone, a roof made of slate. You thought you were so fucking powerful, so fucking clever, so fucking superior. You laid it all out for me the minute I walked in the door. Larchmont said fire or water would blow you away. He didn't know how to deliver it. But I do."

Turning away, he opened the patrol car's trunk, reached into the darkness, and felt the familiar shape of the Army-issued M-42 flame thrower and its two cylindrical fuel tanks. The tanks held eighty pounds worth of volatile chemicals, liquids and gases so highly flammable and explosive that even fifty years after its perfection for use against the Japanese in World War II, the formula for the chemicals in the tanks was still a highly classified secret.

Sutton ran his hands up from the tanks to the trigger housing on the long metal tube that served as the weapon's barrel. Working by touch he pressed the trigger, then locked it in a full-on position with a rock he'd found that morning out in the National Guard armory's parking lot. Technically, the flame shower should have been spewing out a blazing arc of flames; it wasn't. Twelve hours earlier, after stealing the M-42 from the armory, he'd semineutered the weapon by cutting the wires running from a battery in the trigger housing to a spark ignition system at the end of the barrel. With its trigger pressed into a full on position by the rock, the flame thrower was now violently spurting out the contents of its two fuel tanks, filling the large trunk with a liquid and gaseous compound more volatile than hot nitroglycerine.

As he started to step back from the trunk, his right hand grazed against two rough wooden boxes each containing eighteen pounds of dynamite in the form of twenty-four twelve-ounce sticks packed in sawdust. Like the flame thrower, Sutton had found the dynamite in the National Guard armory, where it had been stored by the county's road construction crew.

He slammed the trunk shut and wiped flecks of dry spit from his lips. There was nothing more to do.

It was time.

He turned and looked down the hill at the mortuary a final time. The walking devil-army of corpses was closing in on the humans by the Mercedes. Larchmont was kneeling at the bottom of the steps, still holding on to his computer and fighting off the efforts of Jenny McKenzie and her daughter to get him into the car. Mark Childress and John Cable flanked the struggling trio. Cable had a tire iron in his hand and Childress was holding a tire jack. The weapons were tiny and pathetic in comparison to the mass of cadavers coming for them.

Those people in the parking lot had become important to Henry Sutton. As he wished them well, the finality of his own pending act welled up in him like a great black wave. He bit his lip in an unconscious effort to check the self-pity heaving up within him. But then the mass of emotions inside him died when he noticed some of the corpses had broken away from the group attacking the humans and were now trying to work their way up the hill toward him.

"That cuts it . . ." he said to no one in particular. Then he turned and looked at his patrol car. "Let's get it on."

He shattered the opaque spiderwebbed rear window with his fist, cutting himself to the bone, but didn't notice. He walked to the car door and, without conscious thought, said, "Hail Mary, full of grace . . ."

He opened the patrol car's door and got in behind the wheel.

". . . the Lord is with thee. Blessed art thou amongst women . . ."

He turned the key. The powerful engine exploded to life with the roar of close thunder. He released the parking brake, dropping the transmission into reverse and pushing down hard on the brake pedal, holding the bucking car high on the hill for a moment longer. He turned, draping his arm over the seat and looking out the clear back window. Then he lifted his foot from the brake and jammed it down hard on the gas.

"Holy Mary, Mother of God . . ."

The car threw itself off the crest of the hill. It crashed down hard on the slope and began charging wildly down the hill like a black horse gone wild. Tires spinning wildly in reverse, its engine screaming, the car continued to pick up speed as it careened down the hill. Granite statues and huge tombstones exploded under its onslaught, and all the while, Sutton kept the car on course, guiding it with one hand, surprised at how easy it was to steer a car rocketing backward down a hill.

". . . Pray for us sinners, now and at the hour of our death . . ."

The Horrcove mortuary loomed up and grew huge in the rear window. Just before the car hit, Henry Sutton said, *"Sweet Jackie, don't let it hurt . . ."*

It didn't. By some miracle Henry Sutton died a microsecond before the collision.

The back end of Sutton's magnificent patrol car slammed into the stone foundation of the Horrcove mortuary at better than a hundred miles an hour. The car's weight, speed, and terrible momentum propelled it through the stone wall and deep into the home's interior before the explosion occurred.

The dynamite and volatile liquid in the trunk exploded with all the fury and power of a plugged volcano. The fiery explosion blew the first and second floors through the slate roof and vaporized anything and everything within the confines of the massive stone walls.

Lost instantly in the sunlike inferno were six huge ornate coffins housed in a large vaultlike room in the basement of the mortuary. Five of the coffins contained creatures of unspeakable descriptions.

The sixth coffin was empty.

Alexander and Bartholomew Horrcove were standing on their home's veranda with their eyes closed, heads bowed, and hands clasped together when the massive wave of flames exploded out the open doors behind them. Before either had a chance to move away, a rolling ball of fire engulfed both. Shrieking incoherent screams, they emerged from the inferno and started down the steps, two twin torches still holding hands. Halfway down the stairway, they collapsed, and their bodies, more carbon than flesh, crumpled into blackened lumps of nothing.

Flaming timbers and huge pieces of slate rained down on the figures trying to get Martin Larchmont off the steps. All had been knocked to their knees by the impact of the tremendous explosion, but now John Cable was up and running toward Larchmont so he could help Jenny and Charlcie McKenzie get his friend into the car.

Mark Childress clambered to his feet with car jack still in his hand. But suddenly there was no enemy to ward off. The army of cadavers was collapsing all around them, dying a second time.

Relieved, but still frightened, Childress began moving toward the people at the bottom of the steps. He never made it; a fist-sized piece of slate from the roof struck him on the back of the head, sending him sprawling facedown in the gravel.

The two women and Cable were struggling to get Larchmont to his feet when the first violent earthquake tremor knocked them to their knees. They tried to get up and a second tremor more violent than the first sent them sprawling.

From his knees Cable looked up at the heavy fortress walls which still encircled the blazing inferno. He could see the walls of the mortuary swaying like wheat in a slow breeze. He screamed at Larchmont. "It's over. They're dead! We've got to get out of here before the walls collapse on us!"

Larchmont was a man possessed. He broke away, got to his feet, and scrambled for the computer. "It's our only hope!" he screamed. "The computer'll kill the brothers and the demons. It will!"

Cable rushed past Charlcie, running to his friend on the stairs and trying to break the grip the older man had on the steps and the computer. Larchmont's mind couldn't accept the Horrcove brothers' death and seemed oblivious to the reality of their plight, the reality of the huge fire-weakened stone walls jutting up high over their heads. He pushed Cable away, kicking out at Charlcie and Jenny.

The earth lurched again, and this time a huge fissure, wide as a riverbed, split the ground apart just beyond the stone lions. Then, like a huge black snake, the V-shaped head of the moving trench began zigzagging across the parking lot toward the humans as if it were alive and seeking out the survivors of the holocaust. Ripping the asphalt apart, the widening oncoming fissure tore the earth apart and tore the earth out from beneath everyone standing in its path. Then it disappeared under the massive torch of the burning home. The violent cleaving caught Cable, Charlcie, Jenny, and Larchmont by surprise. One instant they were standing on firm ground, the next instant the ground was gone and they were tumbling down into a wide trench along with an avalanche of stones and dirt.

Their fall into the fissure was short and painful, and they ended up in a tangled mass of arms and legs at the bottom. Charlcie and Jenny screamed, and Cable felt some ribs and his left forearm snap. Gritting his teeth against the pain, he scrambled to his feet and didn't like what he saw.

They were trapped in a trench five feet deep, six feet wide at the top. The massive stone wall of the front of the Horrcove mortuary looked as if it might collapse on them at any second. If it didn't, the huge granite columns jutting up from the porch high above them to support the massive portico would. He didn't know much about earthquakes, but he did know if another tremor struck, the fissure they were in could reclose and crush them like a vise.

Cable set to work like a man possessed. He grabbed Jenny McKenzie with his good right arm, hefting her up and throwing her out of the trench and onto safe ground. Charlcie followed.

Then he grabbed ahold of Martin Larchmont. He jerked him to his feet, boosting him up until the older man's upper torso was on safe ground and only his feet dangled down into the fissure.

Cable knelt down, grabbing Larchmont's ankles. He was about to lift him up and out of the trench when a powerful downblast of wind coming from directly overhead knocked him to his knees. Dirt and stones flew about like shrapnel as overhead a giant set of wings beat the air and earth into a nightmarish frenzy.

Still clinging to Larchmont's legs, Cable looked up and saw nothing but a black blinding cloud of swirling dust and dirt. Suddenly an unseen force tried to drag Larchmont's legs out of his grasp. Cable hung on and cried out as his arms were nearly torn from their sockets. It was like a nightmarish tug-of-war contest and his unconscious friend was the rope.

The pulling then stopped. The wind faded, and the cloud began to settle. The only sound Cable could hear was the sound of Jenny McKenzie's terrified never-ending scream. He pushed Larchmont's legs up unto the asphalt, then clambered out of the trench to join his friend. Rolling over, Cable got to his knees and scanned the orange and black sky for whatever had tried to take his friend from him. Then he saw it. He saw it and accepted it for what it was: a beast with wings, a giant flying gargoyle that belonged on the roof of a cathedral in Notre-Dame. Cable's only bleak thought was that one of the demon creatures had escaped the holocaust brought on by Henry Sutton. It must have sensed the threat and flown away just before Sutton rammed his patrol car into the side of the mansion.

It swooped in low, making hideous cawing sounds like an angry condor. The garish light from the fire illuminated the creature's protruding eyes, its fanglike teeth, and its expression of hate and vengeance.

As it closed on them, Cable's eyes widened. In the bright orange light he could see the creature's giant twelve-inch-long talons wet with blood and strips of human flesh. Suddenly he knew . . . oh, God, he knew what those talons had done to Martin Larchmont.

Jenny McKenzie screamed as the creature flew past. Then it began to circle high over the burning building. Still on his knees, Cable finally looked at his friend. Martin Larchmont was lying on his side. His eyes were open. He looked a little confused, but he wasn't in pain. At least not anymore, Cable thought, as he looked down at the hideous gaping wounds in Larchmont's upper body. John Cable sighed and closed Martin Larchmont's eyes before looking up into the sky, trying to find the creature that had done this to his friend.

It was out there, flapping its wings and circling them slowly, methodically, taking its time while it decided which human it would tear to pieces next.

Cable scrambled to his feet, running to Charlcie. He grabbed her and literally threw her into the old Mercedes-Benz. Turning, he ran to Jenny McKenzie as the creature started its attack like a heavy winged dive bomber. It was coming in low and close to the ground, its giant talons extended and locked in place like steel lances. Jenny McKenzie had run over to Martin Larchmont and was on her knees beside the man when Cable came in from behind and dived on her, throwing the full weight of his body on top of hers, crushing her to the ground and protecting her body with his as the beast came for them.

Explosions of dust and stones were stirred up from the creature's wings as it came in low and close to the ground in its attack on them. Its talons missed him by inches and it screamed its horrible disappointment with shrieking caws of frustration that split the night like train whistles.

Instantly Cable was on his feet, trying to pull the hysterical woman toward the car. Pushed into shock by what she'd seen, Jenny pushed Cable away and screamed something about Martin needing her. Out of the corner of his eye, he saw the winged beast whirl in the air, readying itself for another run on them. He knew he wouldn't be able to get Jenny to the car in time. He released her and looked around for something, some sort of weapon that he could use against this mythical creature.

The power, the gut burning rage he felt within him, was something he'd never known before. There was nothing he wanted to do more in the world than meet this creature head on and destroy it. Kill it. Make it suffer for what it had done to Martin Larchmont.

Halfway through a slow gliding circle, the creature angled its wings in preparation for another attack. Cable looked around for a weapon. Seeing the tire iron he knew it wouldn't work. It would be like going against an alligator with a matchstick.

The monster was starting its approach, wings moving with the sounds of rapid thunder. Behind him the computer, still in its briefcase with its impotent program and strange machinelike voice, droned on. Cable whirled around, looking at it. It was heavier and bulkier than the tire iron, and it was all there was. He sprinted for the metal briefcase as the flapping sounds grew louder and louder.

Grabbing the heavy metal briefcase by its handle, he turned to face the creature. It was thirty yards away and coming in like a helicopter gunship, its talons extended, its eyes locked on the prostrate grief-stricken Jenny McKenzie.

Dr. John Cable, the quiet man of theory, began running toward the monster, screaming meaningless threats he could barely hear above the roar of the creature's wings. Suddenly distracted, the creature slowed its descent and hovered above the prostrate woman. Its narrow, slitted, snakelike eyes sought Cable out and found him. Still hovering above Jenny McKenzie, the creature glared at Cable.

John Cable skidded to a stop and returned the winged beast's withering glare. "Come to me," he whispered. "Come for me, fucker."

It was almost as though the creature had heard Cable's whispered words. It screeched at him, increasing the speed of its wings. And then it did come for him.

Still gripping the metal briefcase, Cable broke into a hard full-out run straight at the beast. The creature shrieked at Cable, flapping its wings harder as it charged down on the human.

It was nearly on top of him, just a few feet away, when Cable hurled the vibrating briefcase at the snapping giant beak. He threw it in a stiff-armed fashion, putting all the strength he could muster into the throw. The handle left his hand smoothly and he saw the case arch away, saw tints of orange and yellow from the nearby fire gleam off its metal sides and knew there was no way he could miss the demon from this distance.

He had the time to throw himself on the ground and

cover his head, but he didn't. Instead, he faced the creature and waited.

The heavy briefcase soared through the air, then smashed into the creature's beaked face. Both the winged creature and the briefcase seemed to scream out in hysterical unison, a double-edged scream composed of strange words and hellish caws.

Disoriented and stunned, the creature veered, spinning down on Cable. A talon the size of a rail spike hooked Cable just below the eye and split his flesh. A hurricanelike wind from giant beating wings knocked Cable to his knees.

Looking up, Cable watched the flying creature pitch and yaw, veering first to its left, then to its right as it attempted to gain altitude. Something was wrong with it. It was confused; disoriented. It whirled in the air, then veered toward the flaming mansion. It tried to change its course to avoid a collision and couldn't. It flapped its wings harder, frantically hoping to clear, to fly up and over the high red hot walls.

It didn't make it; it crashed headlong into a massive flaming stone wall just above the entrance to the Horrcove mansion.

There was a tremendous explosion, then a second explosion. Burning flesh and hot stones rained down on the driveway as the massive front walls of the mortuary slowly toppled backward into the center of the burned-out shell of the old building.

Odd, Cable thought as he got to his feet. The creature had probably saved their lives. If it hadn't flown into the wall, the front of the Horrcove mortuary would have toppled forward, down on them.

A moment later the three remaining outer walls of the Horrcove mortuary collapsed, resulting in a billowing cloud of fire and smoke that seemed to symbolize the final destruction of anything and everything that had ever been a part of the Horrcove brothers' legacy.

A numb and silent Charlcie McKenzie helped carry

her mother to the car. With Cable's help, Mark Childress was able to get up and walk to the Mercedes.

After everyone was in the car, Cable paused to survey the surrounding destruction. The mortuary was a pile of burning rocks, the driveway littered with bodies. He saw the remains of Lynn Langley and avoided looking at the tiny body of Martin Larchmont. He didn't feel much at that moment. He was too numb, too stunned to feel much of anything. But he knew that one day soon his grief would come and it would be immense. The man had been his friend, and more. Martin Larchmont had been the father John Cable had never known.

"Take care, Martin," Cable said softly.

The fire consuming the mansion illuminated the hill next to it. Clearly visible were the tire tracks Henry Sutton's car had made as it had carried itself and its driver down the slope and into the Horrcove mortuary. Standing beside the old Mercedes with dry eyes, a broken arm, and a cheek cut to the bone, Cable pushed aside his feelings for Larchmont and tried to think of something to say to Sutton. The words just wouldn't come. He could think of nothing to say, or maybe, he thought, as he tried to fight back the tears, there was too much to say . . . too many says to say. "I saw what you did. I saw you give your life away. I don't know if you know it, but you beat them. You destroyed the brothers and their legacy, and we're alive because of you. . . ."

Gripping the roof of the car for support, Cable lowered himself into the driver's seat. Charlcie was in the back of the car, holding her mother. Childress was asleep in the passenger seat, his head resting against the window. Puzzled, it took Cable a moment to remember that sleep was often a symptom of a concussion.

Steering and shifting with one hand, Cable awkwardly drove the big Mercedes out of the cemetery and down through the winding streets of Ravina. The ride to the Ravina County Hospital took nine minutes.

Epilogue:
Part One

Jenny McKenzie died of a massive coronary two hours after being admitted to the Ravina County Hospital.

Dr. Mark Childress was hospitalized for a possible concussion. Thirty-six hours later, he was discharged but forbidden to leave the hospital by a number of county, state, and federal law officials all intently interested in getting to the bottom of whatever was going on in Ravina. At one point, when the investigating officials were in the cafeteria on a coffee break, Childress perused his unopened mail. One letter was from a laboratory in Los Angeles, and with some interest he opened it. The letter contained the laboratory's analysis of the granulated tissues surrounding Lynn Langley's fingernails and teeth. The analysis was essentially a statement of bewilderment and accusations: it stated that the submitted tissues had undergone some sort of complete metamorphosis on a molecular level. The laboratory director took pains to point out that a molecular restructuring could not occur unless massive amounts of radiation were introduced into the tissues. The sample they'd received contained no evidence of radiation intrusion whatsoever.

The remainder of the report was a battery of questions along with a thoughtfully written postscript suggesting that Doctors Childress and Seafront might have accidentally erred and submitted something other than human tissue for analysis.

There was a second letter on his desk from the same laboratory, and Childress knew it carried another confusing analysis of the tissues and bodily fluids of Deputy Robert Calms. After tossing the still sealed letter away, Mark Childress picked up his phone and responded to a job offer he'd received from a private hospital in Portland, Maine. The telephone conversation with the recruiting hospital's personnel director was brief; Childress accepted the job, agreed to the salary, and told the director he'd have to give two weeks' notice to his own hospital. Without the blessings of the state and federal investigating officials, Mark Childress would leave for Maine fifteen days later.

It took Colonel William Seafront less than two weeks to have his medical retirement papers processed and approved. When that was done, he moved his wife and children off post. His retirement from the Air Force was mandatory; he didn't have a choice. One could not suffer a fifty-percent loss of hearing in both ears and remain in the Air Force. That's what had happened to William Seafront. A bizarre computer accident had deafened him in both ears. Still, he was lucky, far luckier than an Air Force computer technician who'd lost a hundred percent of his hearing in both ears.

The accident happened when a miniaturized computer-receiver housed in a metal briefcase came into contact with a winged demon from hell. The collision of flesh and electronic wizardry had resulted in an explosion so intense that the wave of energy flowing from the hospital's computer to the briefcase had been reversed. The highly amplified high-pitched wave of feedback slammed back into the hospital's computer like a super charged bolt of lightning, blowing out the computer's internal components and microchips in less than a tenth of a second.

The laserlike intensity of the sound that had burst out into the computer room during that tenth of a second knocked the computer technician off his chair and shattered his eardrums. Seafront, who was standing some yards away, leaning against a wall, only had his eardrums ruptured, losing only fifty percent of his hearing.

Six weeks after he retired, Seafront, with the aid of two hearing aids, entered the peaceful world of private practice. Never wanting to do another autopsy again, through with forensic pathology forever, Dr. William Seafront went into family medicine in a small clinic in a small town in northern California.

John Cable was admitted to the Ravina County Hospital for multiple injuries. He had a compound fracture of his left forearm, numerous broken ribs, and a severe facial laceration that required twenty-two stitches to close. Twenty-four hours after he was admitted, his attending physician gave the green light to a large flock of law officers who would have eaten Cable alive if it would have brought them closer to solving the mysteries they were investigating.

They asked Cable hundreds of pertinent questions; John Cable gave them back hundreds of half-giggled, half-slurred meaningless answers. It wasn't that Cable didn't want to cooperate; it was that he couldn't. Both he and the investigating officials were victims of Cable's attending physician's belief that people in pain should not feel pain. The doctor was also a firm believer in alleviating pain with Demerol. One shot every three hours. In the state he was in, John Cable was simply too stoned to give the officials and investigators his name and birthdate, let alone any information on the mysteries in Ravina.

The interrogations of Childress and John Cable finally

stopped seventy-two hours after the fire at the Horrcove mansion. The interrogations stopped because Andrew Slatkin, the night watch commander with the Ravina Police Department, came to the hospital a little after six in the evening with a letter that had been delivered to his home a few hours earlier.

The letter he carried was the one Henry Sutton had written in the McKenzie living room just prior to the last sunrise of his life.

Slatkin, now the acting police chief of Ravina, used his newly acquired authority to order the county, state, and federal officials into the hospital chapel. After everyone was seated, Slatkin placed the thick letter on the dais of the small pulpit, explaining who it was from. Then he began to read Sutton's letter.

Henry Sutton started his narrative with the deaths of Lynn Langley, Deputy Robert Calms, and Louellen Mae Harnes. Next came a terse description of his encounter with the Horrcove brothers and an equally terse description of the death of Jackie Fairmont. That was followed by a description of the resurrection of Louellen Mae Harnes and her second death in the hospital parking lot. After detailing how Deputy Gaylord Bender had died when he'd answered the phone, Sutton went on to tie it all together.

Henry Sutton covered it all. He included the observations and enigmatic findings of the autopsies Childress and Seafront had performed. He described Martin Larchmont's theories; Jenny McKenzie's findings; even recalled much of what Ben-Admid Tomar had written on the tin scroll.

It was all there: the deaths, the mysteries, the horror, the explanation, and Martin Larchmont's plan to use a computer to destroy the creature-demons and the Horrcove brothers.

Near the end of the letter Sutton explained why he felt Larchmont's plan would not work and went on to talk about what he intended to do if the professor's plan failed. Slatkin had read the letter earlier in his home. He knew what was coming next and his voice seized up with emotion as he read how Sutton thought the demons and their guardians could be destroyed by fire, and how he planned to carry that fire into the home of the Horrcove brothers.

At one point Slatkin could almost hear Henry Sutton laughing quietly in the background when he came to that part of the letter where Sutton wished Slatkin well in his efforts to explain to the local National Guard commander just exactly what had happened to the M-42, the company's flame thrower.

Andrew Slatkin almost broke down as he read the final page. This part of the letter was not meant for anyone else, but Slatkin read it anyway, wanting his audience of FBI agents and state police investigators and county detectives to know what kind of a man Henry Sutton was. This was a man who was in control. This was a man who knew what he was doing. This was a man who in his letter told Andrew Slatkin where he would find a check payable to him for five thousand dollars. The money was to be used to secure the services of a competent and crafty lawyer who would make sure that everything Henry Sutton owned—including the profits from the sale of his house, his savings, his insurance benefits—everything would be channeled into a trust fund for Courtney and Brook Fairmont, the twin daughters of Jackie Fairmont.

Sutton ended his letter with a simple request. He gave Andrew Slatkin the name and address of Jackie Fairmont's older sister, the woman who was now taking care of both girls. He asked Slatkin to use the money from his estate to make sure their needs and best interests were met. "Use the lawyer, Andy," Henry Sutton had written. "Use the lawyer to make sure the girls get everything I have and everything Jackie has. I don't like lawyers any more than you do, but if you find a good one, pay him well and look over his shoulder. Make sure the girls get what's theirs.

"Thank you, Andy. Sorry for the inconvenience."

His rigid audience stared up at Slatkin in stunned open-mouthed silence. Andrew Slatkin looked back at them like a fierce fundamentalist preacher. "So now you know what happened, what *really* happened. But I'd be careful with what you've heard. Two minutes from now this letter won't exist. That being the case, if you mention it in public or to your superiors, you'll either be declared incompetent or crazy. I chose to read it to you for two reasons. The first has to do with the survivors. I think the time has come to leave Cable, Charlcie McKenzie, and the doctors alone."

Slatkin delivered his next words as if he were swinging a machete. "The second reason is I'm going to need all the help I can get in covering up this mess."

As a result of Henry Sutton's letter, the bureaucratic investigators not only left Cable alone, they started treating him like one of the creature-demons Sutton had written about. Their nervous and frightened attitudes proved to be contagious. Within hours the hospital staff began treating the closed door to Cable's room as if it were a living creature capable of biting off any hand that pushed it open.

Cable didn't mind. He needed the time alone. He stayed in the darkness of his room and forced his mind not to think. He forced himself not to feel. And failed. In spite of the Demerol, in spite of his efforts, he relived that night at the cemetery time and time again. He also relived Martin Larchmont's death time and time again, always feeling pain and grief. Especially grief.

He kept his room dark for two days and two nights. During that time he began to refuse the offered Demerol and most meals. At the end of that span of time, he still wasn't healed and still not over his grief for Larchmont.

But he was better, improving, and most important, he was clear-headed.

As he started to gain control of himself, starting to come out of the darkness, he realized he'd been in the hospital for five days and hadn't seen or heard from Charlcie. He buzzed a nurse, asking the nervous woman about Charlcie McKenzie and only receiving vague elusive answers that told him nothing.

Concerned, Cable watched the nurse leave the room. As the door was shutting, he heard her strike up a conversation with an FBI agent who'd tried to interrogate him a couple of days earlier. On a hunch, Cable forced his stiff body out of bed, padding across the floor and putting his ear to the door. What he heard chilled him to the bone. Charlcie McKenzie had helped admit Cable, Mark Childress, and her mother to the hospital with a stoic strength that impressed the staff and police. Afterward, she sat in the hospital waiting room, trying as best as she could to answer the questions being hurled at her by a mob of frightened deputies. Throughout it all, she remained composed, her posture erect and her hands folded in her lap. She maintained that poised position even after a doctor and nurse came to tell her that her mother had passed away.

The deputies gave her the better part of a half hour to come to grips with her loss before they started questioning her again. Only this time she didn't answer their questions. She didn't even try to speak. She just sat there, her eyes focused on a small set of plastic praying hands sitting on top of the waiting room's television set.

Minutes later one of the deputies noticed the woman's hands had assumed the same pose as the hands on top of the television set. More important, it occurred to the deputy that the pretty wide-eyed woman hadn't blinked, or moved her eyes away from the praying hands since hearing about her mother.

A few minutes later Charlcie McKenzie was in an elevator on her way up to the fifth floor, where the hospital maintained its emergency services ward for the mentally ill.

Five days after her admission to the hospital, Charlcie's condition had improved to the point where she could talk if she felt like it, but hadn't. She knew what was going on around her, knew what was happening to her, but she simply didn't care.

Sutton was dead. Larchmont was dead. Childress was dead. Her mother was dead. And she knew John Cable was dead. She'd seen him collapse in the emergency room, blood spurting from his head. He was dead and the doctors were keeping the news from her until she was stronger, better able to handle it.

A turnip-shaped psychiatrist had been by to see her several times since her admission and was with her now. Irritated or intimidated by Charlcie's continued silence and lifeless affect, the psychiatrist was trying to explain why he was making arrangements to have Charlcie transferred to a small psychiatric hospital in San Luis Obispo, a hospital specializing in long-term care. In the one-sided dialogue that followed, he explained that the ward she was on was for short-term patients, only those who could be treated and released in seventy-two hours or less. He took great pains to point out that they'd already broken regulations by allowing her to remain as long as she had. Then he began urging her to sign some documents covering her transfer and admission to the San Luis Obispo hospital, adding tactfully that if she didn't sign, he and the hospital social worker would have a local court judge sign the documents for her. At no time did he use the words *commitment* or *incompetent* but the words were there, apparent in everything he was saying, and written all over his face.

Charlcie sighed, allowing her eyes to go out of focus while she just sat in the chair as the doctor babbled on. . . .

The nurse talking to the FBI agent outside of Cable's room was not as tactful as the psychiatrist. Wanting to impress the good-looking FBI agent with her meager grasp of medical terms, she used the words *commitment, incompetent,* and *catatonic* several times.

The coarse descriptive words about Charlcie's condition and her whereabouts drifted through the hospital door and slashed into Cable like a sword. The words jolted him out of his self-imposed isolation and burst his bubble of self-pity. He whirled away from the door and bolted toward the closet. He dressed rapidly in the same clothes he'd worn on the night he'd gone to the Horrcove cemetery, oblivious to the fact that the clothing he was putting on was torn, dirty, and brocaded with dried blood.

Moments later John Cable walked out into the hospital's corridor. His appearance horrified the staff. In his blood-splattered jeans and jacket, he looked like a Safeway butcher; the lacing of black sutures running down the side of his face hinted at a close ancestral relationship to Dr. Frankenstein's monster.

He stopped only once on his way to the elevator. He stopped at the nurses' station. The words he uttered to the startled nurse behind the counter were direct and bordered on being ominous. "Call Mark Childress . . . tell him to meet me on the fifth floor now."

The heavy wooden door to the psychiatric unit was locked. A simplistic overly worded sign informed visitors they should push the button beside the door. In response, someone inside the ward would push another button, and when the visitor heard a buzzing sound it meant the door was unlocked and the visitor should enter quickly.

Cable pushed the buzzer. Nothing. He waited a full minute, then pushed the buzzer again, not realizing the staff on the ward were grouped around the day room's television set, keeping up with their favorite soap opera. No one moved to return Cable's signal.

Thirty seconds later their program was interrupted by the sounds of the ward's locked door being cleaved in two by Cable's boot. The noise surprised them; the act shocked them. No one ever breaks *into* a mental ward.

Dr. Mark Childress emerged from the elevator just in time to see Cable kick in the door. He was able to catch up with him just as Cable was about to rearrange the face of a male psychiatric technician. While Childress calmed the staff down, Cable worked his way down the hallway, accompanied by the sounds of doors being violently opened, then slammed shut.

Cable found Charlcie in the psychiatrist's office.

The psychiatrist was still trying to get Charlcie to sign the transfer and treatment papers when a visage of doom entered his office. The doctor took a hard look at the man's blood-splattered clothing, scarred face, angry eyes and crawled under his desk.

Charlcie glanced back at the intruder two times. The first look was to assess what kind of intrusion had caused the doctor to disappear. The second glance was one of surprise, recognition, tears, and heartwrenching emotion.

She ran into Cable's open arms with such energy that Childress, who was standing out in the hallway observing the reunion, winced at the impact. As Cable held the crying, smiling woman in his arms, he murmured something almost inaudible to her.

Childress wasn't sure, but he thought he heard the words: "leaving now" and ". . . Canada." Go for it, Childress thought, then smiled at the psychiatrist whose eyes were barely visible above the desktop. "I'll fill you in later," he explained.

Childress accompanied the couple to the admissions office on the first floor and stood behind them while Cable gave the clerk his home address in Vancouver, Canada, promising in writing to pay for the door he'd broken. Then Childress cosigned the discharge papers, hinting loudly that the county would probably pay their medical bills, and walked them out to the parking lot.

Someone had boarded up the front door of Jenny McKenzie's home with a large piece of plywood. They got in through the back door, packed, and before they left went across the street, hiring a fourteen-year-old boy to look after the ferns in Jenny McKenzie's greenhouse. The amount they arrived at was twenty dollars a month. He was paid for six months worth of work in advance.

Two hours after leaving the hospital Charlcie McKenzie and John Cable drove out of Ravina. It was misty in Portland, rainy in Seattle, and snowing in Vancouver. At no time during their journey up the coast did they encounter the slightest trace of fog.

Epilogue:
Part Two

On the day following the fire at the Horrcove cemetery, agents from the FBI, detectives from San Luis Obispo, and investigators from the California State Police arrived in Ravina. The intensity of the early part of their investigations rivaled the intensity of the fire that had vaporized the funeral home. However, their zeal was short-lived. Within forty-eight hours all the investigators were confused, angry, and in some cases, frightened. They had come to ease the plight of a panicked and scared town, come to investigate the mysterious disappearances of two children and several strange unexplainable deaths. It wasn't until their investigation was well underway that they actually came up with a full body count and realized that five members of the Ravina police department were dead as a result of whatever was going on, and that only added to their fear. They had come confidently, expecting to solve the mysteries quickly. What they found were not facts and answers, but chaos and riddles leading to questions that led back to more riddles. It was a classic Gordian knot shrouded in body bags, darkness, and fog.

It was at that point when the acting police chief,

Andrew Slatkin, ordered the investigators into the hospital's chapel and then read Henry Sutton's letter. Some of the men in the chapel believed what they heard. Others didn't. But because of Slatkin's leadership and Sutton's letter, the men in the chapel produced a near first in the annals of law enforcement: the state, federal, and county investigators dropped their desire for one-upmanship and banded together in an effort to cover up the mysteries and the horrors that had come from the Horrcove mortuary.

Six days after the fire a hearing was held at the Ravina Civic Center. The conference was closed to the public but open to certain members of the media. At the hearing the officials stated that the damage done to the Horrcove cemetery and mansion was the result of a faulty gas main. They offered up evidence which suggested that accumulated vapors was the only plausible explanation for such an intense fire. A federally employed geologist then went on to add that the powerful gas explosion had triggered a small undetected earthen fault located deep within Horrcove Hill. The snapping of the faultline's edges had caused a minor earthquake that had registered 2.2 on the Richter scale.

He postulated that the earthquake was the primary reason behind the slippage of the hill's topsoil, thereby laying open to the environment—so to speak—the remnants of many graves.

Halfway through the meeting a reporter who'd done his homework before coming stood up and suggested the theory was a "cover-up," adding there were no gas pipes within a mile and a half of the cemetery. The reporter was then hustled out of the meeting and confined to a jail cell for sixteen hours. During those hours some very highly placed state and federal officials conferred with the reporter's editor. The editor then had a heart-to-heart discussion with his employee, and in the end the reporter surrendered his Xeroxed copies of the local utility maps along with his desire to file suits against the officials who'd taken him into custody.

Near the end of the hearing it was announced that commendations of the highest order were being awarded posthumously to Deputies Gaylord Bender, Larry Griffith, and Sheriff Henry Sutton. An award for civilian valor was also being given to Professor Martin Larchmont. The four citations would note the men had given their lives in a valiant attempt to save two elderly men from a fire that was destroying their business and residence.

Twenty-four hours later the four men were publicly eulogized in a large ceremony open to the public at Ravina's only other cemetery, a piece of reclaimed swampland called Highland's View. The four coffins on display at the cemetery were empty. The intensity of the fire had—it was said—reduced the bodies of the rescuers to ashes. What was never publicly revealed was that the various powers involved in the investigation had in fact discreetly hustled the remains of Bender, Griffith, and Larchmont off to a seedy mortuary in San Luis Obispo where the remains were cremated. The actions were deemed necessary and justifiable by the involved officials, given the public's need to feel secure and comfortable in their homes.

An article on the first page of Ravina's newspaper described how a nurse named Elizabeth Bates had been the victim of a tragic hit and run accident in the hospital's parking lot. That large amounts of broken glass and flecks of automobile paint had been found in the parking lot gave credence to the hit and run theory. As to the fact that the woman's body had been found in the hospital's basement near the morgue, the newspaper theorized the woman had survived the impact of a speeding car, then staggered into the hospital, where she had died of her injuries before getting help.

On the afternoon Elizabeth Bates was laid to rest in the Highland's View Cemetery, other bodies were being buried at the Horrcove Cemetery. Louellen Mae Harnes's father was buried—again. Her second husband was buried—again. Lynn Langley was buried—again. In all,

OUT OF THE NIGHT

OUT OF THE NIGHT

an uncounted number of bodies, corpses, and cadavers, many of whom had been buried upward of twenty to thirty years earlier, were buried—again.

The bodies were buried by a platoon of nervous National Guardsmen. The clothing worn by the grave diggers and pallbearers would have been disconcerting to the relatives of the dead. All of the men were wearing standard anticontamination suits, complete with Plexiglas helmets and air-filtration systems. The astronautlike garb was worn as protection against the strains of lethal bacteria that can be present in old graves that contain human remains never embalmed. However, bacteria was the least of the National Guardsmen's worries. Their real fear was based on unbridled and rampant rumors that had circulated among them since their arrival. The rumors were basically theories about what could have caused such massive destruction to the cemetery, the graves, and the funeral home. Speculation ran from alien creatures from outer space to a coven of witches. Because of the rumors, the guardsmen worked as rapidly as possible. No time was taken to identify the cadavers and bodies, and all the dead were reburied in a large hastily dug mass grave not far from the remains of the mortuary.

As it does in all unsolved kidnappings, the FBI continues to keep open files on the cases of Michael Shehane and Anthony Fiori, Jr. Neither file contains much information, and while six FBI agents were present in the chapel when Andrew Slatkin read Henry Sutton's letter, none of the agents said anything about the dead sheriff's letter in their final report.

As for Sutton's letter, it no longer exists. True to his word, Andrew Slatkin did indeed destroy it.

A week after the Horrcove mansion burned to the ground, the National Guardsmen finished their jobs in the cemetery. The corpses were gone, all the old but open graves had been filled in, and the newly dug mass grave had been covered over with quicklime and dirt, then camouflaged with a copse of newly planted birch trees. The quarantine placed on the cemetery by the Environmental Protection Agency, the county Department of Health, and the California Department of Health was lifted. The National Guardsmen were debriefed and sent home. A day later the various health departments met with the Ravina City Council. It was decided that no future burials would take place in the Horrcove Cemetery; the earth on the hill was too fragile, too unstable; the same thing could happen all over again if the newly discovered faultline were to suddenly become active again. The decision was firmly applauded by the owners of the Highland's View Cemetery.

When it was finally reopened to the public, the Horrcove Cemetery received a surprisingly few number of visitors. Initially, morbid curiosity seekers, interested in looking at the remains of the home where six men had lost their lives, far outnumbered those who came to place flowers on a grave. Visible to all who entered was the giant black hole at the base of a steep knoll. As time passed some wondered why no grass or weeds grew among the charred stones and rubble, but then these visitors knew nothing about the remains that had once been home to the Horrcove legacy.